Nora Roberts is the number one *New York Times* bestseller of more than 200 novels. With over 500 million copies of her books in print, she is indisputably one of the most celebrated and popular writers in the world. She is both a *Sunday Times* bestseller in the UK and a number one bestseller in Australia.

By Nora Roberts

Many of Nora Roberts' other titles are now available in ebook and she is also the author of the In Death series using the pseudonym J.D. Robb.

NORA ROBERTS

NIGHT WORK

PIATKUS

PIATKUS

First published in the United States in 2022 by St Martin's Press
First published in Great Britain in 2022 by Piatkus
This paperback edition published in 2023 by Piatkus

1 3 5 7 9 10 8 6 4 2

A CIP catalogue record for this book
is available from the British Library.

ISBN: 978-0-34943-019-5

Printed and bound in Great Britain by
Clays Ltd, Elcograf S.p.A.

Papers used by Piatkus are from well-managed forests
and other responsible sources.

MIX
Paper from
responsible sources
FSC® C104740

Piatkus
An imprint of
Little, Brown Book Group
Carmelite House
50 Victoria Embankment
London EC4Y 0DZ

An Hachette UK Company
www.hachette.co.uk

www.littlebrown.co.uk

For Jason and Kat
My Theater Kids

PART ONE

THE BOY

A boy's will is the wind's will,
And the thoughts of youth
are long, long thoughts.

—HENRY WADSWORTH LONGFELLOW

Every one can master a grief
but he that has it.

—WILLIAM SHAKESPEARE

Chapter One

WHEN HE WAS NINE, and his mother had her first deadly dance with cancer, he became a thief. At the time, he didn't see it as a choice, an adventure, a thrill—though he would consider his career all of those things in later years. Young Harry Booth equated stealing with surviving.

They had to eat and pay the mortgage and the doctors and buy the medicine even if his mother was too sick to work. She did her best, she always did her best, pushing herself even as her hair fell out in clumps and the weight melted off her already thin frame.

The little company she'd started with her sister, his crazy aunt Mags, couldn't keep up with the cost of cancer, the sheer magnitude of the dollar signs needed to deal with what invaded his mother's body. His mother was the backbone of Sparkle Sisters Cleaning Service, and even with him pitching in on weekends, they lost clients.

Lose clients, lose income. Lose income and you had to find money to pay the mortgage on the cozy two-bedroom house on Chicago's West Side.

Maybe it wasn't much of a house, but it was theirs—and the bank's. His mom hadn't missed a stupid payment until she got sick. But banks didn't much care about that once you started falling behind.

Everybody wanted their money, and they added more money onto it if you didn't pay up on time. If you had a credit card, you could buy stuff like medicine and shoes—his feet kept growing—but then all that made more bills and more late fees and interest and stuff until he heard his mother crying at night when she thought he slept.

He knew Mags helped. She worked really hard to keep clients, and she paid some of the bills or late fees with her own money. But it just wasn't enough.

At nine, he learned the word *foreclosure* meant you could be out on the street. And the word *repossessed* meant people could come take your car.

So at nine, he learned the hard way that playing by the rules as his mother had didn't mean much to the suits and ties and briefcases.

He knew how to pick pockets. His crazy aunt Mags had spent a couple of years on the carny circuit and learned a few tricks. She'd taught him as kind of a game.

He was good at it, damn good at it, and put that talent to use. The right and wrong his mom had so carefully taught him didn't mean much either when she was puking in the bathroom after her chemo, or tying a scarf around her bald head to drag herself off to clean somebody's fancy lakefront house.

He didn't blame the people in the fancy lakefront houses, or in the slick penthouses or shiny office buildings. They'd just had better luck than his mom.

He rode the trains, wandered the streets, picked his marks. He had a good eye for them. The careless tourists, the guy who'd had one too many belts at happy hour, the woman too busy texting to mind her purse.

He didn't look like a thief, the slim, young boy just shy of a growth spurt with a mop of wavy brown hair and heavy-lidded deep blue eyes that could radiate innocence.

He could flash a charming smile or slow-walk a shy one. He

might cover that mop of hair one day in a backward Cubs fielder's cap (his dork look) or tame the mop into what he thought of as the private school slick-down.

During the period his mother was too sick to know what was going on, the mortgage got paid—Mags didn't ask; he didn't tell—the lights stayed on. And he had enough to pore through the secondhand stores for what he thought of as a wardrobe.

An old school blazer, dress pants, a faded Bears sweatshirt. He sewed pouches and pockets inside a secondhand—maybe thirdhand—winter coat.

And he bought his first set of lock picks.

He kept his grades up. He had a bright, thirsty mind, studied, did his homework, and stayed out of trouble. He considered starting a business himself—charging for doing assignments for others. But Harry understood most kids were blabbermouths.

Instead he practiced with his lock picks, and used the computer in the library to research security and alarm systems.

Then she got better. Though still pale and thin, she got stronger. The doctors called it remission.

That became his favorite word.

For the next three years, life hit normal. He still picked pockets. He shoplifted—very carefully. Nothing too expensive, nothing identifiable. He'd worked out a nice arrangement with a pawnshop on the South Side.

They had a mountain of bills to carve through—and the money he made tutoring fellow students didn't carve enough.

Besides, he had a taste for it now.

His mother and Mags built up their business again, and for three years in the summers, Harry cleaned and scrubbed and cased houses and businesses.

A young man with an eye on the future.

Then when the mountain of debt had been whittled down to a hill, when the worry lifted from his mom's eyes, cancer came back for another dance.

Two days after his twelfth birthday, Harry broke into his first house. The terror he'd felt that he'd get caught and dragged off to prison, and the trauma of it would join hands with cancer and kill his mother, evaporated the moment he stood inside the quiet dark.

In later years, when he looked back, he understood that that was the moment he found his purpose. Maybe it wasn't a good purpose, one acceptable in polite society, but it was his.

He stood, a tall boy now after that longed-for growth spurt, staring out the wide windows at the moonlight spearing across the lake. Everything smelled of roses and lemons and freedom.

Only he knew he stood here. He could touch anything he wanted, take what he wanted.

He understood the market for the electronics, for the silver, for the jewelry—though the good jewelry would be locked up. He hadn't yet figured out how to crack a safe. But he would, he promised himself that.

He didn't have time or the ability now to haul away all the shiny things.

He wanted to just stand there, just bask, but pushed himself to work.

Most people, he'd learned, don't think anything about gossiping in front of the help. Especially if that help is a twelve-year-old scrubbing the kitchen floor while you and your neighbor plan some charity event over coffee in the dining room.

So, keeping his head down, his ears open, and his hands busy, Harry learned about the client's neighbor's husband's stamp collection.

She laughed about it.

"It's become an obsession since he inherited his uncle's collection last year. Can you believe he just spent five thousand on one of those things?"

"On a stamp?"

"That doesn't count the temperature and humidity controls

he's had put into his home office where he keeps them. He used to joke about his uncle's hobby, now he's all in. He's haunting auctions and online sites, added his own albums. Now it's an investment, and that's all fine. I mean, what do I care if he has a bunch of silly stamps in his desk? But he's looking up auctions and dealers in Rome so he can check them out when we go next month."

"Let him buy his stamps," the client advised. "You go buy shoes."

Harry filed it all away and decided the universe sent him a big, bright sign when the friend talked about hauling boxes for the event to her car.

He approached the dining room, all innocence. "Sorry, Ms. Kelper, I'm done in the kitchen. Um, did you need some help carrying something?"

"Actually—Alva, this is Harry. Harry, Ms. Finkle could use some help from a strong back."

He flashed his grin, flexed a biceps. "I can give you a hand before I go up and help my aunt finish upstairs."

So he walked with Ms. Finkle to the big, beautiful house next door with its big, beautiful views of the lake.

And got a firsthand look at the alarm system when they went inside. No dog, he noted, always a plus.

"Um, are you moving, Ms. Finkle?"

"What?" She shot him a glance as they crossed the wide foyer. "Oh, the boxes. No, we're holding a charity event, a silent auction. I'm in charge of collecting the items."

"That's really nice of you."

"We have to do what we can for the less fortunate."

I hear that, Harry thought, noting the open floor plan, the turn to the left. And the double glass doors—closed—with a manly office space behind them.

He carried out boxes, stowed them in the back of a shiny white Mercedes SUV.

And though he wanted it—could've used it—he refused the offer of a five-dollar tip.

"It's for charity," he said. "But thanks."

He went back to work, spent the rest of a sunny summer morning with his hands in hot, soapy water.

He and Mags took the train back to his house in silence because today was chemo day, and Mags spent the ride meditating and holding one of her magic stones to stir up healthy vibes. Or something.

Then, with his mother in her candy-pink headscarf, they rode to the hospital for the best day and worst day.

Best because the nurse—Harry liked the nurse better than the doctor—said his mom was getting better. Worst because the treatment would make her sick.

He sat with her, reading out loud from what they called their C-Day book. She kept her eyes closed while the machine pumped the medicine into her, but he could make her smile, even laugh a little when he changed voices for different characters.

"You're the best, Harry."

She murmured it while Mags sat cross-legged on the floor at her feet. Imagining, she'd told them, bright white light blasting the cancer.

As always on the best/worst day, Mags made some sort of dinner she claimed had healing properties and smelled almost worse than it tasted.

She'd burn incense, hang crystals, and chant and talk about spirit guides or whatever.

But as crazy as she was, she always stayed the night on chemo day, sleeping on an air mattress on the floor beside her sister's bed.

And if she knew how often Harry snuck out of the house, she never spoke of it. If she wondered where he came up with an extra hundred dollars, she never asked.

Now he stood in the Finkles' lakefront house in the breathless quiet. He moved through it soundlessly, though there was no one to hear if he'd stomped his way to those double glass doors.

Inside the office he breathed in the air that smelled vaguely of smoke and cherries. Cigars, Harry decided as he spotted the humidor on the wide, ornate desk.

Curious, he lifted the lid, sniffed. He lifted out a cigar, mimed taking a few important puffs. For the hell of it—he was twelve, after all—he put it into his backpack.

Then he sat in the high-backed leather chair the color of port wine, swiveled back and forth, scowled as he imagined a rich man might when conducting a meeting.

"You're all fired!" He jabbed a finger in the air, snorted out a laugh.

Then got down to business.

He'd come prepared to deal with a locked drawer, but apparently Finkle considered his home too secure to bother.

Harry found the albums—four in all—and, using his penlight, began to go through them.

He wouldn't take them all. It didn't seem fair, plus, it would take too long to move them. But in the past three weeks, he'd done a load of research on stamps.

Finkle had mounted his on black, acid-free paper, used the glassine sleeves to protect them. He had the tongs, but Harry wouldn't risk those. Without practice and skill, he could tear or damage a stamp and lower the value.

Most sleeves had four stamps across and six down. He chose one from the first album and carefully transferred it to the binder he'd brought with him.

One from each album seemed right, so he replaced the first album, opened the second. He took his time with it, and since Finkle had a handy spreadsheet in each album listing the stamps and values, he didn't even have to work very hard.

He'd just chosen the sleeve from the final album when lights flashed on against the other side of the glass.

With his heart banging into his throat, he closed the desk drawer on the final album, grabbed the last sleeve, and took it with him on his slide under the desk.

Somebody was in the house. Somebody besides him.

Another thief. A grown-up. Three grown-ups. With guns.

They stormed into his mind, three men, dressed in black, packing heat. Maybe they didn't want the stamps. Maybe they didn't even know about them.

Sure they did, and they would come in. They'd find him and shoot him in the head and bury him in a shallow grave.

He tried to make himself smaller, imagined himself invisible. And thought of his mother getting sicker and sicker with worry.

He had to get out, get past them somehow, or find a better place to hide. He started to count to three. On three, he'd crawl out from under the desk.

The blast of music had him jolting so he rapped his head on the underside of the desk hard enough to see stars.

Inside his spinning head he said every forbidden word he knew. Twice.

The second round he directed at himself for stupidity.

Thieves didn't turn on the damn lights, and didn't blast out music.

Somebody was in the house, okay, but not a ring of thieves with guns who'd shoot him in the head.

Carefully—especially careful since his hands still trembled a little—he put the sleeve into the binder, closed it into his backpack.

He combat-crawled out from under the desk and, with an eye on the glass doors, away from the light. Along the journey he spotted a guy—older than he was but not old—in boxer shorts.

In the kitchen, pouring what looked like wine from a bottle into a couple of glasses. He'd nearly made it to the shadows when the girl danced into view.

In her underwear. In that lacy bra thing and that thong

deal—like in the Victoria's Secret catalogue that his friend Will's mom got in the mail, and he and Will and some of the guys pored over whenever they could.

Bright red against her skin, and her butt was right there. Just right there. And her breasts were all up there over the top of the bra, sort of jiggling while she shook her shoulders and rocked her hips.

They'd see him if they looked toward the doors, but he couldn't move. He was twelve and male, and the instant woody locked him in place.

She had black hair, long, long black hair she lifted up, then let fall again as she grabbed the wineglass. Drinking, she danced toward the guy. He was dancing, too, but was nothing but a blur to Harry's eyes.

There was only the girl.

She reached a hand up her back, unsnapped the bra. When it fell, every ounce of blood in Harry's body throbbed to his groin.

He'd never seen an actual girl's actual breasts. And they were amazing.

They swayed and they bounced in uncanny time with the music.

He had his first stunning orgasm to Fall Out Boy's "Dance, Dance."

He feared his eyes rolled clear out of his head. He feared his heart stopped. Then he just wanted to lie there on the gleaming hardwood floor for the rest of his natural life.

But now the guy was all over the girl, and the girl was all over the guy. They were doing stuff, lots of stuff, and he was peeling off the thong thing.

And Jesus, she was all the way naked. He could hear her making sex noises over the music.

Then they were on the floor and they were doing it. It! Right there, with the girl on top.

He wanted to watch, more than just about anything. But the

thief inside the boy knew now was the time to get the hell out. Get out while they were too busy doing it to notice.

He eased the door open, belly-crawled through it, then used his foot to nudge it closed behind him.

The girl was practically singing now: *Terry, oh God, Terry!*

Harry went from belly crawl to crab walk, breathed deep, then ran for the door. He heard her scream of ecstasy as he slipped outside.

He used the hike to the train to relive every moment.

He fenced the stamps for twelve thousand dollars. He knew he'd have gotten more if he'd known more. And if he wasn't a kid.

But twelve thousand equaled a fortune. And was too much to keep hidden in his room.

He had to go to his crazy aunt Mags.

He waited until they were alone. His mom insisted on helping, but she was only up to light cleaning work on one house a day, and on Thursdays, they had two.

He helped Mags strip the linens from the single guy's slick, party-time apartment. An all-day rain lashed at the windows as they worked. Mags used the client's stereo system to play some sort of New Agey crap.

She wore a T-shirt she'd tie-dyed in purple and green and the hair she'd recently colored a kind of deep maroon bundled under a green kerchief. She had dangling stones at her ears and a rose quartz crystal—for love and harmony—on a chain around her neck.

"I want to open a bank account."

He glanced over as she bundled sheets into the hamper. Her eyes were blue like his and his mom's, but a lighter shade, and dreamier.

"Why's that, pal?"

"Because."

"Uh-huh."

She unfolded the contour sheet, and together they snapped it, then started to fit it onto the bed.

Harry knew she could leave it just like that. To the "Uh-huh" that stretched into forever.

"I'm almost thirteen, and I've saved up some money, so I want to have a bank account."

"If all of that were true instead of part of it, you'd be talking to your mom and not me about it."

"I don't want to bother her."

"Uh-huh."

They repeated the process on the top sheet.

"I need an adult to go with me, probably sign stuff."

"How much money?"

If she went with him, she'd find out anyway, so he looked her straight in the eye.

"Almost fifteen thousand."

She stared hard back at him. The tiny blue stone on the side of her nose glinted.

"Are you going to tell me where you got that kind of money?"

"I've been tutoring and doing odd jobs, and cleaning houses. It's not like I spend much of anything."

She turned away to get the duvet, black as midnight, soft as a cloud. And said, "Uh-huh."

"It's my money, and it can pay off some of the bills, and some of the mortgage. We're getting all that past-due crap again, and a guy came to the door—a collection agency guy. She said I had to go to my room, but I heard enough."

She nodded as they floated the duvet onto the bed, then started casing the pillows.

"You're a good son, Harry, and you're not going to Dana with this because she wouldn't go for it. Too many questions, but I've got a few before we come to an agreement."

"Okay."

"Did you kill or hurt anybody to get the money?"

"No." Genuine shock radiated. "Man!"

She arranged pillows just so on the bed. "Are you dealing drugs—even pot, Harry?"

He happened to know Mags smoked pot when she could get it, but that wasn't the point. "No."

She gave him a long look with those dreamy eyes. "Are you selling yourself, honey? Sex?"

His jaw didn't actually hit the floor, but it felt like it. "Jesus! No. That's just— No."

"Good. Color me relieved. You're such a good-looking boy. Prime bait for some, so I worried a little there. You think I don't know you sneak out at night?" She carted over the shams.

"I was hoping you had a girl, or met up with some of your friends for fun." Studying him, she toyed with her crystal. "Whatever you're doing, you're doing it for your mom. I love her as much as you do."

"I know."

"I don't know why the universe put this shadow on her, and I'm not a fan of money bringing the light. But it does, for her, seeing as she worries too much about the bills."

Stepping back, Mags eyed the landscape of the bed before nodding approval.

"You don't want a regular bank account. You want a broker-age account. Money makes money, that's the sad state of it."

Mags had some weirdo ideas for sure, but Harry also knew she was nobody's fool. So he listened, he considered.

"A brokerage account?"

"Are you planning on . . . saving more?"

"Yeah. It's not just the bills. The last time the guy fixed the furnace he said it couldn't be fixed again, and we'd need a new one this winter for sure."

"Brokerage account. I dated somebody who does that kind of work. Too straightlaced for it to go anywhere, but he'll set us up."

She crossed to him, laid her hands on his cheeks. "You're a good son and a smart boy." She patted those cheeks. "Keep it up."

They heard about the Finkle Stamp Robbery when Ms. Kelper watered her deck plants. He felt Mags's cool sidelong gaze on him as she washed the glass deck doors and he polished the stainless steel appliances.

"I'm really sorry to hear that," Mags said. "Were they valuable?"

"Apparently, but what's worse is their son Terry was supposed to be taking summer courses in college, but blew that off and partied for a week while they were away. In their house. I had to tell Alva I saw the lights, heard the music, the cars. So it was probably one of his friends, or a friend of a friend—you know how those college parties go—who took them."

A sign, Harry thought as he made the Sub-Zero fridge gleam. Like Mags would say, the universe shined a light.

And his mother got better.

WHEN HE WAS SIXTEEN, Harry fell in love with a doe-eyed blonde named Nita. She supercharged his dreams and made him float down the hallways at school. He tutored her in Spanish—no charge—helped her with her algebra homework.

They went to movies, or for pizza, sometimes solo, sometimes with Will and his girl du jour. He asked her to prom; she said yes.

He cut back on his work—the cleaning and the lifting locks—to spend more time with her. After all, they'd gotten the new furnace, paid down the medical bills, stayed current on the rest.

He kept his hand in, of course, cleaning with his mother and Mags on Saturday afternoons. He averaged two B&Es a month, and added to his account.

They still had bills to pay, after all. And college was around the corner.

His mother liked Nita, loved having his friends hang out at the house watching DVDs or playing video games. His junior year of high school would always be one of his fondest memories.

For prom he pooled money with Will and sprang for a limo. He bought a pink rosebud wrist corsage and rented a tux.

When he stepped out of his bedroom, Dana pressed her hands to her face. "Oh, oh! Just look at you. Mags, it's Booth, Harry Booth. No martinis tonight, son of mine. Shaken or stirred."

"Scout's honor." He held up two fingers, then crossed them to make her laugh.

"Pictures!" She grabbed her phone, but Mags snatched it from her.

"You go stand with that handsome boy of yours. God, Dana, he looks just like you."

"Love of my life," Dana murmured as she tipped her head to his shoulder.

He wrapped both arms around her, pulled her closer. "Best mom in the history of moms."

She turned, brushed a hand at his hair. "You got so tall. My baby's all grown up, Mags, and on his way to the junior prom. Come on, we need one of you and Harry."

Dana and Mags switched places. Mags rose to her toes as if to kiss Harry's cheek. She whispered, "I slipped condoms into your right jacket pocket. Hell of a lot better safe than sorry."

That night, after the magic of the prom, during the after-party at Will's, Harry took Nita's virginity, and she his, on the cool tile floor of the guest bath.

He began his last high school summer as happy as he'd ever been.

Before summer ended, cancer came back for one last dance.

Chapter Two

HARRY NEVER DOUBTED HIS aunt's love for her sister. The woman's past included the carny circuit, communes, and covens. She'd ridden her thumb around the country, worked—briefly—as a Vegas showgirl, a performance artist, a magician's assistant, and a waitress at a truck stop, where she met the man she referred to as her first ex-husband.

But Mags caged up her wanderlust for a decade to stick by her baby sister. She cleaned houses and apartments and office buildings, and even in the good times rarely spent more than a handful of days away and on her own devices.

In the bad times she was a rock—a colorful one, but solid. She never missed a doctor's appointment or chemo day. When Dana was too weak to manage for herself, Mags bathed her, dressed her—refusing to let Harry help.

"A son doesn't give his mom a bath," she decreed. "Not when she's got a sister."

But he understood how deep and wide that love ran when cancer took his mother's hair for the third time.

He and Dana made dinner together. She was having a good day, a pretty strong day. Maybe he worried about the dark circles that haunted her eyes, or how thin she felt—like skin over loose bones—when he hugged her, but her color was good, the eyes above those circles bright and happy.

He'd finished his homework, and Mags was coming over around eight. He could go out without worrying, hang out with Will awhile. Then he had a house to case before he came home.

So a good day took a turn into the weird and amazing when Mags strolled in two hours early.

The woman who loved dying her mass of waves crazy colors, who often braided beads and feathers through it, stood with her bald scalp covered with glitter.

The spoon in Dana's hand clattered to the floor.

"Oh God, Mags! What have you done?"

"It's a look, right?" Mags posed, one hand on her hip, the other behind her ear. "The glitter makes it, I think. I used rainbow glitter as a tribute to my gay and lesbian friends, enemies, and strangers, so it's double the pow."

"Your hair, your beautiful hair."

"I donated it—another pow." She pointed a finger as Dana began to cry. "Knock that off. What's for dinner?"

"Mags, Mags, you didn't have to—"

"I don't have to do a damn thing. Free spirit here, and I do what I want when I want to." She crossed to the kitchen as she spoke, sniffed at the skillet. "Smells good."

"It's—it's got chicken in it. You're a vegetarian—"

"Not today. Today I'm a bald carnivore, so there better be enough for me."

"There's enough." Because he feared he might cry, too, Harry moved the skillet off the heat before it burned, then wrapped an arm around each woman, hugged them in. "There's always going to be enough."

After dinner, when Mags dragged his mom into her particular form of Scrabble—bonus points for best made-up words—Harry studied himself in the bathroom mirror.

He liked his hair. Actually put off haircuts as long as he

could get away with it because they always cut it shorter than he liked.

And he really liked the way Nita played with it.

But he understood what Mags had done was a gesture of love, support, and, hell, solidarity.

So he picked up his electric razor—he didn't trust himself with lather and a blade on his face. He took a lot of deep breaths until he saw more determination than fear in the eyes looking back at him.

After he took the first long swipe—almost straight down the middle—and the thick waves fell, he had to bend over from the waist, clutch the vanity.

His legs buckled, his stomach twisted, and his breath just stopped.

"Holy shit." He forced himself to look again and watched his own eyes bug out. "Holy shit. No going back. Get it over with."

The second pass brought on the same reaction, but he held steadier for the next, and the next.

The razor wasn't the best, and he figured he'd probably cut its life expectancy by half.

It left a stubble, but he figured it was the thought that counted.

He looked . . . really weird, he realized. Not like himself at all. It occurred to him he'd have to wear a ski cap for his nightwork, but he considered the possibilities of more radical appearance changes, and how they could add to his bag of tricks.

He cleaned up the mess, then studied himself again. And realized something else.

How his mother must feel when she looked in the mirror. She didn't have a choice about losing her hair. The cancer and the treatments took that choice away from her.

When she looked in the mirror, she saw that loss, that lack of choice, and someone who didn't look quite like her.

"Another reason Mags did it," he murmured. "So she could feel and see and know what Mom does."

He slipped into his bedroom, changed his shirt. Then tried on a pair of the glasses—clear lenses—he sometimes used to change his look. Switched to sunglasses.

Narrowed his eyes and imagined himself with a soul patch or a goatee. He might be able to make some facial hair bits with his own hair and some of the stuff they used in the theater department at school for plays.

Pleased with the possible side benefits, he stowed the bag of hair, grabbed a ball cap.

When he came out, the sisters were deep in the game.

"Oxmoana? Come on, Mags."

"The plaintive cry of a constipated ox, or that of a female ox in labor." Mags smiled, fluttered her eyes as Dana rolled hers. "Seven-letter bonus, on double-word score, plus the bonus-bonus. I'm kicking your ass, Dane."

"Yeah, well, I can beat that. I can beat it. Hold on."

Harry stood back, watched his mother rearrange her letters, and felt the love for both of them just blow through him like a warm wind.

"I'll just add an *s* to your word for a field of constipated oxen, and go up with q-r-a-z-i-e-s. Qrazies, a couple of bald women drinking cheap wine and making up words for Scrabble."

Dana picked up her glass. "Now who's kicking whose ass?"

"The night is young."

"I'm going to leave you qrazies and go hang with Will."

"You have fun, baby, and . . ." Dana trailed off as she turned. She slapped both hands over her mouth as her eyes filled. "Harry. Oh, Harry."

"What?" He looked down, smiled. "Whew. I thought I forgot to zip my fly."

"I can't believe you—you weren't even bald as a baby. He came out with a headful of hair. Remember, Mags?"

"Yeah, I remember. Want some glitter, pal? I got plenty."

"I'll pass, thanks."

"Oh God, look at us." Tears streamed as Dana began to laugh. "Would you just look at us." She gripped Mags's hand, reached for her son's. "I'm the luckiest woman in the world."

Nita cried, and not in a sweet, supportive way.

"How could you do that! You didn't even talk to me about it first."

"It's my hair. Or was."

She got that look in her eye, one that warned him they were going to have an actual fight.

"How would *you* feel if I cut off my hair, or dyed it blue like some weirdo?"

"It's your hair."

"Oh, easy for you to say, because you know I'd never do anything like that."

"I don't care about your hair. I care about you. And I did it for my mom."

She took a big, audible breath, the way she did when she considered herself really reasonable against his screwups. He'd learned over the past eight months he screwed up a lot on Nita's scale.

"I'm sorry about your mom, you know I am. It's awful what she's going through. I hate it, so much. And I understand you have to help her work, and be there for her so we can't spend a lot of time together, or go out as much as other couples do."

"But."

There was, Harry knew, always a *but* when she pulled out Reasonable Nita.

"But it's our senior year, and the homecoming game and dance is next week! Next week, Harry. Your hair's never going to grow back in a week. How are we supposed to go to our last homecoming with you looking like a freak?"

That snapped it. He hadn't known you could fall out of love in a single moment.

"My mother lost her hair. It's the third time she's been there. I guess that makes her three times a freak."

"You know I didn't mean it like that, and that's a stupid thing to say. Your mom—she's a victim. You did it on purpose, and didn't even ask me first."

He hadn't known when you fell out of love you felt so cold.

"My mom's nobody's victim. She's a fucking warrior. And I don't have to ask you, or anybody, about what I do for her. And this?" He pointed to his head. "This doesn't come back until hers does. Since that makes me a freak, and you don't want to be seen with one, we're done."

Shock widened her eyes an instant before they filled. "You're breaking up with me? You shave your head and you break up with me, right before homecoming? You can't do that."

"Shaving my head didn't have anything to do with you, and you made it clear you don't want to go with me the way things are."

"I already have my dress!"

"So wear it or don't. Not my problem."

"You can't just . . . We're having sex."

"Not anymore."

He walked out on her, and felt both cold and free. He decided swinging by to see her on the way to Will's had opened his world.

Everything had been fine when his mother was in remission. But they'd started to get rocky when the cancer came back, when he hadn't been able to take Nita out as often or give her as much attention as she'd wanted.

She'd been subtle about it, he thought now, just enough to make him feel guilty and torn.

Well, no more of that.

Maybe he'd miss having a girlfriend, and he sure as hell would miss the sex—when they'd managed it. But he had plenty to fill his time. School—and he still had hope of a scholarship to Northwestern—friends, work, his mom, his nightwork.

Hands in pockets, head down, mood sour, he trudged his way to Will's. He knocked on the door of the cheerful white bungalow.

Will's dad answered, stood in his Bears sweatshirt, angled his head.

He plucked Harry's cap off, grinned.

He said, "Dude!" then scrubbed a hand over the stubble. "I can smooth that out for you if you want."

"You can?"

Will's dad ran a hand over his own smooth dome. "I got the skills." Then he laid a hand on Harry's shoulder, and his eyes went a little misty. "You're a stand-up guy, Harry Booth. Get your skinny white ass in here."

CRISP, COLORFUL FALL TOOK a hard turn into the gray and white of winter. And winter punched down with brutal fists, blew its icy breath over the city as if determined to freeze it in place.

The new furnace did its best, but the aging hot-water heater gasped its last on a February morning that dawned at minus eight.

Harry had enough socked away for a new one, though he had to lie to his mother about getting a deal on the unit and the labor. It wasn't the first lie he'd told her that winter, and wouldn't be the last.

He told himself she looked better, and once they got through the winter, once she could get out, walk in the fresh air again, she'd bounce all the way back.

His acceptance letter from Northwestern and the scholarship perked her up. She could happily pore over the college brochures, haunt their website, and spend whole evenings making lists of what she thought he'd need in his dorm room.

But he'd done the math.

"I'm going to commute the first year. Live at home. Free rent and laundry services."

"I want you to have the whole experience. You're the first in our family to go to college. And such a good one. I want—"

"I'll have plenty of the experience—and not have to bunk with somebody I don't know. After I check it all out, make some friends or whatever, I can think about living on campus next year."

"But you'll miss all the activities, the parties."

"Now you want me to go to drunken college parties?"

She smiled a little. "Sort of. I want you to have a life."

"I've got a life."

"And spend too much of it on me. I know it costs more to live on campus, and the scholarship won't cover everything, but we can take out a student loan."

"Next year."

She sat back. "I've been looking into taking out a second mortgage."

"No."

Now she folded her arms over her thin chest. "Harrison Silas Booth. Who's in charge around here?"

"Well, Dana Lee Booth, you said you wanted me to have a life, and having one means making my own decisions. My decision is to live at home the first year."

"First term. The first term, Harry, that's a good compromise. You'll know your way around by then, you'll make friends."

"You sure are anxious to cut me loose."

She reached out, laid a hand over his. "I want my bird to fledge. I want to see you fly, Harry. You take the first term to find your way, then we'll figure out the rest."

"First term, but you ditch the idea of a second mortgage."

"I can agree to that. We'll look into student loans. You could get a job on campus. It's such a beautiful campus."

Because it made her happy, he let her rhapsodize.

But he had a job, and once she was settled for the night, he'd go to work.

A couple of young professionals spending the cold heart of February in their vacation home in Aruba had a very nice collection—his and hers—of designer watches.

Bvlgari, Rolex, Chopin, Baume & Mercier, TAG Heuer. And, his information told him, a couple of Graff.

He doubted they took everything with them.

But if he bombed there, people who collected five-figure watches had lots and lots of other goodies to choose from.

He hoped for the watches—one from each; he wasn't a monster. If one of those included a Graff, he could turn them and cover medical, household, and college expenses for months.

He'd been inside the house the previous spring when the owners interviewed the Sparkle Sisters to do a deep-cleaning job but hadn't hired them, so he knew the layout. He knew the security system, and could beat it.

And he knew the Jenkinsons had two safes—one in their home office, one in their master suite walk-in closet.

That one would hold the watches.

He'd made an investment and bought the same brand. He'd rented a small storage space, like a holding center for items waiting to be moved. And in it, for weeks, he'd practiced the art of safecracking.

They hadn't gone top-of-the-line, probably lucky for him, but Harry thought he had a knack for the art. With his new skill, some luck—and the coming six to ten inches of snow he took as a sign—he'd start college in the fall debt free. Or close.

He worried about leaving his mother, even for the two hours—three, tops—the job would take him. What if the storm knocked out the power? What if she got sick and called for him?

What if, what if?

But if he pulled off this job—and he damn well would pull it off—he could eke out the take slowly, paying things down, tell her he'd taken on some extra tutoring.

He'd think of something.

So he took the train, just a teenage boy bundled up to the eyeballs like everyone else on a gusty, snowy night in Chicago.

He got off a full stop before his destination, put the thick-framed glasses he'd worn on the ride in one of his inside pockets. Switched the football ski cap for the hockey one, and trudged a half mile through the bitter.

Anyone with any sense, or without thieving on their mind, was tucked into the warm at one in the morning. His only concern on the half-mile hike was the possibility of a patrol car stopping to see what the hell he was doing out.

Went to see his girl, you know. Heading down to the El to go home. No problem, Officer.

But he didn't see any patrols, and when he reached his destination, kept walking with purpose.

You go furtive, he figured, people pay attention.

He didn't hesitate, but walked straight to the front door.

The locks posed no real challenge, as they'd gone for decor instead of serious security with the single cylinder and basic dead bolt in Venetian bronze.

They fell for him inside a minute.

He slipped out of his boots, stepped in on his thick socks, stuffed the boots into a plastic bag, counting the seconds in his head.

Shut the door, lock it, and move straight to the alarm box.

They'd gone basic there, too. He opened it, clamped it off, then stood and let the silence surround him.

His favorite part, he could admit. Beyond the prep, the practice, the study came the moment when he could just stand in the silence and his pulse tripped with the thrill of it.

The stealing, the payoff? That was just the work.

But that moment, that silence, that was his.

So he took it, then he moved.

Straight up the stairs, double doors on the left, and to the closet on the right wall.

A lot of clothes—a hell of a lot of shoes. These two were crazy clothes hogs. But he could admire the man's suits—that fine, fine wool—and the shirts with the monogram on the cuffs. The soft leather of designer shoes.

He admired, too, the woman's collection of sweaters. Cashmere, merino wool. He felt a tug of temptation, wanted to take one—just one—for his mother. So warm and soft.

But that would bring questions, and he didn't want to lie about a gift.

Instead he played his light over the safe. And smiled.

"Hi there. I've been working with your brother for a while now. Let's get acquainted."

He shook his head as he got out his stethoscope. "Basic combination lock. They should've done better."

His first step was to find the combination length. To make sure all the wheels disengaged, he turned the dial clockwise three times.

He put the bell of the stethoscope beside the dial and began to turn it counterclockwise. When he heard the first two clicks, he stopped, noted down the number on the dial.

He reset, repeated twice more to be sure.

"Good start."

Moving the dial counterclockwise, he stopped it opposite his first number. Started back—slow, careful—to where he'd parked the wheels, listening for clicks, noting down the number until he heard no more.

A four-number combination, he thought.

And now his math skills—who said you never used algebra in real life?—came into play.

He drew two line graphs, labeled them. X-axis for starting point, y-axis for the right contact point.

He reset the lock, then put it at zero.

He worked in silence—just those clicks—worked patiently, noting down each contact area, then graphing the points, x-value, y-value.

It took him thirty-three minutes of painstaking work, careful listening, exacting math to identify the four numbers.

8–9–14–2.

Now he needed the sequence. He started to try the numbers as written down, then stopped.

"It's a date. Jesus, it's Valentine's Day. Probably their first date or something. In '98. Could it be that easy?"

A four-digit combination could mean close to two thousand variables. No way he'd hit on the first.

But he tried it. 2–14–9–8.

And when he pulled the lever, the door opened smooth as silk.

"Oh shit! Just like that."

The thrill nearly rose to the level of that first, strange, outrageous orgasm at twelve.

He pulled out his stopwatch, hit the button.

"Thirty-five minutes, twelve seconds. Not bad, but I'll get better."

He drew out a glass-topped case—no lock—that would hold a dozen ladies' watches. It currently held seven. And one was the Graff.

He took it out, shined his penlight over it.

He'd never held anything that cost so much. And there was beauty here, he could see that. The way the diamonds fired under the light, and the sapphires mated with them gleamed.

He'd learn more about gems, he promised himself. They had, well, life in them. More fun than stamps or old coins.

He put the watch in the pouch he'd brought, put the case back, took out the next, and studied the men's collection. He settled on the Rolex—a classic for a reason—then replaced the case.

He drew out other cases—cuff links, earrings, bracelets, necklaces. Small collections, he supposed, but impressive.

And tempting.

Gotta get home, he reminded himself, and he still had to go by the storage place, stow the take.

But in the end, his fingers simply reached for a pair of square-cut diamond earrings. Small but classy, and probably not easily traceable.

He closed the safe, spun the dial. Checked the area to be sure he left nothing of himself behind.

He retraced his steps and was walking through the thickly falling snow less than an hour after he'd stepped into the house.

And with, he figured, about two hundred thousand in his backpack.

He was going to push for twenty percent. He'd take ten, but he'd push. And maybe get fifteen.

And with thirty thousand, he'd knock back a shitload of the medical bills.

In the spring, they'd have that fresh air—and the heating bills would vanish. Maybe, just maybe, he could talk his mother into taking a vacation in the summer. They'd sold their old car long ago, but they could rent one. He had his learner's permit. He'd taken the course in school, and Will's dad took him out in his car so he got practice. He could get his license, they'd rent a car, and they'd drive to the ocean.

She'd told him how much she wanted to see the ocean. Plus, sea air was supposed to be healing and all that.

They could get a motel near the beach for a few days. The drive to and from, that would be vacation, too. They hadn't had a vacation since . . .

Since cancer, he thought, then shoved it away.

He'd had a great night, no point in spoiling it. Time to look ahead to spring, to summer, to college in the fall.

But winter held on, and March went out as ferociously as it came in.

By the middle of April, he decided Chicago had become the ice planet Hoth.

Then slowly, spring began to crack winter's icy grip.

They threw open the windows, let the air in. Sure, they had to close them at night or freeze to death, but it was a start.

Harry felt hope bloom like the crocuses his mother had planted when he'd been a little boy.

He was even seeing a new girl. Alyson. Science nerd, but totally cute. Nothing serious; he didn't want serious before he started college. But he had a prom date, and that mattered.

He walked home in the almost balmy air, juggling his night's schedule in his head.

Homework—had to keep those grades up—a little more research on precious gems. Dinner—maybe he could talk Mom into ordering pizza.

And he had a potentially lucrative target he wanted to take a closer look at.

He walked into the house, mood high.

"Hey, Mom! I'm grabbing a snack. Figure I aced my chem test today. I got a crapload of homework, but I'm all over it."

He had a bag of Doritos in one hand, a can of Coke in the other when she came out of the bedroom.

"You used to want a folded-over PB and J after school."

"Times change. I need the carb and caffeine rush for the calculus and the paper I have to write for . . ."

It got through that high mood, the way she looked at him cut right through it.

"What's wrong?"

"Let's sit down, Harry."

"Mom."

"Please. Let's sit down. How about you bring me one of those Cokes?"

He made his mind blank; it was all he could do. He poured hers into a glass over ice because that's how she liked it. Then he sat at the kitchen table with her.

"I went in for a PET scan today."

"What? You didn't tell me you had one coming up. I go with you."

"You have school. Mags went. And I didn't tell you, baby, because the doctor wanted one. He wanted one because . . . Baby, the chemo's not working this time."

"No, they said it was. They said."

"It was, for a short time last fall, into the winter, but not anymore, Harry, and not for a while."

He'd known, hadn't he? Inside he'd known. The circles under her eyes, deeper, her energy sliding away like the flesh on her bones.

"They'll try a different treatment."

"Harry." She took both his hands. "It's spread. They've done all they can do."

The hands holding his felt like bony feathers. So light, so thin and sharp. "I don't believe that. You can't believe it either."

"I need you to be brave for me. It's not fair. I shouldn't have to ask you to be brave. None of it's been fair. It stole your childhood, and I hate that. I hate it. I'm not saying I won't fight, I'm not saying that. But we're stopping the chemo."

"Mom, please—"

"It might buy me a couple months, months where I'm sick from it. But that's all. I want the time I have left with you where I can be your mom, at least for most of it."

She squeezed his hands hard. "Six months. Eight or nine, maybe, with more treatments. I'd go through it a hundred times, Harry, if it meant I could watch you grow into a man. Graduate from college, fall in love, start a family. But I can't. My heart wants that—you're my everything—but my body won't let me."

"You beat it before."

"Not this time. Help me make these six months good ones."

"You beat it before," he repeated.

When she put her arms around him, he was a child again. And the child pressed his face to his mother's breast and wept.

Chapter Three

ON THE LAST DAY of school, the last page, as Harry thought of it, of a twelve-year chapter of his life, he heard hysterical laughter spilling out from the open windows of the house where flowers bloomed in painted pots beside the front door.

She laughed more now, his mother, and looked so much brighter, happier, he could convince himself—almost—they'd beaten the enemy inside her after all.

She planted flowers. She cleaned houses, played music, went shopping. She bought a new dress to wear to his graduation.

She said every day was a gift, and he tried to see it her way.

But sometimes, in the night, in the dark, he thought each day that passed was one less.

Today he heard her laughing—giggling, he thought, like one of his classmates.

Former classmates now.

He walked in to see her and Mags at the kitchen table laughing their asses off.

Mags's short skullcap of hair blasted a sapphire blue.

That was no real surprise, but his mother's short new growth in bubblegum pink knocked him back.

The two of them grinned over at him.

"What do you think?" Dana asked.

"I—I think you look like Easter eggs. If they had them on Mars."

That brought on more insane laughter.

"I've got enough of both colors to do yours. I can mix them for a nice purple. You got a kind of George Clooney Caesar do going," Mags observed. "Purple would set it off."

"Hard pass."

Dana rose and got a Coke out of the refrigerator before he could get one for himself. "I'll cover it with a scarf for graduation. Don't worry."

He took the Coke, bent down to kiss her cheek. "You will not. I bet nobody else is going to have a mom—and an aunt—with pink and blue hair."

She leaned in for a hug.

So thin, so thin. He pushed that away, and reminded himself: Here, she's here. She's happy.

"Mags ambushed me with it after we finished the Gobbles' house. And I thought, what the hell. And in all the excitement, I forgot!" She clamped her hands on his face. "It's the last day of school. My baby, my six-foot-two baby just had his last day of high school."

"Uh-oh, I need to go put some sentimental music on."

"It's already in my head," Dana told Mags. "I can still see you, my little man, in your red jacket, carrying your Scooby-Doo lunch box when I walked you to your first day of school. And when we got there, you just said, 'Bye!' and walked right in by yourself. Fearless. You were always fearless."

He remembered it because he remembered everything.

"Got that from my mom."

"I'm going to fix you a snack. You must have a party to go to tonight. Are you going with Alyson? She's a nice girl. A smart one."

"She's a nice girl, and smart, but I've got a date with somebody else tonight. Actually, two somebodies."

Dana stopped, turned back. "You're not going to spend the first night of the rest of your life with me and Mags."

"I think I get to decide how I want to spend the first night of the rest, and I made plans."

"What kind of plans?"

"My plans. We've got a couple hours, so time for that snack—make enough of whatever for all of us. Then I'm going to mow the lawn."

Which would take, like, ten minutes, considering the size of it.

"It's a surprise," he continued, anticipating the questions. "What you're wearing's fine. You're going to want a sweater maybe, or a jacket, but that's it."

"A mystery," Mags said. "A mysterious surprise. I already like it."

They didn't have a clue even when they boarded the train, and he refused to give hints. But as they got closer and more people piled on wearing caps and jerseys, Mags gave Harry a quick shoulder punch.

"Wrigley. Night game against the Marlins."

"Maybe."

"You don't really like baseball," Dana began. "I've never understood where I went wrong, but—"

"I like it okay. But my ladies love it."

"This is great. This is awesome. Man, I should have my blood-stone pendant for energy. No, no, the black onyx." Mags dug through her purse. "I have to have something in here. My lucky Cubs hat's at home, but I can visualize it. Who's pitching? I can't remember who's pitching."

"Mitre," Harry told her.

"Okay, oh well. I'll visualize hard."

He loved the way they talked about the game around him, on the train, on the walk to the stadium, and under the big red sign.

He loved the buzz from them, and everyone else.

"My treat," Dana said. "For the last day of school."

"Too late." Harry pulled tickets out of his back pocket. "Already done, for the women who got me through the last day of school."

"Harry, those—those are box seats. You can't—"

"Already done. And everybody's getting a new lucky hat."

"Don't spoil the boy's plans." Mags gave Dana's hand a squeeze. "Take the gift."

"You're right, you're right. We didn't even get to a game last season, and now? Box seats. Oh, Mags, look. First base side, right behind the dugout!"

He bought them caps, and one for himself.

And heard his mother's reverent sigh as they walked into the stadium and the green grass, the rich brown mound, the white baselines filled the world back to the ivy-covered wall.

"We're practically on the field. I can smell the grass! Mags, remember when we used to watch games from the rooftop?"

She gestured to the buildings outside the walls.

"Sure I do. Uncle Silas would take us up there, ply us with hot dogs and root beer. I've told you about Uncle Silas, your grandmother's brother."

"I got his name in the middle."

"You sure do. He fell in love with a woman who didn't love him back, and he pined for her until he died. Never married. He had a heart attack when you were just a baby."

Harry knew the story. Mags and Dana's father had taken off when Dana had still been in diapers. Their mother had worked in her brother's butcher shop, raised her two girls.

She'd been killed by a stray bullet in a drive-by shooting when Harry's mother had been seventeen.

The same age, he realized, he was now.

"He might've had a wonky heart, but it was a sweet one. Those were good times." Mags patted Dana's thigh. "Real good times."

"They were." Dana breathed deep. "This is an even better one."

They ate hot dogs, drank beer. Though he didn't have much of a taste for it, Harry sipped some from his mother's cup.

Solidarity.

They cheered, they booed, argued calls.

His mother looked radiant—that was the word that came to his mind. She sprang up to watch the flight of a long ball, hooting when the center fielder caught it a few feet shy of the wall, moaned at a strikeout.

The sun went down; the lights came on.

More through accident than design, he caught a foul that lined straight at him. And that had his mother up and dancing.

"Fast hands," Mags said, shooting him a knowing look. "Sharp reflexes."

After he shook the feeling back into his hand, he presented it to Dana. "Your souvenir, ma'am."

Whether it was the lucky caps, the bloodstone Mags dug out of her purse, or the Cubs' solid night, Mitre pitched a shutout, and the boys walked off the field with fourteen runs.

Harry didn't have his mother's passion for the game, but he knew a purist wouldn't rave over a fourteen-to-zip nine innings.

She leaned her head against his shoulder as they sat, as people filed out.

"You know what beats a summer night at Wrigley?"

"What?"

"Nothing."

They got off the train a stop early, bought ice cream cones, and walked Mags to her apartment.

As they walked the few blocks to home, he put an arm around his mother's shoulders just like she had once put hers around his.

"I bet you're tired."

"A little," she admitted. "But a good tired. It was a terrific surprise. You've always been my very best surprise. You never ask about your father."

"What's to ask?" he said, and genuinely meant it. "He doesn't matter."

"He does, because without him I wouldn't have you."

She leaned against him, sighed. "I should tell you because you should know. We were young. I was so sad when we lost my mother. Mags was mad, but I couldn't push out of the sad. Uncle Silas tried so hard, but he was grieving, too. Anyway, there was the boy and he wanted me. I wanted him. We didn't love each other. I don't want you to think he broke my heart, because it wasn't like that."

They turned to the house, and she stopped at the door. "Let's sit a minute."

She lowered to the stoop with the flowers blooming on either side.

"We were only together for a few weeks, had already drifted apart when I realized I was pregnant. He'd started college, Mags had gone off to be a carny, and I was working in the butcher shop. It's going to sound odd, but I didn't panic or wonder what to do. I was thrilled from the first moment. Young, foolish, but thrilled. And all the sad just melted away.

"I had to tell the boy, but I wasn't surprised by his reaction. I couldn't blame him for it, and I never have."

She looked over at him, her eyes tired but level. "You shouldn't either, that's why I'm telling you. He was barely eighteen, just starting his life, like you're about to. We didn't love or want each other. I know I could've pressed him to contribute, and maybe I should have. But I didn't want to. You were mine, and why should you have someone in your life who didn't want you, when I did? He'd resent you, and me, the way I realized my father had come to resent my mother and Mags and me. No, I wasn't going to take you there. That's a painful road."

"I wouldn't want it any other way, if that's what you're asking me."

"Good. That's good. Anyway, Mags came back a few weeks

before you were born, was right there when you made your debut. She came back again when Uncle Silas died. I wish you could remember him, Harry, but you were just a baby. He adored you. He left enough for me to put a deposit down on this house. Then we started the business, got it going pretty good once you were in school. And here we are."

She leaned into him. "I had the best gift, the greatest love, come out of all that sad. I just want you to remember that. And?" She gave him a big, noisy kiss on the cheek. "No sad tonight."

"I know I don't remember him—Uncle Silas—but I know him through you and Mags. I remember all the stories you've told me."

She smiled, tapped his temple. "Magic memory."

"Yeah."

And he knew he'd never forget sitting with her on the front stoop on a summer night with her pretty flowers beside them.

She wore her pink hair and her new dress to his graduation, and with Mags's help threw a party for him and his friends.

But as June faded into July, the dark circles haunted her eyes. And he could see the pain above those circles far too often. When she could barely cross a room without running out of breath, it was his turn to tell her to sit down so they could talk.

"I made a decision."

She sipped at the odd tea Mags insisted had healing properties. "About what?"

"I'm taking a gap year."

"Harry—"

"No, you listen." He knew she couldn't fight him, and part of him hated that, hated knowing she'd grown too weak to fight.

"A lot of people do it, and that's what I'm doing. Mags needs me to keep the business going. You need me. And I need to be here. I need it, Mom. Northwestern's not going anywhere."

"Your scholarship. You worked so hard."

"It'll hold over."

"I'm sorry." She squeezed her eyes shut. "I'm sorry that I can't argue with you. That I can't make you go. I wanted to watch you walk into college the way you walked into elementary school. I wanted that. I hate this. I hate knowing I'm not going to be there for you. Listen . . ."

She had to take a moment. It was one of the bad days, and they both knew it.

"I talked to Anita at hospice this morning. She's been great, and she understands I don't want to go into the hospital. I want to stay here. You'll need help."

"Mags and I can take care of you."

"Don't I know it. But if you need help, they're there. I've made arrangements. I wrote everything down. I know it's hard for you to talk about this, but we need to."

"Okay." It made him feel sick and scared, but he just nodded.

"Cremation, that's what I want. No big ceremony or anything. You and Mags, you can decide where to spread the ashes. Whatever and wherever."

His stomach tightened into sweaty fists, and the heat slicked his body like a second skin, but he nodded again. "Okay, don't worry."

"I had your name added to the house, I did that months ago, so it'll be yours. You should sell it. We've got some good equity in it. You should sell it to help with college. Property values are going up, and there're a lot of buyers who want to take a place like this and gentrify it."

She reached for his hands, and he felt the tremor in hers.

"Don't you waste that brain of yours, my baby. You're so crazy smart. You go to college. You find your passion. Explore. Travel—see places. All kinds of places. You're tough, Harry. Smart and strong, and you're kind. I did a damn good job."

"Yeah, you did."

"Be there for Mags. She may be your crazy aunt, but she's never let us down." She pushed the tea away. "Even if she does try to pour this crap into me."

"How about a Coke?"

She smiled. "I'd love a Coke."

As summer faded, so did her strength.

Mags moved out of her apartment and spent her nights on the air mattress beside her sister's bed.

Harry spent his days cleaning houses with Mags and using the money from any nightwork to pay a professional aide to care for his mother when they couldn't.

In the fall, most of his friends left for college. The pang he felt came and went at odd times. When he took out the trash or tied his shoes or hit the library for another stack of books to read to his mother.

They bought a wheelchair so they could take her out in sunlight and fresh air. But even in the glory of an Indian summer, she got chilled if they stayed out beyond an hour.

By November Dana's world contracted to her bedroom. She ate little, slept long. They'd rented a hospital bed, and moved the old dresser into the living room so they had room for two beds, two chairs.

Friends and neighbors and clients sent flowers or food or both. He'd never forget that Will's mother came by three or four nights a week after work to sit with her, whether or not Dana slept through the visit.

"Take your aunt out and buy her a coffee," she told him.

So they escaped the house that smelled too much of flowers and sickness and walked in the sharp November air.

Mags took his hand. "Honey, we have to let her go." He tried to pull his hand away, but Mags clamped down. "It's love holding her here now, for you, and for me, too. She's suffering. The medicine helps with the pain, but it doesn't stop it. The pot helps with the nausea, but it's still there. She's drifting from minute to minute, caught between worlds now, and hanging on to this one for us."

He wanted to curse her, shove her away. But he stared straight ahead, seeing nothing. "She said every day's a gift. And she was asking Mrs. Forester about Will when we left. She picked out a new book to start tonight."

"She's got such a strong will, and such a huge love for you. It's a crap thing for me to say to a boy who just turned eighteen. But she won't move on until you tell her you'll be okay."

"So you're ready to just let her die."

It was Mags who let go of his hand. "No. I'm never going to be ready. But I know she is."

They didn't speak any more about it, or about anything as they circled the block, and the resentment inside him built like storm clouds. He had plenty more to say, and promised he'd say it all after Will's mom left, after his own mother slept.

He'd be damned if his crazy, stupid, selfish aunt would tell him what to do, feel, think. And if she was tired of helping take care of her own sister, she could go to hell.

He'd do it all himself.

When they walked back into the house, Mags went straight to the kitchen. "I'm going to heat up some soup for Dana. Do you want some?"

"No."

Will's mother came out of the bedroom. "We had a nice talk." She moved over to hug Harry. "Don't be upset if she thinks you're home on a college break now. She's a little tired and confused."

"Okay, it's okay. Mrs. Forester, I really appreciate you coming to see her like this."

"Your mama and I, we've been friends since you and Will started kindergarten." She gave him a quick, extra squeeze. "I'm going on home, Mags," she called out. "You let me know if you need anything."

"I will. Thank you, Keisha."

She gave Harry's arm a pat. "You take care of each other now."

He'd take care of everything, he thought. Including telling his aunt where she could stick her advice.

But first they needed to work together to get some food into his mom. He knew how to focus, how to set everything else outside the walls of that focus and get a task done.

He took off his jacket, had started to hang it up when he heard his mother talking. Not calling for him, just talking. And laughing.

Jacket still in hand, he walked to the bedroom.

She leaned against the elevated back of the bed, her eyes too bright. She wore the red sweater Mags had knitted over her pale blue nightgown. And she smiled at him.

"Hi, baby! Welcome home. I was just telling Uncle Silas you were coming for the weekend. He's got center-cut pork chops on special, and he'll bring some over for dinner."

He stumbled over what to say, just stood there. And Mags breezed in with a tray. "I hope there's mashed potatoes to go with them, and no spinach."

"Peas. And crescent rolls."

"I get to whap the can on the counter."

"You always get to."

"I'm the big sister."

"I'm not really hungry right now," Dana said as Mags spooned up some soup.

"For Mrs. Cardini's minestrone? Your favorite."

And Harry felt shame—it just washed over him in a hot flood as he watched his aunt spoon a little soup into her sister's mouth.

"She makes the best."

"She does. And Harry's going to start reading your new book while you eat. What's this one?"

"We got the story of an ordinary man's extraordinary journey. Adventure! Redemption! Love!"

"Sex?"

"I'm not reading sex out loud to my mom and aunt."

"Your boy's a prude, Dane. But he knows how to give a dramatic reading."

"He's studying books in college, and he'll be in the school plays again. I can't eat any more, Mags." She turned her head away. "I got my suitcase out, didn't I? Did I finish packing? I need to finish packing."

Mags set the spoon down, put the tray aside. Harry saw the tears wash over the blue of her eyes. "You're all set."

"Oh, good. Oh, sure, I see." She smiled at something only she could see across the room. "All packed and ready to go. You'll be too busy to miss me, baby, with college and everything."

Still smiling, her eyes so bright, and sunk so deep, she reached for his hand. "I'll send you postcards. You can make a scrapbook. I always meant to make a scrapbook. You'll be okay, right, Harry? You're all grown up. You'll be okay while I'm gone on my trip."

He took her hand while tears burned behind his eyes. "Yeah, I'll be okay."

"You and Mags will look out for each other."

"Yeah, we will. You don't have to worry."

"I'm a little tired. I'll finish packing later."

She closed her eyes, and as she drifted to sleep, Mags rose and picked up the tray.

"I need a drink," she said, and walked out.

When he came out, she'd poured two glasses.

"Crap box wine is still wine, just like crap pizza is still pizza. If you don't want any, I'll drink your share."

"I'm sorry." When she shook her head, he plowed on. "I'm sorry for how I acted, what I said, and the worse things I thought."

"She's your mom."

"She's your baby sister."

Mags gulped down wine as tears spilled down her cheeks. "I'm so pissed off, so fucking pissed off at whoever's in charge. What's the point or purpose in making her go through all this? None, and I don't care what anybody says."

She dropped down at the kitchen table, used the heels of her hands to swipe at tears, and smeared her mascara. "The last few nights she's been talking to Uncle Silas or our mother. And— and she's happy when she does that. I don't care if you believe she really sees them. Everybody's entitled to believe whatever as long as they don't pound you over the head with it. But I believe it. I believe they're waiting for her."

He sat, tried the wine. Marginally better than cheap beer, he decided. "I don't know what I believe. But I know you were right before. She's fighting for us, and it hurts her, it's taking everything away from her, and you were right. She needed to know I'd be okay."

"I don't want to let her go."

"I know. We're doing it for her."

"I need to ask you not to go out at night until . . . I wouldn't be able to reach you if . . ."

"I'll be here."

Two nights later, she slipped away while he read to her and Mags knitted an endless scarf.

SHE HADN'T WANTED A funeral, so they didn't have one. People still came to the house and brought flowers or food or both. He was surprised how many clients made that journey or sent sympathy cards.

On a cold, blustery night in November, he broke through the security at Wrigley Field and led Mags to what would've been home plate during the season.

"I figured you must be doing something like this—breaking and entering—but I didn't figure you were so damn good at it."

"Looks different empty, and heading toward winter. But she'd like this, right?"

"She'd love this. It's the right place for it. Chicago girl, through and through."

"Okay then. Do you want to, like, do something, say something?"

"Her spirit's already flown. Let the rest fly with her. It's enough."

He opened the box, held it high. And let the wind carry the ashes.

"Look at her go, Harry. Part of her will always be here, cheering on her Cubs. They'll never know how lucky they are to have her. But we will. We do."

"We do." He watched the wind take the ashes, carry them, swirl them.

When they rode the train home, Mags patted his leg. "What are you going to do with the house?"

"You can live there as long as you want."

"Can't do it. For now, until you decide, sure. But I couldn't live there without her. I don't want Chicago without her, not once you decide. You could start at Northwestern, maybe even next month."

He shook his head. "Can't do it. It's the same for me. I don't want to be here, not without her."

"Where, then?"

"I don't know. Maybe just somewhere warm at first. Away from the damn cold. What about you?"

"I've got a line on an old VW Bus."

He turned to stare at her. Her hair was currently the color of a ripe eggplant. "You're kidding me."

"I am not. I'm thinking west. And I can start up my phone psychic business again. Madame Magdelaine knows all, sees all."

"I'll buy you a decent car."

"The Volkswagen Bus is a classic for a reason, pal. I have fond memories of previous encounters in same."

"Then I'll get you the damn Bus, make sure it's restored and in good condition. I'm not going to visualize you broken down on some road in the desert. Let me do this for you—from her. She'd want me to."

"You're not going to make me cry on this train. You have that kind of money?"

"I have enough, and I'm going to sell the house, so I'll have more."

"She wanted college for you. Harry, she wanted that so much."

"I'll get there. That's a promise."

He knew he should wait until spring—better real estate market—but he put the house on the market. Then sold it in just under two weeks for five thousand over asking. He bought himself a secondhand Volvo—low mileage, good condition.

Clearing out the house—all his mother's things—was the hardest part of it. But when it was done, he stood with Mags in the little front yard. She wore the red sweater and a pair of his mother's earrings.

Her VW Bus—two-toned, red and white—sat in front of his black Volvo.

"That is one boring car, kid."

"Boring cars don't get noticed. You'll be racking up tickets before you get to Iowa."

"The day I can't charm a cop out of a ticket's the day I pack it in." She turned to him. "We need to make a pact."

"Okay."

"Once a year—more is fine, but at least once a year—we meet up. I come to you, you come to me, we meet somewhere, doesn't matter. And we spend a few days. You're all I have left of her, Harry. You're my family."

"Let's pick the first date now—location to come. Before is fine, but let's say April first."

"April Fool's?"

"Easy to remember. We meet up April first. Want to pinky swear it?"

"Let's try this instead." She wrapped around him. He smelled his mother on her—his mother's favorite shampoo—and just buried his face in Mags's hair.

"It works. Deal is sealed. Try to stay out of trouble."

"What fun is that?" She eased back, cupped his face. "You call me anytime. If you need somebody to post bail, I'm your girl."

"Same goes. Are you ready?"

"For adventure? Always. Have some of that, Harry. Have some adventures. April first," she said as he walked her to the VW. "Don't make a fool out of me."

"Deal's sealed. I love you, Mags."

"I love you." She climbed in, slipped on rainbow-lens cat's-eye sunglasses. She had some crystals and a peace sign dangling from the rearview mirror. She took one of the crystals and passed it to him through the open window.

"White moonstone, for safe travels."

"Where's yours?"

She pulled the chain from under her shirt. "Peace out, pal."

She started the car—ran like a top—and drove away. He waited until he couldn't see her, then got into the Volvo.

He thought, what the hell, and hung the crystal on the rearview.

He took one last look at the house.

Then he drove away without turning back.

Chapter Four

HARRY TOOK INTERSTATE 65 across Indiana. As besides Illinois, Indiana was the only other state he'd ever been in, he wanted out of that, too.

Someplace else, somewhere new, anywhere warm.

He stuck to the highway, kept the radio blasting and the heater rolling. And felt a lift, a physical lift when he crossed into Kentucky. He took an exit at random. He'd make a pit stop, and maybe just wander the state for a while.

"Bluegrass State—actually commonwealth," he corrected, pulling out some factoids filed in his brain. "Capital's Frankfort. Ah, horses, bourbon, fried chicken, Derby, blues, Fort Knox."

Fort Knox had him wondering what he'd do with gold bars if he pulled off a heist. Awesome bragging rights, except bragging would send you to a Kansas institution. Leavenworth. Or Kentucky's version thereof.

Besides, you couldn't stash gold bars in your backpack.

He stopped to empty his bladder and fill up the Volvo, bought Doritos—still a favorite—and a Coke.

He liked the look of the hills, a roll he'd only seen in pictures or movies. He imagined them summer green, rising and falling, behind fields of grazing horses.

Maybe he'd enjoy a little rural living. Maybe.

But though the air didn't bite, it still had enough of a snap in it.

He drove on, aiming south, and when the Doritos didn't fill the hole, hit a drive-through at McDonald's for a Big Mac and large fries.

The lady, about his mother's age, handed him the bag with a smile. "There you go, son. You enjoy that now, you hear?"

He found her accent warm and wonderful.

"Yes, ma'am."

Enjoy it he did, chowing down as he crossed into Tennessee.

"Whiskey, Elvis, Dolly Parton, tobacco farms, barbecue and blues, and the Smoky Mountains."

For a boy who'd never been more than two hundred miles from home, it was like exploring a foreign country. A whole world of other.

And along with the secret sauce he tasted freedom.

He considered heading southwest to Memphis and paying Graceland a visit. He couldn't claim to be a major fan of Elvis, but iconic had appeal.

Another time, he decided, and headed southeast.

He'd had a vague plan to drive to the ocean. He'd never seen an actual ocean. Why not check that box first?

His first look at the Great Smoky Mountains had him gaping like a tourist in Times Square. Since the ocean wasn't going anywhere, he aimed for the mountains first.

Before, *vast* meant the plains outside the city. The endless flatlands where the wind streamed and tornados swirled. Now it meant the stunning rise of green peaks and the valleys below.

Clouds wisped through them. Yes, like smoke, and the sun slanted down, winter thin. He had his first experience with switchback roads, and took it easy mostly because he wanted to see everything all at once.

He climbed and climbed, pulled into overlooks to step out

and take it all in. He snapped pictures with his phone. He'd text them, he thought, to Will, to Mags.

He stopped again as day faded toward twilight, and this time took the small bottle from his backpack.

He hadn't told Mags he'd taken some of his mother's ashes before they'd gone to Wrigley. He'd planned to spread them into the wind by the ocean, but he thought he'd release some here.

Share this with her.

"We're really high here, almost six thousand feet. Just look how they keep going, like folding their way to North Carolina. So, it's been a pretty good first day. Four states. And I guess I'll go find a motel or whatever. But first . . ."

He uncorked the bottle and shook out some of the ashes. The mountains took her flying.

In the gloaming, he got back into the car, faced the challenge of driving in the mountains at night.

At one point he stopped dead, mouth falling open in shock as he watched a bear—an actual bear—lumber across the road like he was heading home after a hard day's work.

He decided to head for the nearest civilization.

He found a motel tucked in what he supposed were the foothills. The single-story spread of it consisted of cinder-block walls painted red, a gravel parking lot, and an attached diner with a neon sign that read EATS!

That sold him, as he was starving again.

He checked in with a man who had an impressive beer belly under a white T-shirt and a gray-flecked brown beard.

He paid for a single night, in cash, got a key, and learned, when he asked, the diner closed at ten.

His room, he saw when he carted his duffel and backpack inside, boasted a single bed covered with a green-and-blue-floral spread, a single dresser on which sat a clunky-looking TV, a green carpet, beige walls.

He had lamps on stands on either side of the bed and a tiny

bathroom, which, to his very experienced eye, actually looked more than acceptably clean.

He pulled the shade down on the window, then turned on the TV for company while he stripped.

He unwrapped the complimentary sliver of soap and took a long shower.

Nobody knew who he was or where he was, and he found that fascinating. Freeing. He'd let Mags know, send the pictures, but otherwise he was no one and everyone all at once.

He dressed, scooped his fingers through his hair. It had grown back into a mop again, and he was fine with that.

He felt like he'd walked through a movie set when he stepped outside. The humming ice machine, the two vending machines, the smell of pine in the cold air—not Chicago cold, but still too chilly for anything but an overnight stop. The sound of TVs muttering behind closed doors.

Inside the diner, that feeling hit full bloom.

The hard, bright fluorescent lights threw everything into relief. The long counter with pie or cake stands stacked up and the open kitchen behind it.

The air smelled of grease and coffee and frying meat. Two waitresses, one about his age, the other old enough to be her grandmother, wore pink dresses with white aprons.

Orange vinyl covered the seats of booths and chairs and backless, circular counter stools. Tables of white Formica held napkin dispensers, condiment caddies, and upside-down coffee mugs.

A couple in a booth looked exhausted as they tried riding herd on their two little kids. Traveling for the holidays, he decided. Maybe over the river and through the woods to Grandmother's house.

The two men arguing football over what looked like meat loaf he pegged as locals.

A mix of both scattered around with a plastic Christmas tree twinkling in one corner beside a juke box where—oh yeah, perfect—Dolly Parton begged Jolene not to take her man.

"You just grab yourself a seat now, honey," the older waitress called out. "We'll get right to you."

He took a booth and plucked the laminated menu out of the holder on the condiment caddy.

"Want some coffee, handsome?"

He looked up at the grandmotherly type with the name tag that read MERVINE. She had red lipstick and redder hair.

Her accent took a turn from the McDonald's lady's. Mervine's sounded like she should sing like Dolly.

"No, ma'am, thanks. Can I get a Coke?"

"You sure can. Traveled a ways, haven't you?" She picked up the pair of coffee mugs. "From up north."

"Yes, ma'am. Chicago."

"That's a ways. You want more time with that menu?"

"Ah, I guess."

She put a hand with the mug handle around her thumb on her hip. Angled her head. "I'm gonna tell you what you want."

"You are?"

"I got a knack. Now, you tell me if I'm wrong and you're a vegetarian or some other kind of tarian, but what you want is the chicken and gravy, mashed potatoes, and green beans. You're gonna get corn bread with that, and we make it right here. You trade that Coke for a good sweet tea, and you'll have yourself a meal, good-looking."

"That sounds . . . really good."

"Guaranteed." She winked at him before she walked off. "Darcia, get that pretty young man some sweet tea. Herschal, y'all get me a hot yardbird swimming, a mound of murphy, and side the greens."

He ate every bite and drank two glasses of sweet tea.

Dolly plunked a fat wedge of apple pie with a scoop of vanilla ice cream melting on top in front of him.

"Ma'am—"

"Pie's on me. You need some meat on those bones. If there's a man in this world doesn't like apple pie with ice cream, I've yet to meet him. And I've met most of them."

"You still haven't met him," he said, and made her laugh.

"You've got sad eyes, handsome. See if that pie don't put a smile in them."

He left her a twenty-dollar tip and figured he wasn't the first to fall a little in love with her.

He thought about walking off the pie, thought about the bear, and went straight back to his room.

He did a few push-ups. He didn't know about meat on the bones, but he sure as hell wanted to start putting on some muscle.

He took off the bedspread because who knew how many naked asses had sat on it before, then got a book out of his duffel. He turned the TV back on to fill the unfamiliar quiet.

He sent the text and relaxed when Mags reported back she'd stopped for the night in Nebraska.

After bunching the pair of lumpy pillows together, he cracked the book open.

He woke, still dressed, light on, TV muttering, and the wail of a kid howling he wanted cartoons.

It took him a minute to remember where he was. Groggy, wondering what the hell a kid was doing outside his room in the middle of the night, he walked to the window.

When he pulled back the side of the shade, the sun blasted his eyes. After slapping a hand over them, he let the shade fall back, blinked. Looked at his watch.

Nine-thirty? He'd slept almost twelve hours. He couldn't remember the last time he'd slept eight hours, much less twelve.

Then again, he'd never driven more than an hour at one time before, or driven up mountains.

He cleaned up, hauled out his stuff, bought a Coke and a bag of chips—breakfast of champions—from the machines, and was on his way east by ten.

HE EXPECTED HE'D FALL in love with the ocean when he got there. And there was a hell of a lot of North Carolina between the Tennessee border and the Atlantic. He'd calculated the fastest route would get him there in eight or ten hours, depending on how often and how long he stopped. But he decided almost immediately he didn't want or need fast.

He expected to fall in love with the ocean, but he hadn't expected to fall in love with the mountains.

If the Smokies seeded an infatuation, the Blue Ridge and Appalachians set the seeds to bloom. Instead of the highways, the interstate, he toured the byways. He enjoyed the rise and fall, the climb and descent where around every turn the world opened to a new vista.

He stopped awhile at Lake Norman—it was no Lake Michigan, but pretty enough. He liked the trees, and the December quiet while he ate a burrito he'd picked up at a mini-mart.

He consulted his map, decided he'd take a swing through something called the Uwharrie National Forest, then take a detour up to Chapel Hill, check out the college campus.

If it looked promising—he definitely wanted college at some point—maybe he'd find a motel in the area, get a feel for it all.

He'd head for the coast the next day, or the day after.

The forest provided a brand-new wonder. Since he already regretted he hadn't taken the time to walk any of the Smokies, he parked at one of the well-marked trailheads.

He took his phone, his keys, his half a bottle of Coke, and a Kit Kat bar, then the born-and-bred city boy set off in his Chucks to hike the trail.

It smelled of pine and wild, and compared to December in Chicago, the shadowy high fifties felt like spring. He couldn't get over the quiet. He would've said he'd grown up in a quiet neighborhood, but it equaled madhouse compared to forest quiet.

He heard a couple of birds, saw a squirrel scamper up a tree, and came to a stream where water gurgled over rocks.

He wondered if he might end up in a place like this. Not year-round, he thought as he followed the trail. But maybe like a vacation place. A hideout.

He'd need another place, in or close to an urban center. Somewhere. A guy had to earn a living, after all.

Atlanta maybe, or Miami. Houston or Raleigh.

He'd probably know it when he saw it. And someday, absolutely someday, he'd fly to Europe. Florence and Paris and London. Madrid and Prague and all of it. Just all of it.

A lot to learn and a lot to earn before that someday. But right now he just wanted a walk in the woods and a trip to the ocean.

He walked more than an hour before he heard anything but that silence, those strange-to-him forest sounds, before he heard anything that said human.

An engine—a couple of them.

The little he'd read about the forest on his phone told him he heard off-roaders. Something else he'd never done, and would try someday.

But right now it felt like an intrusion into his hike, so he headed back.

When the buck crossed his path, he stood struck with wonder. It stared back at him haughtily. No other word for it, Harry thought as he slowly, carefully slipped his phone out of his pocket.

The minute he took the picture, he was struck again, by the many sharp points on the antlers. If Bambi—people forgot

Bambi was a guy—decided to charge, Harry figured he'd end up full of antler holes.

"I'm cool. We're cool, right? I'm just heading down this trail."

The buck made some sound. It might have been derision, dismissal, or disgust, but the important thing was he strolled off the trail and into the trees.

"Good. That's good. We're all good."

And Harry covered the rest of the way back to his car at a light jog.

He'd wanted to explore, he reminded himself as he started the car. He'd wanted some adventure. Well, mission accomplished.

He drove to the university, and found yet another love.

It was big and sprawling, and he'd need big for the furthering-his-education plans. It was beautiful with its classic, dignified buildings, its green quads, and he wanted beautiful if he could get it.

As Will liked to say, Harry yearned to learn, and he could picture himself here satisfying that yearning. For a semester or two, he thought as he got out to wander.

Just another college kid in high-top Chucks, worn jeans, and oversize jacket.

Thousands went here, he thought, crossing the quads, sitting in auditoriums for lectures, hurrying down halls to classes.

He could be one of them.

Maybe in the spring, or the fall if he took the full gap year. But he wanted what they served here.

Knowledge.

As he had in the forest, he walked and he studied.

He blended with a group walking between classes and slid right into a building, and a library.

He wandered the stacks, smelled the books. And no one paid any attention to him.

By the time he'd taken his informal tour—covering only a fraction of the campus—he knew he'd spend some of his college life right there. To seal the deal, he walked to one of the shops and bought a UNC hoodie.

Lots of shops, he noted, restaurants, clubs, college hangouts. And as he drove around the area, added some very nice homes to that list. Nice houses where people had nice things an enterprising young man could liquidate.

He chose another motel, had a decent pizza with sausage and black olives. He settled in for research with his laptop.

He made a list of courses he wanted to take. After four years in high school, his Spanish was pretty damn good, so he figured to switch to French to start. English lit, of course, art history because if—no, when—he expanded to stealing art, he needed to know what to target. More computer classes. More math. He'd want some gemology eventually. He could take a brush at engineering.

No joining clubs, no frats, no serious girlfriends. No dorm life. He'd have to live off-campus.

Theater kids, he thought, always ended up really tight-knit. So no trying out for plays, though he missed that a lot. But maybe he could slide through a semester—just one—in tech, or costume, or makeup.

Satisfied with his emerging plan, he did his nightly push-ups. Maybe he'd buy some dumbbells when he had a place, get serious about building some muscle.

In the morning, he donned his new hoodie, checked out, then hit one of the campus coffee shops. He ordered a latte and a bagel, mostly because it seemed like a college thing to do.

He ate outside, watching college life stream by, admitting to his envy for it. And listening to the voices.

The locals had a flowing sort of accent that he practiced in his head as he toured another section of the campus. Snatches of conversations ranged from Professor Hardass to party at the dorm to getting through till winter break.

He slipped in and out of buildings and, though he felt bad

about it, lifted some jock-looking guy's wallet. Since the mark wore Air Jordan XXs that ran close to two hundred bucks, he didn't feel all that bad about it.

He couldn't very well forge a student ID unless he had a template.

He waited until a rest stop beyond Raleigh before he took out the wallet.

Carson Edward Wyatt III. It wasn't really right, but the name and the smirky smile on the ID wiped out even a whisper of feeling bad. C.E.—because Harry just bet that's what they called him—had a North Carolina driver's license, so a native son. He had an American Express Gold Card, a Platinum Visa, two Trojans, and a hundred eighty-two dollars in cash.

Harry took scissors out of his backpack, cut up the driver's license, the credit cards. He pocketed the cash and the condoms, divided the pieces of the credit cards and license between two trash cans.

The wallet—a Fendi in black leather—could replace his own. He tucked the student ID away in the backpack along with the fresh cash. After switching out the contents of his old wallet, he tossed that into the backpack.

He made it to Nags Head with the Pamlico Sound behind him and the Atlantic in front of him. He knew he had to find a room, but he walked over the dunes, across the sand, and just stood.

The water rushed toward the sand, deep green capped in white as the wind whipped at it. It whipped at him, too, snapping at his sweatshirt, tossing through his hair.

The green faded toward blue, then the blue deepened as the water spread out and out and out to the end of the world.

It rolled up, slapped, curled back into itself, then did it all again. Again and again. Circling gulls cried out, and some small, skinny-legged birds danced along the wet sand.

Other people walked the beach. A youngish couple with a big, beautiful golden retriever on a red leash. An oldish couple who held hands like lovers, a dad with a grinning toddler riding his shoulders, a long-legged woman in running gear, feet slapping the wet sand as she put in her miles.

He saw the remnants of a bonfire with the charred wood like black bones. And a tiny, translucent crab that scuttled into a hole in the sand.

He sat on that chilly sand, watched the waves, smelled the air, let the wind blow over him.

As the sun dipped in the west, the eastern sky deepened, and so did the sea.

When the first stars came out, he stood up to walk to the water. He slid a hand into his pocket, closed it over the bottle that held the last of his mother.

He hadn't thought it would be hard, letting this last part go. It had been the point, hadn't it, of coming to the sea? But the grief struck so sharp he could only stand there and mourn.

"Son?"

Trapped in misery, he hadn't heard anyone approach. And when he turned, he saw cop. He tried for his best nothing-to-see-here, but his voice trembled a little.

"Yes, sir."

"I got word you've been sitting out here a couple hours or more."

"Yes, sir. I've never seen the ocean before. I was just sitting here taking it in."

"Uh-huh."

He had a grizzled look to him, tufts of gray hair, weathered, ruddy face, and no-bullshit eyes.

"How old are you, boy?"

"Eighteen. I've got ID." He'd done the stupid, Harry admitted as he took out his new wallet. He'd stood out.

"Harrison Booth, from Chicago, Illinois." The cop nodded over it, handed the wallet back. "A long way from home, aren't you? Family here with you?"

"No. I'm on my own. Officer—"

"Deputy. Deputy Prince."

"Deputy Prince, I wasn't hurting anyone. I just wanted to sit on the beach."

"Uh-huh. Got any drugs on you?"

"No, sir."

"Well, I'd sure like to see what you got in that pocket."

"Deputy—"

"Dark out here now, even with the moon. Cold with it. Why don't you just show me what you got in that pocket, and we'll get out of the dark and the cold."

He could refuse, Harry thought. Then somebody with eyes like Deputy Prince would find some reason to haul him in.

He took out the bottle.

"Now, what's in that thing?"

"It's—it's the last of my mother's ashes. She died. She had cancer and she died, and she always wanted to see the ocean."

Prince looked into Harry's eyes. Harry knew his had filled, but he'd be damned if he'd cry in front of a cop.

"You came all this way to give her that?"

"She was my mother."

"It's a hard loss, a mother. Lost mine two years back and still feel it. I'm sorry for your loss, Harrison. Have you got a place to stay?"

"Not yet. I'm going to find a motel, maybe stay a couple days."

"Drive south about a quarter mile. You'll see the Gull's Nest on your left. You tell them I sent you. It's a good, clean place, and it's off-season rates."

"I will. Thanks."

"Don't stay out here too long. It's just gonna get colder."

The deputy walked back over the sand. When he stood alone on the beach again, Harry faced the sea, opened the bottle.

"We made it, Mom. I miss you, but I'm okay. I'm going to be okay," he said. "Bye." And let the ashes go.

Chapter Five

HE STAYED FOR THREE days, setting his alarm every morning so he could walk down to the beach and watch the sunrise. He took what he judged as better than decent pictures of the elegant majesty of light spreading in reds and golds and shimmering pinks over the plate of the sea.

He ate amazing barbecue and discovered the joy of hush puppies.

Then he packed up and drove south on 12 to Hatteras. He took pictures of the lighthouse, because . . . lighthouse, checked out the beaches. Quieter by far than Nags Head or Kitty Hawk. If he came back this way, maybe he'd rent one of the cottages or splurge on an oceanfront house for a week.

But for now he drove to the end of the island and the ferry to Ocracoke. Another first, driving his car onto the boat, getting out to stand at the rail while it chugged its way over the sound. He watched the wake spear behind them, the gulls fly overhead.

Once they docked, he drove to the other end of the island and boarded the big ferry in the harbor, bound for Cedar Island. From Hatteras he could've driven to the mainland via roads and bridges, but the ferry rides meant he could just sit back or stand up and see, and feel and smell.

For the first time in years he didn't have a solid plan, or need one. He had nowhere he had to be, nothing essential that had to be done.

That had to change, he knew it, even looked forward to it. But for now it was moment to moment, and he liked it.

On the mainland, he drove the coast as much as he could, winding and wandering, stopping when the mood or hunger struck. Another motel, another diner.

He learned in his handful of days in North Carolina that hush puppies equaled awesome, you could keep your grits, cheesy or otherwise, and he'd pit their barbecue against the world's.

He crossed into South Carolina on a bright December afternoon warm enough to have the windows open.

Capital, Columbia. Cotton, Fort Sumter, Clemson.

Beaches. Lots and lots of beaches.

He spent a day exploring them, ate fried chicken—they knew what to do with a chicken. He practiced his regional accents and fabricated a story for the waitress when she asked where he was heading.

"Home for the holidays, ma'am, from college down at UF—ah, University of Florida."

"You've come a ways already. Where's home, honey?"

"Kill Devil Hills—the Wright brothers?"

"How about that? Well, you drive safe now, and have a nice Christmas with your family."

"Can't hardly wait to see 'em."

By the time he hit Georgia—peaches, Atlanta, peanuts, Jimmy Carter—he decided to spend a few days in one spot, and Savannah struck just the right note.

He loved the gnarled trees, the cobbled streets, the waterfront, the graceful architecture, and the strangely easygoing vibrancy.

He booked a room at the Thunderbird Inn because he liked the name, the look, and the easy walking distance to the historic district. He petted a carriage horse—the firsts kept coming—and picked a couple of fat pockets on strolls under silvery Spanish moss.

He spent Christmas Eve eating pulled pork and nachos in his room while he researched a very promising house—mansion—an easy walk away.

It paid to keep eyes and ears open for an opportunity. The Carlyse family was hosting a big, bust-out party tonight, followed by a Christmas brunch for close friends. Then they'd fly out—their own jet—for their annual ski trip in Vermont. Where they had a second home.

It seemed to Harry they'd not only be well insured, but could afford to lose a little something to offset his travel expenses.

He read article after article on Jeb Carlyse—fourth-generation Savannahian, wealthy businessman. It appeared some of those ships that went in and out of the port were at least partially his. His wife, Jaylene, came from money, too. They had the mansion in Savannah, the lodge in Vermont, a beach house in the Caymans. And there, Harry bet, there was some offshore tax-dodging hanky-panky going on. They had three children, son J.B., age twenty-nine, engaged to an heiress, naturally. Son Josuah, age twenty-six, working in the family business, and a daughter, Juliet, age twenty, attending the University of Georgia in Athens.

Big patrons of the arts, Harry read as he munched on nachos. Extensive art collection. The house, on the historic register, opened partially to tours one day every spring. Because of that he found plenty of photographs.

Plenty more of the Carlyses attending galas, and Jaylene's really nice taste in jewelry.

He decided to take a Christmas Eve walk, check out the house. If he could get close enough, maybe assess the alarm and security system.

He changed into a decent shirt and his newest jeans. Strolling, he enjoyed the Christmas lights, the sounds of music and voices.

More than one party tonight, he thought, and found his mind starting to slide back to Christmas Eves of the past.

The tree in the front window—always the same spot with the dopey felt Santa he'd made his mother in grade school prominently hung. Stockings on coat hooks, Christmas music playing.

"Jingle Bell Rock" meant dancing. Springsteen's "Santa Claus Is Comin' to Town" meant singing the refrain at the top of your lungs.

He didn't want to think about all of that now, didn't want to dwell on spending his first Christmas alone. Prepping for some nightwork was a better use of his time.

He heard the party from half a block away, and saw the lights before that. The graceful three-story brick shined in all-white lights, and the trees dripping with moss twinkled with them. Music poured, and it sounded like a live band to him.

People spilled out of the house onto the veranda, the balconies, even the sidewalk with their champagne flutes and highball glasses.

And man, they dripped, too. Diamonds, rubies, emeralds.

Talk about the best Christmas ever. He could make enough in a five-minute pass to put himself through Harvard.

He stopped, as he suspected many others had and would, and studied the tableau.

The windows gleamed with light and the people moving behind them. Cocktail dresses, slick suits. He counted three trees, one on each floor, decorated and sparkling. Poinsettias—white ones—marched up the walk and steps with little lights inside the pots. Greenery tied with huge red bows and more tiny lights twined up the columns of the veranda.

"What do you think?"

He recognized Juliet Carlyse from his research, though he thought she looked better in person. She'd cut her hair, one of those pixie deals, and it suited her, that pale gold crown, the long neck, the big blue eyes.

"It's beautiful."

"Not too much?"

"Nothing's too much at Christmas."

She smiled, took a sip from her champagne flute. "Do I know you?"

"I don't think so. Do you want to?"

It made her laugh. "Maybe. Well, come on in."

"Oh, I was just walking by. I'm not invited."

"I live here, so you're now invited." She held out a hand. "Juliet."

"Silas"—he decided on the spot—"Silas Harrison."

"Come on in, Silas Harrison. Let's get you some holiday cheer. What are you doing out walking alone on Christmas Eve?"

"Just taking in the city. My first time here."

"Is that right?" She walked him right into the house that smelled of pine and perfume and candle wax.

The entrance foyer soared up; more poinsettias glimmered with lights on their march up the curving staircase. A big round table held the biggest arrangement of red and white roses he'd ever seen or imagined. People milled everywhere.

To the right a wide doorway opened to more, and a simmering fire with a mantel alive with greenery and candles, the towering tree sparkling in the big window.

Servers in white shirts, black pants, and red bow ties carried trays of drinks and finger food.

Juliet snagged two flutes from one. Set her mostly empty glass down. "Merry Christmas."

She tapped her glass to his.

"Merry Christmas."

"Hungry?"

"Actually, I just ate, but thanks. Is everyone friendly around here?"

"Hospitality is a religion in Savannah. Where are you from?"

Since he'd used his South Carolina accent, he went with it. "Florence." Straight shot up 95, he remembered. "I'm heading down to Jacksonville to surprise my grandparents. I figured to get there tonight, but hit more traffic than I planned for. So I'm here until morning, as I didn't want to get there so late I'd scare them instead of surprising them."

"Aren't you the sweetie?" She gave him what could only be interpreted as the flirt eye. "Traveling alone?"

"With my brother. He's moping back in the room, talking to his girlfriend because I dragged him along with me." The story flowed right out of him. "We lost our daddy last summer, and our mama back when Willy was a boy, so it's just the two of us."

"I'm so sorry." She laid a hand on his. "It's good of you to go see your family, and I don't expect he'll mope for long. Let's get you in the spirit. There's dancing upstairs."

She led him to the staircase.

"So what do you do back in Florence?"

"Right now I'm doing carpentry work. My father's company. I'm taking a gap year with all that happened, but Willy'll be off to college in the fall, God willing, and I can go back to Carolina. UNC. How about you?"

"Home for winter break. University of Georgia. Family tradition." She took his hand, led him up the next set of stairs.

"This house is amazing."

"We take pride in it."

His original plan had fallen along the lines of getting in, straight to the master bedroom and the safe he'd concluded he'd find. He'd assessed the locks and the alarm pad as Juliet led him through, knew he could beat them.

But now it seemed simpler, and somehow more polite, to just palm a piece of jewelry off a handy wrist or neck and be done with it.

Not hers, he thought, because that would be downright rude,

though she wore a trio of very nice diamond bangles on her right wrist and a Chopard on her left.

She hailed a man in a dark suit and red tie he recognized as Jeb Carlyse. "Daddy! I found this stray wandering the streets and brought him in for some cheer."

Carlyse laid a hand on his daughter's shoulder and gave Harry a steady once-over.

"Is that so? Where did you stray from?"

"Florence, sir, on my way to Jacksonville and my grandparents. We're just stopping for the night in Savannah, and . . . I'm intruding."

"I invited you," Juliet reminded him.

"What do you do back in Florence?"

"Carpentry. I don't have the skill my father did, but I know enough to say the millwork here is extraordinary."

"His daddy passed last summer, so he's tending to his younger brother until he starts college. Then Silas here can go back to UNC."

"You're in Carolina?"

"Yes, sir. I'm going back in the fall once Willy's settled."

"And what are you studying there?"

"Daddy, how much longer are you going to grill poor Silas just for coming in for a drink and dance?"

"This might be the last."

"I'm a lit major. Like most lit majors I'm planning to teach to keep the wolf from the door while I write myself the Great American Novel."

That got a faint smile and a little nod. "Southern thrillers?"

Harry laughed. "Why, yes, sir. Does it show?"

"It's what I do. All right then, you've got your drink, go and have your dance. Enjoy the party."

"Thank you for your hospitality, Mister . . . Sorry, I don't even know where I am."

"Carlyse. Try the shrimp mousse. It's damn tasty."

"Dance first." Juliet tugged him toward what he saw was an actual ballroom, decorated to the nines, with a live band rocking it out and the balcony doors wide open.

So he danced. He was good on his feet, as his mother had loved to dance and he'd been her usual partner. He kept the drinking to half a glass, though he found the champagne a lot tastier than the shrimp mousse.

He picked out a couple of marks, then one fell into his lap, almost literally.

She tumbled into him on the dance floor, a woman somewhere in her forties, he gauged, who hadn't kept the champagne anywhere near half a glass.

She wore a tight silver dress showing off impressive breasts. Her chestnut hair had started to tumble out of whatever updo it started in, and her brown eyes laughed up at him.

"Oops!" Then she locked her arms around him. "Since I got him, Juliet, I'm stealing him. This boy has the moves! Show me some moves, cutie-pie!"

He held her upright, sent Juliet a mildly panicked look for effect. She just rolled her pretty blue eyes.

"You go on, give Miss Mazie a spin. Then I'm taking him back, Miss Mazie."

"If you can get him!"

Not flat-out drunk, Harry decided as he gave her that spin. But she was heading there. While she giggled, flirted, hung on to him, he snapped open the safety on her bracelet, flipped the clasp, and had the very nice set of diamonds and sapphires sliding into his pocket.

When the music ended, she said, "Whew! You do have the moves. Juliet's wasting your moves on the dance floor, you ask me."

"Now, Miss Mazie." Juliet peeled her off Harry. "Shame on you for embarrassing my guest. Now I'm taking him back."

"Don't waste him, child." And she wandered off to find someone else to give her a spin.

"She really should get some air."

"Oh, she'll be fine. Happens every year."

He gave Juliet another dance to cover himself and because he just wanted to.

"I really have to get back. I never expected to be out this long."

"Tell you what, if Willy's still up and moping, bring him back. We'll party the mopes out of him, and, trust me, this is going on all night."

"I might just do that. I'd like to do that."

She walked him down to the second floor, then turned away from the staircase.

"Just give me another minute."

She led him down a wide corridor, into a room. Her bedroom, he realized when she nudged him inside, closed the door, leaned back on it.

"I bet Willy can handle another little while, and I'm so bored with these parties. Got any ideas how to take care of that boredom?"

"Ah, maybe, now that you mention it."

"Right here." She smiled as she just pulled her dress up and away, stood in the tiniest of black bra and panties. "Right now. Bang me up against this door, Silas. Good, hard, and fast."

"Talk about merry Christmas."

He thought about the bracelet in his pocket, took some care so it didn't fall out. Then he accommodated her.

He walked back to the motel in a daze. If not for the weight of the bracelet in his pocket, he'd have sworn he dreamed it all. When he reached his room, he sat on the side of the bed and relived it all. Especially the last part.

The part where she'd wrapped both her legs around his waist, dug her nails into his shoulders. When he'd come it had been an explosion.

He hadn't known it could be that fast, that intense, that hot.

If he had one regret, it was knowing he couldn't go back and do it all over again.

But he pulled out the bracelet, got his loupe, studied the stones under the light.

"Oh yeah, merry Christmas, and happy New Year."

He set his alarm—best to be gone at first light—and crawled into bed.

PLANS TO HEAD SOUTH and check out Florida, maybe spend a week or two exploring the beaches, possibly all the way to the Keys, changed. No point winding his way toward Jacksonville when he'd pointed an arrow at it. Just in case somebody put a missing diamond and sapphire bracelet and some dude who'd danced with its drunk owner together and wanted to chat.

Instead, he spent his first Christmas Day on his own cutting across Georgia to Alabama. Because he didn't want conversation—What're you doing all alone on Christmas, boy?—he hit a vending machine for road food and snacked on chips, peanut butter crackers, Oreos, and Hershey bars while he traveled the rolling hills of the Piedmont.

Hyped on carbs and sugar, he crossed the Chattahoochee and drove straight through to Montgomery and a half-assed motel, where he slept for twelve hours.

He thought about Juliet of the sunny cap of hair and supple legs winging her way north to ski. It all seemed like a dream until he studied the bracelet.

While he calculated he'd put enough miles between himself and Savannah, he didn't want to risk trying to sell the goods so soon.

He learned to love the South, the feel of it, the food, the voices, and the slow, easy pace of the byways.

He spent New Year's Eve in Mobile, watching the ball drop in Times Square in his motel room while he ate cold pizza. After crossing the border into Mississippi, he spent New Year's Day enjoying the beach on the Gulf of Mexico.

He considered settling down right there for a while, maybe getting a job, picking up some nightwork. Instead, he pawned the bracelet in Biloxi, and moved on.

Then he drove into New Orleans, and fell in love.

It had everything: the water, the voices, the food, the music, the architecture. And tourists with fat wallets, not to mention a historical district loaded with mansions.

It had Tulane—smaller than he'd wanted to risk for slipping into a college for some classes, but he thought he could manage it.

After two days of exploring the French Quarter, he learned he could walk into the humblest of holes-in-the-wall and eat like a king. A stroll down Bourbon Street after dark meant music pumping out of doorways, and tourists drunk on Hurricanes he could relieve of watches or wallets with a simple bump and snatch.

Taking the leap, he rented a furnished apartment on Burgundy Street, opened a local bank account, and—though it cost him—acquired a damn good fake driver's license all under the name of Silas Booth.

The enterprising soul, one Jacques Xavier, who'd sold him the ID had a cousin, a tarot reader who worked as a bartender at night. Dauphine LeBlanc had wide, soulful eyes and a flood of black hair.

She didn't mind if he hung out at the bar some nights, listening to the music, drinking Cokes or sweet tea, and trolling for marks.

She wore snug, colorful shirts and chains of crystals. The crystals prompted him one night halfway through January while the band oozed out deep, dark Delta blues to tell her she reminded him of his aunt.

She pursed her pretty, full lips, angled her head. "You sit there, *doudou*, and say you look at all this fine and see your *tante*?"

"No, not like that. She's into crystals, and she's working as a phone psychic. And she's terrific."

And Mags didn't feature in any of his sex dreams, where Dauphine had starred a time or two. At twenty-two, she treated him a little like a stray dog who came to the door. Kindly, with occasional and vague affection and no ties whatsoever.

But then he wasn't looking for ties.

He drank his sweet tea, enjoyed the music as she worked the bar before she came back down and topped off his glass.

"You should come into the shop so I can read your cards."

She wouldn't do it for free. Her cousin had told him Dauphine had a hard line on the issue. Do a free reading for one, and it opened the door for the flood of friends and relations to want the same.

"Maybe. Sometime."

"I already see what I see. I come from a line, and we know what we know. You see plenty, too." She leaned over. He had a generous view of her excellent cleavage, but since he'd been raised better, he kept his gaze on her face.

"Like the table there, with the man so white he glows while he sweats through his fancy shirt and drinks whiskey sours. You see, as I see, the big, ugly gold watch, and the woman he's with and whose leg he strokes under the table isn't his wife."

"His wife's home somewhere like Toledo while he brings his side piece with him to the convention here where he can play big shot on his expense account."

Dauphine tapped her finger on the back of his hand. "You see, I see. But why Toledo?"

"Thereabouts, anyway. His accent."

"Ah, *bien sûr*. Yankees, they all sound the same to me. You have good ears, I think."

An idea struck, so he went with it. "How much would you charge to teach me French?"

She waved him off, moved down the bar to fill orders. He'd learned, even on the short acquaintance, to just wait.

The band went up-tempo, and feet started stomping. A group of four—college-type girls, he concluded—came in and crowded at the bar.

Dauphine would card them all, and it occurred to him if any of them had a fake ID, it might be courtesy of her cousin.

Dauphine came back, put a plate of crawfish boulettes and Creole mustard sauce in front of him. She'd charge him for it, but he couldn't complain.

"What you want to learn French for?"

"I like to learn."

She eyed him while she mopped at the bar. "What kind of French you want to learn? You got French like in Paris, you got Louisiana Creole, you got Cajun French, and more."

"All of it, or as much as you know."

"We do this. I give you one lesson, one hour, fifty dollars, and if I think you're an imbecile, *c'est tout*. If I think you're not wasting my time and your money, we go on. Twenty-five dollars each lesson."

"Deal. You won't think I'm an imbecile."

She didn't look convinced but nodded. "Tomorrow night, eight. You have dinner and a good bottle of wine for me. One hour, no funny business."

That night before he went to bed, he put the gold watch—a Gucci—and the cash from the wallet he'd tossed in the space he'd made beneath the floorboards under his bed. He'd hold on to the watch for a few weeks, where it could keep company with a very nice pair—about two carats each—of ruby earrings, a cuff of rainbow sapphires, and a TAG Heuer Aquaracer.

Once he sold them—not all at once, of course, and not all in the same place—he'd add to his bank accounts. He'd never have to worry about someone taking away the roof over his head, or if Mags had enough to get by.

He settled in with one of the books on art history he'd borrowed from the library—with a card. He thought the day was fast approaching when he could expand his nightwork to art.

He had to pay somebody to buy the wine, as even his fake ID had him underage. He decided to cook. He liked having a kitchen and often tossed a meal together. But he wanted something a little better—or more adult than mac and cheese or a burger. Since he didn't think he'd developed the skills to try a Cajun or Creole meal yet, he fell back on one of his mother's standbys for company.

In the days when they'd had company for dinner.

He hit the farmers market for red potatoes, found some early asparagus, bought a baguette, some chicken, and a small praline cheesecake.

He wouldn't hit on her, he thought as he quartered the potatoes. She might laugh him off—humiliating—or refuse to continue the lessons. And he wanted French in his pocket.

So he made the meal, and if the steps and the scents brought his mother into his apartment, it didn't hurt as much as it had. He found some comfort in it.

He set the table, put out the flowers he'd bought. He didn't light candles, didn't put on music—sent the wrong message. When she knocked—precisely at eight—he concluded prompt would be part of his lessons.

She wore a body-skimming black dress and red heels that put her nearly eye-to-eye with him. Nearly a month had passed since his brief and intense sex in Savannah, so he thought he could be forgiven the spike of lust.

"*Bonsoir*," he said. "*Bienvenue*."

She nodded. "*C'est bon.*"

She stepped in, gave the tiny apartment a quick glance. "You keep it clean. I have three brothers, all slobs. Their rooms always smell like dirty socks and moldy bread. Yours smells like good cooking. Did you cook or pretend to?"

"I bought the bread and the cake. I made the rest."

She wandered the few short steps to the kitchen. "Where did you learn to cook?"

"My mother."

Those soulful eyes went straight to his. "She's left us? I have ears, too," she added. "I hear sorrow."

"Yeah, last year."

"*Je suis désolée*." She touched her heart. "I think you've done her proud with this cooking. Now pour me some wine. *Divin*— Louisiana French. *Du vin* in formal French." She tapped her ear. "You have to listen to hear the difference."

He poured wine for both of them. "The second is, like you said, more formal. I can hear that."

"Then you hear good." She stepped to the window, pointed. "The car? *Un char*, Louisiana French. *Une automobile* in French. But you see, you can blend and mix here—not, I think, in France, but here you can use either or both. It shows you know more than one language. So we who do switch from French, English, Creole because we can."

"You have to be fluent in all first."

"*Mais oui*. The wine is good. *Le vin est bon*."

When he repeated it, she pursed those lips and nodded. "Your accent's good for a beginner. So you can feed me what smells so good. I think talking with dinner is a good way to learn."

He proved not to be an imbecile, so she agreed to come back the next week for half the price, a meal, and good wine.

On the third week they had the lesson over his first attempt at crawfish étouffée.

"You could get a job as a cook. I know places."

"It's no fun if you have to do it. And I'm slow at it, only got a handful of things I can make. Besides, I'm not looking for legit work yet. I asked my aunt to come for Mardi Gras, and I want to show her around, have the time for her."

"*Tu as un bon coeur*." She tossed her mass of hair back as she looked around the apartment. "You're clean, and you have a pretty face. I tell you not to move on me, and you don't. You have manners. I think you know this from the lessons, and the song. *Voulez-vous coucher avec moi?*"

He picked up his wine, took a careful sip. "I'm a heterosexual male. You're beautiful, sexy, fun, smart, and you've got that body. You've really got a body. So. *Absolument.*"

"I don't want romance. I don't have time for it. I like you—a friend, a clever friend. If you fall in love with me, I'll break that good heart. And be sorry for it."

"I don't want romance. Ah . . . *Je ne suis pas prêt. Je vous aime.*"

"*Je t'aime bien*," she corrected.

"*Je t'aime bien*," he repeated. "Maybe you'll fall in love with me, then I'll be sorry to break your heart."

"We're safe there." She held out a hand. "*Amis.*"

"*Amis*," he agreed.

"Is your bedroom clean like the rest?"

"Yeah."

She got up, held out her hand again. "*Montre-moi.*"

Chapter Six

THE LONG, WILD PARTY that was Mardi Gras began for him with Mags's arrival. Maybe only a couple of months had passed—though it felt longer—but he found himself ridiculously happy to see her.

His crazy aunt with her maroon hair streaked with candy pink enfolded him in arms tanned from the desert sun. The inside of her right forearm now bore a compass tattoo with a red heart in the center.

"What's this?"

"The symbol of my wanderlust." She gripped him again, hard. "With all the miles you've put in already, you might get one yourself."

He really didn't think so.

"I'm going to get one of my spirit animal when I decide what it is."

"I thought it picked you."

She just laughed, pulled back to study his face. "You look good, pal. Jesus, you're taller. You've got another inch on you."

"Maybe."

"Maybe, my butt. I figured you'd stopped sprouting. Now, let's see this place of yours."

With her bags—a pair of enormous floral duffels—dumped by the door, she stepped away to survey the apartment.

"Nice, very nice for our boy's first apartment. Great location, nice light. I like the art, the French Quarter street scenes."

"Those are mine. I didn't mean I did them," he said when she turned to stare at him. "The place came furnished, but I hung some pictures I picked up. Bought," he qualified. "Lots of artists in the Quarter."

"Shows good taste, and supports local artists. Sparkle clean, too."

"I guess that's in the DNA."

"Oh yeah. I miss her so much."

"I know. Me, too. I didn't tell you, but I took some of her ashes with me. There was this spot in the Smokies where I let some go, then this beach on the Outer Banks where I sent the rest out to the ocean."

Mags let out a sigh, then pointed to herself. "Painted Desert, Pacific."

"Really?"

"I guess we're more alike than either of us figured, Harry."

"I'm Silas here."

"Right."

"Let me put your bags in the bedroom, then I'll give you a tour, take you to lunch."

"I'll take the couch."

"My Mags doesn't take the couch in my place." To settle it, he hefted the duffels and walked them into the bedroom.

"Okay, this is adorable. I'm all about the slanted ceiling, and look at you with Maxfield Parrish prints on the wall."

"Flea market, out of a calendar or something."

"More good taste."

It wasn't a room you could wander, given the size, but she did a turn. "And daffodils on the dresser. For me. Somebody raised you right. Silas."

"Two people raised me right. Or right enough."

She gave the light stubble on his cheek a rub. "Better give me that tour before I get sloppy and ruin my makeup."

"You've never made it here before?" he asked as he walked her out.

"First time. I think the universe decided I should have my first experience in New Orleans—and at Mardi Gras—with my nephew."

"How's Vegas?"

"Warm and lively. But I'm going to give Santa Fe a try. Heading there when I leave."

"What about the phone business?"

"That's the beauty, my friend." Outside, she took a deep gulp of warm, humid air. "As long as there's a cell tower, Madame Magdelaine's in business." She laid a finger on her tattoo. "So she goes where the spirit drives her."

"Desert winds for you."

"Apparently. And heat, humidity, and water for you."

"Yeah, so far. But I think I have a thing for hills, mountains, too. For a city, this hits the bell. I want to try New York, DC, San Francisco, and I may have an excuse to see Santa Fe, but this is the highest rung city-wise. Because it's not a city, not this part of it anyway. It's an experience."

Tourists swarmed the shops, the streets, the bars. They tossed coins in the hats and instrument cases of sidewalk musicians as the sounds of horns, accordions, a cappella voices wound through the air.

They strolled along cobbled streets under lacy balconies strewn with flowers and gold and purple beads. He introduced her to his favorite carriage horse and waited while she hunted in a shop selling crystals and candles and incense to add to what he knew was her already heroic collection. Waited again while she selected a Mardi Gras T-shirt.

Before she could drag him into another shop, he steered her

into a cramped, fragrant restaurant most tourists wouldn't give a second glance.

Mama Lou's held a dozen tables and offered counter service. Lunch meant every chair or stool would have an ass in them, but he'd arranged a table.

Little Lou, Mama's daughter, hailed him when he stepped in.

"Where you at, *cher*! *Assis-toi, assis-toi*. Mama! Silas is here, *avec sa tante*."

She scurried over, a bony fortysomething with gleaming dark skin and a headful of braids, while he shuffled Mags to the table by the single tiny window. The prime spot.

Little Lou rose on her toes to kiss his cheek. "Mama wants to meet Miz Mags. She got one big crush on this boy."

"Mutual. Mags, this is Little Lou, Mama's daughter, and the second-best cook in the Quarter."

"'Cause Mama, she comes first." She let out a laugh. "I'll get your drinks right away. Silas wants his Coke, *c'est vrai*?"

"*Merci. Vin blanc pour ma tante, et une bouteille d'eau pour la table, s'il te plaît.*"

"*Bien, bien.*" She scurried off.

Mags leaned over the little wooden table to poke him in the shoulder. "When did you start speaking French?"

"I've been taking lessons. Here comes Mama. She's like no one else."

Mama Lou, a wide-hipped woman who topped out at five foot nothing, sashayed around the little tables like a queen in her white bib apron and pansy print dress. At sixty, her brown skin remained smooth and her haunting green eyes sharp.

Silas rose, and as he had after he'd first tasted her jambalaya, took her hand and kissed it.

He stuck with French—formal French because he knew it pleased and amused her. "Mama Lou, *permettez-moi de vous presenter ma tante*, Magdelaine Booth. *Et merci, merci beaucoup de l'accueillir. Elle m'est chère.*"

She gave him a nod, then a pat on the cheek. "*Bien, cher.*" Then she offered Mags a hand. "This is a good boy," she said in a voice that flowed like liquid flowers. "My daughters, they are too old, and my granddaughters too young, or I'd steal him for one of them. I'd take him myself, but *mon mari* would punch his pretty face for it."

"Can't have that. Thank you for helping look after him. I like knowing he's in such good hands."

"Still too skinny."

"Yes, but not as skinny as he was."

"You've come for Mardi Gras, so *laissez les bon temps rouler.*" She shifted just enough for her daughter to serve the drinks. "Now, Tante Mags will have the gumbo, and Silas a shrimp po'boy. And you split so each has some. And bread pudding for dessert. Bon appétit."

Mags watched her sashay back to the kitchen. "Like no one else, you said, and you're not wrong. Does she always tell you what you'll eat?"

"Only when she likes you."

"Okay then." She picked up her wine, sipped. "Not bad. Now, tell me about this French business. How do you learn to have conversations like that after a few weeks?"

"A really good teacher."

"I guess. I remember you always aced Spanish and could rattle off like a toreador. The magic memory's handy. A college class, adult education?"

"Private tutor. A friend. You'll meet her tonight."

"Oh." Mags drew that syllable out, meaningfully. "A friend."

"Yeah. You'll like her. She's a tarot and palm reader. Tends bar a few nights a week."

"A friend, with benefits?"

His answer to that was a shrug. "It's nothing serious, on either side."

"Good. You may speak three languages now and run your

own life, from what I can see pretty damn well, but you're still too young for serious. I've got to ask, it's my job, but are you thinking about college?"

"I'm thinking about auditing or taking a few classes at Tulane. After Mardi Gras, and maybe next fall if I'm still here."

Little Lou brought out their lunch, added a basket of hush puppies.

"Holy God, that's a lot of food."

"You don't go hungry at Mama's."

Mags sampled the gumbo. "All right, this is amazing." Then a bite of her half of the po'boy. "And again. Are you looking to move on anytime soon?"

"I don't know, I just know, not yet. I gave myself a tour of the University of North Carolina when I was up there, and that's a strong pull, so eventually. I'm looking at some others. I'm not looking for a degree, Mags, just learning more about what appeals to me."

"I'm the last person to argue that one. You're not happy yet— me either. It takes as long as it takes. But I'll say you're in a good place, and not just on the map. Me, too. So good for us."

That night, they walked the parade route. They caught beads, tossed beads. Mags, being Mags, danced in the street with total strangers. They ate shrimp kabobs and hot beignets while they cheered the floats.

A man in nothing but a jester mask and purple boxers did a boogie on a balcony and earned some applause.

"Where has this been all my life?" Mags shouted over the din.

He steered her into the bar where Dauphine and a second bartender mixed, poured, and served, and tonight's band played zydeco.

Dauphine spotted them and called out.

"Tito, you've warmed that stool long enough. Get up and let the lady sit."

A robust man with sleepy eyes stood, turned to bow at Mags.

"Why, thank you, sir."

"Mags, this is Dauphine, my friend and French tutor."

"If you mix drinks as well as you teach French, I've got to have me one. Silas is spouting off like he was born here."

"He has a gift for languages, I think, but more to learn. What can I get you?"

"You pick. It's Mardi Gras in New Orleans, and I'm up for anything."

"I like an adventurer." The two women studied each other a moment, then Dauphine nodded. "I know what you need." She called out in French to the other bartender that she was taking a short break with friends, then took out a cocktail shaker. She chose lemon wedges and mint, poured in something from a bottle before she began to muddle it.

"So, Miz Mags, are you enjoying New Orleans?"

"I'd be crazy not to. Are you from here?"

"I am. All my life is here."

"This week probably isn't as much fun for you."

"But profitable." She added a scoop of crushed ice, something from another bottle, some club soda, then began to turn the shaker back and forth. "You do physic readings, by the phone."

"Yep. Profitable."

Dauphine grinned at her. "Do you read the cards?"

"I do a spread while I'm talking to the client. Silas says you read the cards for a living."

"At Five Fold." She poured the drink into a lowball glass, topped it with a sprig of fresh mint. "Taste. If it's not right, I'll make you something else."

Mags sipped, smiled slowly. "Magic! What is it?"

"A Creolo. Sophisticated and refreshing, as I think you are."

"Oh, I like your friend, pal of mine. Let's have dinner tomorrow. Take us on a date, Silas."

"Um. Sure."

Dauphine smiled at her, got out a fresh bowl of bar nuts. "He cooks. He cooks good."

"He was always better at it than me. Cook us dinner, cutie."

They bonded. They bonded fast and they bonded strong.

For the next three nights, Mags out-partied him, and topped off the night at the bar testing out a new cocktail.

On the first day of Lent, and Mags's final night, he made them jambalaya—and attempted hush puppies for the first time.

He didn't have to add much to the conversation when they got together. They talked movies, books, art, fashion, and, despite his presence, men. If they, and they did often, veered into sex, he made himself scarce.

It was just too weird.

"I'm going to take out the trash," he said as they huddled together at his little table. "And maybe take a walk."

He stepped out and walked around the block a couple of times in the post-party quiet of the Quarter.

When he came back, it surprised him to see Dauphine reading Mags's cards.

"How much are you charging her?"

"We're doing a trade. I read hers, she reads mine." Dauphine reached over to take Mags's hand. "She watches over you. You see? I think she always will. This is female strength at the root, and the sorrows of the past, the change, the endings that hover still. But she's with you. And here he is, the son you shared. I have a little piece of him for now, but yours is for always. He looks ahead, ambitious, restless. So do you, look ahead to the next and the next. His feet might one day plant, but yours, they wander unless love plants them. And even then, love must be willing to go with you."

She smiled, traced a finger over a card. "Love isn't a goal, but a wish. I feel the same. It's a gift you can open or leave tied and wrapped. It must be a choice or it doesn't hold for you.

Voyages and journeys, and you must have the wheel. Security? What's the point without the adventure, the new, the next?"

He came over to watch, as he'd never seen her do a reading. He knew the cards only because Mags had sometimes fiddled with them.

"You may travel as you will, and alone physically, but you take your roots with you. You know how to transplant them, to grow where you want, until you want somewhere else. This is freedom. I admire that. And the bounty you have? Your cup never runs dry. Love fills it, again and again."

She sat back. "You're a fortunate woman, Mags, and one who brings the fortunate with her."

"My sister gave me a gift. Not that I knew what the hell to do with it at the time. Not that I didn't like babies and kids. Dana was a mother down to the bone. I think I was born to be an aunt. It surprised me to see some of me in Silas. The brains? I don't know where the hell he got those. Or the scary memory."

"I could ask you about some Cubs' outfielders' stats and you'd rattle them right off."

"That's not scary memory, pal, that's baseball. Let's have another glass of wine, Dauphine, and I'll read yours."

Dauphine smiled. "Let's."

AFTER MAGS DROVE WEST in her VW Bus, Silas made his way to Tulane. He had his paperwork—carefully, even meticulously generated—and Silas Booth's backstory firmly in place. It didn't take much work to gain permission—with fees paid—for the few courses he wanted to audit.

Through the rest of February and right up to April first, which he spent with Mags in Santa Fe—he kept his head down and his mouth mostly shut and studied English literature, the Impressionists, and computer programming.

He felt, almost, like a regular undergrad, walking the leafy green campus, strolling by azaleas exploding with color. Though not required of him, he did assignments, wrote papers. And he learned.

His French lessons with Dauphine progressed to evening conversations and occasional sex. He learned computer hacking from Jacques, through his own reverse engineering, and stumbled onto an online course on Italian.

It seemed like just the thing to add to his résumé.

Then as warm, moist spring slid toward hot, drippy summer, he met Sebastien Picot.

He sat on a bench at the Fly in Audubon Park, out of the syrupy hustle of the city, and watched the great river and the steamboats that plied it.

Behind him people picnicked or tossed Frisbees or just napped on the grass. He wore his Green Wave T-shirt—just another college kid on a steamy May evening.

He'd come to meet Jacques, at his forger's and sometimes fence's request. Since he'd started prepping for another job— the wealthy grandmother of a student in his lit class who loved to brag about her grandmama's jewelry—he planned to discuss the liquidation of the multistrand diamond necklace his mouthy classmate looked forward (with considerable glee) to inheriting.

Jacques plopped down beside him, held out a hand for a low five. "My man."

If Silas's build ran thin—he had the dumbbells, and worked on that—Jacques was a scarecrow in basketball shorts. Even sitting still he pumped off energy. Silas figured Jacques burned off more calories taking a nap than most did jogging a mile.

"Not your usual spot, bro."

"But one of yours."

It was, Silas agreed. The wide brown river rolled, and at sunset everything tripped over into magic.

"Got someone wants to meet you."

When Silas shifted his gaze from the river to Jacques, Jacques held up both hands and grinned. He wore a near permanent grin, showing large white teeth, but when he meant it, he all but gleamed.

"Would I mess you up? Known this one since I was working the change raising on tourists. Got a proposition for you, so you take it or leave it, *ami*. I'm just here to stand his bona fides is all."

"What's he paying you?"

Jacques let out a hoot, shook his head so the twists that circled his head like a crown shook with it. "This here is friend to friend, *ça va*? If you take the proposition, and it all works, I get a fee. You don't want, you don't want, and we cool."

He was sleeping, now and again, with Jacques's cousin, and he knew that counted in Jacques's code. So he shrugged. "I'll listen."

"*Bien.*" Jacques held up a hand, turned it back and forth.

Silas watched the man hobble toward the bench. His right foot wore one of those thick medical boots and he used a cane. Otherwise, he looked fit and about fifty.

He had a little scrappy-looking bowlegged dog on a leash.

He hit maybe five-seven, with a weathered face boasting a trim goatee. A little silver threaded through the sunstruck blond of an impressive mane of hair.

He sat on Silas's other side, let out a whoosh as he took the weight off the booted foot.

The dog sniffed at Silas's Chucks suspiciously.

"He don't bite much. *Assis*, Bluto, you old *coullion*." His Cajun accent managed to be sharp and lazy at the same time. "A fine spot, this, even got a little breeze going."

"I'm gonna get on." Jacques rose. "Leave you two to get acquainted. *À bientôt* now."

Sebastien settled back like a man with all the time in the world. "That boy, he shoots off energy like a rocket ship. Got a quieter way about you. Sebastien Picot," he continued without offering to shake hands. "I'm an admirer of your work, me."

"What work is that?"

Sebastien just smiled, kept looking out at the river as Bluto sat—but continued to sniff at Silas's shoes. "A man in my position, with my experience, he best know the competition, or more friendly-like, a colleague. We got some mutuals, you and me, *mon ami*. Jacques, and Burdette up in Baton Rouge, Michelle in Lafayette. They careful, as you know, what they say and who they say it to. Me, they know a long time, so when I ask, they answer."

"Ask about what?"

"*Mais*, some pretty baubles finding their way out of one place to another. Finding their way smart. I like smart. Me, I think, this one's young to be so smart. Smart not to leave bread crumbs, smart to take a little and not all. Elegance here, I think, when I study these journeys. Baubles, *c'est bon*. I've helped many baubles on their journey in my time. And art *aussi*. Cash, what is this but paper. No elegance. You take, *bien sûr*, if it's just there for the taking, but the baubles, the art. This is elegance."

Silas didn't see setup, not with Jacques involved, but he let the silence hang when Sebastien finished.

They sat, a minute, then two, while the river rolled and the sun began to dip.

"I have a client, me," Sebastien continued. "There is a very nice painting he wishes for his collection. Now it's in the collection of another, you see? A private collection where it made a journey at one time from a public one in London. You know London?"

"I know where it is."

Sebastien laughed, and the sound was a rusty saw on old wood. "I wasn't part of this journey, but I knew of it. Very elegant. Before you were born, I think. *Mais* this painting is no longer in London, but here in New Orleans, in this private collection. The client wants it, and I agreed to arrange this. I've taken, what you'd say, a deposit for the work. I have done the preparation for the work. A challenge, but I am good at what I do."

"Okay. Well, good luck."

"*Malchance*, this is what I had." Sebastien leaned down to tap the boot. "The work needs the nimble, and I am in this fucker for five more weeks. The painting must take its journey next week. This client, he pays very well, but he is . . . hard. I would return the deposit, but this wouldn't be enough for him. I would have more than a fracture of the ankle if he's not satisfied. I don't want my bones broken, so for this, I need a partner."

He told himself he wasn't interested, told himself to walk away. Instead, he pointed at the boot.

"Take it off so I can see."

"*Alors*." Sebastien hissed a little, but bent over, unstrapped the boot. And gingerly lifted out his foot with its storm cloud of bruising. "Hairline, they say, and I say fuck them."

"How'd you do it?"

"I could say I did it leaping from a window to avoid a jealous husband, but I tripped over the goddamn dog. A man gets up to piss in the night because he had a lot of wine, and trips over his own dog. And now I need someone with brains and skill to help this painting make its journey or I'll have my legs, my arms, could be my neck broken."

"Lift up your shirt."

Sebastien sighed, but lifted the shirt. "You're smart to be careful. I don't need stupid." Without being asked, he emptied his pockets. "Jacques would never betray you. Your heart knows this truth, but we have to heed the brain, *oui*?"

"I work alone."

"The same, me, almost always. You make a mistake, it's yours. You run your mouth, it's yours. And the fee, it's yours. But this job, this time, this client. I can't do it alone."

"What's the fee? You're thinking how much to shave off it. How much will draw me in. Don't. I've been doing what I do half my life."

"*Non!*" Equal parts astonished and impressed, Sebastien goggled at him. "You would be a bébé!"

"Nine. Circumstances, not your business. Don't try to con me."

Sebastien poked a finger into Silas's chest. "You I like. I could say less, but I have a big need. I have a deposit of ten thousand—and this I keep, as the client came to me. When the painting makes its journey to him, is authenticated—and this I also handle—he will transfer the fee to my account. One million dollars, American."

Silas couldn't breathe for a minute, not after the hard thump his heart took on the way to his guts.

"What the hell is the painting?"

"It's known as *Sun Rising over the Thames*. Turner painted it in his mature phase, an abstraction. A small painting, two feet square. It's made many journeys and was once in another private collection in Germany before being taken by the Nazis. More journeys and it was donated to the Tate, in London. Now it rests in a secure room in this private collection."

He knew a little about Turner from his studies, and promised himself to learn more. "It's going to be worth more than a million."

"*Mais oui*, but this is the fee, and handsome enough for such as me. I will take eighty percent, and the deposit, as I have done the preparations and the client is mine, and I must teach you, I think, some of the skills you have yet to master. From my share, I pay Jacques one thousand for the introduction."

He couldn't imagine what would be close to two hundred thousand. He couldn't imagine seeing that much from a single job. But that didn't mean he'd settle for first offer.

"I'll be doing the actual job, taking the risk. Even split—you keep the deposit."

Sebastien let out a snort. "I have thirty years' experience, and have already invested near a month on this. I have the equipment. Seventy-five–twenty-five."

"I have two good ankles, and you're pressed for time. Sixty–forty."

He'd been more than ready to take seventy–thirty, but didn't flick a lash when Sebastien held out a hand.

"Done."

Silas accepted the hand, and began the next leg of his own journey.

Chapter Seven

BY THE TIME HE went to dinner at Sebastien's home the next night, Silas had thoroughly researched Turner as well as the heist in 1983 that had relieved the Tate of *Sun Rising over the Thames*.

He'd also grilled both Jacques and Dauphine about Sebastien.

Jacques deemed him solid, reliable, and honest in the way of thieves and con men. Dauphine termed him a charming reprobate who couldn't be trusted around women or a locked door.

Silas considered what he could do with a fee breathlessly close to half a million.

He could go to college, he could travel. He could buy better equipment for his nightwork. And when the Volvo died, buy something that wasn't used.

He didn't want a big, fancy house, but he could send some money to Mags if she did.

But first, because ten years of experience taught him not to count the take before the work, he had to prepare and he had to learn.

He brought wine because that's what you were supposed to do, and thought he'd be damn glad when he didn't have to pay somebody to buy it for him.

Sebastien lived in the bayou, but not as Silas expected, in a little shack or cabin. He had what looked like a cozy cottage with white walls and bright red shutters surrounded by flowers with views of the water and the cypress knees poking out of it. A pirogue swayed at a short dock.

The cottage had a covered front porch with a pair of rocking chairs flanking a square table. Wind chimes and what he knew were spirit chimes sang and rang in the breeze.

A red pickup sat on the gravel between the cottage and a shed.

Music blasted out of the open windows of the cottage, and the dog barked its head off.

Silas stood a moment, admiring the water, the shadows and light.

And saw the knobby back of an alligator cruise by.

"Shit! Holy shit."

He backed up a couple of feet before he turned to step onto the porch and knocked.

"Come on in now, and wipe your feet first. *Ferme ta bouche*, Bluto!"

The dog stopped barking when Silas stepped in, but raced over to give his shoes a sniff, then stare at him with hostility.

He'd call the cottage *cozy*, and figured his mom would've said *cluttered*. But cheerfully.

He thought the walls might be cypress, and they held driftwood art, a cuckoo clock, pencil sketches of nudes. The living room with its bright blue sofa and bright red chairs led straight back to the kitchen, where Sebastien stood with a bib apron over his baggy jeans and T-shirt.

"You're in for some luck, *cher*. I caught me a couple nice catfish 'bout an hour ago. Gonna blacken 'em up. Go good they will with my potato salad and fried okra."

The dog ran over to a basket full of balls, rubber bones, the tattered remains of what had been stuffed animals. He snatched out one of the bones, hopped onto a chair with it. Then stared at Silas as if daring him to do something about it.

"What you got there?"

"Wine. Ah, a Shiraz, but I think it's supposed to be white with fish."

"These cats ain't gonna care 'bout that. Bring it on in so we can open it up."

He walked back to a kitchen, where pans and tools hung on the wall. Bottles and jars crowded together on open shelves. Dishes and glassware jumbled in glass-fronted cabinets. A bunch of wildflowers shot out of a jug on the square kitchen table.

Sebastien doused the filets in God-knew-what, but the scent made Silas's nose itch.

"Corkscrew on the wall there, glasses back there."

While Silas worked on opening the wine, Sebastien washed his hands in the deep sink, then walked over to turn the music down a few notches.

"I saw an alligator right out front. In the water, but right out by your dock."

"Probably Pierre. He likes his evening swim."

Silas wondered about partnering up with somebody who named an alligator.

"He'd take your dog in one swallow."

"Bluto, he's too tough to eat. And he got a charm on his collar wards off the *cocodril*."

"Okay."

Not his weird little dog, Silas thought. And despite the fact he figured he could drop-kick Bluto an easy fifty yards if necessary, the dog was just scary.

"Have you done many jobs like the one coming up?"

"They come, they go." Sebastien took a hit of wine, then pulled a couple of eggs out of a snow-white refrigerator, began to whisk them in a bowl.

"Jacques said you've never been caught."

"*Mais . . .*" He began slicing up pods of okra. "Only once. Me, I'm about your age, I'm thinking, and working with my second cousin on my *maman's* side, Louie. We gonna take some baubles on a journey out of a fine house in Metairie. Louie, he's not too bright under the skull of him, but he's family. And what's that boy do but wander off in that fine house, and he done wake up the man of that fine house, and that man he's got him a shotgun."

As he relayed the story, Sebastien dumped the okra slices in the egg to soak.

"Me, I coulda run. Shotgun man's got Louie, and that boy's not too bright, but he's not going to say nothing about me. *Mais*, I can't be running and leaving Louie to take the fall alone, so I step out, hands up. And me and Louie, we do six months."

He picked up his wine again. "And that, *mon ami*, is the last time I work with a partner till now. I think you got plenty of bright under the skull of you."

"What happened to Louie?"

Sebastien smiled as he took a couple of cast-iron skillets off the wall. "That boy got himself married and got a job on a shrimp boat. He got him five kids, and three grandbabies now."

"If you have jobs like this come and go, why do you live here? It's a nice place, but with that kind of regular take, you could live anywhere."

"Maybe have me a big, fine house somebody else wants to sneak into?"

"Nobody knows home security better than a thief."

Sebastien hooted. "You got that on the head. This is home. I was born on the bayou. You know that song."

"I didn't, until I came here."

"My blood's here. My heart. No place else in this world sings for me. I built this place."

"Seriously?"

"With these two hands. Family helped as family does, but it's mine like nowhere else could be."

"It's really good work. I've got a friend whose dad's a carpenter, so I know enough. If you can build like this, why do you steal?"

"*Cher*, I wonder 'bout that bright when you ask the foolish. I got the *envie*, same as you."

"It's not about envy for me."

"*Non, non, envie*. The hunger. I got it for how you think it through, make the steps, for how it feels in the blood when you move through the dark. You ain't got that, there ain't no reason but the greed, and the greed'll do you in."

Silas got that, he got that exactly. *Envie*, he thought. He knew the hunger.

"And I got three daughters, me. My sweet girls, and the three ex-wives I made them with. I give them a good life, good educations."

"Three ex-wives."

Sebastien got out a bowl, dumped cornmeal into it, added salt, pepper, something from one of his jars.

"I love women, me. Love all about them. Any size, any shape, the rich, the poor, the wise and unwise." He worked while he rhapsodized, added oil to a skillet, turning on the heat, dredging the soaked okra through the cornmeal mixture. "They got the fragrance, the flavor, the feel. Mmm-mmm-mmm. Ain't nothing like a female, and every one of them? *Elles sont belles*. I tell myself, You don't go marrying this one, Sebastien, but then I do. I make a good lover, I help make beautiful girls, and I'm a good daddy, me, but a *mari*?"

He lifted a hand with fingers coated with wet cornmeal, wagged it in the air. "*Mais*, we stay friends because we have those treasures we made."

He slid the coated rounds into the hot oil. The air went to sizzle and smoke.

"Catch me the plates there. This don't take long. Gonna get these cats going."

It seemed an odd way to do business, but Silas set the table. At Sebastien's request, he pulled the bowl of potato salad out of the fridge. When the dog raced over and began to dance in place,

Sebastien filled a red bowl with kibble, then cut up a portion of the blackened fish to mix in it.

They sat in the kitchen, windows open to the sounds of the bayou, with Silas nursing his first glass of wine and Sebastien into his second.

"Careful with the wine, are you?"

"I'm driving."

Sebastien tapped a finger on his temple. "Good to be smart and careful. *Mange*."

Silas sampled the fish first. It had a kick, but a damn good one. *"C'est bon. Très bon."*

Everything had a kick, Silas discovered, and a damn good one.

"A man without a woman who doesn't cook goes hungry," Sebastien told him. "I don't like to go hungry, me. Jacques, he says you learn French good, and you got the Spanish, too."

"High school Spanish, but I'm okay with it. I'm learning Italian now."

"Why you learn all that?"

"I guess I've got the *envie* for languages. And they're a tool. Like you can put on somebody else."

"Put on? Ah, *oui*, like a disguise?"

"Yeah, like that."

Sebastien drank, ate, studied his potential partner. "How'd you start off in this work?"

"Jacques didn't tell you?"

"He says it's your story. So you tell me if you want. We have us a *veiller*."

"Vay-yay?"

"*Veiller* is, ah . . . talk with friends, shoot the shit."

The dog finished eating and wandered outside after poking open the back screen door. Silas assumed he wouldn't be a snack for a crocodile.

"My mom got sick, and the bills piled up. Medical—the worst—but mortgage payments and the rest. My aunt and I kept the business going—they had a cleaning business—but it wasn't enough with just the two of us, and I had school. So."

"A son takes care of his mama or he ain't no son. She get better?"

Silas shook his head. "She got better, then got sick again, and better again, and sick again. She died last year."

Sebastien made the sign of the cross, laid a hand on his heart. "I'll light a candle for her in church."

"You go to church?"

"Sometimes I go to church, sometimes the bayou's my church. Angels are everywhere if you look. How'd you start? You lift the locks?"

"Picking pockets."

"Hah. You good at that?"

"Yeah."

"No skill there, me. Locks for me." He patted his narrow chest. "I can sweet-talk any lock to fall for me. They got the digital now, but they don't stop me. This man, with the painting, he lives in a big old plantation house, got him servants and people come to mow the lawn and all of that. Doesn't treat them fine and fair, I tell you this. Cheats on his wife. I had me three wives and never did I step out on any of them. You love women, you have respect. A cheating man's no man."

"Does it matter to you if the mark's a good person or not?"

Sebastien shrugged skinny shoulders. "Job is what it is. But it's *lagniappe* when they a cheating bastard."

"A little something extra."

"*Mais oui*. You dance, *garçon*?"

"Dance. Yeah. Why?"

"The ladies, they like a man can dance—that's one. Dance? It's grace and rhythm and balance. *Tu saisis*?"

"*Oui.*"

Sebastien tapped his boot. "With this, I don't dance, and

such a job needs the grace and rhythm and balance. I clomp, not glide with this. This man who cheats on his woman and is hard to those who work for him has a house with many doors and windows. Many locks and all wired, *tu vois*."

"If I know what kind of system, I can beat it."

"It's a very fine system, but none, as we know, are perfect. *Mais*, inside, this room where he keeps the painting—and other things precious—this is also protected. Like a vault it is inside the office he has there, a big room, also kept locked, opened that office only for cleaning. And this he changes the code for every day—so it's told to me."

"So it's in steps. The house alarm—cameras?"

"Bien sûr."

"Okay. The house system, then the room, then the vault. Then retrace."

"Retrace?"

"I leave everything, put everything back the way it was. Reset the systems. Why let them know straight off you've been in there?"

Sebastien sat back. "This is a clever way. Takes more time, yes, but gains time maybe. All is as it was, except one thing. The painting is on its journey." Then with a nod, he rose. "Come, I'll show you what we have."

He led the way down a short hall and into a bedroom. Since it held two beds—a human one with metal head- and footboards and a dog one—Silas concluded it was Sebastien's.

The cypress walls displayed more pencil art—bayou scenes and female figures. A wooden chair sat in a corner with a pole lamp. Shelves held books and trinkets.

Sebastien went to a sketch of a full-figured woman standing under the lace of Spanish moss. He slipped a finger behind the frame. And the wall slid into the wall.

"Pocket door. You wouldn't see the joint unless you knew where to look."

Impressed, Silas stepped forward to study the space, about two feet by twelve.

A narrow desk held a top-of-the-line computer. A board hung behind it, covered with what Silas assumed were schematics for the current job, a blueprint of the house, timetables, names, dates, a photo of the painting, others of the plantation house and grounds with outbuildings. And, most intriguing, one of a vault door.

"How did you get a picture of the vault?"

"This is not his, but one of the same model."

"I've never worked on one of those."

"There must always be a first."

He stepped in farther and noted the shelves on the bedroom wall inside the hidden space held tools of their trade. The lock picks, drills, stethoscopes, remotes, and cell phones that could be—or already were—converted for use on digital systems.

Gloves, paper booties, ski masks. A freaking grappling hook. Nylon rope, glass cutters.

"Catch me that chair," Sebastien said as he booted up the computer. "Stood too long on this damn foot already."

As Silas went to get the wooden chair, Bluto walked in, went straight to his dog bed. He sat in it and gave Silas his death stare.

"Dogs usually like me."

"He like you fine, else he'd be making a rumble in his throat. He's just showing you who's top dog 'round here. Every place has a weak spot," he began.

To Silas's astonishment, he brought up the house and, using the mouse, took the image on a slow revolve.

"That is seriously cool."

"World changes, you gotta change with it. This here?" He tapped a set of glass patio doors with his finger. "That's where you go in."

They spent an hour on the basics before Sebastien said it was time for a coffee and sunset break on the veranda.

Though he wasn't much for coffee, Silas enjoyed that slow bleed of red and gold light over the river, through the cypress.

Owls hooted, insects sang, frogs croaked, something splashed in the water.

"Bayou, she makes music all night long."

A strange but appealing sort of music for a city boy, Silas admitted. "You don't have much security here."

"I got me this fierce beast," he pointed out as Bluto snored at his feet. "Got Pierre and his family over there. And that little bump you might've noticed coming back here? That's a pressure alarm. I know when someone's coming to my place. But I was born and raised here, my family's here, and people know me. Ain't nobody on the bayou gonna mess with me. And the po-po, they got no reason to nose around here either. If they do, they got nothing to see. Just a man and his dog, living off the land, doing some odd jobs here and there. Never do I break in, me, to a house I work on."

"It was the same with me when I was cleaning them."

After the break, they worked till midnight, going over the steps, the systems, the household habits. They didn't have a dog—always a plus—but a cat. Or a *minou*, as Sebastien called it.

In addition to the cat, the man, his wife, two kids—boy, age twelve; girl, age eight—they had a live-in housekeeper and her husband.

By the time he drove home, his brain and eyes wide open from the single cup of café noir Sebastien had pushed on him, Silas knew every name and location of the household occupants, the distance from the entry point to the locked office, and the distance from that door to the vault.

He knew the house security system, and since he'd worked with one like it, felt confident there. The locked office door didn't worry him overmuch.

But the vault? That was new and fresh and complex. And he only had a matter of days to learn its intricacies and secrets.

Pumped from the coffee, he worked another two hours in his apartment, making his own notes, timeline, practicing with the doctored remote Sebastien had lent him. And practicing with his combination lock.

The vault had a nine-number combination max, and he agreed with Sebastien the mark would use all nine.

Time-consuming.

He could do a three-combo in under fifteen minutes now on most jobs. A nine wouldn't just triple that, he knew. The complexity would add at least an hour more, most likely. Unless he got really, really lucky.

He banked on two hours to break the vault.

In and out, he calculated, in three—three and a half to be safe and sure.

Longer than he'd ever risked, but then the biggest payday he'd ever gone after.

When he finally climbed into bed, he dreamed of endless combinations, and the satisfying click, click of tumblers.

HE SKIPPED HIS WEEKLY French lesson and the possibility of sex with Dauphine and focused on improving his time. He settled for frozen pizza in a city where food was a religion to cut down on any distractions.

With scrap metal picked up in a junkyard he built a low-rent mock-up of the vault door, then spent hours setting and resetting a combination lock. After two nights, he shaved his average time to sixty-seven minutes, twelve seconds.

He determined to do better.

He munched on Doritos and studied the security schematics.

He lifted weights, drank Gatorade, and played every step, every movement in his mind.

When the night came, he told himself he was ready. He reminded himself a job was a job, a series of steps after careful, focused preparation.

He left his car at Sebastien's cottage and climbed into the pickup, along with the dog.

"I drop you where I showed you on the drive-by, and you hotfoot it from there. Ain't nobody much travel that road this time of night, but you see a car coming—"

"I move off the road," Silas finished. "When I'm clear, I turn my phone back on, text you, and you pick me up where you dropped me off."

"You got a cool head, *mon ami*?"

"I'm cool. I've got it," he added. "If we run through it too many times, I'm overprepared. I've got it."

The steamy, moonless night worked in his favor. There'd be security lights on the grounds, but easy to avoid. Windows closed against the heat, the hum of the AC, both little advantages as he saw it.

At one in the morning on a heavy summer night the household should be fast asleep. If not, he'd just have to avoid any insomniacs. If he could hit his best practice time, he'd be in and out inside of two hours. Any complications, he'd still be back in the pickup before even an early riser stirred.

They didn't pass another car on the tree-lined road.

When Sebastien pulled over, he gave Silas one last long look. "*Bonne chance.*"

With a nod, Silas got out, checked the time. And ran.

Tall, lanky, dressed in black, he covered the quarter mile quickly, then stopped in the cover of trees to study the house.

The expected security lights illuminated the lush lawns, silvered the dripping moss. The carriage lights that flanked the wide front door gleamed over the long veranda with its thick columns.

But the many windows, every one, remained dark.

Using the trees, the shrubs, he kept an eye on those windows for any movement as he circled around to the side of the house and Sebastien's declared weak spot.

Roses, lilies, and the summer scent of green perfumed the air as he dealt with the simple lock on the ornate iron handset. Inside what he guessed they called a morning room or sitting room, he went straight to the alarm pad.

First test, he thought, to see if Sebastien knew what the hell he was doing with the homemade reader.

The seconds ticked off as the numbers flashed by on the display. Worst case, he ran.

But the code flashed green.

He closed the door again, quietly.

The air here held perfume as well. Flowers and lemons. And that air held still as he stood, eyes closed, to boost his sense of hearing.

With the blueprints in his head, he moved out of the room, took a short jog to the right and across the massive entranceway with its graceful central staircase.

Another jog, this time left, moving quick and quiet, past another parlor, the billiard room, and to the locked door of the office.

As he got out his picks, something swished against his legs and nearly shot him out of his Chucks.

The orange tabby said, "Meow."

Though it had a sweet face, Silas didn't touch it. He gave himself ten seconds to settle, then dealt with the lock.

The cat slipped in before he could stop it, and pranced over to leap up and perch on the wide arm of a port-wine leather sofa. If he put it out, it might meow more, scratch at the door, or do something else to wake someone up.

Silas closed the door, and faced the vault.

It looked more impressive in person, three feet wide, eight feet tall, gunmetal gray. He knew from the schematics it was nearly thirty years old.

He approached it, laid one gloved hand on its cool metal surface.

Then, clicking on his stopwatch, got to work.

Behind him, the cat watched and purred. He'd gauged the distance to the window—his single escape route if someone decided to come in.

Then he blocked everything out.

He worked meticulously, as he had on his very first—and, in retrospect, incredibly simple—safe job. As each tumbler fell, he felt a quiet ping of satisfaction.

He'd trained himself to make the graph in his head, did his calculations, and moved on.

He stopped once when he heard a creak. Waited, waited, but it didn't come again. Old houses, he knew, had their night voices.

When he gripped the lever, he held his breath. Math never lied, but more than sometimes human calculation could go off.

The lever moved smoothly, and with a long, strong pull, the vault door opened.

He clicked the stopwatch. Fifty minutes flat.

Later, he promised himself, he'd celebrate that personal best.

Still using only the penlight, he swept the room. Twice as wide as the door, he noted, and outfitted with a leather chair, a commode table—looked antique. A crystal decanter and glass sat on the table.

In a room, he saw, decorated with statues—bronzes, marbles, stone—on pedestals. Wide shelves held smaller ones, and displays of gemstones, what he thought might be a moon rock. A fancy egg—possibly Fabergé—a pair of dueling pistols.

Paintings graced the walls. A portrait of a young woman in profile, a landscape of rolling hills and trees painted with autumn glory, a watercolor, an abstract that made no sense to him.

And the Turner, the small jewel of golds and reds and hints of blue.

It was nothing like the photos he'd studied. It was so much more.

It lived, it moved, it breathed. He could *feel* the sun exploding to life over the city, over the river, and vowed he'd go there one day and see it for himself.

It seemed to him the painting glowed as he lifted it carefully—reverently—from the wall.

He was supposed to cut it out of the frame, roll up the canvas, and get out.

But he couldn't do it, not when he could see the brushstrokes, feel the brilliance. Since he didn't know exactly how to get it out of the frame, didn't have time to try to figure it out, he decided to take it with him as it was.

Though he wanted—had the *envie*—to take a closer look at the other treasures in the room, he resisted. He stepped out, started to close the vault door.

And saw that the cat was no longer perched on the couch.

"Fuck."

He started to search, then heard the purr. The cat had made himself at home in the master's chair in his private museum.

Silas tucked the painting under one arm, the cat under the other.

He closed the vault, spun the lock, then set it back on the number where he'd found it.

He set the cat down outside the office, closed the door before it could slither back in. Relocked it. It meowed after him, a little forlornly, when he retraced his steps.

He reset the house alarm, closed and locked the side door, and jogged to the road and into the trees before he stopped to text Sebastien, then jogged back to the pickup spot.

He checked the time, smiled slowly. In and out in seventy-two minutes.

Chapter Eight

HE KNEW THE SOUND of Sebastien's pickup, but kept to the shadows until he saw it pull up and stop.

"Fast work," Sebastien began when Silas opened the passenger door. "What you do? Bring it in the frame?"

"No way I was putting a blade to any part of this canvas. Man, just look at it."

Sebastien rolled his eyes. "We look later. And we better hope no po-po decide to cruise by and want to have a chat while you got that on your lap."

He glanced over as he pulled out onto the road, and Silas stared down at the painting.

"Don't you go falling in love. That belongs to the client now."

"I can fall in love and still do the job."

"Any trouble in there?"

"I met the cat. I nearly shut him in the vault before I realized he'd walked in there. Nice cat." He shifted a little as Bluto—obviously scenting cat—snuffled all over him.

"Other than that, nothing. You were right about the side door. I probably could've gotten through with a celluloid strip, and your reader's solid. You need to teach me how to make my own."

"Do I, now?"

"Yeah, you do. I could figure it out now that I have some time, but you already know. I'm going to take more courses with electronics, IT stuff. I can do basic hacking, but I need to expand that."

"How long it take you to break that vault?"

"Fifty flat. I'm going to get better there. Sebastien, he has a room behind it full of art and gems and antiques. He's got a big leather chair in there so he can sit and admire all of it. Locked away, just for him."

"People like that, they keep us in business."

"If I ever get myself something like this, the real deal? I'm hanging it on the wall, in the open. This client, does he have a room like this?"

"I say this one, he got himself a room make what you saw look like my broom closet."

"I don't get why people like that want to have something so beautiful no one can see but them."

"Don't have to get. Like I said, they keep us in business." But as he turned into the bayou, he sent Silas another glance. "They got no soul, *tu saisis*? They don't see what you see when you look at that. They just want, *c'est tout*. Like you fuck a woman in the dark without knowing her, or seeing her, or feeling her, or having a care. It's just the want, and no soul."

He pulled up at the cottage. "All the money in this world— and they got the most of it—won't buy them that soul. *Mais*, they just gonna want the next thing, 'cause they never gonna see what you see when you look."

They got out, and Silas took one last look at the Turner before handing it to Sebastien.

"You want a drink? You earned it."

"No, it's late. There's a summer class I want to see about auditing."

"That brain don't quit. I'll be calling the client in the morning, and likely taking this painting on the rest of its journey. So tomorrow, or a day or two more if he ain't ready, I'll be putting your share in those accounts like you wanted."

"Okay."

"Ain't gonna screw you on it."

"Never thought you would. Besides, I know where you live." He looked down at Bluto. "And your little dog, too."

Sebastien slapped him on the shoulder. "Maybe we work together again sometime."

"Maybe."

"*Bonne nuit, mon cher ami.*" Sebastien hobbled toward the cottage.

"*Bonne nuit.*"

Silas got in his car, drove back to the Quarter. As he drove through the hot, still night, he realized the biggest thrill of the night wasn't the stunning fee he'd collect. It wasn't even cracking the vault in fifty flat.

It was holding that miracle in his hands and looking into its heart.

The phone woke Silas at quarter to ten and out of a dream about sunrises and sex.

He fumbled for it. "Yeah, what?"

"Rise and shine, *garçon*. You gonna take the journey with me and the painting."

He yawned hugely and tried to engage his brain. "Why?"

"'Cause the client wants to meet you. Get yourself dressed and come on and pick me up. You're driving. It's a ways for me with this bum foot anyhow."

"What's a ways? Where are we—"

But Sebastien had already hung up.

"Shit."

He'd planned to get up when he woke up, seeing as it had been damn near morning when he'd fallen into bed. Then he'd hoped to see about talking himself into a summer class.

He didn't especially want to meet this client, but he sure as hell wanted the fee. He grabbed a Coke, showered while he drank it to wake himself up.

He got out his newest—and cleanest—jeans, then decided most of his T-shirts wouldn't do, since he hadn't done any laundry in over a week. He put on one of his three good shirts, rolled up the sleeves.

He grabbed another Coke, his wallet, keys, and sunglasses, and headed out the door eating a Pop-Tart.

When he arrived at Sebastien's, he saw—and accepted— that Bluto would go along for the ride. Sebastien had the leash hooked to his belt. He carried the painting, wrapped in thick brown paper, a go-cup of coffee, and his cane.

The dog hopped right in, gave Silas a glare, then jumped into the back seat. Silas secured the painting in the back with the seat belt.

"You been to Lake Charles?"

"No."

"Today you do. Best you get on 10. Not so pretty as the byways, but faster."

"Why does he need to see me?"

"You don't ask a man like this why. We go, we get paid, we say *au revoir* till the next time he wants something."

Silas turned the car around and started out. "You don't like him."

"Don't have to. You like everybody you work for back when you clean houses?"

"No."

"There you are. I have to tell him I got me a young partner to do the work because of my foot 'cause he don't give me time to heal up and do it myself. I tell him I don't give the young partner his name or nothing, and he got no reason not to believe that. You don't want to go lying to this one, *tu saisis*? But today he says, bring you. He knows this job, it takes finesse, and skill, so I think he decides he wants a look at you."

"Fine. Whatever."

Sebastien frowned out the window for a time.

"Now you're gonna know his name, and his face, and one of his fine houses. Maybe that's a good thing for you. He has those wants. But he isn't a good man."

"You already said."

"I don't get the painting for him when I say I get it, he'd bust me up good. Pay somebody to bust me up. I don't get it because I make a mistake, get myself caught? He don't worry about that 'cause he knows I don't say nothing about him. Ain't worth my life."

"He'd kill you?"

"My guts tell me that, for sure they do. And I hear things that tell my head that. Can't say *absolument*, but my guts and my head say what they say, and I got three daughters not yet grown. I'm saying to you, 'cause I've got this fondness for you now, watch where you step with this one."

"We're delivering the painting, so there's no problem."

"Not this time. And me, I've taken things on journeys for him many times, many years. But he wants more, and bigger, *oui*? More special. I tell him true if what he wants I can't get, and no trouble. One day, he might not say no trouble if I say I can't get. But now, we work fine."

"Who is he?"

"Carter LaPorte."

"That's his name, not who he is."

"Rich, and born that way. A man who lives a life of privilege and plenty. More than plenty," Sebastien considered. "Excess, *oui*? He wears a mask very well, *tu saisis*? Of the civilized, the sophisticated, and the elegant. But under the mask is the ruthless, and the cruel."

"Why do business with him?"

"He wears the mask very well," Sebastien repeated. "And pays always without the negotiating after the job. Many will. I have three daughters." He shrugged, as that answered all for him.

"This is a man who holds rubies in his hand, but they aren't enough. Never enough. Someone else has emeralds, so he must have them. He must have more than another, more than he has, always more. And the best, the biggest, the most precious."

"So, he's greedy. One of my rules is don't be greedy. It's a good way to get caught."

"Men like LaPorte, they don't worry about getting caught. They have all the power. He sees what he wants, and takes—one way or the other. He has a woman—the most beautiful, most desirable—but he tires of her, or sees another, or sees—more this, I think—a man with a woman who is beautiful and desirable, so he must have her. Because she is with another. Possessions, and a woman is, for him, only another possession.

"He does not marry. Be wary of a man who doesn't keep a woman—or, as it goes, another man—in his life. A love. Without a love, there are only things."

Sebastien played a little tattoo with his hands on his thighs, giving Silas his first clue. Sebastien feared LaPorte.

"You're afraid of him."

"I'm a man of sense, me. *Mais*, I have fear of him. Be a man of sense, *mon ami*. I tell myself always this is the last job I do for him—"

"Don't ever say it's the last job, on anything. Hard rule number one. That's when it all goes to shit and you get caught."

"You have rules?"

"Yeah. Don't get greedy. Don't ever say this is the last job. Don't even pretend to have a gun. Don't steal from somebody who needs it more than you do. Run when you have to—and keep a go bag ready so you can."

"A man of sense. What, I wonder, will LaPorte make of you?"

"He can make whatever he wants, as long as he pays."

Sebastien directed Silas off the interstate to the lakefront. He had Silas stop so he could walk Bluto as, he explained, Bluto wouldn't be allowed out of the car at the mansion.

Silas spent the time looking at the lake, wondering what it would be like to live in a house with that view. What kind of house he'd have. Lots of windows, he decided, so he could see the water from all of them. Maybe a little sailboat at the dock. A secure room, of course, and bigger than Sebastien's.

One day, he thought. He couldn't really imagine himself living in a house right now, much less owning one.

But one day.

In short order, he learned LaPorte didn't own a house. He wouldn't have called it a mansion. What he saw ranked as an estate.

Mediterranean style, its red-tiled roofs had multiple levels. Its golden stone walls jutted with balconies and wide terraces, with its long covered veranda facing the lake.

It looked like an exclusive hotel with perfect lawns, lush gardens, old-growth trees.

Silas imagined the security system presented a hell of a challenge, and wished—fleetingly—he could pit himself against it.

But another rule? Never steal from a client.

The iron gates slid open to a gate or carriage house with the same stone, same red-tile roof as the main.

"Security—three men. Armed," Sebastien told him. "On twenty-four-hour rotation."

"Good to know."

"Security in the house as well. What you would call a butler is ex-military. The housekeeper? She was Mossad. Head grounds-keeper? Expert in mixed martial arts, and so it goes."

"Smart. Tech's easier to beat than actual people."

He stopped at the carriage house when a man in a suit stepped out, held up a hand.

"We get out. Open the trunk. They check the car, and us."

"For what?"

"Weapons, devices. And because they can. They will take our phones. We get them back when we leave."

"Seriously?"

"He is a careful man, LaPorte."

Silas decided not to argue with an armed man who looked as if he could snap him into small pieces without breaking a sweat.

He handed over his phone—and felt oddly naked. He held out his arms as the man wanded him the way they did at airports. He submitted to the pat-down.

Quick and invasive.

The guard had another device for the car—inside, outside, under.

"You're clear," he told Sebastien.

"Does he do that to everybody?" Silas asked when they got back in the car.

"I cannot say. I haven't been invited to a soirée, me. You park over there, by the garage. In the shade."

"That's a garage?"

"He has many important cars."

Since the garage was bigger than the house he'd grown up in, Silas didn't have any reason to doubt that.

"Leave the windows down, one quarter, for Bluto. You wait." He tapped Bluto between the ears and produced a small rawhide bone from his pocket.

When they got out, Sebastien retrieved the wrapped painting. "We go to the side, toward the back, the servants' entrance, as we are servants to his mind."

As they started down the wide path of golden pavers, a woman stepped out of a side door. She wore unrelieved black. Her raven hair coiled at the base of her neck and left her glorious face unframed. Her eyes, deep and brown, flicked over Silas.

She carried a tray of glasses, a small bucket of ice, and a pitcher of what looked like lemonade.

"Mr. LaPorte is in the courtyard. I will take you."

"*Merci.* May I carry that for you?"

"I have it."

Her accent, very slight, made Silas think she might be the ex-Mossad agent. One thing for certain: She was really hot.

Sebastien sent him an eyebrow wiggle signaling he agreed.

The path opened up to an enormous courtyard. The grand house's expansive golden walls tucked it into a wide U. Beyond it lay a pool with sparkling blue water, another small house, and spectacular gardens, a grove of trees. He saw lemons, limes, oranges.

Silas pegged LaPorte as the slim man with wavy gold hair sitting at an umbrella table. He wore a white suit, white shoes, and dark-lensed sunglasses.

Silas knew he needed to form an impression, to remember details. But it wasn't easy, as the other occupant at the table was a stunning redhead in the tiniest bikini known to man.

It was emerald green, and showed off all but a few inches of a spectacular body. She wore a band of flashing diamonds around her left ankle, and tipped down amber sunglasses to peer at him out of eyes the same color as those tiny scraps of material.

"He has a new one," Sebastien said under his breath. "The last was a brunette."

LaPorte gave the redhead a pat on the arm, murmured to her. She pouted a little—in a way that had Silas actively willing himself not to drool.

Then she rose and donned a brightly floral and transparent wrap of some sort. It swirled around endless legs as she walked to the house.

A shame, Silas thought, but her departure helped him focus on LaPorte.

Despite the dark lenses, he knew LaPorte studied him, assessed him. Just as he assumed the man knew as much about him already as he'd been able to dig up.

He decided his best strategy was to say little and listen well.

"So, Sebastien, you've brought your young friend."

His voice held the South, the wealthy South.

"*Mais oui*, as requested."

LaPorte didn't rise, offer to shake hands, but sat as the housekeeper replaced the used glasses, ice bucket, the half pitcher of lemonade with the fresh.

She filled three glasses with ice that crackled as she added the liquid.

Sebastien waited until she'd carried the tray away.

"And the Turner."

A man held open a door for the housekeeper, then walked toward the table.

The butler? Silas wondered. He looked military—the posture, the way he moved. Saying nothing, the man took the wrapped painting and went back across the courtyard into the house.

"Sit," LaPorte invited. "We'll have some lemonade while the painting's authenticated."

"*Merci.*"

"I haven't yet heard of an unfortunate burglary. While my acquaintance would be reluctant to report such a theft to the authorities, I would surely hear of it."

"My young friend is very . . . tidy in his work. No trace of him left to find. I think perhaps this acquaintance hasn't as yet visited his personal gallery. He will be surprised when next he does."

"Did you take anything else?" LaPorte looked directly at Silas.

"No. I was hired for the Turner. I took the Turner."

"I'll know if that's true."

"Then you'll know."

"Tell me how you did it."

"No."

Under the table, Sebastien put a hand on Silas's knee. Squeezed. LaPorte's mouth tightened as he sat back.

"I'm paying you. You answer to me."

"You're paying me for the Turner. You're not paying me for my methods. They're not for sale."

"Everything has a price."

No, Silas thought, and believed it absolutely. But he said nothing.

"You're young. You'll learn—if you live long enough. I could contact the authorities, tell them you came here today with the Turner, tried to sell it to me. They'd have many questions, and would never believe a man such as myself would be a part of such a thing, or associated with such as you or Picot."

"You could. Then you wouldn't have the Turner."

LaPorte let out a quick laugh that had nothing of humor in it. "Oh, there are ways and ways."

At its signal, LaPorte picked up the phone on the table. He listened a moment, then set it down again without saying a word.

He smiled a little as he sipped some lemonade.

"What if I tell you the painting you brought me is a forgery?"

"*Monsieur*," Sebastien spoke up. "This is not what was said on that call. You tease my young friend."

Bait, Silas thought, but held his tongue.

"Indulge me. What would you do?" LaPorte asked Silas.

"Leave. Then find a way to steal it back. It might take years, but I'd work on it."

Now LaPorte laughed and actually seemed to mean it. "He has spine. I'll see the transfer is made, as agreed. Sebastien, give me a moment with the boy."

"*Monsieur.*"

"A moment with the boy." That voice turned the air to ice. "I'll send him out to you, unharmed."

"It's fine. I'll meet you at the car in a minute."

"He's under my care," Sebastien said as he rose. Using the cane, he crossed the courtyard and turned onto the path.

"An interesting man, Sebastien, and a clever one. Our association has been mutually beneficial for some time."

LaPorte sipped again, gazed out over the pool, the gardens.

"But he's older than he was, and not as quick on his feet. He called on you because of that. I think the transfer should be more for you than I imagine he negotiated. What's your percentage?"

"Between Sebastien and me."

"I'm offering you a bigger cut. It's my money. I think eighty percent for you, twenty for him. I'll need your banking information."

"You pay Sebastien, he pays me. That's the deal we made."

"I'm changing the terms. You barely know him, and I think I'm offering you double or more than what you agreed to."

"I appreciate it, but you pay Sebastien, he pays me. That's the deal."

LaPorte tipped down the sunglasses, peered over them with cold hazel eyes. "Loyalty can be bought, too."

"If it can, it's not loyalty." He rose. "Thanks for the lemonade. Enjoy the Turner. It's really beautiful."

"One day you'll regret not taking a bigger cut," LaPorte called out as Silas walked away.

"I don't think so."

He understood Sebastien's fear now, now that he felt that deep cold in his own belly. It occurred to him the hot housekeeper or the stoic butler or the rigid carriage house guard—any or all of them—could bash his skull in—Sebastien's, too—and dump their bodies in the lake.

Nobody would know the difference.

He figured LaPorte knew the same.

Sebastien didn't speak when Silas got in the car, or when they drove to the carriage house to retrieve their phones. He waited until he had Silas pull over yet again to walk Bluto.

"What did he want?"

"To give me a bigger cut—cut you out down to twenty percent."

Sebastien nodded as Bluto lifted his scraggly leg and pissed like a racehorse.

"And what did you say?"

A trace of the anger—anger born of fear—lashed out. "What do you take me for? We made a deal."

Sebastien let Bluto walk and sniff, sniff and walk as he gazed out at the lake.

"Many who had made a deal would have taken this new one."

"Then I'm not many."

"No, *cher*, you're not. He would not be pleased."

"I get that. Nobody says no to him. I thought about agreeing, figuring we could fix it between us the way we said after, but fuck that, Sebastien. The only reason he wanted me here—no, two reasons—one to try to screw with me, and the other to screw over you."

"You're new, and interesting to him. A puzzle to him. He may contact you directly for another job."

"Maybe I'll take it, maybe I won't. Will he pay what he agreed, and the way he agreed?"

"He will because there will be something else he wants to possess. You're a rich man, my friend. And still, we go back to the Quarter, and I buy you a fine dinner."

"Tell me one thing first. If it had been reversed, and he offered you the new deal. Would you have taken it?"

Sebastien looked him straight in the eye. "I would not, no. I would not. Friends are a precious thing. And me, I am not of the many. Now, we go feast."

They walked the dog back to the car, and Sebastien sighed as he sat. "The woman? The red-haired woman? Ooh la la."

Chapter Nine

BY THE TIME HE turned nineteen, Silas spoke four languages, and had a rudimentary handle on Russian. Concerned by Tulane's small campus, he shifted to online courses, and while he learned what he wanted to learn, he discovered he didn't get any genuine buzz out of it.

He learned more from Sebastien about electronics and how to circumvent them, more from Jacques about computers and hacking than he did in any structured class.

He spaced out his nightwork, pacing himself, and spreading out from New Orleans up to Baton Rouge, over to New Iberia and Lafayette. Too much nightwork in one area gave the po-po, as Sebastien called them, too much to sniff at.

At Christmas he got a small tree, decorated it. He strung lights in the windows, and knew it was time to move on.

He spent part of Christmas Eve, happily for both of them, with Dauphine in bed.

While they lay lazily naked looking at the lights around the bedroom window, listening to the revelers still partying in the Quarter, she reached out to take his hand.

"When are you leaving?"

He didn't pretend not to understand. "After Mardi Gras, I

think. Mags wants to come back for it, and there's no real hurry or anything."

She sat up, shook her hair back. He liked watching the dark cloud of it shift and settle.

"My generous friend gives me these for Christmas." She tapped one of the ruby drops at her ears. "But he doesn't fall in love with me."

"Promised not to. I love you, and that's different. But it's real."

Leaning down, she gave him a light kiss. "I have a love for you, and always will."

When she rolled out of bed, Silas sat up. "Do you have to go right now?"

"No. I've got a little bit of time before I go to Mama's. You could come, you know. She loves you, too."

"I'll be there for Christmas breakfast. Then I've got Christmas dinner at Sebastien's mother's, which I'm warned lasts half the day and most of the night."

He paused, regretting watching her dress. Still. "It's good to have family at Christmas. I feel like I do here."

"And that is always, too. Now, put your own clothes on. I have another gift for you."

"Another. I still can't believe you bought me new Chucks."

"The others all but fall apart. You could spend some of your money on yourself, *cher*."

"Yeah, I'm thinking about it."

"Where're you going when you leave?"

"I was going to head up to North Carolina and the university, but I think I'm just going east into Texas. Never been there. And Texas A&M's as big as they get."

"How much smarter do you need to be?"

"There's always more to learn."

"Like what you learn from Sebastien, from Jacques."

"Yeah, that. *Et de toi*."

She smiled at him as he pulled on jeans. "Not so skinny as you were."

"I'm going to seriously miss the food here."

"You'll come back. I know this even without reading the cards. But we'll go out, sit, and I'll read them now."

He stopped short in the act of dragging on a T-shirt. "You will?"

"You never ask me to read them for you."

"Because you're spooky at it."

"Tonight, I'll read them. No charge because it's Christmas and a gift." She pointed at him. "It's rude to say no to a gift."

He dragged the shirt on, thinking no, she didn't always need the cards to read him.

He knew the routine, and sat to shuffle the cards she took out of her purse. He made the cuts, then watched as she laid out the spread.

"This doesn't surprise me." She tapped the central card representing him. "The Magician. Clever, creative. One who seeks new opportunities. You connect with the spiritual and material realms. You're a man of the earth who knows there's more. There's power in you, so you seek the knowledge to use that power. And here is Strength crossing you. You see the woman with the lion—you have many women in your spread."

"They can't resist me."

"So much of the strength in you—both courage and compassion—comes from the women who forged you. You're fortunate in them, for you'll need strength, the energy and kindness of it, on your journey. You know this inside yourself already.

"Above you, the Page of Pentacles. Youth, ambition, a desire for knowledge and for the journey that leads to finer things. He looks ahead, you see? Always ahead to what's next. You won't settle for some time to come. And here, below you, the Queen of Cauldrons, a woman of kindness and a giving spirit. Your mama here, *cher*, and Mags as well, who gave you the foundation."

She looked at him with a smile in her eyes. With love in them—the sort that came from true friendship.

"If women are drawn to you, it's not just your pretty face. I might have slept with you for your pretty face, but I wouldn't love you as *mon cher ami* without the rest."

"You helped change my life. Not just the French lessons and the sex. The friendship." He took her hand. "I had good friends in Chicago, but I had to leave, and I don't know if I'll ever really reconnect with them. I will with you."

"You will. I won't allow it otherwise. Here, behind you is The Tower. Loss and trauma and grief. We know what this is for you, and while behind you, it's always part of you. It's part of the strength, the foundation, the heart of you.

"And before you, the Empress."

"She looks rich. Do I sleep with her or steal from her? It's a rule not to do both."

"This is respect. But no, she symbolizes control here, a need to control your actions, and more your heart. You still don't look for love—true and lasting. She is power again, and wiles. Material wealth, both the need and the achievement."

"I like that part."

"And still it's not things you want, even a new pair of shoes. It's the knowing you can have, and the loss behind you so influences what you see and need ahead. For now, it may be you need this guard on feelings. For here, this card is your feelings, for now."

"Yeah, I never like that one. Death."

"How many times do I tell you, this isn't physical death, and in this spread, with these cards, this is your thoughts of loss—in the leaving—and the freedom in the leaving. The change, the end of this phase, the start of the next. No, you won't settle for a time, and what comes soon won't be the only change to come. The only end or beginning. You look ahead."

She tapped the Page of Pentacles again.

"And here you have influences and surroundings. The Queen of Swords. This is, again, your caution, but also a woman to come. One you'll hurt. Another kind of loss, and a parting. Trust won't come easily after this, and neither forgets."

Dauphine looked up at him, reminding Silas why he'd never asked her to read his cards. Spooky, he thought again. The spooky was all over her.

"Sometimes, we look ahead and don't see what waits and wants right in front of us. Your journey takes you on and away—maybe to protect her or yourself, but the sword pierces hearts. A wound can strengthen as you've been strengthened by wounds. And they can harden. Take care, *mon ami*, not to harden."

"I don't want to hurt anybody. Sounds like bullshit coming from a thief, but—"

"Not from you. Here we have your wishes and goals. Pentacles again—a kind of coin, *oui*? The Nine shows a woman again, and she is content. A wish for that contentment, for accomplishments, fulfillments, and the ability to make it so. Wealth, yes—in the material and in the spirit. Luxury, for you, is that contentment and security. And it comes to the last card—the outcome."

He saw The Lovers, and gave her a leering grin.

"This isn't sex." She wagged a finger at him. "Or not only. It can be love—real love—and unity—with deep emotion. But it also symbolizes loyalty and understanding, a choice to give those, to overcome something lost and embrace what is found.

"I think, *cher*, the Queen of Swords may come back to you, or you to her, then the choice will be for both of you. You have what you need—what was given to you through strong, loving women. You seek what you need on the journeys as you look ahead, start and finish, finish and start. And if you use all you have, all you gain, all you are, you'll have what you need most at the end."

He studied the cards, then Dauphine. "That wasn't too spooky. In fact, it was a pretty awesome gift. Thanks."

"It has one more part."

She gathered the cards together, shuffled them, then spread them out. He'd seen her do this, too. Knew he'd pick one and she'd add it to the reading. Kind of a top off.

So he picked one, held it up to face her.

Her expression brought the spooky back.

"Jesus, which one is it?" He turned it around. "Okay, the Devil. That can't be good."

"This is an enemy. You choose your friends, your lovers. But an enemy chooses you. He is ruthless and cruel. Full of greed. If he tempts you, turn away. Don't let him choose you, or he'll scar you. He'll take all you are and all you can have, so turn away."

"No problem."

"Promise me." She grabbed his hand, gripped it hard. "Promise."

"I do. Absolutely. No deal with the devil."

Deliberately, she took the card, put it back in the deck. "Some don't recognize the devil until the deal's struck. Keep your eyes open, *mon ami*."

When Mags came for Mardi Gras, he'd already packed most of his things.

Not that he had a lot to pack. It occurred to him he didn't go for things so much because, right now, they'd just be more to pack when he needed to move on.

Mags had gone for electric-purple hair, which she wore straight as rain, with bangs. She should've looked weird. Instead, she looked fabulous.

And her bone-crushing hug felt like home.

"I think you've finally stopped growing. Six-three?"

"And a quarter. Yeah, I think I've topped out."

"Now look at these." She gave his right biceps a playful squeeze. "Getting ripped, pal. Even better, I see more happy here." She tapped a finger to his cheek.

"Seeing you makes me happy."

That earned him another hug. Then she nodded to the duffel in the corner. "You're really leaving?"

"I'm sliding into Texas A&M in a couple weeks. A transfer for Lee Harrington from Florida State to be closer to my parents, since my father's sick. I can handle the tuition, so why not jump in?"

"You've got it all worked out."

"Yeah, everything's set. New Orleans has been good for me, but I'm juiced to see what's next."

"Got a place to stay yet?" she asked as he carried her bags into the bedroom.

"I checked out some apartments online. Dorms wouldn't work, but I can get a place near the campus. Huge campus."

"I took a little detour on the way here to get a look. It'll swallow you up."

"That's the plan. When you cruise through right, you don't make waves. How about a walk before we meet Dauphine and Sebastien for dinner?"

"I'm in. Can't wait to meet this Sebastien."

HE EXPECTED MAGS AND Sebastien to get along. He hadn't expected them to Get Along. He didn't know how to feel about the fact his aunt and the man he realized had become a kind of father figure actively flirted right in front of him.

And the dog—because of course Sebastien brought Bluto along—sat and gazed at Mags with adoring eyes.

It actually put him off his gumbo.

He tried to ignore it as the crowds grew thicker, the mood wilder, the music hotter. He snagged beads as he'd once snagged a foul ball at Wrigley. He sipped a little of Dauphine's takeaway daiquiri—just not his drink—and went back to Coke.

He figured it was an experience of its own to be cold sober in a crowd of the tipsy and outright drunk. It marked his second Mardi Gras in New Orleans, and likely his last as an actual resident, so he wanted to embrace it.

It didn't bother him when Mags and Sebastien started to dance. Lots of people danced—alone, in groups, whatever. Lots of foot stomping, shoulder and hip shaking going on.

Then the cheerful, wine-soaked boogie eased into an unmistakable Sexy Dance. Bodies rubbing, undulating, hands—God! Hands, hands! Worse, they were really good at it. Rhythmic, sensual, loose as water.

"My eyes. It's burning my eyes."

"Better close them then, *doudou*," Dauphine suggested. "'Cause looks like they're just getting started."

She wasn't wrong. He knew they both had moves. He'd grown up with Mags, and he'd been to *fais-dodos* at Sebastien's mother's place.

But seeing the two of them put those moves together—with each other—changed things. Worse, they drew their own little crowd, the kind that let out approving sexy noises and kept the time with hands or feet.

Mortifying.

Then they capped it, just capped it right off, ending the dance wrapped around each other like *kudzu*, and in a serious lip-lock that had the crowd whistling, cheering. When Dauphine joined in, he felt alone on a rocky island of shock.

Beads fell like rain, candy tumbled down like gold-wrapped hail.

And when Sebastien whispered something in Mags's ear, she let out that big, crazy laugh. And pinched his ass.

It got worse when he lost sight of them. His own fault, he admitted, as he'd averted his eyes to keep them from bleeding during subsequent lip-locks.

"Where'd they go?" Panicked, sincerely panicked, he tried to laser his vison through the moving wall of people. "Where'd they go?"

Dauphine just shrugged. "Wherever they want. You got no worries, *cher*. She's with Sebastien."

"That's my worry."

With a laugh, she wrapped an arm around his waist. "Do you think a woman as full of life and passions as Mags doesn't have sex?"

"I don't think about it. I don't have to think about it because she's out west and it's not in my face. This is in my face, with Sebastien."

"Would you rather she snuggle up with a stranger to you, or someone you know?"

"That's a trick question." His height gave him a small advantage as he looked over the rolling waves of the human sea. "Shouldn't I be able to spot that hair? It's electrocuted purple."

"Come, I'm going to buy you a walk-away wine, and one for me. Put your worries away, *cher*. Sebastien will see her home safe."

Apparently home safe meant three-seventeen in the morning. Silas knew the exact time, as he heard Mags giggling—jeez, giggling—outside the apartment door, and Sebastien's rumbling chuckle in response.

He heard nothing for the next several minutes, and willed himself not to imagine what happened in the silence.

He'd walked Dauphine home around two, then had done a solo search through the revelers before giving up and going home.

Where he'd sat or sprawled on the couch in a pair of sweat shorts. Waiting.

Finally Mags slipped in, shut the door. Shook back her disordered purple hair.

And spotted him.

She grinned, then widened her eyes.

"Uh-oh, did I miss curfew?"

"Funny. I was worried. You didn't answer your phone."

"Probably because I left it on the charger in the bedroom." She went into the kitchen, poured herself a big glass of water.

She brought it with her to sit in the chair across from him. Drank deep.

"Where'd you go anyway?"

"Oh, here and there. Got out of the crowd awhile, had a drink in a bar, listened to music. Did some dancing. Had some key lime pie."

"You know, Sebastien has three—count 'em, three—ex-wives." She studied Silas over the rim of her glass as she drank again.

"And each one gave him a beautiful daughter. Are you worried he'll want to make me number four, or I'll want to make him my second ex-husband?"

"I just, you know, want you to know how it is."

"Pal, I've known how it is since before you were born. Does that make you think I'm too old to have sex with a very interesting man?"

"No." Not exactly.

"Good. I'm going to bed—what a night! Sebastien's picking me up about noon tomorrow. He's going to fix me lunch at his place and take me for a ride in his pirogue."

"There are alligators. Actual alligators."

"Looking forward to seeing one. Night," she said as she walked into the bedroom and shut the door.

SILAS FOUND HIS LAST days in New Orleans really strange. Clearly, his aunt and his friend were—to borrow a word of his mother's—smitten.

It seemed a more harmless word than the phrase *hot for each other*.

He couldn't claim Mags didn't spend time with him. They had breakfast together every morning. They took walks, just hung out. And because he'd soon head off to college, she insisted he buy some new clothes. Which meant shopping.

While he focused primarily on jeans, T-shirts, he bent to

her insistence on a couple of what he considered dress shirts because they had a collar and sleeves. He started to balk when she handed him a leather jacket.

"I don't need—"

"Not about need. Put this on."

Rather than waste time arguing, he shrugged into it. Okay, so it felt really awesome, but he still didn't need it.

"Yeah, that's what I'm talking about." She took his shoulders, turned him toward a mirror. "Slick and sexy."

Maybe. Yes.

Black, with a pointed collar and angled pockets, it hit him at the hips. And the sleeves—often an issue, as he had long arms—worked.

"You look damn good, pal, and you know it."

"Yeah, it looks pretty good." He hadn't expected that, or that it made him feel good.

Then he looked at the price tag. "Holy shit!"

"Get what you pay for, and this is damn good leather. Nice and gooshy. You'll wear it for years. I'm buying it for you."

"No." The idea had him swinging around to face her. "No way. Look, I've got the money."

"I know you do, but that's not the point. I'm buying you your first leather jacket." She cupped his face. "Don't let it be the last you hang in your closet."

She stepped back. "You make me proud."

"Aw, Mags."

"You make me proud," she repeated. "And that's a good thing for me, as you're what I've got. Now, you're going to buy yourself a couple of decent belts—one black, one brown."

"There's nothing wrong with this one."

She would not be denied.

Nor would she be denied when she pushed him to pick up a few lightweight sweaters and a pair of black leather boots.

Nor when she unpacked his duffel, tossed several items of

clothing into what she called the It Goes Pile, then neatly packed his new stuff.

"There." She dusted her hands together. "Duty done. Now let's go party and do your last night in New Orleans up right."

"I didn't say I was leaving tomorrow."

"Who knows you? Your head's already moved on. Your heart needs this last night."

He'd said goodbye to the people who mattered. Dauphine—in a slow, sweet hour in her apartment on an afternoon Mags spent with Sebastien. To Jacques, to Mama Lou and Little Lou and everyone else he'd connected with.

He'd say goodbye to Sebastien tonight.

"I was thinking maybe I'd head out when you did tomorrow. Follow you west awhile."

She took out a lipstick, and with a skill he'd never understood, applied it perfectly without a mirror. "I'm not leaving tomorrow. I'm staying a few days more."

"Oh. I thought—I can tell the landlord. I—"

"I don't need the apartment, cutie."

"But— Oh. Oh. Really? You're going to stay with Sebastien?"

"For a few days. I'm going to be able to say I lived in the bayou."

She walked over, hooked an arm through his. "Party time. I already miss you, so let's party hard."

When he thought about that last night, it came as a blur of movement and color and sound, of Mags and her purple hair and crazy laugh, of Sebastien dancing to zydeco, Bluto howling with the *muris*. And Dauphine in a red dress.

New Orleans had taught him a lot. And it had cradled him when he'd needed it, opened worlds for him, offered him friendships.

He'd miss it, the lazy, wet heat of it, the slow voices of it, the constant beat of music, and the people who'd welcomed him in.

He'd find his way back to it, he knew that absolutely.

But now, as he started his journey west, he didn't look back. He looked ahead.

TEXAS DIDN'T SPEAK TO him like New Orleans, but the university did. It swallowed him up, just as he'd wanted. And he learned. He kept his head down, carefully made a handful of casual friends. He dated a few women who didn't want serious any more than he did.

He expanded his nightwork, added to his bank accounts—and bought another leather jacket.

He didn't go back to New Orleans for Mardi Gras. His heart wasn't ready for it. But he hooked up with Mags on spring break and booked a hotel suite for them on the beach in San Diego.

In his second term, he'd traded in his tiny apartment for a two-bedroom, and used the second as a kind of office.

He learned basic accounting because he needed to handle his own money, and took a course in playwriting because he thought he'd find it interesting.

He did, and also learned—despite one of his mother's dreams for him—he really couldn't write. Or he couldn't sit still long enough to write.

When he knew he'd hit the time to move on, he forged transcripts and transfers, using the name Booth Harrison.

He didn't look back as he headed out of Texas, and he wasn't in a hurry to get there. He'd have the whole summer to settle in, gauge his ground, maybe even find a little house to rent. He could afford it, and he'd grown tired of apartment life.

He wanted a yard, grass to mow himself, and room.

He had time, and had decided he was ready to see what Carolina had to offer him.

Chapter Ten

IT STRUCK HIM AS it had before, the sights, the sounds, the feel of Chapel Hill. He felt an affinity, as he did for New Orleans. And though he couldn't afford on the budget he'd worked up—time or money—to rent a house on the lake, he found what he was after.

It reminded him, a little, of the house where he'd grown up. He'd have to furnish this one, but that's what flea markets were for. He wasn't after fancy or permanent, just livable.

And it had a yard, some trees and bushes.

He bought a lawn mower before he bought a bed.

He could walk to campus if he didn't mind a two-and-a-half-mile hike—and he didn't. But he bought a bike.

The neighbors on his right, a couple in their thirties, had a kid about four and another on the way. On his left was a couple in their sixties who had two adult children, a couple of grandkids, and a golden retriever named Mac.

He made a point of being congenial to everyone, keeping his grass mowed and the music down.

Here, he was Booth Harrison, originally from Chicago, as he deemed that safe enough now. A senior at Carolina, a lit major, with double minors in theater and romance languages.

He wove in enough of the truth to keep it simple. He'd lost

his mother, had an aunt out west, and he'd wanted a place in a quiet neighborhood so he could focus on his studies.

He liked to cook, and bonded with Miz Opal, the grandmother next door, over recipes.

He helped Jackson, the guy on the other side, screen in their back porch. Jackson had recently passed the bar, but didn't know a hammer from a screwdriver.

By the time classes started, he'd fully immersed himself in his new identity. With his own tools, he installed a gun safe in the unfinished basement. There, across from the aging furnace, he kept his nightwork tools and the bounty from it behind sturdy doors with a good digital lock.

He'd found enough nightwork over the summer—outside his own neighborhood, of course—so the tuition didn't sting too much.

He rode his bike the first day on a warm breezy morning. And felt instantly at home when he secured it and joined the throngs of students.

He figured if he hadn't been a thief, he might've been a professional student. Maybe a teacher—though teaching seemed like a lot more work than studenting.

He enjoyed his first theater class tremendously, and congratulated himself on the choice. He'd fill in more of what he'd already learned in Texas and New Orleans on makeup and costuming, and the requirement of monologuing or acting out scenes would only polish up his skills in becoming who he needed to be.

He learned quickly that the stern-eyed professor in his French class equaled tough and challenging. No English permitted in class, at all. All reading—*en français*—and all essays written. Straight off she assigned reading "*Le Savon*," a poem about soap by Ponge—a dead French poet—with a paper analyzing it, line by line.

He couldn't say he was thrilled to analyze a poem about soap, but it was the French that counted.

He had enough time between classes to grab a slice of pizza and a Coke, and ate his first lunch alone on a bench watching campus life.

He wasn't looking to make friends, particularly, and intended to keep, as always, partying to a minimum. Some parties, some dating—because otherwise you stood out.

And the whole idea was to blend.

On impulse, he signed up for the Shakespeare Club because it sounded interesting, and his next professor headed it up. A couple of hours, one night a week, he thought.

That way, like the theater classes, he'd make himself a couple of little circles. People to hang out with at lunch, or have a beer with.

He walked into the classroom—more like a lecture hall than his smallish French class. He chose a seat, not in front, not in the back, not precisely in the middle, but close.

As others filed in, he took out his tablet, his mini-recorder, and his notepad. He always covered all the bases.

He liked the hum of students talking or just settling in, the smell of somebody's takeaway latte, someone else's gum—definitely cherry.

A guy with a thick flop of brown hair falling over his forehead and toward his horn-rims slid in next to him.

"Saw you in Jones's class this morning, right? R.J. Doyle."

"Yeah, how's it going? Booth Harrison."

"Going good, bro."

The way he said *bro* pegged him as a geek. Booth liked geeks. And the accent said native—but probably more along the North Carolina coast.

"Lit major?" Booth asked him.

"Nah. Theater major, but if you want to do Shakespeare, and I do, Professor Emerson's your man. Well, you know that if you're a lit major."

"Transfer from Texas A&M. It's my first day here."

A flip of the flopping hair, a shove of the glasses. "No bull? Big jump for your senior year, yeah?"

"I guess. I was ready for a jump. I had a major breakup last year, and wanted new. So far, I really like it here."

"You came to the right place." R.J. lifted a hand, waved and signaled to somebody. He said, "Yo!" which had Booth suppressing a grin.

Total geek.

The guy who wandered over had skin the color of that somebody's latte, eyes like roasted chestnuts, and a head full of long dreads.

With his sharp cheekbones, full lips, and arched brows, Booth thought it was a face made for a magazine cover. He'd noticed the new guy in his first class due to that striking face.

"Zed Warron, Booth Harrison, just transferred, lit major."

"Welcome then. Where'd you come from?"

"Transferred from Texas A&M."

"You don't sound like Texas."

"Chicago."

And Zed, he thought, came from the mid-Atlantic. Maryland maybe, or Northern Virginia, DC.

"I got cousins in Chicago—freaking cold winters. Cubs or Socks?"

"Cubs."

"Stay away from my cousins when you go back. They'll take you to the ground. Socks fans, major."

"I'm a live-and-let-live sort."

"Trust me, with baseball, they ain't." He got out a MacBook, booted it up. "Y'all ready for this?"

"Born ready," R.J. claimed, and the geekiness was irresistible.

The professor came in, took his place at a podium, and shuffled through some notes.

Booth instantly decided if he ever posed as a college professor, he'd fashion himself after Bennet Emerson.

A lot of thick hair—leaning chestnut, like Zed's eyes, but with a liberal dash of silver at the temples. A perfect goatee, short, trim, also liberal with the silver. Soft green eyes behind the lenses of steel-framed glasses.

He wore a brown jacket over a white T-shirt and jeans.

Booth filed the details away, then scanned the room—almost full—as a handful of stragglers came in.

Then he saw her.

He'd think countless times through his life of that single moment. The moment she'd walked into the room, into him, and left him just a little breathless.

She was beautiful, but not stunning and sultry like Dauphine or candy-box perfect like a girl he'd dated awhile in Texas. Tall, but not overly, maybe five-eight, he judged, and wand slim in her black leggings and hip-skimming blue-and-white shirt.

She had hair braided back the color Titian made famous—that golden red that took a master to create. Her skin was milk and rose petals. He couldn't be certain of the color of her eyes as she took a seat on the aisle, leaned over to murmur to another girl who'd obviously saved it for her.

But he knew when she smiled at her companion she had a wide and perfectly shaped mouth.

"Good afternoon," the professor began. "And welcome to the World of Shakespeare."

Booth heard the voice—an attractive baritone that carried well, and pegged the prof as a native—but he had to force himself to look away from the girl, because his ears rang.

He switched on his recorder, did his best to tune in as Professor Emerson gave an overview of the course.

He wished he'd brought in a bottle of Coke or water, or anything, because his mouth and throat were dry as dust. His heart just kept pounding against his ribs.

Crazy, he told himself, just crazy. He'd never had a reaction to a woman like this. Interest, attraction, a nice lust spike, sure, but nothing—ever—that made his entire insides tremble.

He told himself to stay away from the redhead. Keep clear of her, because this couldn't be good.

R.J. leaned over, whispered, "Caught ya looking, bro. Miranda Emerson, the prof's daughter."

Booth made some sound, made some notes he'd never be able to decipher later.

He'd steer very clear, he promised himself. Getting involved with the professor's daughter was no way to blend.

He visualized placing the image of her in a box, then closing the lid. It helped enough so he could concentrate, even take legible notes.

After class, the last of the day, he went along with R.J. and Zed for nachos and beer. He thought the noise, the smells, the company might help erase the image of the redhead from his brain.

Plus, the nachos hit every right note.

"Either of you know anything about the Shakespeare Club?"

R.J. pointed a thumb at his own chest, then pointed at Zed. "Vets. We get to go deep into a play, and the prof lets the discussion roll, you know? And once a month, he has it at his house, with pizza and lots more. That's the best."

"You in that?" Zed asked him.

"I signed up. I'm just not sure with the workload I'll have time for it."

"Make time." Zed scooped up more cheese and guac. "It slides right into the course, but it's more casual, more freewheeling. What're you going to do with the theater minor?"

"That's more for the fun of it. I just like it, and the rest of my load's pretty tough stuff. And speaking of, I've got to get to it."

"A group of us have a house on campus. We'll hang sometime." R.J. tipped up his beer in toast.

"That'd be great. Catch you later."

A damn good first day, he decided as he made his way outside. He liked his classes so far—he'd reserve judgment on the French lit class—he'd made a couple of contacts, and he thought he'd enjoy hanging around with them now and then.

The campus was perfect, the weather incredible, and he'd slipped right into the rhythm as he'd hoped.

Then he saw her again. What were the freaking odds of seeing her again on a campus this size? But there she stood by one of the fountains with a group—three other girls and a couple of guys.

She wore sunglasses now, so he still couldn't make out her eyes. But he knew, just knew, they'd be amazing.

He cursed himself for not giving the group—and her—a very wide berth. Instead he walked by them, near enough to hear her voice.

Warm and fluid, like a summer rain, and with a smoky kind of laugh at the end. She said, "I can't believe anyone would *do* that."

Now her voice, her laugh etched in his memory like her face. And just when he'd started to close it out.

He kept walking, just kept walking. And because he lost track, had to double back for his bike.

He used the ride home to try to erase her again. Actually considered asking Sebastien to send him some *gris-gris* to break the spell. Because it felt like a spell.

He didn't even know her. She could be a total bitch, a total snob bitch. He decided to paint her that way in hopes of breaking the spell.

Miranda Emerson. He bet her dad named her for *The Tempest*—that would fit. But instead of being innocent, sweet-natured, and naive, she turned out cold and cruel and smug.

He'd nearly talked himself into it by the time he got home. Miz Opal and Papa Pete, as he'd been told to call them, sat on their little front porch drinking what he knew would be sweet tea.

He thought they looked like a scene out of a movie. A good, heartwarming one without too much cheese.

Spotting him, Mac galloped over. As he crouched to wrestle with the dog, Booth thought of Bluto.

"You're a real dog," he murmured. "Not some weird little mutant dog."

"How'd you do your first day?" Miz Opal called out.

"Good. It was a real good day."

"Come on over here and tell us about it, have something cold to drink."

"Thanks, but I've got a heavy load to lift tonight." Because he knew they'd appreciate it, he continued. "I have to read a poem about soap in French, and analyze it."

"About soap?" Papa Pete let out a hoot. "Boy, you're making that up for sure."

"God's truth. I'm getting that one over with first thing."

"I like soap; it slips and slides. When you're dirty, it'll clean your hide."

Laughing, he gave Mac a final rub. "Miz Opal, I think you're twice the poet this French guy was." With a wave, he went into the house.

He found the poem more interesting and clever than he'd figured on, and actually enjoyed the challenge of composing his analysis in French. He started on the paper for his Shakespeare class, which made him think of the redhead, so he broke to fix something to eat and clear his mind.

He appreciated the structure. Work on assignments, make some dinner, deal with the dishes, more assignments. Chill out with a little TV or music while he researched areas of his nightwork.

About one, he changed, checked and rechecked the tools selected for the job. He loved his quiet neighborhood, but the downside of quiet meant someone might hear him turn over the engine in his car.

He had a story ready for that—when he couldn't clear his head and sleep, he took a drive. But he didn't like the idea of needing the story, so he coasted silently down the block before starting the car.

The target house, eleven point two miles away, would be empty. He knew this, as the occupants, Jack and Elaine Springer, posted photos—heavy on the food—of their trip to Italy daily.

You had to love social media.

While morning spread over Rome's Spanish Steps—Jack and Elaine had a fine view of them from their hotel—he parked half a mile from what he thought of as their McMansion.

It was a big if uninspired Colonial with a decent, and easily circumvented, security system. Since the goal was stamps, something Jack posted about—and discussed on several message boards dedicated to collecting—Booth considered the job a sort of return to his roots.

Nearly ten years of experience had him inside the house a lot faster than his younger self, but once in, he revisited that sense of wonder, the slow, spreading thrill.

He'd never been inside, of course, but he brought the blueprints he'd accessed into his mind. He went straight to Jack's first-floor study/office, where the philatelist kept his collection in leather binders in a display cabinet. Inside one lived an 1840 Penny Black—the world's first adhesive postage stamp. Not mint, according to Jack's windy discussions, but with four clear margins.

He'd decide that for himself once he got a look at it. If Jack, like many on social media, exaggerated, he could make other choices.

He found it easily enough, as Jack proved to be an organized collector. Definitely not mint, Booth decided as he studied it with his magnifier. And while three of the four margins were very clean, the fourth was questionable.

And that lowered the value—and his payday—considerably.

Still, not crap, he thought. He started to take down another album, search for his second choice, when he stopped to look closer at the painting over the small gas fireplace.

He didn't like the art—all hard colors and shapes—but when he played his light over the frame, he spotted the hinges.

"A classic."

He swung the painting out, and smiled at the small safe with its four-number digital lock.

"I mean, I'm standing right here. It would be wrong not to take a look."

He reached into his tool bag. He'd never been a Boy Scout, but he valued their motto. He came prepared. He took out the magnet housed in a good gym sock. He had other methods, but this one left no trace, and when it worked, it usually took under a minute.

Or, in this case, eighteen seconds of running the covered magnet over the safe door.

A lot of papers inside, but the ones that interested him were all green. Ten neat stacks of banded fifty-dollar bills. A thousand dollars a stack.

He considered the possibility of pulling in twice that for the stamp—or stamps—against the bird in the hand.

He could take both—cash and stamps—but that broke the greed rule. He made a new rule on the spot.

"Always take the cash."

He put the money in his bag, closed the safe, swung the ugly painting back in place. He said goodbye to the Penny Black, replaced the intact album.

In under an hour since he'd coasted down the block, he locked ten grand in his basement safe.

When he climbed into bed, he thought about the best ways to disburse his take. Then he thought about the paper he'd started to write on *Henry V*, and the political comparisons to today's world.

He thought he had a handle on the angles he wanted to

explore, and let them play through his mind as he started to drift.

And ended up dreaming of the redhead.

HE SHOULD'VE KNOWN SHE'D be in another one of his lit classes. He'd chosen the school not only for that pull he'd felt but because of its size.

And there she sat in his contemporary lit class, with that hair in a fancy braid, and this time just close enough that he could see her eyes—sea green with a dark ring around the iris that made them impossible to ignore.

Or nearly, as he concentrated on doing just that. He'd come to learn, to discuss books, to go inside them. Not to obsess over another student.

Then she turned her head and looked at him. He thought maybe his focus on ignoring her had flipped some internal switch, but she turned, looked directly at him for ten painful seconds.

Smiled, just a little, just enough to make his heart twist, before she shifted away again.

The rest of the class was a blank for him. He'd have to rely on his recorder, replay the whole damn thing. Though he made sure to avoid her at the end of class, he didn't relax again until he settled into his class on stage makeup—also applicable for film, television . . . and nightwork.

He finished up his day with a dance class. Also applicable for nightwork. It took grace and nimble feet to deal with motion sensors. And he'd come up against them, no doubt, if he expanded to bigger jobs.

Other than the redhead—and he'd get over it—Booth rated his first week at UNC the best he'd ever experienced.

He gave himself a break Friday night, hung out with R.J., Zed, and a few more of the theater gang.

On Saturday, he mowed his lawn, cleaned his house—lifelong habit. He threw a Frisbee for Mac awhile, then rescued his other neighbor from his attempt to hang the porch swing he'd bought for his wife for their anniversary.

Honestly, the guy was not just pathetic but dangerous with tools.

Booth found a rhythm in those first few weeks, balancing the demands of higher education with easy friendships and the simple fun they offered. With the challenges and timing of what he genuinely considered his job.

He spread that work out, toggling between writing papers, completing assigned reading, and doing the research and prep work necessary for a successful career in thievery.

He decided on no more than a single job per month—two if something just fell into his lap.

And looking ahead, as the cards read—he started researching plans for spring break.

Not to the beach with a bunch of other college students, but Italy, with Mags. Maybe he'd been inspired by Jack and Elaine—or that easy ten-thousand-dollar night—but he wanted to see Florence, and he wanted Mags to see it.

Since he hadn't read about or heard on his scans of the local news stations so much as a peep about the missing cash, he wondered if maybe Jack hadn't accumulated that ten grand by strictly legal means.

Either way, the bulk of it was now carefully invested, and would go a long way toward covering a couple of first-class airfares and a two-bedroom suite in a first-class hotel.

He'd see how well his Italian held up on its native ground, see all that art, eat that amazing food. And wouldn't it be a kick to try a little nightwork in a place where English wasn't the primary language?

Something to think about.

Months off though, and he had to concentrate on the now.

He planned to slide out of the Shakespeare Club—especially when he learned that the first meeting would take place at Professor Emerson's home.

She'd be there, most likely, and it wouldn't be as easy to avoid her as he'd managed to date.

But R.J. and Zed ganged up on him.

"No way, bro, you gotta go." R.J. waved the last half of his panini as his flop of hair fell back into his face. "You're getting it all—insight, camaraderie, and prime eats. The prof always has prime eats."

"And if you signed up—you did," Zed reminded him, "then don't show? He's going to ask you about it."

"Why would he care?"

"The man does," Zed assured him.

"I've got a really heavy class load, and I've got a paper to finish on King's *The Stand*. Plus I've got one to do on another dead French poet. Tell me why the hell I took that class?"

"Didn't you say you aced the last one of those? The soap guy."

"Yeah, but—"

"Balance your life. Zed says you gotta zen." He swiped a fry through a pool of mustard—a departure from norm Booth couldn't get behind. "Scared of the prof's daughter?"

"Who? What? Why would I be?"

"Dude. You don't look at her so hard you might as well go up and nibble on her neck."

"Come on, man, that's bogus."

"Truth." R.J. polished off his panini. "You can pick us up at the dorm, since you've got the best car. We'll pool it and protect you from Legs Emerson."

"Legs?"

"You've been not looking hard enough to see she's got 'em up to her eyeballs," Zed pointed out. "Zip on by about six, and that makes you the DD for the night."

Not drinking wasn't a problem, but not looking hard enough to be noticed was. Time to fix that.

"Fine. But if I tank that French paper, I know who to blame."

PART TWO

THE THIEF

Chapter Eleven

THE REDHEAD—HE TRIED REALLY hard not to think of her actual name—wasn't just there. She answered the door. She answered it wearing one of those breezy summer dresses—the sort where most guys didn't really notice the dress itself but just the fact it was thin and breezy and showed off a lot of legs and arms.

No braid tonight, so that sunset hair just fell all loose and wavy past her shoulders. Almost bare shoulders.

Those sea-green eyes smiled; the wide, naked mouth curved.

"Hi. It's R.J. and Zed—I remember you from last year."

God, she had a voice. He'd heard it a couple of times in class, and once on campus, but this was different. This was intimate, and right in front of him.

And as they had that one time in class, those eyes shifted to his.

"And who's your friend?"

"This is Booth Harrison. Transfer student. Lit major, theater minor." R.J. gave Booth a companionable pat on the shoulder.

"Welcome, Booth. Miranda."

When she held out a hand, he thought: Oh Jesus, now I have to touch her.

He made it quick, though he managed the single, firm shake well enough. "Nice to meet you."

"We have some other classes together, I think. Anyway, come on in. Most of us are here."

He tried to concentrate on the house and not the way she moved through it. Fluid, like her voice.

He'd already pegged it as both dignified and arty, and given the neighborhood—lake view—the size, the careful maintenance, decided the professor had some family money somewhere.

It wasn't like Jack and Elaine's—not a McMansion—but an old, gorgeous, quirky Victorian.

He crossed it off any potential list for his nightwork. It might have been just the sort of place a man in his line found a nice treasure or two, but he didn't hit on his teachers.

Just rude.

He noted the art—classy, interesting—and the furnishings from the foyer and into the living area ran to antiques. Heirloom stuff.

At least a dozen people already mingled in the living room. A large space that made him think a couple of parlors had been opened into one room somewhere along the way.

But they'd preserved the really excellent woodwork and ceiling medallions. They'd whitewashed an old fireplace, flanked it with floor-to-ceiling cabinets full of books, photos, trinkets.

"You like old houses?" she asked him.

"What? Ah, yeah, actually."

"Me, too. I'm the fourth generation of Emersons to live here. So, y'all remember where the kitchen is? Drinks and snacks are set up in there. We've got a few more coming, so take your time."

Even as she said it, the bell rang again. And she turned and went to answer.

He fell for the house. They hadn't opened it all up, but left that Victorian warren of rooms. Until you hit the kitchen, where it opened up again with walls the color of toast, wide glass doors leading to a patio and the lawn and gardens, then the lake behind it.

A huge galvanized tub sat on a table and held drinks—beer, wine, water, sodas—in a bed of ice.

Pizza and all sorts of easy food spread out on a big center island.

R.J. grabbed a plate. "Prime eats. Did I lie?"

Booth settled on a Coke. He didn't like the feeling of a nervous stomach—he never got nervous. But since he felt it, he didn't want to put much into it.

He knew some of the others from classes, recognized a handful by sight. He reminded himself of the purpose for joining.

To learn, have a little fun. And to make some casual connections.

Lone wolves didn't blend.

The redhead sat on the floor talking to the jock-looking guy he'd seen her with on campus and the girl who'd saved her a seat that first day. Definitely a trio, he concluded. When the redhead laughed and gave the jock guy a friendly elbow bump, he wondered if they were a thing.

The possibility should've relieved him. Instead he felt a quick, nasty twinge he thought must be jealousy.

Another new sensation he didn't like.

He saw the professor, who'd perched himself on the arm of a sofa. Even in jeans and a T-shirt—no jacket—and gesturing with a bottle of Amstel Light, he looked like a college professor.

Booth spotted a handful of folding chairs set up on the other side of the room, and headed there. It made him part of the group, but just a little apart. And suited him.

The chatter didn't end when the professor pushed to his feet, but it died to murmurs.

"Welcome to our first meeting of the year. Some of you are here because you're Shakespeare fans, some are hoping to improve your grade, and some because you heard about free food. Valid choices all. I see some familiar faces and some new ones. I don't know all your names as yet, but I will.

"The rules of the road are few. Keep your area clean, recycle all bottles and cans, if you break it, you bought it. Otherwise, all opinions and interpretations are, again, valid. They may be disputed. Those disputes are also valid. And lively discussions don't have to cross over into rude."

He sat again, gestured again. "Discussions this term will focus on the romance in Shakespeare's work, the humor and conflict in them, the wit and words, and how those relationships depict the era in which they were written, how they resound with or jar against today's sensibilities. To start us off, tonight we'll take a look at Beatrice and Benedick, potentially contrasting them with Hero and Claudio."

He paused a beat. "And if you don't recognize those names, haven't read *Much Ado*, you need to brush up your Shakespeare."

"Brush up your Shakespeare," R.J. sang in a surprisingly strong voice. "Start quoting him now."

Ben laughed, waved a hand. "And if you don't recognize *that*, rent the movie. Though when we get to Petruchio and Kate, we'll open the windows to clear the smoke pumping out of Miranda's ears. If the Bard lived today, she'd have many, *many* choice words for him over *Shrew*."

"Sexist bully violently and psychologically tortures a strong woman until he crushes her into a compliant doormat."

"And other words to that effect," Ben finished with a grin for his daughter. "But another time for that. Let's start with Beatrice, another strong woman—smart, shrewd, acerbic, with a gimlet eye toward the male of the species—and that we see from her lines."

"'I had rather hear my dog bark at a crow, than a man swear he loves me.'"

"And how's that not sexist?" the jock guy objected.

And, Booth noted, they were off and running.

A lot of cross talk, points, counterpoints. The group tossed quotes around like confetti, in big, colorful bunches.

He didn't intend to say much, if anything, this first round. It paid, in his opinion, to know who's who and what's what before wading in. You learned more, he thought, by listening, observing.

The redhead had a lot of opinions, and wasn't shy about expressing them. He also determined, in about two minutes, she was scary smart—at least in this area.

Zed had squeezed into a chair with a girl named Jen—black-framed glasses, no-nonsense straight black bob deal. The jock guy—Phil—took on all comers, but in a low-key sort of style. The third of the trio—Hayley—had to be on the debate team, as she'd take either side of a point and argue it out for the sake of it.

The professor didn't insert himself often, but let the conversations roll. Booth decided it was the sign of a good teacher, and a confident leader.

R.J. went out and came back with another bowl of chips, and handed Booth another Coke.

"Thanks." And because he was tuned into the discussion as he opened the bottle, he spoke without thinking.

"Claudio didn't actually love her."

Ben looked over, tilted his head. "Because?"

"What? Oh, sorry. I was just thinking out loud."

"Finish the thought."

Stuck, he shifted in his chair. "I mean, how's that love? He's duped by Don John—and everybody knows Don John's an asshole—into thinking Hero's banging some other guy. Why doesn't he head right up there and deal with it? He waits until the wedding, condemns her—doesn't say what the hell. And he's fine if she dies for it. Even her dad's fine with it. But nobody's saying how about the guy banging her? Nobody's saying get a rope for him. How's that love? She's just a woman, right, nice to look at, and he can get another. Benedick and Beatrice meet and stand on even ground. Hero and Claudio don't."

He wished he hadn't noticed how the redhead smiled at him when he finished.

"He thought she betrayed him, on the night before their wedding."

This from Hayley the debater.

"'Thought' is the word, isn't it? He never asks, never demands an explanation. And he doesn't believe her when she denies it. He's passive, and so's Hero. They're solid foils for Benedick and Beatrice."

"Hero should've told Claudio to stuff it. Thanks for nothing, you dick," Jen continued.

"Right? And maybe how she'd rather marry Dogberry. At least he knows he's an ass."

That got a laugh Booth found surprisingly satisfying.

That brought on a couple of the theater kids acting out some lines from Dogberry and the watch.

"Let me ask you this before we wrap it up. Sorry, you're in my Monday and Thursday class."

"Booth. Booth Harrison."

"Right. Very solid paper on *Henry V.* Will these two couples, those four crazy kids, make it?"

"Sure, I think so. Benedick and Beatrice are crazy about each other, they've both got brains and won't ever be bored. Claudio and Hero will just passively drift through, follow traditions, break no norms, and they'd be fine with it."

"I have to agree, and on that note, pick up your debris and get out of my house. Next week, on campus, same time. We'll discuss the relationships in *Midsummer.* Adding some magical hijinks as another wedding approaches."

People shuffled up, gathered their debris, and the noise level rose with it. Out of long-ingrained habit, Booth started gathering up what others left behind.

"I hope we didn't scare you off."

"Oh, no, sir. It was good. You even started with my favorite comedy."

"I've a particular fondness for it. You're doing excellent work in my class. It wouldn't hurt to participate more."

Shit—stood out.

"I guess I'm more absorbing right now."

"Don't wait too long. I like hearing my students' voices."

He disposed of the trash he'd picked up, kept the half Coke for the ride. And since the redhead huddled with the jock—had to be a thing there—managed to get out of the house without running into her again.

Some of the kids lingered outside, hanging out on the lawn, the sidewalk. Some climbed into cars, others straddled bikes, and some, he imagined, would hike the mile and a half to campus.

"Hey, Booth, do you mind giving Jen a ride back?"

Zed had his arm around her shoulders, but it struck Booth as more companionable a move than romantic. Either way.

"Sure, pile in."

"Thanks. Your first meeting, right?"

"Yeah. I liked it."

"We've got a Drama Club that meets the first Tuesday of the month. You should join. How come you guys haven't talked him into the Drama Club?'

"Rejected," R.J. told her.

"One at a time. I've got a full class load this term."

"Gotta have an outlet."

Jen chatted all the way back in a manner that told him the three of them knew each other well.

"I can drop you at your dorm," Booth told her. "No problem."

"No dorm, thanks. I live with these guys. No sexcapades, just five of us living in platonic chaos. You hooked up?"

"Ah, no."

"Bad breakup in Texas," R.J. supplied.

"I hear that. I'd ask you out because you're really cute, but you're not my type."

That had him glancing in the rearview, as R.J. had grabbed shotgun. "Okay, why's that?"

"I am a petite Asian goddess at five-one. And you're a long, lean machine. What are you, six-three?"

"And a quarter."

"See. We'd look stupid right off with a foot and a quarter difference. So more Platonicville."

"You could wear heels."

She laughed, slapped Zed on the leg. "I like him. You told me I would."

He liked her, too, the free-wheeling way of her, and drove home after the drop-off, pleased with the whole evening. Now that he'd shipped the redhead and the jock, he could put her out of his mind all the way.

SHE AMBUSHED HIM THE next day. He never saw it coming, and walked right into it.

She waited outside the class, then just blocked his way.

He said, "Hey. Hi."

"Hey. Hi. Let's go get coffee."

It stumped him, so he was slow off the mark. "Actually, I need to—"

"You've got an hour and a half before your next class. Me, too. Let's get coffee. I'm buying."

Rude, in his mother's world, was a four-letter word. "Okay. Do you need something?" he asked as she took his arm, pulled him along.

"Yeah, coffee. I overslept this morning—I hate when that happens—and barely had time to knock down a single cup on the dash."

"No, I meant from me."

"I do. I have a burning question."

She hadn't had time for the braid either, he thought, but had managed to pull her hair back in a long, sleek tail. And flipped it back as she looked at him.

"Okay."

"Do you believe in reincarnation? You know, we live many lives until we get it all the way right?"

It didn't come close to any question he expected. But since she was leading him along—she obviously knew just where she wanted to get her coffee—he considered the answer.

And thought of his mother, how short her life had been, how hard so much of it turned out to be.

"Yeah. There has to be more than one round."

"I think so, too. So I'm wondering—second burning question—if I did you wrong in some past life, and that's why you don't like me. I'm generally considered pretty likable, but maybe in that past life I strangled your dog."

"I don't think you strangled my dog or anyone else's."

She gave him a long, knowing look with those fabulous eyes. "Past lives are tricky."

"And anyway, I don't don't like you. I don't know you."

"Now's your chance." She aimed straight for a café among the shops, eating up ground on those long legs. "I liked what you said about Cláudio and Hero, so you get that chance."

The place was packed with students and staff craving coffee, muffins, cookies the size of dessert plates.

"I don't really drink coffee. Much."

She stared at him with those oddly amazing green eyes. "And yet you stand and breathe and function." She stepped up to the counter. "Miranda for both. Café Americano, extra shot."

He figured that was enough espresso to drive an eighteen-wheeler cross-country.

"Do your eyes bug out like an electrocuted cartoon cat after you drink that?"

"We'll find out."

"Vanilla latte."

"Ah, a coffee wimp."

"Accepted."

She paid, and they shuffled aside to wait.

The whole place smelled like coffee—a scent he'd never found translated satisfactorily to the actual drink. But even through it, he caught her scent.

Light, fresh.

Because he did, he reminded himself he'd hooked her up with the jock. Phil. Phil the jock.

"So . . . where's Phil?"

She arched one eyebrow—the left. He'd noticed she had that skill—quirk—whatever. And she took her phone out of her pocket to check the time.

"I think he's got his film studies class about now. Why?"

"No reason. I just figured since the two of you were . . . a thing."

She smiled that smile, then turned to grab their drinks when they called her name. "Let's take these outside, out of the noise. A thing," she repeated, as he got the door. "We do have a thing. It's called friendship. We clicked in sophomore year. Sophomore because I took enough college-level in high school and in summer courses to come in as a sophomore. He's really smart, funny, athletic—starting quarterback this year. And he's crushing pretty hard on this grad student right now. Chad."

"Oh."

"He's not my token gay friend, just my friend. Any problem with that?"

"No. Jeez, no." Except it made him a mess again.

"Good, I draw a hard line at bigotry in any and all forms. So," she continued as they walked. "Transfer in your senior year. Why's that?"

"If you spent two minutes around R.J., you already know."

She laughed, gestured to a vacant bench. "Bad breakup. Most of us have had one, but we don't usually move to another state."

He blended stories on the spot. "I wanted a change. I'd toured the campus before, and I really liked it, but . . . My mother died."

"Oh, Booth, I'm so sorry."

She meant it, he could feel it when she put a hand over his.

"It was all hard, and after my aunt—my mother's sister, she'd been with us through it all—we both wanted out of Chicago. She was looking at New Mexico, so since Texas was on my list, I took it. It's a great school, but when I had the excuse, I guess, to switch, I took it. And it feels right here."

"Preaching to the choir, as I basically grew up here. How about your father?"

"Never in the picture. Your dad's great."

"Top dad in the world of dads."

He needed to know more. He didn't want to, but needed to. "Your mom?"

"Mmm. Long story. Short version? She fell out of love with us, wanted someone and somewhere else, so she left."

"Now I'm sorry."

"No, actually, it worked out best for everybody. She's living the dream in Hawaii—the big island—with Biff." She'd slipped on sunglasses when they sat down, and now tipped them down to peer at him over the tops. "That's his actual name."

Shit, shit, shit! He liked her.

"Well, he has to live with that."

"He does. They do. And my father and I are—as she sees it—stuck in the muck of academia. I guess we just like the muck."

She took a long, slow drink of her coffee, tipped her head back to the sky. "So, Booth Harrison from Chicago via Texas, what do you want to do with your life?"

"Right now? Learn. I like learning."

"Me, too. What's wrong with us? And what do you do for fun that doesn't involve learning?"

Break into houses, he thought, crack safes, bargain with fences.

It might've been his job, but that didn't mean it wasn't fun.

"I like music, and hanging out with the dog next door. Mac, golden retriever. He's pretty great. I like to cook."

Down went the shades again. "You cook?"

"Yeah. I learned when my mom was sick, and I have some friends in New Orleans and spent some time there. I got better at it."

"My dad and I fumble around the kitchen. We actually hired someone—Suzanna—to come in twice a week and make meals so we don't starve. Well, now that we've established I didn't strangle your dog in a past life, you can show me your culinary skills sometime. Meanwhile, I have some prep for my next class."

This time she lifted up her sunglasses, tapped a finger under her eye. "Did they bug out?"

"No. They're beautiful."

She slipped the glasses back in place. "Luck of the DNA lottery. Good talk," she said as she rose. "See you around?"

"Yeah, sure. Thanks for the coffee."

"That barely qualifies as coffee, but you're welcome."

She left him there, sitting on the bench, looking down into what barely qualified as coffee.

And he knew he was sunk.

Since avoiding her now seemed stupid, Booth did his best to keep any encounters brief and casual. He'd come to UNC to learn, and to have the best experience he could in his final year of college.

Though he'd already started looking at some postgraduate classes. After all, when he finally let go of college, he'd probably need to get some sort of day job as cover for his actual career.

He could start a cleaning company. God knew he had the experience. And he'd taken some accounting and some business courses at A&M, so he had a handle on that.

But this year he'd earmarked for the sheer pleasure of learning what appealed.

Two months in, he held solid As, a small circle of friends, and a routine that satisfied him.

Then R.J. and Zed dragged him to a football game.

He didn't dislike football; he was completely neutral on the sport. While his mother and Mags had supported the Bears, they hadn't done so with the same fervor they devoted to the Cubs.

Sports just hadn't been one of his interests, but he'd learned—especially in Texas—that if a guy didn't want to stand out, he warmed a seat at a few football games and cheered for the home team.

And when the Tar Heels met the Cavaliers on the home field, you showed up at Kenan Stadium wearing school colors.

He did his job, wore a school hoodie, cheered for the mascot—a live ram named Rameses. He ate a very decent pulled pork sandwich, yelled, booed, or cursed at appropriate times along with around fifty thousand others.

And thought, with some regret, of all the empty houses ripe for the picking on this cool, clear night in October.

He knew enough about football to see that while Phil the jock was on his game, the defense was sorely lacking. As a result, the Tar Heels ended the first quarter up seven.

They made it ten to seven at halftime, which boosted the sprits of the home team crowd.

Since Zed busied himself flirting with his current date, and R.J. and Jen argued with surprising passion over a flag thrown on the Tar Heel's offense in the last minutes of the half, Booth decided to stretch his legs.

And there she was.

In a stadium of fifty thousand, he ran right into her.

She wore jeans, a school hoodie with her hair tumbling down her back. People milled and flowed around her as she leaned against a wall and finished texting someone on her phone.

She tucked it into the kangaroo pocket of her hoodie.

"Football fan?"

He started to say sure, then the truth came out of him. "No, not remotely. Peer pressure."

She pressed her palm to her chest. "Friendship. Well, and family. If my dad somehow whacked off his own right arm before a home game against Virginia, he'd tell the ambulance to detour here first."

She held up a finger, pulled out her phone. "That's him now, asking me to pick up some fries before I go back. He nervous eats at these games. He's got a friend who went to the University of Virginia, and they place a serious bet on any game."

"Really?" The professor hadn't struck him as the gambling type. "How much?"

"A shiny quarter. The same quarter—the lucky quarter. A coveted prize for seventeen years and counting." She gestured to one of the concession stands. "Hang with me while I do my daughterly duty. I heard you were tutoring Ken Fisher—he's the right tackle, or left tackle. Or something. Phil told me you were helping him with his French class."

People milled around them. He didn't notice.

"Yeah, he needs a foreign language credit, and he's having a hard time with it. Professor Relve asked if I would. He's got her for French 101."

"Phil says it's helping. Ken's got to keep his grades up to keep his scholarship and stay off the bench. Do you have time to take on one more?"

His heart tripped a bit. "Do you need some help?"

"Me, no. *Je parle français très bien. Mais j'écris français très mal.* Conversational, no problem, but the reading, the writing, I'm not good enough to help Hayley, and she's struggling." She ordered the fries, turned back to him. "Do you have time, and what do you charge?"

"I could see what I could do. Ken's paying twenty a session."

"Sounds right. Let me know, okay? She seriously tanked her last assignment, and she's freaking."

Maybe he'd found his day job early. "I've got time between classes on Mondays—nine-thirty to ten-thirty, and on Wednesdays one to two. Thursdays, same as Mondays. If any of those work."

"I'm booking you for her."

"Okay. If she changes her mind—"

"She won't. Freaked. Hayley doesn't tank assignments. Give me your phone."

She pushed the takeaway box of fries at him as she took it. "Putting my number in your contacts. Just text me if anything changes with you."

"Got it." He didn't mean to ask, knew it was a mistake, a terrible idea, but he did it anyway. "Do you want to maybe grab a pizza sometime?"

She smiled, did that single eyebrow raise. "Yes. But I'd really like to come to your place for dinner and see if you can really cook."

Bigger mistake. Much bigger. But . . . "Sure. Ah—"

"How about tomorrow night. Does seven work?"

"It could work."

"Great." She took out her phone again. "I need your address."

In a kind of daze, he gave it to her. "Well . . . any, you know, allergies or things you don't like, won't eat?"

"No allergies, and if you cook it, I'll eat it." She took the fries back from him, shook the box. "I have to get back before these get cold. I'll let Hayley know about Monday. And I'll see you tomorrow."

"Yeah, see you tomorrow. Hope your dad wins his quarter."

She tossed a sparkling look over her shoulder. "Not as much as he does."

In the same daze, Booth made his way back to the stands.

What the hell had he done?

And what the hell was he going to cook?

Chapter Twelve

IT THREW OFF HIS entire Saturday routine, which told him maybe, just maybe, he'd already settled into a rut.

It wasn't as if he'd never cooked for a girl—woman—before. Dauphine might've been the first outside of family, but she hadn't been the last. Though he'd kept that particular move mostly in reserve for when both parties knew—or certainly assumed—the evening would end in bed.

That wouldn't happen here—he'd firmly decided that one. Besides, this equaled a first date. If it really was an actual date, and he had to admit Miranda kept him continually off balance.

Maybe they were just pals. Platonicville. That would be best all around. Her father was one of his professors, for God's sake. Talk about sticky.

Still, he wanted to impress her with the meal. Nothing fancy though, he thought as he rejected a half dozen menus. Fancy was just bragging.

But nice, something nice.

He decided, finally, on pesto pasta with grilled chicken. He'd use farfalle so nobody had to wind or slurp. Plus, farfalle looked cheerful, casual. Pasta was casual.

It was all casual.

He still had his Saturday cleaning, so he hit it early and hit it hard while the dough for the Italian bread rose.

He did all his usual Saturday chores, baked the bread, then went shopping for what he needed for dinner.

Then he made himself sit down and work on a paper for his own French class. Shifting from that he went downstairs, set a timer, and worked on improving his personal best on combination locks.

It helped, keeping his hands busy, his mind focused. And still by the time he took a shower, started dinner prep—and a soft, light rain began to fall—he admitted he was a wreck.

He should've done some yoga. Mags swore by it, and whenever he tried it, it zenned him out. Plus, it kept the body limber, and someone with his career choice needed to stay limber.

Too late now, he thought as he wondered if he should light some candles, put music on. Or if that was just too much.

He decided the candles worked because the rain made it gloomy. Just cheering it up, like the farfalle.

At 7:02—not that he was watching the clock—the knock came. And his stomach clenched. Not like a fist, but like two fists wringing out a wet rag.

She wore one of those dresses with a short denim jacket over it. Little raindrops glimmered on her hair.

He'd never wanted anyone or anything as much in his life.

She held out a small bouquet of flowers. "I thought about wine, but since I didn't know what you're cooking, I didn't know what kind to steal from my father."

He stepped right back into the daze as he took the flowers. A first, he thought. No one had ever brought him flowers.

"Thanks. Come on in."

"It's a nice house, and wow," she added as she stepped in. "So clean it sparkles." When he laughed, she quirked that eyebrow.

"Family joke, I guess. My mother and my aunt had a cleaning company. The Sparkle Sisters."

"Great name for it." She wandered the living room.

Pretty sparse, he realized now that she stood in it. But absolutely clean.

"I grew up cleaning houses, so . . . habit."

"He cooks, he cleans. You must like living alone off campus."

He just shrugged and fell back on the line he'd used all summer. "I like having the space—a yard—and the quiet when I'm working. Studying."

"You've got that. Why don't you show me what smells so good?"

He walked her back to the kitchen, watched her wander again. Nothing much to see, he thought, beyond the ancient Formica countertops, the clunky cabinets. Considering the size, he'd hung a pegboard and taken a page from Sebastien's book, hung up kitchen tools.

"This is where you live more than out there."

"Yeah, I guess I do."

"And it's Italian." She gestured to the plate of antipasto on the counter. "Always a top fave."

"I've got some wine to go with it if you want some."

"Not technically legal until April, but I would."

He didn't have a vase, but had an iced tea glass that would do. He stuck the flowers in, poured the wine.

"Okay, you're not perfect."

"I'm not?"

"You don't know how to arrange flowers." She took the wine, then set it down to fuss with the flowers. "Hayley's thrilled, by the way. She got the lowdown from Ken. He says you're a kick-ass tutor, which is high praise from Ken."

"I did some in high school, and here and there. Ken's motivated, but the grammar's killing him. We're working on it."

"Too bad you're not a math major. I know some people struggling there."

"Actually, I used to tutor math."

169

She glanced up, then took a pepperoncini from the plate, bit in. "This is, like, calculus and advanced algebra." When he shrugged, she did that eyebrow thing. "Really?"

"Math's just numbers, formulas, and logic."

"I can't say I ever felt that way about it. But I never have to take another math class in my life." She tried an olive. "This is good. Anyway, if you want to add to the tutoring, I know a couple people."

"Sure, I guess."

She leaned back against the counter as she sipped her wine. "Are you thinking about teaching?"

"No, not really. Right now, it's about learning. You?"

"Maybe. I'd like to write, but there's that whole earning a living thing in there."

"Write what?"

"Big, sprawling, juicy novels." She sent him that smile. "Which takes time and talent and probably luck, so I may end up teaching big, sprawling, juicy novels other people wrote."

Maybe, he thought, but she struck him as beyond motivated. She struck him as driven.

"But you'll write anyway."

"It's what I like best. You must read something besides Shakespeare."

"Anything and everything. One day I'll read *Big, Sprawling, and Juicy* by Miranda Emerson."

Laughing, she shook back her hair. "Doesn't every lit major want to write, even secretly? Don't you?"

"My mother hoped I would. I'm okay at it—just okay—and it doesn't pull at me, you know?"

"Yeah, I do. What does? Pull at you?"

Dark, quiet houses, he thought. Locks to be lifted, safes to be cracked. "Too many things, maybe, so I can't settle on one. I like figuring things out, how things work. People, too. How do they work? Languages—I like learning them. It's figuring things out.

Theater. How do you take this story, this setting, these people and make it all work?"

"Back up." She circled a finger in the air. "Languages? More than French?"

"Yeah, well, Spanish and Italian. I'm pretty solid now in Russian and Portuguese. I think I might try Farsi."

And he was telling her too much, he realized. Because it was all so easy.

"Hungry?"

"I'm making inroads in the antipasto, so I must be."

"I'll get the pasta going."

He already had the water heating, so turned it up to bring it to a boil.

She sipped her wine, moved over to lean on the counter by the stove. "How do you say that in Italian? You know, boiling the pasta?"

"*Buttare la pasta.*"

"Of course, you could've made that up, but it sounds right."

He'd wrapped the bread in a cloth, and now uncovered it to put it on a cutting board.

"Where'd you get the bread?" Her hip bumped his as she moved over to sniff it. "You did *not* make the bread."

He didn't know if he felt goofy or proud. "Baking bread's one of my zen things."

"Shut up!"

When he starting slicing it, she grabbed a piece from the board, bit in. "Well, God! This is awesome. Maybe you should open a bakery."

"Are you kidding? Do you know how early bakers have to get up every day? Middle of the night, basically. And baking for a living cuts deep into the zen."

"I guess it would. But you could, and that's the thing. Dad and I bake cookies together every Christmas. Trust me, we couldn't open a bakery."

She watched him add the pasta to the boiling water, get out a colander, wide bowls.

"You're the first male to ever cook—or attempt to cook—dinner for me other than my father."

"Really?"

"Really. I'd ask if I can help, but I'm just going to stay out of your way."

She did just that while he got out the cherry tomatoes he'd already halved, the container of pesto he'd made, more fresh basil, a hunk of fresh Parmesan.

She nibbled from the antipasto plate while he sliced the grilled chicken he'd kept warm in the oven, mixed the pasta, chicken, pesto, tomatoes in a bowl.

"Did you actually make the pesto from the basil?"

"That's how it's done."

He cut slivers of it, to garnish the servings he'd arranged in the bowls, then grated the Parm over it.

He poured a little balsamic over the olive oil in dishes for dipping. Put it all, and the bread, on his table.

It looked good, he decided. Damn good. And she looked just perfect.

"Okay, *buon appetito*."

"I heard that." She sat, immediately took a forkful of the pasta. "Okay. Well, wow. You know, when I invited myself to dinner, I figured you'd toss something on a grill, maybe bake a couple of potatoes—which is all fine. This is amazing. And delicious."

"You're the first person I've had over for an actual sit-down dinner."

"Is there another kind?"

"There's taking some Cajun potato salad over to a neighbor's cookout, or sharing some leftover spaghetti with the kid next door."

"Now I have to ask what's Cajun potato salad."

"Something else again. A friend of mine in New Orleans gave me his secret recipe for his Cajun spice mix."

"I've never been to New Orleans. Is it as wonderful as it looks in movies, sounds in books?"

"It's like nowhere else. I felt steady there, easy there, when everything went rocky. You should go sometime. It's not just a place. It's an experience."

"I'll put it on the list. Where else have you been?"

"I'd never been anywhere before, so I took a long road trip on the way to New Orleans, then to Texas. I drove through the Smoky Mountains. Chicago is, you know." He drew a flat line with his hand. "So I'd never seen anything like them, and I'd never seen the ocean, so I drove the coast some, went to the Outer Banks. Water pulls me. Water and hills."

"We stayed in a house on Hatteras a few years ago for a week in the summer. It's beautiful."

"Where else have you been?"

"England." She tore off a hunk of bread, dipped it. "My dad, right? Shakespeare. Ireland, because Yeats, Joyce, and so on. Gorgeous and green. Maine. And if you like the ocean, you should see it from one of those rocky Maine beaches."

"I'll put it on the list. Where do you want to go you haven't been?"

"Top pick? Florence—the art, the architecture, the food, the sun. The shopping."

He'd stopped feeling nervous and self-conscious. Stopped worrying about what to say—and what not to say. He felt more easy sitting at the little table with her while the sound of rain pattered outside than he'd felt anywhere in life.

"You hit one of mine. In fact, Mags and I are going over spring break."

"Mags?"

"My aunt."

"Lucky you! You must be tight with your aunt. What does

she do now? Does she still have the business since she moved to New Mexico?"

"No, actually . . ." He could've said anything, but went with truth. "She's a phone psychic."

He waited for the reaction, expected laughter, possibly derision. Instead he got wide eyes and a light punch on the shoulder.

"Get out! Seriously? Does she read palms? You can't read palms on the phone, can you? Tarot cards?"

"Yeah, that, and vibes or something."

"This is amazing. Wait." She pointed at him. "You don't believe."

"You'd have to know Mags to . . . You do? In psychics?"

"'There are more things in heaven and earth, Horatio.' We went to Stonehenge when we were in England, and this—much smaller, but incredible—stone circle in Ireland. If you didn't feel the 'more' there, you'd never feel it."

They talked, and talked, and it was all so easy. He couldn't pinpoint the moment when the nerves vanished. Everything just glided.

Books they'd read, movies they'd seen, music they liked, and more as they ate pasta and bread, then scoops of gelato. They talked while she helped—insisted on—with the washing up, then more as they sat awhile longer, her with a sparkling water, him with a Coke.

Just past midnight, she sighed. "I need to go. This was really just perfect. I wish I could reciprocate by offering to cook you a meal, but I like you, so I can't subject you to the horror of it."

"We could grab that pizza sometime. Or you could just come back."

"Both sound good. Let's try this. Pick a movie. I can take you to a movie without risk of giving you food poisoning. That way, I can invite myself to dinner again with a clear conscience."

"Okay. How about tomorrow night?"

She rose to pull on her jacket. "Monday's better for me.

I've got a paper due Monday morning, and it still needs some polishing."

"Monday works." Any Monday, he thought as he walked her to the door. Any day, anytime. Ever.

"Pick the flick, text me." She tossed her hair back, looked dead in his eyes. "Thanks for dinner. It was wonderful."

When she opened the door, he saw the rain had gone to a mist. It floated, thin, cool, and beautiful. She stood in the open doorway, her back to it, and simply took his breath away.

"I have to ask you a question."

"Okay."

"I think I'm a pretty decent judge, and I judge you're into me."

"Who wouldn't be?"

"Scores," she said easily. "But I judge you are. I've given you a few openings, and you don't go through them, so I invite myself over. And we've had, oh, a good five hours or so alone in your house. Good food, good company—again in my judgment. But you don't make a move."

And there, once again, she'd thrown him off balance.

"I wasn't sure if you . . ."

"I could've moved on you—not at all opposed to that. Equal rights and all that. I wondered if you're just not over that bad breakup."

"The what? Oh. No, no. No," he repeated. "That's all done."

"Good to know. Maybe you don't have any moves."

Off balance and knocked back, he led with pride. "I got moves. I've got some damn moves."

"Maybe you should show me one. Just one," she added, holding up a single finger. "Doesn't have to be your best. I'll certainly grade on the curve, as you might be rusty."

Irritated, as she'd certainly intended, he moved in, gripped her hips, then with his eyes on hers, slid his hands up her sides. Slow. Until he'd gathered her against him. Close.

Only then did he lower his mouth to hers.

It was hard not to take too much, not to feast when he'd wanted and wanted and wanted. But he could float here, like the mist floated beyond them. Float on the taste of her, the feel, the scent, the everything of her.

Not take too much, follow the no-greed rule, and just bask in the moment. Having her arms around him, having her lips answer his, hearing that low hum in her throat.

Her hands slid up into his hair as the kiss spun out. And because his hands wanted to touch, to take, too much, he cupped his on her face, changed the angle of the kiss. And let it spin out once again.

When he eased back, he looked into her eyes, those sea-witch eyes.

"That's a good move," she managed.

"I thought about starting with this one."

He turned her, pressed her back against the doorjamb, and with her pinned between it and his body, took a little more. Now he could feel her heart pounding, her pulse jumping, and the single, quick tremble that shuddered through her.

"Also a good choice."

He liked knowing her voice wasn't quite steady, nor was the hand she pressed to his chest to create a little distance between them. "Ten out of ten, no curve needed. Now I really have to go."

"Or you could stay." He touched her hair, all that beautiful fired-gold hair.

"I want to more than I thought I would, so I have to go. I have a rule about first dates, and I really want to break it, so I can't."

"We had coffee that one time."

She laughed, shook her head. "Definitely doesn't count. Rules is rules," she said, and sidestepped him. "Let's try that movie, maybe the pizza or whatever."

"I get rules. I've got some of my own." And one, carved in stone, was to respect a woman's choice. "Monday night."

"Monday night."

He watched her walk through the mist to her car, watched her drive away.

And he thought: This is what they're talking about. In all the books, this is what they meant. This was falling in love.

WHEN SHE GOT HOME, Miranda hung up her jacket, very carefully. She walked up the steps, very quietly.

She knew her father's bedroom light was on, as she'd seen it glowing when she pulled up. But he often fell asleep reading in bed, his glasses sliding down his nose, the book open on his lap.

Not tonight.

He sat up, wearing a Tar Heels T-shirt, and shut the book he held when she peeked in.

"You know," she began, "I'm too old for you to wait up for me."

"You'll never be too old for that. Besides, I wasn't. I'm reading a very good book on a rainy Saturday night. How was dinner?"

She crossed the room to sit at the foot of the four-poster that had been his grandmother's. "He baked bread."

Ben frowned. "You mean from yeast and flour?"

"Yes, he said it's a 'zen thing.' And he made this amazing pasta—with pesto he also made from scratch."

"You can do that?"

"He did. His house—it's cute—and it's so clean I feel like I need to hose down my room in the morning. His mother and his aunt used to own a cleaning company, and he helped clean houses. Oh, oh, his aunt—he calls her Mags—she's a phone psychic! I can't get over it. You can tell he loves her, not just the sure, I love my aunt, but loves her."

She got up, wandered to the window to look out at the misty night.

"And he used to tutor math, too, so I'm going to tell Nate to contact him. And he doesn't just speak French, but Italian, Spanish, Russian, Portuguese."

Ben shifted in bed. "Are you sure he's not inflating some of this, baby?"

"He's not. You sort of have to pry things out of him to start. He's not shy, but he's cautious. I had to bait him into kissing me."

"Oh, Miranda. How many more gray hairs do I need?"

She came back, pressed her lips to his cheek. "As my father, you'll be pleased to know that when he could've taken advantage—and sorry, there's another gray hair, he could have—he didn't. He didn't press, he didn't push, he didn't sulk. He's got what you always say is so important."

"A solid core."

"Exactly. He's special, Dad. There's something different about him, and I want to find out more. I'm taking him to the movies Monday night."

He took her hand, rubbed it between his. "You'll be careful."

"You know I am. I was raised right."

"I like him. He's extraordinarily bright, well-mannered without being too stiff or shiny about it. We'll have him over for dinner sometime. Suzanna will cook, then I'll grill him like a fish."

"Seems fair." She kissed his cheek again. "Don't read too late. You know you'll nod off, then you get that thing in your neck."

"When you're right, you're right. Good night, sweetheart."

He waited until he heard her door close, then set the book aside.

He hadn't—precisely—waited up. He'd been reading. But now that the center of his world had come home safe and sound, he could sleep.

Maybe he'd worry a bit first about his little girl's starry eyes when she'd talked about the boy, but he could sleep.

"Six languages?" Ben muttered when he turned off the light. "At his age? We'll see about that one."

Chapter Thirteen

BY MONDAY, BOOTH HAD three more students. He'd need to juggle his time, but he'd always been good at juggling. He set up in one of the student study areas with Miranda's friend Hayley. And quickly learned she had a tighter grip on French than the football player.

More, he found out she was deadly serious about improving her grade, and, due to that, along with her frequent stumbles on French reading comprehension, he learned her favorite word. *Merde*.

"Okay, that's time. Look, you're solid on conversational. You need to wire up for translating and comprehending the written. So, homework."

"Merde."

"Yeah, and still. Do, like, a journal entry. Pick a day, or make it up. How would I know? But writing it out's going to help you read blocks of text. And hit the foreign section in the library, pick a French translation of a romance or mystery novel."

She slitted her eyes at him. "Romance because I'm a girl?"

"You'd rather I said read Cervantes or Dumas?"

"Been there, done that. Sucked."

"I hear you. What I want is for you to read something that's been translated from English into French."

"Got it. And this didn't actually suck. Plus, after this, I totally get why Miranda's into you."

There went that heart skip again. "Is she?"

"Please." With an eye roll, Hayley gathered her things. "I wouldn't say it if you didn't already know it. Have fun at the movies tonight."

"Thanks. See you next time."

He grabbed his backpack, thinking he'd grab a Coke to sustain him through his next class. He ran into Ben on the way.

"Booth, got a second? Miranda tells me you speak Italian."

He nodded because all he could think was Miranda talked about him with her dad. A good thing? A scary thing?

He decided the answer was both.

"Do you read it?"

"Yeah, I—"

"Great. I don't." Ben dug into his own bag and pulled out a scrap of paper. "Can you translate this for me?"

Booth took it, scanned it. "Yeah, it's Dante, from the *Inferno*. You'll know it in English because it gets tossed around a lot. 'Do not be afraid; our fate cannot be taken from us; it is a gift.'"

"Ah, of course. Then again," Ben said as he took the paper back, "most of us wish, sometimes, we could return the gift."

"If you did, everything else changes with it."

"True enough. I hear you're doing some tutoring. French, calculus, global authors—Jane Austen."

"Yes, sir. That sort of happened."

"Calculus and Austen. Quite the combination. Let me ask you something, Booth."

He didn't freeze, but braced. He hadn't faded into the background the way he knew he should have. When you stood out, people noticed, and had questions.

"Eidetic memory or just a wide range of interests?"

Definitely not the question he'd expected. "It can be both."

"It can. I thought I detected the memory."

"It's just something else that happened."

"It's rare, and valuable. Definitely a gift you wouldn't want to return."

"Sometimes remembering every detail isn't a big plus."

Studying him, Ben nodded. "I suppose you're right. Come to dinner tomorrow night."

"Sorry?"

"To dinner, Booth. Tomorrow. Seven. Thanks for the translation."

Ben strolled off; Booth stayed rooted to the spot.

He should cancel his movie date. In fact, he should head home, pack up, and take off. There were other places, other colleges. There was always somewhere else to slide into.

But he did remember every damn thing. He remembered what it felt like to sit and talk to Miranda, to hear her laugh. What it felt like inside him when he kissed her.

He knew what it felt like to belong again, to have friends again, something he'd avoided since New Orleans.

He didn't want to give it up. He didn't want to give her up. He'd let down his guard, more than a little. But he'd handle it, he'd adjust.

Dante claimed fate was a gift? Fine. He'd figure out how to use it.

A MOVIE DATE, SHARING popcorn, kissing the girl good night might have ranked as usual for most guys, but for Booth, they hit top of the list. Everything about her hit top of his list.

He knew about chemistry, biology, endorphins. Just as he knew what drew him to her wasn't as basic or elemental as science.

If having her in his life, if creating a life that had her in it proved to be a mistake, he'd deal with the consequences.

He considered dinner with her father the first of those consequences. He prepped for it the way he'd prep for a complicated job. He found articles on meeting the parents. Of course, he'd met Professor Emerson, but the same concept applied.

He read Ben's bio, read the papers he'd published. Even as he prepared for the job he'd earmarked for Thursday night, he considered his wardrobe for dinner, appropriate topics of conversation, and his own personal story line.

He arrived promptly at seven, already wishing the night over.

Then she answered the door and reminded him why he'd prepped for torture. She wore dark jeans and a sweater that reminded him of the pines that covered the hills in the Smokies.

When she smiled, everything inside him went bright.

"And he comes bearing gifts. I'm going to guess the flowers are for me, the bourbon's for my father."

She took the flowers. He'd gone for red roses to keep it all classic.

"Come on back while I put them in water." Then she took his hand, squeezed it. "This won't hurt too much. Promise."

He didn't believe that for a minute, but the house charmed him as it had before, and he imagined what it must be like to call such a place home for generations.

Ben stood in the kitchen, sharpening a carving knife.

"Don't worry. It's not for you." One eyebrow winged up, just like his daughter's. "Yet. We're having roast chicken."

"Smells great. Thanks for inviting me. I heard you like good bourbon."

"I do." Ben set aside the knife to take the bottle. "Woodford Reserve. A fine choice. Will you join me in a glass?"

"Actually, I'm driving, so . . ."

"Correct answer. I hope you brought an appetite. Suzanna outdid herself. I hear you're quite the cook."

"I like to cook."

"My claim to fame in the kitchen is carving. I'm an exceptional carver. Miranda is a very fine stirrer."

"And chopper," she added as she finished arranging the flowers. "I'm an excellent chopper and a slightly above-average peeler."

"There aren't many meals you can make without stirring, chopping, or peeling."

"No doubt Suzanna did all of the above. Why don't we get started on the results?"

The chicken rested on a platter Booth recognized as Wedgwood. Ben did have an expert hand at carving, and with the table already set—fancy style—for three, they sat in the dining room.

He had a glass for water—still or sparkling—and one for wine. He took half a glass of wine, an amount he thought acceptable.

Ben toasted. "Here's to the end of midterms. How'd that go for you, Booth? I know you aced my class. That was an excellent paper on the gender roles in *Macbeth*."

"Thanks. I know it sounds like sucking up, but I really enjoy your class."

"I don't object to some sucking up, but I can tell you enjoy it. What sparked your interest in Shakespeare?"

"We watched *Henry V* on TV—the Laurence Olivier one—when I was a kid. It had all those battles, and the inner conflict, the redemption. Mostly the battles, really. So I got this big collected works out of the library."

"How old were you?"

"Eleven."

"Shakespeare featured in some of my bedtime stories."

Ben smiled at his daughter. "You're never too young."

"The language, the rhythm of it, it would be soothing."

Ben wagged his fork at Booth. "Exactly. The same can't be said about my lullaby singing. What attracts you to language, Booth?"

"It's not just communication. I mean, that's key, sure, but it's culture, too, and it's personal, even intimate. How it's used, how it sounds or looks."

"Looks?"

"On the page, or in sign."

"Do you sign?"

"I'm okay at it."

"Learning sign's on Dad's list. He never seems to have time for it."

"Maybe you could teach me. Coach tells me Ken got a B on his last French test, and that's up from a C minus. You must have the spark. The teaching spark."

"Mostly it's just finding the soft spots and filling them in. And Ken's really motivated. He wants to go pro."

"You like football?"

"'Like' might be a strong word."

Shaking his head, Ben ate some chicken. "Sadness. Miranda tolerates it."

"'Tolerate' might be a strong word." She gave her father that eyebrow lift.

"And yet more sadness. When she was twelve, Miranda nagged, begged, wheedled to get her ears pierced."

"He'd set thirteen as the line, which is arbitrary."

"Teen being the line. I lowered myself to a bribe. If she'd watch the game with me Sunday afternoon, I'd take her to get holes punched in her ears."

"And when I kept the bargain, I didn't cry during the piercing, as he'd warned me I would."

"I cried a little."

She laughed, leaned over to rub Ben's hand. "He really did."

They looked just right together, Booth thought. They were just right together. It brought on a quick pang for his mother because it reminded him how they'd been just right together.

"So, tell me, Booth, what are your plans? What do you aim

to do with all these languages? Teach, build a career as an interpreter, become an international jewel thief?"

He covered that jolt by taking a bite of carrot. "I haven't decided, but I could combine all three. Use the teaching as a cover, and assist the authorities with my language skills as I travel the globe stealing diamonds."

"Just diamonds?" Miranda wondered.

"I could specialize. They come in all sorts of colors, cuts, carats. But right now, I'm thinking maybe grad school."

"What field of study?"

Because the grad school portion was true, he went with truth on the rest. "That's the problem. Narrowing it down. I like school. I like the structure and the purpose, but it's a big menu, and hard for me to pick one or two things from it."

"If you decide on grad school here at Carolina, I can always use a good TA. It would give you a taste, and you'd see if the spark you obviously have catches fire."

A teaching assistant. And for the father of the woman he really hoped to sleep with?

"I don't know if I'd be any good at it. I've only done the one-on-one. With that, you can really focus in."

"Something to think about. A lot of lit majors hope to write."

"I'm not that good at it. Creating something's different from analyzing something someone else created. My mother . . ." He started to trail off, then pulled it back. "She hoped I might write. She loved to read. I took some courses, but—"

"But?" Ben prompted.

"They have all these rules, and depending on the instructor, they can be pretty adamant about them. Then you read something, and it seems to me the really good books, the ones that suck you in, don't follow all those rules. Then I'm trying to read with all those rules in my head, and it killed it for me."

"But you obviously didn't stop reading or enjoying books."

"No, I just stopped doing it with the rules in my head. I think you just have to know how to tell a story your way. I don't have that—what you said—that spark."

Ben looked over at his daughter. "He gives good answers."

"Have you finished grilling him yet?"

"Baby, I've barely filleted him. I'll grill him over dessert."

Maybe he felt a little heat over apple pie. Ben wanted to know bits and pieces about his life in Chicago, his time in New Orleans, in Texas, traveling.

Since he'd prepped, Booth had already picked and chosen what to say, how to say it.

When they got to Mags over coffee—a Coke for Booth—Ben was fascinated.

"She traveled with a carnival."

"For a while, yeah."

They sat in the living room now, the fire simmering low.

"When they lost their parents, their uncle took over. Then Mags took off with the carnies, and my mom worked in her uncle's butcher shop. Then I came along, and Mags came back to help out. Their uncle died, and they started their cleaning company."

"The Sparkle Sisters," Miranda filled in.

"Yeah. Sometimes Mags said a client's house had bad vibes, so she'd bring in crystals and white sage. Chant. She does that."

"And now she's a phone psychic."

Since Ben said it with delight, Booth grinned at him. "She's unique."

"If she comes to one of our visitor weekends, I hope you'll introduce me. It's personal, but you don't mention your father."

"He opted out before I was born."

"Ah. Well, I can sincerely say it's his loss." He looked back at Miranda. "I approve. And now I'm going to pour myself two fingers of excellent bourbon and take myself upstairs. You're welcome here, Booth, anytime."

Booth rose as Ben did. "Thank you, Professor, for the meal, and everything."

"Ben. Around here, you can make it Ben. And think about the TA position. I think you have a talent for it." He bent down, kissed the top of Miranda's head. "Good night, baby."

"Night, Dad."

When he left and Booth sat again, Miranda turned, took his face in her hands, and kissed him until his head swam.

"Invite me to dinner Friday night."

"Come to dinner Friday."

"I'd love to." She kissed him again. "I'll tell Dad not to wait up."

IT FELT LIKE THE longest week of his life. He had a full class load, what had evolved into a fairly challenging tutoring schedule, and basic household chores he simply wasn't wired to ignore.

Added to it, he had the final preparations and execution of a job inside a nicely rehabbed old Colonial involving a diamond and emerald necklace. Gaudy, but since he'd break it down for the stones, taste didn't apply.

He had a generous three-hour window to get in, crack the safe, take the gaudy, and get out. Since the couple, off to their daughter's wedding rehearsal dinner, neglected to set the house alarm, the whole deal—one he'd spent two weeks planning—took him less than forty-five minutes.

That gave him enough time to pop the stones, box them up for FedEx—inside a jar of Nivea face cream. He'd ship them off to Sebastien, who, for a small carrying charge, would pass them on to a contact.

The system worked.

And the take would cover grad school tuition.

Finally, Friday blew in on a kicky wind that rattled the trees. It made Booth wish he had a fireplace, just for the atmosphere.

He decided if he ever had a house of his own, it had to have a fireplace.

Since he wanted to give Miranda a taste of New Orleans, he had jambalaya in the pot and corn bread keeping warm in the oven. And this time he wouldn't feel stupid lighting candles. He even had the blues playing low on his iPod.

A quick internal check told him he felt excitement instead of nerves when her knock on the door finally came.

She wore jeans and boots and a sweater the color of crushed blueberries. Instead of wine or flowers she carried a little overnight bag.

"If things don't work out, it'll go back in the car with me." She set it just inside the door. "What smells so good?"

"Jambalaya."

"Really? I've never had it. I'd say I can't wait to try it except . . . Can it hold awhile?"

"Sure."

He wanted to kiss her, but she wandered around his living room.

"Great, because I'd really like to see if things work out." She turned back to him. "I'm a little anxious—that's the best word for it. I'm not sure I could handle dinner without knowing."

This time, he realized, she had all the nerves. So he walked to her, gathered her in, laid his mouth on hers. He sank into the kiss, just let it take them both away.

She put a hand on his cheek, looked in his eyes. "I think things are going to work out just fine."

"If you change your mind—"

"I'm not going to change my mind."

"I was going to say," he continued, taking her hand to lead her to the bedroom, "if you change your mind, I'll never be able to eat jambalaya or corn bread again."

"I can't be responsible for that."

He kissed her again. "Lights on, lights off?"

"Oh. Well . . ."

"Let's go with candles." He'd set out a few, in anticipation and hope. As he lit them, something struck him, and he looked back at her, more than a little panicked.

"It's not, like, your first time, is it?"

"No. Two semi-serious boyfriends, so not my first time." The lifted eyebrow and smile told him her nerves were draining again. "You?"

"No."

"I see you don't toss out a number."

"No," he said definitely.

"I'm going to take that as I'll be in good hands."

"This feels different."

"Yeah."

And right, he thought when he drew her against him. Just right in every way.

He wouldn't rush, not when moment to moment was its own small miracle. The way her mouth moved against his, the glide of tongue, the merging of breath.

He'd remember it, all those small miracles. The scent of her hair, the feel of her skin, the rattle of branches in the wind outside the window.

She tugged at his sweater; he tugged at hers.

Then she laughed, stepped back. "I need to take off my boots."

"We'll get to them." He pulled her back, stripped the sweater over her head. Incredibly, perfectly, the scrap of bra mirrored the color of her sweater. "You're just beautiful. God, you're just beautiful."

He scooped her up, laid her back on the bed. He let the kiss deepen, let his hands begin to roam.

Slowly, though slow was a struggle. Easy, though easy proved hard won.

Snooks Eaglin's "Teasin' You" murmured in the air, a quiet, steady beat as he pressed his lips to her heart.

The thrill rocketed straight through her, left her both wild and weak. She'd expected a rush—had been more than ready to match that pace—and this long, thorough exploration woke every nerve in her body.

Good hands, she thought. She was in very, very good hands.

She could float under them, ripple like a river as she took the gift and did her best to return it.

He had such a long torso, lean, taut. Smooth skin, surprising muscles that bunched and released under her hands. She wanted, more than she'd known she could, and finally dragged his sweater away.

He flicked open the clasp of her bra one-handed, made her shiver.

"Good trick," she managed, then arched, moaned when his mouth claimed her breast.

With tongue, teeth, lips, he took her to the edge.

Then his hand slid down, and his fingers unfastened her jeans with that same canny skill. He had only to press a hand to her center to fling her headlong off that edge.

"I'm going to get your boots off."

His lips moved down her now, lighting countless fires.

"I don't care, I don't care, just don't stop."

"I do. I need to get you naked."

Even as he yanked them off, his tongue swept over her, lightly inside her. The orgasm shot through her, a hot, wet bullet that left her dazed, crazed.

He took her over with his hands, his mouth, and she knew he hadn't just stripped away her clothes, but everything.

And she didn't care.

When he started to unfasten his jeans, she reached out.

"Let me. Let me." She fumbled a little, let out a breathless laugh. "My hands are shaking. It's crazy."

No, he thought, it was perfect. Having her hands on him, the way her hair glowed, quiet fire, in the candlelight, the way she trembled because she wanted, like he wanted.

Then he lay over her, and their mouths met again, hungry now, greedy now. She opened for him, wrapped around him, long limbs, speeding heart.

He'd remember the way her hair spilled over his simple white sheets, and how the magic of her eyes met his. He'd remember how her breath caught when, at last, he slid inside her.

And he'd remember when they moved together, what coursed through him was more than pleasure, more than need, more than triumph.

It was finding a treasure, something precious, something without price. Something he'd only dreamed of.

Chapter Fourteen

HE WISHED HE COULD write poetry or music, or paint. Surely he'd compose an epic poem, a soul-stirring song, create a masterpiece with what now lived inside him.

She lay with her head on his heart, and he knew if he lived to be a hundred, he'd never know a more beautiful moment.

"It really worked out."

She made him laugh, and with the laugh, everything in him felt free. "I don't know, we should probably try it again, a few times, to make sure that wasn't a fluke."

"Sensible." She gave his chest a quick rub. "You know, you hide all this pretty well."

"My astonishing sexual talents?"

"Those, too. The muscles. You're pretty ripped for a thin guy. When I caught you looking that first day in my dad's class, I thought, that guy's got a really pretty face. And if I spotted you on campus, I'd think, tall guy, classic lanky build. I thought you were a dancer."

"What? Why?"

"The way you move, kind of catlike, athletic, but not in the sporty sort of way. Like a dancer."

"Just my natural, and again astonishing, grace. I didn't want to like you."

"Now it's my turn." She lifted her head to study him. "What? Why?"

"Because the minute I saw you, everything else stopped, faded away. Then my world did a one-eighty. Turned upside down. Seriously pissed me off."

Smiling, she shook her hair back. "That's the biggest compliment in the history of compliments."

"I decided you had to be a snobby, arrogant bitch so I could stop thinking about you. Then you weren't, so that screwed that."

"Sorry?"

He shook his head. "Not sorry."

"Me either. I did a lot of thinking about you, too. This mysterious guy with the navy-blue eyes slipping around campus like a shadow."

"I'm not mysterious."

"Little bit. And I like puzzles. My dad would say you have lots of layers. Very interesting layers. Crazy smart, and that's from someone who's pretty damn smart herself. Clicks with the nerds—and that's a real click, even though you're not a genuine nerd yourself. But likes to live alone, off campus, away from the action. Older, here and here, than most," she said, tapping his heart, his temple.

"You sure you're not a psych major?"

"Just a wannabe writer who likes figuring people out. After all, I'm going to write about people. And seeing as we're naked in bed, figuring you out is important."

"I'm pretty sure I'm in love with you, if you haven't figured that out."

She laid her head back on his heart. "I'm pretty sure I'm right there with you. It's scary."

"Yeah, it is. But it's . . . it's really great, too, because I've never felt like this, about anyone. And I've never asked anyone if we can just see each other and nobody else."

He felt her lips curve as she turned to press them to his chest. "That's already a given for me."

"You make me happy, all the way through. It's been awhile since the happy's made it through all the layers." Happy, content, hopeful, he stroked her back. "Hungry?"

"Starved."

"Let's go eat, then maybe we can take a walk. Then we can come back and try this all again to, you know, eliminate the fluke factor."

"I'm for all of that."

"Just one thing," he said as he sat up with her. "If it turns out you don't like jambalaya, the whole thing's off."

"That's very strict."

"Somebody told me recently rules is rules."

It turned out she liked it just fine.

AT THE AGE OF eight, before his world crumbled, Booth wrote a story—a school assignment—about a boy granted a wish for a week full of Saturdays. The story, which earned an A plus, convinced his mother her son would one day become a writer.

While that fond maternal hope would, in Booth's more realistic view, never come to pass, the story, and the boy's joy in it, remained his personal pinnacle for pure joy.

The short weekend with Miranda topped it. They walked his quiet neighborhood under the autumn moon, exchanged dreamy kisses under its tender light. And though afternoon clocked in before they got out of bed on that magical Saturday, he fixed her breakfast. He agreed to buy a coffee maker if she'd spend the day with him.

With her approval, he settled on a French press. They talked about taking in a matinee, ended up renting a movie and watching it snuggled up on his living room sofa. And made love there as the credits started to roll.

And she stayed, showing off her chopping skills when he made fajitas for dinner.

When he lay beside her Sunday morning, he thought of that

boy in the long-ago story, and the perfect bliss of waking on yet another Saturday.

"We could pretend it's Saturday again."

She had her head on his heart. He wasn't sure he'd ever linger in bed again contentedly without that sensation.

"Can we pretend we don't have papers due tomorrow on *The Merchant of Venice*? That Professor Emerson cracks the whip. And I need to take another hard look at my revenge story for my writing class. Then . . ."

She broke off, lifted her head, and gave him a narrowed-eyed stare. "You finished the Shakespeare paper, didn't you? You bastard."

"It needs a final polish."

"I could hate you right now. I've barely finished the first draft. And, crap, it's nearly noon. I really have to go."

"You could work here."

She slid up enough to kiss him. "I'm liking the scruff," she murmured. "And I don't think either of us would get much work done if I stayed—added, all my stuff's at home." Lazily, she wound some of his hair around her finger. "Do you think this, all this with us, will settle down any?"

"I sure hope not."

"Me, too. I really have to leave. I'm going to hop in the shower first."

Because he hopped in the shower with her, she didn't drive away until almost two.

And he, a man who prized his solitude, felt completely alone.

He had plenty to fill his time until he saw her the next day. That paper did need a polish, and he needed to work out lesson plans for his tutoring gigs. Domestic chores, some nightwork research.

He turned on music, got started. And with every task, he thought of her. She'd filled the spaces he'd thought he'd wanted to keep empty.

She made him think almost as much as she made him want.

He wondered if she'd move in with him. Rushing things, sure, but maybe in a few more weeks . . . Then he thought of his actual career, and his tools, his work space in the basement.

How could she live with him when he had those secret places?

They'd figure it out. That's what people in love did, he thought. They figured things out.

He could quit—maybe. He thought he could quit. Or at least take a break. Like a test. He'd never thought about setting aside his real work, work he'd done for more than half his life now.

But he could try. For Miranda, he could try anything.

She texted him, and brightened his entire day.

Taking a break between Portia and Revenge. Decided I do hate you.

He texted back.

Add the pound of flesh to your revenge story. I miss you.

Too late for the lb of flesh. More like a bucket of blood.
I miss you, too. Music at Club Caro tomorrow night.
You want?

Sounds good.

See you in the morning.

I'm seeing you everywhere. It's weird. I like it.

She sent him a heart and lips pursed in a kiss. And signed off.

He could take that break, he told himself. He could set his work aside. Maybe even try out a civilian sort of job.

When he finished the schoolwork, the lesson plans, had his

house in order, he thought of his work in the basement, and the research he'd started on a coin collection.

If he was going to set all that aside, he might as well start now. He could take a walk, read a book. He could text R.J. and see what he and Zed were up to.

He figured the knock on the door came from one of the neighbors.

Nothing prepared him for opening the door to Carter LaPorte or the big, burly guy standing one pace behind him.

"Hello, Silas. Oh, no, it's Booth now, isn't it?"

"What are you doing here?"

"Manners dictate you ask me in. We'll discuss that."

"I was just heading out."

LaPorte's lips curved in a smile. His eyes didn't reflect it. "Change of plans."

Booth noted the dark Mercedes sedan at the curb. He'd need to come up with a story about that, when the neighbors asked. And they would.

But he couldn't risk an altercation in the doorway. Especially since the bodyguard could, no question, break him in half.

"Make it quick." He stepped back. "I have friends waiting."

"Friends. Yes, you've made quite the little circle here, haven't you?"

In his steel-gray suit and carefully knotted tie, LaPorte scanned the living room.

"I'd expected more from a young man with your talents. It's quite—usual, isn't it?"

"I'm a college student."

LaPorte pinned Booth with one long stare. "We both know you're much more than that. You've done quite well for yourself since we last met."

LaPorte walked to a chair, sat. Spread his hands. "I have connections. And my connections have connections. I would love some coffee."

Booth thought of the French press he'd bought with Miranda. For Miranda. He'd be damned if he'd use it for LaPorte.

"I don't do coffee. What do you want?"

The icy fury blasted. It could do more damage, Booth thought, than fire and flame.

"You can start with respect for your elders. David here is an expert in convincing people to show respect. Shall I ask him to show you?"

Because he didn't want a black eye, broken fingers, or worse, Booth sat on the couch. "You're here because you want something. I have people waiting, and your time's too valuable for you to waste."

"Better. I have a business proposition for you."

"Sebastien—"

"Isn't equipped for this. Don't interrupt. There's a small, exquisite bronze, a female figure titled simply *Bella Donna*. It was auctioned at Christie's in New York recently and is now part of a private collection. It, along with a few other pieces from this collection, will be on display at the Hobart Museum in Baltimore. The collector is a native son. The showing runs from November first through the end of January. I need you to acquire this piece for me, for which service you'll receive one point five million dollars."

Careful, Booth warned himself. "I appreciate the offer, Mr. LaPorte, but I'm a full-time student here, in North Carolina. More, I've never taken a museum. Only private homes. I'm not the right person for this job."

"I disagree. The Hobart is a private museum. Essentially, a private home. You'll have several weeks to prepare."

"I live here, go to school here."

"Things change, as you well know." At his ease, LaPorte gestured with one hand, then settled back in the flea market chair in his rich man's suit.

"Now, while your pursuit of higher education is admirable,

of course, we both know it leads nowhere. And I could end that pursuit so easily. Some interesting information in the right ears. Who is this Booth Harrison, really? How is he paying his tuition? Why did he leave the university in Texas? Ah, wait, he didn't, as those records are falsified.

"What would your little circle of friends, and that very attractive redhead, think when they learn who and what you really are? A drifter, a thief, a liar, using them as cover?"

"I'm not using them as cover. Threatening me doesn't make me right for this job. And the fact is I can't do that kind of work anymore. I have a full class schedule, I'm tutoring. We're about to go into tech on a play. I can't steal a bronze in Baltimore no matter how much you offer me."

LaPorte leaned forward. "Do you think you can just switch it on and off?" He snapped his fingers. "You are what you are. You'll go to Baltimore, make yourself into who you need to be, as you've done before. And you'll acquire the bronze."

"I can't. Look, nobody turns down that kind of money if they have a choice, but—"

"How's your aunt?" Folding his hands, LaPorte sat back. "The last living branch on your family tree, isn't she?"

He knew the taste of fear, and it filled his throat now. He knew the heat of outrage, and it burned through him as he pushed to his feet.

"She has nothing to do with this. I need you to leave."

The bodyguard clamped a hand on his shoulder. Booth tried to shrug it off, but it gripped like iron as it shoved him down again.

"You may want to give her—Mags, isn't it? Charming. You may want to give her a call. She's had a break-in, a very destructive one. Fortunately she wasn't at home when it happened.

"This time," he added. "It would only take a word from me. A single word to put her in the hospital. To put her in the ground."

Outrage couldn't compete with the fear. "Why would you do this? You could get someone else."

"If I wanted someone else, we wouldn't be having this conversation. You're quite the student—Booth—so learn this. I'm the power, you're the tool. You have a function. Fulfill your function and reap the reward. Fail, reap the consequences."

"Why now?"

"You made an impression on me. I haven't required your services again until now. *Bella Donna*, the Hobart Museum. I'll expect you to deliver her to me by February first, latest."

LaPorte nodded at the bodyguard, who tossed some wrapped bills on the coffee table. "Ten thousand, more than enough, I believe, for your travel and living expenses. It will, naturally, be deducted from your final fee, due to your behavior."

He rose. "I'll get out of your way. I'm sure you'll want to be on the road to Maryland very soon."

"If you hurt Mags, I'll kill you."

LaPorte just flicked a glance at the bodyguard.

The backhand came fast. Later, Booth would think he'd been lucky it wasn't a fist, but when he spilled to the floor with half his face on fire, he didn't feel lucky.

"Mind your manners."

They left him there, and he stayed where he was until he got his breath back, until the ugly sickness in his belly passed.

He fumbled out his phone, called Mags.

"Hey, pal."

Her voice—a little rough, a little breathless—made him squeeze his eyes shut. "Hey, Mags, how's it going?"

"Like piss down my leg, that's how. I got home about an hour ago. Somebody broke in here—broad damn daylight—and busted up my sweet little house."

"Are you all right?"

"Yeah, yeah. It doesn't look like they even took anything. Just busted things up. The cops think it might've been somebody after drugs—of which I don't have any. Except a little pot, stashed away, which I didn't tell the very cute officer of the law. Or maybe somebody who's pissed at me, but I swear to tiny baby Jesus, I haven't pissed anybody off lately. I'm doing some in-person readings here and there, so maybe somebody didn't like the read. I don't know. They broke the vase. You know, your mom's pretty blue vase with the hummingbirds on it."

And she started to cry.

"I'm sorry. It's okay. It's going to be okay. Do you want me to come?"

"No, no. It's just stuff, that's all. Sorry to blubber. I've got the pieces of the vase. I'll make something with them. I should've done what you told me and gotten an alarm system. There's just nothing . . . Anyway, I will now. So tell me something good. Perk me up."

He tried to think of something good when everything was wrong. He told her about Miranda, and felt his heart break as he did. It just broke away from his body, because he knew that perfect weekend was it.

He'd never have it again. Never have her again. Never have anything again.

When he set down the phone, he sat where he was, on the floor.

He knew what he had to do. If he did what he had to do, Mags stayed safe.

He got up, and did it. He packed his clothes, his tools, cleared everything out of his work area.

He had a blooming bruise on his jaw and cheekbone he covered carefully, thoroughly with makeup.

He couldn't just take off—they'd look for him. And look into him.

He sent a text to R.J. after he'd loaded up his car.

Family emergency. I have to take off and now. Don't know when I'll get back—may not. Rent's paid through May. Use

the house if you want. I'm leaving the keys with Miz Opal.
If I don't make it back, take the furniture. It's not much, but
somebody can use it.

The return text came as he walked to the neighbor's.

Wtf, bro? What happened? You're just booking?

Yeah, I have to. My aunt needs me and now. Gotta go, and
it looks like a long haul, so use the stuff. I'm probably going
to be out there for a few months anyway. Really gotta go.
Can't text and drive.

After he sent the text, he turned off the phone, then knocked
on the neighbor's door.

He spun the tale, had to add an accident, his aunt needing
surgery and rehab, and whatever came to mind. Miz Opal teared
up, but she took the keys.

And hugged him before and after she bagged up some peanut
butter cookies for him.

He got in the car, waved to Miz Opal, Papa Pete, Mac, then
drove.

He didn't think of Miranda. He couldn't let himself think
of her.

He just drove, kept his mind blank and drove straight
through, North Carolina into Virginia, Virginia into Maryland.

He had none of the anticipation or fascination he'd felt with
his drive south and east from Chicago. None of the looking
ahead.

The life he'd toyed with building? A fantasy. He saw that now.

LaPorte was a man of lies and arrogance, but he'd said one
true thing.

Whatever name he used, Harry, Silas, Lee, Booth, he was
what he was.

As Harry Williams—a nod to his childhood and his old friend—he checked into a motel, let the exhaustion come and take him under until morning.

And in the morning, late in the morning when he woke and turned his phone back on, he saw text after text, voice mail after voice mail.

Miranda's first voice mail logged in at eight-twenty-eight. He didn't listen to it—couldn't. He could see, clearly, how she'd looked for him in class, and R.J. telling her he'd gone and why.

She followed up with a text.

Booth, I'm so sorry about your aunt! I hope she's okay. Text or call as soon as you can. So worried. Love shooting straight at you.

There were countless others after that, but he didn't read them all. He knew what he had to do.

Just seeing these, sorry, he texted back. Mags is holding her own, but it's going to be a long haul.

He left it at that, just that, and, knowing what would come next, took a shower so he wouldn't hear the phone ring.

He dressed—good sweater, leather jacket, good jeans. He applied the facial hair carefully. Stylishly scruffy goatee, dark blond to go with the wig. He gathered it back into a stubby tail, then tried various glasses until he settled on wire rims.

He changed his backpack for his messenger bag.

Once again, he turned the phone off—best not to be distracted—and headed out to take his first look at the Hobart.

Then he'd find a good furnished apartment nearby, or, if he gauged the job would take more than four or five weeks, a small house.

Harry Williams was a freelance writer, a trust-fund baby from Baton Rouge, researching Baltimore for a story. A loner, a serious man of twenty-three.

Wealthy, privileged, and a little bit of a prick.

He made his way to the Inner Harbor, noting the traffic patterns—horrible—the feel of the area—touristy. He used public parking and walked several blocks in the chilly November wind. Considering the wind, he stopped in a shop, bought a navy scarf, and wore it out.

It added a touch of arty, he thought, which worked.

The Hobart nestled among the higher-end shops and restaurants and was, as LaPorte had said, a private residence.

Redbrick, white trim, two stories, and likely a basement. Double front doors, gleaming windows, the brass plaque all spoke of dignity.

He noted the security cameras, the lights, and the little discreet sign that warned the premises were protected by Guardian Security.

Thanks for the tip, he thought, and went inside.

Wide-planked hardwood floors, security cameras, motion detector—smart. All open concept to display the art on walls, in cases, on pedestals.

He paid his fee—on the stiff side—and, along with about five other people, began to wander.

One uniformed security guard visible. Another, he assumed, monitoring the cameras. Most likely at least one night guard, so something to keep in mind.

He made notes, as a writer would, on various paintings, sculptures, pottery.

He got his first look at the lady in question, and she was beautiful. Sinuous, he thought, sensuous with her elongated body, the head with its flowing hair tilted to look over her left shoulder.

She held her left hand out, arm cocked at the elbow, palm up. As if she said: Take it, take me. If you dare.

He had to dare.

After making some notes, he strolled off.

He spent seventy-five minutes casing every inch of the space, then strolled out to inspect the neighboring buildings, the street, escape routes.

Midafternoon he used an Internet café to look for rentals, and bagged himself a decent row house less than two miles from the target. He wrangled a three-month lease, paid the hefty deposit and the full three months—part of his negotiation.

He bought a few groceries and moved right in.

The place needed work, he thought, but he didn't care. It was clean enough, and he let himself find a little pleasure in the working fireplace.

He put everything away, setting up his tools and work supplies in the second bedroom.

He put a frozen pizza in the oven, got a Coke, and turned on his phone.

It rang almost immediately.

"I'm sorry, I'm sorry," Miranda said the minute he answered. "I know I'm filling up your voice mail and text, but I'm so worried."

"Yeah."

"How's your aunt, how are you? What can I do?"

"She's stable." He kept his voice neutral, and a little brisk. "I'm okay. I'm not the one who got crashed into by some asshole texting and driving. Nothing you can do."

"Is that what happened? Oh, Booth. What hospital is she in? We could send flowers."

"She doesn't know you." He put a chill in this round, and hated himself. "Look, I've got to get back in there."

"Could you call me later, fill me in a little? We're all thinking about her, and you. If—"

"I appreciate it, okay? I'm really busy, and I don't have time to talk you through it. She's going to need months of rehab after she gets out of here."

Her voice changed, too, and he heard the hurt in it. Felt it carve into him.

"We just want to help, Booth, any way we can. Even if it's just someone to talk to. I could fly out for a few days and—"

Pressing a hand to his face, he fought off the drowning emotions, the need, even the image of her in his head.

His voice snapped, cold and sharp.

"Jesus, get a grip. We had fun, right? We had a great weekend and all that. But that's it. I've got real shit to contend with here, and that doesn't include dealing with you making a few dates and some good sex into some romance novel."

"That's . . . that's an awful thing to say, and it's not like you."

"Guess you didn't know me. Gotta go."

He hung up, then leaned over to put his head between his knees.

She'd hate him now. Then she'd forget him. He'd just be some asshole she'd fallen for—briefly—in college. A mistake. A lesson learned.

A mistake all around, he told himself. A lesson learned on both sides. He'd never let himself get that close to anyone again. Time to focus in, do what had to be done. Just like always.

When the timer dinged, he got the pizza out of the oven.

He took it and the Coke upstairs, booted up his computer.

He got to work.

HE TOOK THE LADY on Christmas Eve.

He'd gone back in once, using a different look—long, straight brown hair, full beard, tinted glasses, a temporary tattoo of a peace sign on the back of his right hand. And he'd sort of slouched his way through while he'd added more details.

What burned him, when he trolled the neighborhood at various times of the day, of the night, was how clear it became LaPorte hadn't needed him, specifically, for the job.

LaPorte had ruined his life, or the life he'd started to imagine, because he'd just wanted to. Because Booth had once said no to a man who demanded absolute obedience.

Another lesson learned.

At two a.m. Christmas morning when kids dreamed of Santa, Booth slipped through the shadows and the lights out of camera range. He disabled the system for thirty-two seconds. Anyone monitoring would see it as a glitch, and if they came out to check around, he'd keep clear.

He studied the thin red beams of the motion lights, waited to see if he heard anyone, anything.

He thought he heard voices, prepared to move and fast, then recognized George Bailey on the bridge with Clarence. *It's a Wonderful Life.* The guard entertained himself with a Christmas movie, and who could blame him?

Booth danced over red lights, sprayed camera lenses with black paint on his way to the lady. She had weight, but since he'd read her full description, expected it.

He actually heard the security guard cackle and call out, "Run, George, run!"

Shaking his head, Booth lifted the statue into his backpack before he retraced his steps. Another short glitch, and he was on the sidewalk and fast walking to his car.

He'd already packed up his things—just a guy heading home for Christmas.

Chapter Fifteen

CHRISTMAS AFTERNOON, WITH THE sun beaming through the windows, he stood in LaPorte's impressive office in the impressive house in Lake Charles.

Fueled with anger, resentment, he'd driven straight through. He hadn't slept in thirty-six hours. Rather than fatigue, he felt wired.

"You surprise me. I hadn't expected to see you so soon, and on Christmas Day. Another hour or so, you wouldn't have found me at home."

Saying nothing, Booth set the backpack on the big mahogany desk next to an antique inkwell.

He'd remember this room, he thought, and everything in it. The Georgia O'Keeffe over the fireplace, the bookcase behind the desk full of treasures rather than books. The jade horse, the Ming vase, the Daum peacock.

All the treasures.

Because one day. Maybe one day.

But for now, he took the statue from his pack, set it down.

"Ah, and there she is."

Booth saw it—the greed, the satisfaction of possession—as LaPorte trailed a finger over the bronze face, down the body. "She's lovely, isn't she? Strong, sexual, almost fierce. A woman,

I think, who knows the needs of men, and meets them when she chooses."

He walked to a ten-sided glass cabinet—a Victorian vitrine, Booth remembered from his study of antiques—and took out a decanter.

"A drink to commemorate the moment?"

"No." Booth took out a paper, set it down beside the statue. "Wire the money there."

"Your manners don't improve."

"It's business. You got what you wanted. And you didn't need me for the job. You didn't have to upend my life for this job."

"I disagree." LaPorte poured the bourbon into a short crystal glass. "And, I believe, in the end have done you a great favor. Your skills continue to impress, and I'm pleased to have such a well-oiled tool in my very exclusive toolbox."

He toasted Booth, sipped. "I will, of course, need to have the bronze authenticated before you collect your fee. As I'm engaged this evening, and you weren't expected, I'll arrange for that tomorrow."

"Then wire the money tomorrow." Booth turned to leave.

"So trusting. I might keep the bronze and your fee."

"You won't. I know where you live."

"I could say the same. But not to worry, you'll have your fee. I always pay my debts." He toasted again. "Until the next time. And Merry Christmas."

"Just wire the money."

WHEN SEBASTIEN RETURNED HOME after midnight from a long, raucous Christmas at his mother's, he found Booth's car in front of the cottage.

And Booth asleep on his couch.

"You break into my house, *mon ami*?"

Booth woke to find the dog staring holes through him, and Sebastien standing with a wide grin and two loaded paper bags.

"Sorry. I needed to sleep."

"How come you don't tell me you're coming?"

"I wasn't sure about it."

When Booth sat up, rubbed his hands over his face, then just left his face in them, Sebastien's grin faded.

"*Cher*, you got trouble all over you. Did you have a job go bad?"

"No, nothing like that."

"Bet you need to eat. I got enough food from the family table to feed the whole damn bayou. You come on and sit. I'm gonna fix you up."

"Thanks."

Sebastien started unloading the bags, and the scent of food hit Booth's empty stomach like a hammer. He took the plate Sebastien loaded with ham, fried chicken, biscuits.

"I'm gonna warm up the red beans and rice, and some of these taters. And you tell me what you're doing eating in my kitchen instead of snuggled up with that girl you told me about. The redheaded girl."

Booth just shook his head, but Sebastien didn't need words to see.

"Ah. Sometimes love, it turns away from us."

"I did the turning. I had to. I had to make her hate me."

"Why?"

"LaPorte," Booth said, and told Sebastien everything.

"*Picon!* Fuck him to hell and back again. I don't take the work up north, not in many years, this is true. But he has others. For him, you're like the statue. He wants to own you."

"Yeah, I got that."

"We're gonna figure this out, *tu saisis*? You go back to your college and your girl, you make things up with her."

"I can't. He'll use her, Mags, you, anyone I care about to get to me. And next time he might not settle for busting up some furniture."

"What do you want to do? What you want, I'm with you."

"I picked up some prepaid phones. I'm sending one to Mags, and leaving one with you. I'll give you the number of mine. I've already ditched my other phone. It's probably overkill, but he's got a long reach. He can't use me if he can't find me. There's no point in hurting people I care about if he can't find me."

"Where you gonna go?"

"I'm going to drive to Atlanta, sell my car. It's time for that anyway. Change my name, again, and use some of his goddamn money to book a private plane. They don't x-ray your luggage and stuff. Gotta buy some good luggage. Some casual designer clothes, that sort of thing. Look the part of somebody who can fly private from Atlanta to Paris. I'll start in Paris, then we'll see."

"Rich young Frenchman—rich family. You're going to be Paris French, so put on the snob. Louis Vuitton luggage, and you buy Italian shoes, sunglasses."

"I got it."

"You let me know when you get there. I'm going to worry about you."

"Don't. I'll be fine. Let Mags know, okay? Tell her I'll call her on the new phone in a few days. I'll be fine," he said again. "I always wanted to go to Europe. It might as well be now."

He pushed up, went to his pack for the phone. "My number's in there, and so's the number for the one I'll send Mags. I'm going to get started. Thanks for the food."

"You don't thank me for that. We're family." He took Booth by the shoulders. "You come here anytime, you hear? And when you feel it's safe for you, I'll come to you, me. Mags and I will come to you."

Sebastien hugged him, slapped his back. "I have three pretty girls. And I have one handsome boy. Why don't you stay tonight, get more sleep?"

"Better to drive at night. He'd figure I'd come here, so it's

212

better to keep moving. Tell Dauphine . . . tell her I'm sorry I couldn't go see her."

On December 30, Henri Metarie boarded a private jet in Atlanta. He had sun-streaked, light brown hair worn in shaggy waves. He had a hip-length bronze leather jacket over a navy cashmere turtleneck, Armani sunglasses—though the sun had already started to set—and snug black jeans.

His Piaget watch—a knockoff, but it would pass—had a black leather band.

He spoke little, and then in perfect English with a clipped Parisian accent. The flight attendant assigned to tend to him told the pilot he seemed bored and snooty.

That would have pleased him.

He landed in Paris on a misty winter morning, and slid through customs as the rich and privileged do. His passport had the numerous stamps of the frequent and international traveler.

Here, it received its first legal one.

"*Bienvenue*, Monsieur Metarie."

He gave the customs agent the slightest nod. "*Merci*."

And with everything he cared about behind him, he walked through the airport and into the next world.

HE SPENT MOST OF his twenties in Europe, exploring, working, even hiking and biking. In France he focused on what Sebastien called baubles, and shifted from a flat in Paris, to a cottage in Provence, to a castle hotel in the Loire Valley.

He took cooking lessons from a student at Le Cordon Bleu, and shared her bed after learning how to prepare the perfect macaroon.

In Italy, it was art, to admire and to steal, as he basked in the glory of the light in Florence, the magic of the canals in Venice, the antiquities of Rome.

He traveled to Greece, and learned the language, to England and Ireland, to Sicily and Tuscany. He learned to travel through

Europe as casually as he'd once ridden his bike through his old Chicago neighborhood.

Once a year, as pinky sworn, he spent a few days with Mags.

He'd pick a spot—a villa in Tuscany, a house in Bar Harbor, whatever appealed. She often traveled with Sebastien, and he'd have those days to catch up on what her life had been.

At twenty-seven, he was wealthy, well-traveled, spoke ten languages, eight of which he considered himself fluent in. He'd seen the world, or enough of it.

And aside from those few days every year, he was alone.

He sat on the terrace of a pretty villa on the coast of Italy, and sipped wine, looked out on the Med and the boats gliding over it.

Mags sat beside him. She'd come alone, as Bluto had, the previous winter, gone to the big doghouse in the sky. Sebastien had a new puppy, just weaned, and hadn't been willing to leave him as yet.

"He's insane over the puppy," Mags said. "I know having Wiley helped him through the grief."

"Like Coyote, right? Wile E. Coyote? He would name his dogs after not only cartoon characters but the bad guy. Sort of bad guy, I guess."

Reaching out, she took his hand, just held it as they sat.

He'd told her she looked fantastic, and he hadn't had to exaggerate. She still wore her hair long and wild, and now flame red with generous streaks of glinting gold.

"I have some news," she began.

"Good news or bad news?"

"I think very good, for me. I'm moving."

"Again?"

She'd left Santa Fe when he'd left the US, and tried on Sedona.

"Again. I'm moving to New Orleans."

That got his attention, and he shifted to her. "You're not

moving into the cottage with Sebastien. I know the two of you . . . I know about that, and I love the man, sincerely, but it's the bayou, and it's—"

"Sebastien and I both like having our own space. Between my business and the fact you keep throwing money at me—"

"You're my family."

"And you're mine, pal. Anyway, I'm buying my own place. Not renting this go-around. It's time to have my own. Dauphine and her man helped me find one. And since Luc's handy, he's going to help me fix it up. My way. It's a nice little place, and I'm going to have a magical shop street level. It's just big enough. Big enough for you to come visit, come stay. I know you haven't been back to New Orleans in years, so maybe it's time, or will be soon."

"Maybe."

"And some more news? Dauphine's expecting."

"Expecting what?"

Mags let out a laugh that turned into a hoot, then hiccupping gasps as she pressed a hand to her ribs.

"A baby, you dumbass."

"A what? Really? Holy shit! Is she happy? Is it good? Is she good?"

"She's ecstatic, and very good. So good Luc's finally convinced her to marry him. Next month. She hopes you'll come, understands if you can't."

Boats glided by on the sea, the wide, blue sea.

"I wish I could. I really do. It's just the sort of thing he'd look for."

"Oh, honey, that fuckhead can't still be looking for you. I swear to God nobody's bothered me. I'd tell you."

"I know you would, but his type doesn't hear no. Or when he does, he has to make you pay for it. And he got a whiff of me in Prague last fall. I got tipped off, but he's still got feelers out."

"You didn't say anything."

"It was a whiff, and that's all he got." He kissed the hand that held his. "Tell Dauphine I wish her the best of everything. With the baby, with Luc. And I'll come back, I will. Soon. Things are getting a little warm here anyway."

"You don't mean the weather."

"They've given me a name. The people who look for people like me. The Chameleon. I like it," he admitted, "but when they figure out your style enough to name you? It's getting warm."

"You could stop."

He made a noncommittal sound. "I was thinking about checking out Rio, getting a look at South America, the Amazon. Maybe a year or two there, or maybe in the States. Thinking anyway. Or Australia, New Zealand. A nice vacation maybe."

"I think you got those itchy feet from me."

He looked at her, his crazy aunt Mags, his family, his constant. No one knew him the way she did. No one else remembered the boy he'd been, his mother, their life.

"Let's take our itchy feet and walk down to the village. You haven't had a chance to do any shopping yet."

"You know me." But she gave the hand she still held another squeeze. "Who'd have thought we'd ever sit here like this, in a villa in Sorrento, with the Med spread all out just for us."

"The world's an oyster, Mags. You just have to pry it open and take the pearl."

A FEW WEEKS IN Rio netted rubies before he headed to Peru for emeralds and a cruise on the Amazon.

He settled a score in Peru and found a way to see one of LaPorte's less refined, and more brutal, tools ended up in a cage.

It felt good. It felt . . . just.

And it sent him away from South America to the South Pacific.

Three months in Australia brought him opals and an interesting little Seurat monochrome. He dove the Great Barrier Reef.

New Zealand was for kayaking and hiking, and the always reliable stamps.

He had a week with Mags and Sebastien on Fiji.

Nine years after he'd landed in Paris for the first time, he returned. Willem Dauphine, an art broker, currently based in London. This time he stayed in the art nouveau splendor of the Peninsula in the heart of the city.

A conservative man, Willem wore perfectly tailored suits, usually with an Hermès tie and pocket square. He kept his dark blond hair short and brushed back, favored tortoiseshell glasses, and clean, close shaves.

He had a small scar along his right jawline, and a pronounced overbite.

He also had a small, furnished flat in another part of the city that served as his work space. He visited museums and galleries, but his target was the Musée National d'Art Moderne, and an exquisite Matisse still life.

There he made an appointment with the assistant director, a fashionable middle-aged woman in a severe black suit who offered him coffee.

Though he found it strong enough to melt the enamel on his teeth, he took it black.

They held their conversation in fluid and formal French.

"Thank you, Madame Drussalt, for meeting with me. I know your time is valuable."

"As all time is."

"Of course. I represent a client who has inherited a collection of art, a private collection, you understand. I have persuaded—or begun to persuade—this client to share this collection with the world."

"And who is this client?"

"I am not yet at liberty to say, but only to divulge that the collection, while small, contains what I consider important pieces of Fauvism. Six pieces in total, which have been in this private collection for two generations."

"I am unaware of such a collection."

"As you would be, madame. It is kept in a private room in a private home. And this, I believe, is not the purpose of art, and so I urge my client to bring out what has been closed away. I am assigned, so to speak, to have a conversation here, as in London, in Rome, in New York, and to take back to my client more details, which might persuade a permanent loan of the collection."

"You wish for us to display this collection, but can tell me nothing of it or your client."

"I wish to persuade my client. This is the first obstacle. I will be frank."

She waved a hand. "Please."

"My client has no true interest in art. I wish to pull her away from selling the paintings, going to auction, where they may, again, be held privately. My client has no need to profit from them, you see. I don't speak to my client of the purpose of art, but of the prestige of a plaque in a great museum, a plaque bearing her name as donor. The publicity generated from such a gift and so on. And with this, my client is persuaded enough to allow me to . . . test the waters."

"I see."

"I live and work in London, madame, but I am a Frenchman. If I could choose, the collection would come here. Still, my priority is to see these works are given to the world. There are others whose priority is the selling of them, or the keeping of them as they are now. I want to take her some assurances on the benefits, to her, of this donation."

"You wish to put conditions on a gift."

"I'm aware of policy, but seek some assurance that if this collection is found worthy, it will be displayed with a plaque." He closed his eyes briefly. "There must be a plaque, and some pomp surrounding the gift."

As if struggling with stress, he rubbed the back of his neck. "I am not at liberty to divulge, but I am sure, madame, you're aware of the exhibition in the Salon d'Automne, in 1905, its controversies. Van Dongen participated, did he not?"

Interest flickered into her eyes. "He did."

"With Matisse, Marquet, and others. It is then, yes, these artists with their bold use of colors were termed Fauves. The wild beasts of art. Van Dongen, we know, moved to Montmartre, was friendly with Picasso. And became a favorite of French society with his portraits.

"You might find it interesting that the grandmother of my client also lived in Montmartre. A strikingly beautiful woman in her day." He paused dramatically. "I have seen her portrait."

"Ah."

"If I can assure you this collection contains works of this importance, I wonder if you can assure my client in turn how they would be received? All, for now, hypothetical."

It earned him a VIP tour, and because of the major art theft in May of 2010, "assurances" regarding security.

HE WENT STRAIGHT TO the flat to work. After checking out of the hotel the next day, he flew to Rome, where he repeated the scenario at the Galleria Nazionale d'Arte Moderna e Contemporanea. There he let it be known he'd been called back to London by the client.

He flew to London, then erased Dauphine, became Jacques Picot, and drove in his newly purchased Mini back to the flat in Paris.

There, with a scruffy beard, long dark hair, John Lennon glasses, a silver stud in his left ear, and a prominent nose, he worked two full weeks on plans for the heist.

And there, he learned LaPorte had gotten more than a whiff.

Later, he'd imagined what might have happened if he hadn't decided to take a walk on a pretty autumn afternoon in Paris, hadn't decided to indulge in a pastry, and wandered by the George V with it.

If he hadn't seen LaPorte sliding out of the limo and, flanked by his bodyguard, greeted by the hotel manager, walking into the grand old hotel.

The hotel within walking distance of the museum. Within walking distance of his flat. To check in only days before he'd planned to steal the Matisse.

The world could be a small place, but not that small.

He didn't run, but kept right on strolling, and cursed himself for returning to Paris, to Europe. He should have crossed it off the list—and now he would.

In the flat, he broke down his equipment, packed, and wiped down every surface. To tie off loose ends, he contacted the land-lord and tearfully told him his grandmother in Nice had died, suddenly and unexpectedly.

As he drove out of Paris, he thought of the weeks of work, the planning, the travel, the damn Matisse, all gone for nothing because one man had decided to own him.

He'd dropped some crumbs somewhere, he thought. Just enough, somewhere, for whoever LaPorte had on his ass to follow.

And but for a pain au chocolat, he'd very likely have been cornered, again. He didn't go back to London, or drive to Nice, but made his way to Calais, where he sold the Mini for peanuts, boarded a train—another look, another name—to Belgium.

He traveled from Belgium into Germany, shedding personas like skin until he was certain he didn't feel any breath on the back of his neck.

He arrived in New York a few days before Christmas and lost himself in the city for most of a cold, lonely winter.

ON FAT TUESDAY, MAGS danced in the street with Sebastien. Traditions deserved respect, after all. The evening was young, but Dauphine and Luc had a toddler to get home to, and Mardi Gras ran all day. They could have danced on the balcony of her pretty house and seen most of the action, thrown their beads to those reveling below.

But not on Fat Tuesday.

She and Dauphine had pulled in constant business that week in the Crystal Ball, the gift shop and physic reading room they ran in the rooms below that balcony.

Life, Mags thought as the music blared and the beads flew, was almost perfect. It would have rung the bell on perfect if she heard from Harry—Booth—Silas—whatever name he carried now.

But he'd warned her communication would have to be spotty for a while longer.

She always carried the phone, just in case, but it hadn't rung or vibrated in more than six weeks. So she carried the nagging worry along with it.

Then it did. It vibrated in her pocket as trumpets blared.

She yanked it out, had to remind herself not to use names yet—in case. She just said, "Hello."

"Hi, Mags. Happy Mardi Gras."

"Oh, pal, it's so good to hear your voice." She gripped Sebastien's hand as she spoke, and the look she sent Dauphine, just a little teary, said it all.

"Yours, too."

"Can you tell me where you are?"

"I'm standing on the balcony of your place. You guys look great."

"Oh my God, you're here! He's here!" She looked up, over, saw him. "We're coming. We're coming right now."

She scooped up Wiley, kept her hand clamped on Sebastien's.

"He's not going anywhere, *cher*," Sebastien told her. "We're just walking on home now." He lifted her hand to kiss it. "Just strolling on home."

She slowed, though she knew he'd never have come if he wasn't sure it was safe.

Dauphine unlocked the door to the shop. Then Mags did run. She pushed the dog into Sebastien's hands, dashed toward the door to the residence, already open, where he waited for her.

He met her halfway.

"Here you are!" Her arms flew around him. "Finally, here you are."

"Missed you," he murmured against her wild, wonderful hair. "And you," he added, looking at Sebastien over her head. "You sure pick ugly dogs."

"Got character, this one."

"He'd have to, to make up for that face."

His gaze shifted to Dauphine's, just held there before he looked at Luc. Maybe an inch or two shorter than he was, but broader in the shoulders. He wore his hair in short twists and had, in Booth's opinion, a world of patience in his eyes.

"Luc, nice to meet you finally. Please don't punch me."

He released Mags to pull Dauphine in, kissed her. Glanced down at the small but visible baby belly. "Both of you. I'm sorry I couldn't make the wedding, or meet Giselle."

She rubbed a hand on his stubble, ran it through the thick hair that fell over his collar. "You'll meet her now."

"I've seen the pictures and videos. She's got your eyes, and attitude."

"Attitude for sure," Luc confirmed.

She stepped back, shook her head. "Still got that pretty face. I'm glad to see it in person again."

"Let's go up. Let's all go up, sit down, have a drink, catch up." Mags swiped at her eyes. "When did you get in?" she asked as they started up the stairs.

"A couple of days ago."

"Couple of days!"

"I wanted to be sure. I'm sure. I like your place, your shop, too. Good security."

"Not good enough."

Booth grinned at Sebastien. "For most it is."

"You'll stay here."

He nodded at Mags. "I'd like to, for a while. You fixed this place up," he said to Luc. "You do good work."

"Only kind worth doing."

They walked into Mags's colorful living room with its forest of pillows, its rain of crystals. Outside the French doors, Mardi Gras rocked.

Wiley, shed of the leash, pranced over to snuggle into a throne of a dog bed. He grinned at Booth.

"This one likes me. He doesn't look as if he'd like to explode my brain with the power of his."

"I'm going to open that champagne you've been saving, *cher*. And I give you this much." Sebastien held two fingers close together toward Dauphine. "And the rest orange juice."

Dauphine patted her belly. "He can handle that."

"A boy."

She smiled at Booth. "So the cards say."

She snuggled into an oversize bright red chair with Luc in a way that told Booth that was their usual spot here.

They looked good together, he thought. Right together. He'd thought the same when he'd seen wedding pictures and family pictures, but seeing them now locked that down.

He heard the distinctive pop from the kitchen, and Sebastien's *Woo!*

"Can you just stay?" Mags asked. "Just settle in and stay? New Orleans works for you."

"It always did. But he's too close here, and he's got too long a reach."

"Curse myself." Sebastien brought in the bottle, glasses, a jug of juice on a tray. "Curse every damn day I ever brought you in on that job."

"Fate's fate. If it hadn't been that, it would have been something else. It's on him, not you. All of it's on him."

"What're you going to do?" Mags took Booth's hand again. "Where will you go? If you go back to Europe—"

"Not there, not for a few years anyway." If ever. "I've got some ideas, some plans, a couple of places in mind." He sent her a reassuring smile. "It's time for that sabbatical."

"I'll absolutely drink to that." She passed him a glass after Sebastien poured, waited until everyone had one. "To a nice, long, happy sabbatical."

Though at the moment he didn't count on happy, he drank.

Two out of three wasn't bad.

Chapter Sixteen

HE'D DRIVEN FROM NEW York to New Orleans in a new Volvo bought nearly as much for sentiment as efficiency. Leading with sentiment, he'd revisited the Smokies and the Outer Banks, and they'd struck him with the same wonder as the first time.

Though he didn't precisely retrace the route he'd taken at eighteen, he used the back roads more than highways, stopped at motels and diners where cash payment didn't raise an eyebrow.

Though it still warmed him, still welcomed him, he understood New Orleans wasn't his place anymore. It was, and always would be, a respite, a place to connect with family and friends, and maybe his younger, more innocent self.

He experienced the sensations of being apart and separate when he saw the obvious connection and affection between Mags and Sebastien. They shared nearly a decade of history he had only pieces of. And seeing Dauphine with her sassy little girl, with another kid cooking, brought on those same sensations.

He hadn't been a part of their daily lives for too long to slide seamlessly back into them. Maybe that could change—if he had time. But LaPorte's headquarters in Lake Charles came too close for anything approaching comfort.

To protect the people he cared about, he had to create more distance.

To create distance meant re-creating himself, again. His past, his present, and for a while, his future.

"A teacher?" Mags said as they sat on her balcony in the cool February sunlight.

"I've used it before. And I can handle high school-level English, and the theater courses."

"I don't doubt that one. Is it going to be enough for you?"

"Don't know, but I've got two potentials. A private high school outside Atlanta, and a public one in Virginia, under two hours from DC."

"Georgia's closer to Louisiana."

"Yeah, there's that." Maybe too close, and that factored in. "Anyway, I've applied for the position, done a few online and phone interviews. Next up is in person. My persona's Sebastian—I'm spelling it the usual way—Sebastian Xavier Booth, originally from Chicago. Double majored in English lit and education, with a minor in theater at Northwestern. I did really well."

"I bet you did."

He stretched out his long legs. "Got my masters, in both, down here at Tulane—where my aunt lives. Stuck it out to get one in theater. Toured Europe between times, and after. Trust fund, you know."

"Oh yeah." She snickered. "We Booths are totally trust funders. Did you ever actually teach?"

"Sure. New York. I considered it a fallback while I tried to break in on Broadway and acting, then discovered it was my true path. But New York wasn't my place. I'm looking for a quieter life, and one where I can connect, have more impact with students."

She reached over to rub his arm. "Are you, pal?"

"Yeah, that quieter life sounds good right now. I'll find out about the teaching part. I liked tutoring, but this'll be a long way from that one-on-one sort of deal. The main thing is disappearing. I don't see LaPorte—or anyone sniffing for the Chameleon—looking at a high school teacher in some small to midsized town."

"And what about your nightwork?"

"We'll see about that. I know how to be careful, and to keep things outside my own nest. Plus, sabbatical, add quiet life, lesson plans, and putting on shows. And all that hinges on me scoring the gig."

"I know you, pal. You'll get the job if you want it. How the hell are you going to pass the audition? They're going to check all this."

"Computers. Technology." He wiggled his fingers. "Magic. I'm leaving you another phone, and I'm going to do some of that magic to your computer. You can expect a contact from both schools. You'll be Dr. Sylvia Fine, the headmistress of the Robinwood Academy in New York. We'll go over all that, but you know the drill. Sebastien's going to handle any inquiries to Tulane, and I'll take care of Northwestern myself. I don't see them going too deep. They'll have my transcripts, letters of recommendation, but we'll cover it."

"Any regrets that you need to cover it?"

"No." He shook his head, shrugged, stretched out his yard of leg. "No point in them. I did what I had to do, then I got to like it. Hell, Mags, I always liked it."

Nodding, she sat back, looked out on the post-Mardi Gras quiet of the neighborhood. "Read any good books lately? Like, say, a southern literary-type thriller set in the world of academia?"

It pinched, more than a little. "*Publish or Perish* by Miranda Emerson. Yeah, I read it. It's good, really good. No surprise. And yeah, I recognized myself in the opportunistic prick and second victim. I deserved my untimely and brutal death."

"No, you didn't." The rare scolding tone made him feel twelve again. "You did what you had to do."

"It can be both. I do regret Miranda," he admitted. "I waver between regretting getting involved with her in the first place and hurting her because I did. I guess that can be both, too."

"It hurt you, too."

"I got through it." Water under the bridge, over the dam, he told himself and always tried to believe it. "We were kids."

"Oh, my man, you had to stop being a kid before you were ten." She looked over at him. "When do you leave?"

"I've got the interview in Georgia Tuesday afternoon."

"Okay then. Let's make the most of the time we have."

They had music and food. He bonded with Luc over home repairs and fell desperately under the spell of the effervescent Giselle.

He sat with Sebastien on the porch of the bayou cottage on his last day, and Wiley napped sprawled over Booth's left shoe.

"This dog's ugly, but he's got excellent taste."

"That old Bluto, he never tried to take a chunk out of you, so he liked you fine enough. Young Wiley here, he likes everybody. He has to grow into more discrimination. You should get yourself a dog, *mon ami*."

"Can't stuff a dog in a go pack when you've gotta run."

"You don't want to hear it, but I look back on that damn job, my bum ankle, and that fucking LaPorte." He shook his head, sighed as the river flowed by. "You did that job so slick! Just a boy, that's the truth, and so slick. Born with that talent, and how're you supposed to not use what comes to you when you're born?"

"The job wasn't the problem. Doing it too well turned out to be."

"Fucking LaPorte. That fucking painting."

"Beautiful work. I can still see it in my head, still feel that wonder and admiration. One day I'm going to steal that and the statue back."

"You stay clear of that pig of a man."

"Oh, I will. But one day he's going to come home to that palace of his and find those gone. And he'll know I bested him. He stole one possible future from me. I'll take what he loves most. Possessions."

Sebastien stayed silent, watched the river. Then he nodded again.

"*Maintenant, mon ami*, if you need help with this, with something else, you call on Sebastien. I'm there for you, me."

"I know you are. You're looking out for Mags, and that covers a lot of ground for me."

"I love that woman. Love her so sometimes my heart, it's too big inside me. So I don't make her my wife. And she'll never be my fourth ex-wife."

That was one way to look at it, Booth decided. A way that clearly worked for Sebastien and Mags. And that's all that mattered.

When he drove away from New Orleans Monday morning, he knew the people he cared about would take care of each other.

SINCE HE INTENDED TO remain at the school that hired him for at least a year—hopefully two—he wore no disguise. He went into the interview as he now thought of himself. Sebastian Booth wore a good stone-gray suit—a Hugo Boss—and carried a leather briefcase. After all, he came from money, as most of the students in the academy did.

Those students wore uniforms, also gray, blazers with the school's logo in red on the breast pocket. No hair color not in nature was permitted, and hair—for boys—had to be trimmed above the collar. Only clear nail polish allowed, no visible tattoos or piercings other than earlobes. Only two earrings—studs only—were acceptable.

He hadn't thought the rigid dress code would bother him. He liked structure, organization, and understood the school of thought that believed such deviations from "the norm" served as distractions to education.

But it did, in fact, bother him, almost as much as the self-satisfied air wafting down the halls bothered him.

Even with the uniforms he could spot the jocks, the nerds, the bullies, and the bullied.

Maybe he could make a difference—which he intended to try to do wherever he landed. But though he found the campus lovely, and the school's architecture interesting, he knew within ten minutes of the interview he didn't want to land there.

Of course, he'd take it—and adjust—if the one in Virginia didn't work out. But he'd take it with an eye to moving on as soon as possible.

He'd planned to stay the night in the area, drive around, walk around, get a feel for the community. Instead, he drove north, and arrived two days early in the interesting town of Westbend—so named, he'd read, as it spread on a western bend of a northern sliver of the Rappahannock.

It had charm with its well-presented Main Street in the downtown/old town section, in its small harbor, with its views of water, forest, mountains.

Enough charm, he knew, to draw some tourists, some hikers, some kayakers and day sailors. It missed being a big draw by a matter of miles. Tappahannock to the south grabbed that bag, as did the water towns along the Chesapeake and the higher-end waterfronts of the Potomac.

But he liked the feel of it. Big enough he could blend, but not so big he'd feel swallowed up.

And should he have to leave abruptly, he could wind his way to 95, and get gone.

He drove past the high school; Westbend only had one, which might be a small problem, but not insurmountable. It didn't have the grace and dignity of the private school in

Georgia, but he liked the solidity of the red brick, and the sprawl of it, the nice grove of trees, the soft roll of grass.

He noted the track, the football stadium—and home of the regional champs, the Westbend Catfish.

He scanned the parking lots—both students' and teachers'—and wound through the campus to drive by the smaller middle school, the elementary.

It all felt . . . normal, he decided.

He circled back to Main Street, parked. He'd walk around, he thought, get that feel. Maybe get a burger.

A gift shop, a bookstore—and damn if they didn't have Miranda's book in the front window. Not all by itself, but there it sat. He couldn't see the photo on the back, but he'd already studied every inch of it. That gorgeous fall of hair, left loose for the head-and-shoulder shot, those sea-witch eyes staring straight out, the wide mouth curved in just the slightest hint of a smile.

He went in because he couldn't resist a bookstore, and liked knowing he'd have one right on Main Street if he landed.

He bought another thriller—he already had hers—with plans to start it in his hotel room that evening.

The very friendly bookseller recommended the Main Street Grill for the burger—just a block down.

He started down the block, then stopped at Westbend Real Estate.

He'd planned—again should he land—to rent at least for a month or two, then consider buying if he felt he'd stick for those two years.

But he hadn't counted on the house in the photo displayed in the window.

A good-size house. Not huge, but certainly bigger than he needed. Not in town, so not walkable to school, and that had been on his list. And with over an acre of land, more than he'd planned on.

Lists and plans went out the window, and he went in the door.

A woman—the only current occupant—swiveled away from her computer and beamed a smile at him.

"Afternoon. Anything I can do for you?"

He pegged her at about his age, curvaceous in a red sweater and with a blunt swing of dark honey hair framing a pretty face.

"The house on Waterside Drive—in the window—caught my eye."

"Terrific property, and it just came on the market this week. Four bedrooms, with one on the main floor that would serve as a home office or study. Master with an en suite—that was recently remodeled. Another full bath on the second floor, a roomy half bath on the main. A bonus outside shower. Original hardwood floors throughout, and in good shape. The kitchen's the centerpiece of the house, in my opinion."

She gave him that smile again. "Do you or anyone in your family cook?"

"It's just me, and I do." But too big for him, he thought. He didn't need all that space.

"You'll love it. Double wall ovens, under-the-counter microwave and ice maker. A little butler's pantry, with sink and wine fridge. Well, you should just see it instead of me sitting here talking it up. How's now?"

"I— Sure, if that works for you."

"Just me here today. My partner's out of the office. I'll just put the sign on the door and drive you out to see it."

"I'd like to take a look, but I don't want to waste your time. I'm here for a job interview, and if I don't get it—"

"Well, welcome to Westbend." She rose, swung on a jacket. "Tracey Newman." She stuck out a hand.

"Sebastian Booth."

"Welcome, Sebastian, and good luck with the job. Showing a house is never a waste of my time. My car's right out back." She gestured, started to lead the way. "What kind of job?"

"Teaching. The high school."

232

"The new English teacher?"

"And theater." Maybe, he thought, the town was too small after all.

"Right. My uncle's assistant principal, so I heard they were looking for someone." She led him out the back to a four-car lot and her compact SUV. "There's some wiggle room on the list price—there always is—but it's fairly steep on a teacher's salary."

"I have other sources of income. Family money," he added after what he deemed came off, as intended, as a slightly embarrassed hesitation.

"Good for you, because it's a sweet property. Coincidentally, Ms. Hubbard—the house belongs to Gayle and Robert Hubbard—is who you'll be replacing when—not if—you get the job. I believe in positive thinking."

She pulled out of the lot, took a side street. "She decided to retire and they're moving to Kentucky to be closer to their daughter and grandkids. Her daughter married a horse trainer down there. Anyway, they've had subs in her classes since after winter break."

She shot him a glance. "I'm going to give you an edge. If you can start pretty much now, they'd lean in your direction."

"I thought it was August."

"I'm giving you an edge. I take it you don't mind being a little out of town."

"Not at all. It's on the water."

"Great views of the river, the hills, the woods. There's a small dock out back—the house faces the road, the river runs behind it. Mr. Hubbard's a keen gardener, so it's got nice curb appeal. Are you in the market for a boat?"

"Maybe a kayak. I like to kayak."

"Rick's Water Sports, the north end of Main. We believe in shopping local."

"Okay."

"So where are you from, Sebastian?"

"From Chicago originally, but I've been teaching at a private school in New York. I wanted a change."

"A private school in New York to Westbend High?" She laughed. "I'd call that a change."

She turned down a gravel road that cut through the woods and opened up to the house.

Two stories, a stone base topped by silvered cedar, it wasn't a box, not with the jut to the south—probably an addition. A covered front porch and, he knew from the photo, a deck on the second floor in the back. A lot of windows, he noted, so a lot of light.

It looked sturdy and simple, warm and cared for, with a lawn he could mow and shrubs and ornamental trees he'd have to figure out.

He thought: Shit. Shit. It's perfect.

Maybe Tracey caught his vibe, because she beamed at him again. "Let me be the first to welcome you home, Sebastian."

She got out, gestured toward the house. "You can see, the property's been well maintained. The interior—you'll soon see Mrs. Hubbard liked strong colors—could use a little buffing up here and there. And you may want to tone down some of those strong colors."

They walked up the three steps to the porch. "The roof's only got five years on it. This porch needs a swing. They took theirs with them. Mr. Hubbard and their oldest son built it, so sentimental."

She punched a code into the lockbox—which he noted and filed away out of habit—to retrieve the keys.

"No alarm system?"

"No, and they lived here thirty-six years without incident. But if you're in the market, I can make some recommendations."

She turned the key—standard lockset, Mission style in matte black, no dead bolt. The door opened into a living room/great room area—with fireplace and a sight line back to the kitchen, which told him they'd likely taken down some walls in the last decade.

He'd been right about the light—it just streamed in—and she hadn't lied about the strong colors.

Mrs. Hubbard had gone with what he decided was something like terra-cotta, and it had impact with the turquoise of the built-ins that flanked the fireplace.

"A bold choice," Tracey commented.

"Brave. Reminds me of my aunt."

"In a good way or a bad way?"

"There is no bad way with my aunt."

"That's so sweet. So. You can see the floors are in great shape, and they run throughout. Mr. Hubbard's a contractor, and they remodeled over the years. It's good work."

"I can see that."

He let her ramble—half bath, main floor bedroom or home office, fully modernized kitchen, where the bold and brave Mrs. Hubbard had gone with a softer blue on the cabinetry and lots of glass fronts, a white granite island, a farm sink, and a back-splash that married the blues and terra-cottas in a pattern that reminded him of Italy.

But what he saw, really saw, was the view through the double glass doors to a slate patio and beyond. He saw the river and its lazy run.

"Laundry-slash-mudroom here, and dining area there. I tried to talk them into letting me stage it, but they waved that one off."

She opened those glass doors, walked him out and around, talking about the grounds, the gardens, the little dock. He heard her data on the furnace, the water heater, and so on. But he knew he'd been sold the minute he'd seen the photo in the window.

The job remained the sticking point.

He asked the right questions, the questions a man who didn't already imagine himself looking at those views for the next year or two of his life would ask, and toured the second floor.

He liked the master, with its atrium doors leading onto the deck, and its more-than-generous walk-in closet offered potential for a private work space. He'd have to live with the choice of lavender walls awhile, but holy shit, he had a bed-room fireplace. Small, gas burning, with a chunky wood shelf over it as mantel.

If and when he deemed it safe for Mags to visit, he had a guest room for her and Sebastien. And yet another bedroom with a walk-in closet. Not as generous as the master, but enough to alter his vague plans. The whole space could work for him.

No basement, and a carport rather than a garage, but an attic space. Another possibility.

"Want to toss out an offer?" Tracey asked him.

"I have to get one first. If I do, yeah, it's what I'm looking for."

"You ready for the interview?"

"I'm ready enough. It's the day after tomorrow."

"How about now?"

"Sorry?"

"Uncle Joe—assistant principal. And I'm in a book club with Lorna—Principal Lorna Downey. Why don't I make a call, then drive you over there?"

"I'm . . . I'm not really dressed for a job interview."

"Around here you are. Just give me a second."

She took out her phone and wandered outside. He heard her say, "Hi, Lorna, it's Tracey. Guess who's taking a look at the Hubbard place?"

He'd planned to get a burger, drive around the area. He tried to avoid impulse because it often led to mistakes, and mistakes often led to five to ten in a state-run facility.

But . . .

Tracey strolled back in, closing and locking the doors behind her. "Principal Downey would be delighted to meet with you now."

"Well, wow. Thanks. I think."

"Tell you what. If you get the job, you buy me dinner. If you get the job and buy the house, I buy you dinner."

He looked back at her, the pretty face, the take-charge attitude. "Sounds like a win for me."

He felt the town suited his needs for a temporary respite. He felt the house more than suited his needs for privacy and ambiance.

The school, when he walked in, checked off the last box.

The kids looked like kids. Ripped jeans, slouchy hoodies, jerseys, the occasional short skirt.

Plenty of hair with colors not found in nature.

As he walked in during the change of classes, the hallways filled with noise. Voices, slamming lockers, pinging phones.

He noted a trophy case and the awards in it. Football, soccer, softball, track, lacrosse, cross-country, basketball.

Sports, sports, and more sports. He spotted one for chorus—all-county—and another for the debate team—regional champs. But sports dominated, and football dominated sports.

He followed the directions Tracey had given him and turned right, then left into the administration office.

The harried-looking woman at the counter gave Booth the eyeball, then flicked a glance back at the boy sulking on the other side of the barrier. "You get on back to class now, Kevin."

He sulked his way out, and Booth caught the faintest whiff of pot clinging to his hoodie.

"Good afternoon." Booth stepped up. "I have an appointment with Principal Downey. Sebastian Booth."

"I know. She's squeezing you in, throwing the rest of the day off schedule." She pushed a button. "Principal Downey, your *un*scheduled appointment's here."

"Okay, Marva. Send him right in."

Marva pointed to a door with the word PRINCIPAL etched on the frosted glass. "I reckon you can read if you're after a teaching position."

"Yes, ma'am, thanks. Sorry about the schedule," he added as he crossed to the door.

Marva said, "Humph."

Before he could knock, the door opened.

He'd researched Lorna Downey and knew she'd graduated from the school she now ran before pursuing her degrees at the University of Maryland. He knew she was a mother of three, grandmother of two. He knew she'd been married to Jacob Po for twenty-nine years.

He knew she was the same age—fifty-two—as the headmistress in Georgia. But that, as far as he could see, was where the similarity ended.

She was short and wiry with her highlighted brown hair whacked into a short cap. Brown eyes studied him as she reached out a hand to shake.

She wore a basketball jersey in the school colors of red and white. She had a tattoo on her ropey left biceps, in Mandarin.

"Mr. Booth, thanks for coming right in! Please excuse the wardrobe and the disarray. We're having a rally for the basketball team."

"I appreciate you fitting me in."

"No problem, no problem." She gestured to a chair before she crossed to her desk—and its current disarray. "Coffee?"

"No, thanks." He always felt obligated to explain. "I don't really drink it."

She nodded as she hit the pot on a hot plate for a mug. "And what planet are you from again?"

"The Planet Coke."

She held up a finger, opened the door of a little cold box. She had a bright red tracker watch on her wrist.

"Only got Pepsi." She offered him a bottle.

"I'll suffer through it without judgment."

She sat, leaned back, studied him over the rim of the mug as she drank her coffee black. "You have an impressive application. Résumé's a little thin with all the traveling you've done."

"Seeing the world, visiting countries where English isn't the first language is another form of education." He gave a slight nod to her tattoo. "'Teachers open the door but you must walk through yourself.' I wanted to try a lot of doors."

"You read Mandarin?"

"A little."

"I didn't notice that on your list."

"Only a little, so I can't claim to be fluent."

"But you are in several other languages. Still, you've opted to focus on English and theater as an educator."

"I did some tutoring in high school and in college, so I knew where I wanted to focus. I didn't know I wanted to teach at all, really. I considered it a fallback sort of thing, until I didn't."

"A man in your position, financially, doesn't need a fallback."

"Travel's educational. It's exciting and it's satisfying, but it's not a purpose. It took me some time, but I figured out I wanted to open doors."

"That's a good answer." She took another long sip of coffee. "I just got off the phone with the headmistress of your school in New York."

"How is she?"

"She seems well, and very sorry to lose you. She had a great deal of complimentary things to say about your intellect, but I could glean that myself by the transcripts. She tells me you have a way of connecting with students, and a skill for reading the room. A true love for education and the arts."

Nice job, Mags, he thought.

"I appreciate all of that. My mother and my aunt gave me the gift of books, the love of stories. Books and theater tell stories, and can draw students in, open those doors, encourage questions, participation, build confidence."

"I agree. And still, Westbend is a long way from New York, in distance, in culture, in pace. And Westbend High's a long way from a fancy private school."

No pushover, this Principal Downey, he thought. And realized he wanted the damn job, *this* damn job, as much as he wanted that damn house.

He wouldn't charm his way into it, not with this woman, and he figured her bullshit meter was fine-tuned.

So straight truth.

"Which is why I'm here. I had an interview with a private academy a few days ago, and I realized immediately, it wasn't a good fit. If they offer me the position and you don't, I'll take it because I want to teach, but it wouldn't be my first choice. I want to teach in a structure that isn't so rigid and privileged, where the students come from the area. Where they live where they learn. I want that sense of community and connection.

"You don't have a Shakespeare Club."

She lifted her eyebrows. "No, we don't."

"You have the Drama Club, and that's important for the students who have that passion. Down on the feeding chain, I expect, and understand, from the football team, basketball, and so on. I get that. But Shakespeare can speak to a lot of young minds if you open the door the right way. And once they walk through, worlds open. I'd like to start one, if I join the staff here."

"I'll warn you it would be on your own time, and a very small group."

"I've got time, and starting small isn't a problem."

She sat back again, swiveled left and right in her chair. "Let's talk a little about your teaching philosophies, and the rules of the road—such as they are at WHS."

They talked another thirty minutes, during which he realized he liked her on a personal level, and he wanted to work with her nearly as much as he wanted the job and the house.

"You're young," she added, "and damn good-looking. Please don't sue me for that observation. They'll think they can eat you alive."

He smiled. "They'll find out I'm hard to chew and tougher to swallow."

She swiveled again. "How soon can you start?"

"Really?"

"They're making mincemeat out of the subs in Hubbard's classes, because they can. And because they can, they're not learning on the level they should be. The spring musical is both important and popular, and they haven't picked the play, held auditions."

"*Grease*. It's relatable because it's about high school. The costumes and makeup aren't complicated. You can tailor the choreography to the skill sets. I'd need to look at the space, see the tech, but that's an easy pick, especially if you're pressed."

She set the mug aside, rubbed lightly at her eyes. "We did *Grease* . . . it has to be ten or twelve years back. I was still teaching, hadn't moved into administration. Big hit. So I repeat, when can you start?"

He decided to echo Tracey. "How about now?"

Chapter Seventeen

IT WASN'T QUITE THAT simple, but it was close.

Within two weeks he bought the house, and moved right in by agreeing to rent it until closing.

He met his fellow teachers, attended his first basketball game, familiarized himself with those who'd be his students.

Instagram and TikTok were treasure troves there, and Facebook filled in from the parental and grandparents end of things.

He did the paperwork and paid the fees to authorize the school's performance of *Grease*, and posted a notice for auditions. Posted another for a Shakespeare Club.

He had to furnish the house, outfit the kitchen, and he shopped local. Slowly, carefully, he began to knit himself into the fabric of the community. Being part of the whole meant you blended in.

Outsiders stuck out.

He felt confident at the head of a classroom, and mildly terrified of producing and directing a high school musical.

Some did try to chew and swallow, but he'd prepared for that.

It started on day one, class one.

The smirking kid in the back of his lit class had a smattering of teenage acne and a bad attitude.

Since the sub had assigned *To Kill a Mockingbird* the week

before, he opened the class to discussion. And the smirking kid called out.

"What's the point of reading stuff by dead white guys anyway? It's got nothing to do with now."

"Actually, Harper Lee's a dead white woman, and I take it—it's Kirby, right?"

He noted the boy's surprised reaction to being addressed by name.

"Yeah, so?"

"I take it you haven't cracked the book as yet or you'd know this particular story has a great deal to do with now. Since you haven't, you can listen to the discussion, which today's going to explore the narration of Scout, a young white girl, and the racial stereotypes, racism, and racial injustice—all of which still exist in the now—she relates throughout the story."

Kirby shrugged, folded his arms over his chest, and closed his eyes as if taking a nap. Snickers ensued.

"And, Kirby, after reading the assigned book, you'll write an essay—five hundred words—supporting your statement, or mine. Your choice."

That popped his eyes open. "You can't make me write that crap and nobody else."

"Write it or don't. Don't? Find another class, because I'm in charge of this one. You made a statement, now you'll back it up or retract it, in a five-hundred-word essay. You're one student in a class of twenty-four, Kirby, and you've wasted enough of everyone's time complaining. I'll add this."

He paused, waiting for the mutters, snickers, shuffling to quiet down.

"A lot of the required reading books might seem out of step, at least on the surface. And not all of them are going to interest some of you, maybe most. So, with that in mind, every four weeks we're doing a free read. You read what you want, and turn in a report on it."

"*Deadpool!*" somebody shouted out.

"Graphic novels accepted."

The kid—Ethan, Booth remembered—stared in shock. "No joke?"

"In this class we respect the written word. We may not agree with the writer, we may not enjoy the story or characters, but we respect the written word, and we're free to express our opinions on a book—positive or negative. Now, back to Scout."

He got through the first day, then the second. He held auditions with the help of the music and choral instructor, and got through those—with some very pleasant surprises.

Vocally, he had some strong voices to work with. On the acting side, a few with actual talent, and more with potential.

And a lot of energy.

He sweated over casting because he remembered what it was like—when he'd still been able—to try out for a high school play, then wait for the posting of the cast, the crew, the understudies.

A week flowed into two, and two weeks into a month crowded with lesson plans, rehearsals, club meetings—he had a total of five for the Shakespeare—staff meetings, grading papers.

He'd known, of course, teaching involved a lot more than teaching, but now he experienced it.

He took time to install a security system, and a secondary one on the bedroom upstairs he used to store his tools and wardrobe and the rest of his nightwork business.

Though he felt a twinge now and then, and a genuine yearning more than once to stand in a darkened house that belonged to someone else, he stuck to the rules of his sabbatical for the remainder of the school year.

He attended graduation, as some of his students wore cap and gown, and decided it served as a kind of graduation for himself, too.

He'd opened some doors, he'd handled more than a few problems, and he'd directed a pretty damn good play. More, he'd enjoyed it all.

Now, with summer vacation around the corner, and some actual time off, he'd do more kayaking on his river, spend a lazy morning or evening now and again sitting on his deck or patio. He'd read for pleasure, maybe have a barbecue for the other teachers and staff.

And if he took a trip to the wealthy DC suburbs and their lovely old homes filled with lovely things over the long summer? A man had to keep his hand in.

HE'D PLANNED FOR A year, possibly two, as Sebastian Booth, high school teacher, avid kayaker, theater enthusiast, and Shakespeare buff.

He liked himself in the role and enjoyed, more than he'd imagined, lighting a spark in a student.

He attended his second graduation and then his third. With his third, he watched Kirby—initial antagonist turned solid B student—cross the stage in cap and gown.

It made him proud, of the boy, and of himself for finding the key to Kirby's particular lock.

On that third summer, he weighed the pros and cons—stay or go.

The pros came easy. He liked his house, the area, the people, the work. And all of that snuggled into a spot just remote enough to keep LaPorte sniffing elsewhere. In fact, it seemed next to impossible LaPorte would continue to waste time and resources in pursuit of a single thief.

But the next to impossible carried weight.

He felt comfortable in Sebastian Booth's skin, and that ranked high. The fact he could see himself remaining in that skin for the long haul straddled the pro/con fence.

Ranking high on the cons? However comfortable the skin, it

didn't allow him to forge serious personal relationships. He had far too many reasons to avoid that basic human need.

Friendships? All good. The occasional and mutually agreed casual sex, no problem. But he couldn't risk real intimacy or a lasting connection.

Then again, he didn't see how that changed if he bailed out and picked it all up somewhere else as someone else.

Here, he had the change of seasons, and he'd seen them all now. The burgeoning banquet of spring, the sticky hot summer, the heartbreaking colors of autumn, and the quiet blanket of winter.

Whenever he went, wherever he went, he needed to find somewhere that gave him the same sense of peace and purpose.

As summer dragged her sweaty feet toward her finish line, he found himself back in the classroom. He looked out at the fresh new faces, the bored eyes, the eager ones.

"Good morning, I'm Sebastian Booth, and this is Language Arts. We'll be exploring various genres of literature, your critical thinking and writing skills. We'll start discussions on the first assigned book, William Golding's *Lord of the Flies*, next week. You can find it in the school library, the town library, at Books on Main, and possibly on a shelf in your own home."

He noted who wrote it all down, who stared out the window or up at the ceiling. And the pair who sat just across from each other who texted back and forth.

"I can make you read those texts out loud to the whole class before I take the phones," he said casually, "or you can put the phones away."

Phones vanished into pockets.

"Good choice."

He decided staying, for maybe just one more year, also made a good choice.

He fell into a routine that took him straight into winter break. Classwork, prep work, club meetings. Auditions, then rehearsals for *Four Weddings and a Funeral*, the senior class play, the various skits and monologues for his theater students. Add the in-depth discussions and debates on *As You Like It* in his now twelve-member Shakespeare Club.

Building sets, building minds.

He had a tree in the window, lights glowing on the eaves of his front porch roof, and a double batch of iced and decorated sugar cookies in a tin to take to Lorna's—Principal Downey's—holiday bash.

He left the house in a festive mood, only more lifted by the brisk air and a killer full moon. He looked forward to socializing with fellow teachers, friends, and others who made up Lorna's wide circle.

He tended to spend most evenings at home, but he never missed Lorna's holiday party, and hosted an annual summer barbecue himself.

He'd drop in for a pizza in town, had become a regular at Books on Main—though he backed off the urging to lead a book club, or just join. Until the depths of winter, he could be seen most weekends kayaking on the river.

He'd seriously considered getting a dog, but managed to fall back on what he determined was common sense and let it go.

Cars already crammed the drive and the street in front of Lorna and her husband Jacob's house.

They didn't stint on decorations. The entire two stories with attached garage winked in lights, as did the big maple that shaded the front yard. Elves scattered under it, and Santa rode his sleigh behind Rudolph on the rooftop.

Christmas might be over, and the world heading fast toward a new year. But here, Christmas lived and lived bright.

He didn't have to knock or ring the bell. An invitation to Lorna's meant: Come on in.

So he did, into lights and Christmas carols. People crowded into the living room and straight back to the kitchen with its long peninsula loaded with food.

Knowing the routine, he greeted and was greeted as he made his way back to the den to ditch his coat, then into the kitchen to put the cookies out on the already crowded dessert table.

Tracey, decked out in Christmas red, came up to kiss his cheek.

They'd dated a little, slept together twice, but both agreed friendship worked better for them.

He'd gone to her wedding the previous spring.

"Merry and happy. You brought those damn cookies, didn't you?"

"Guilty."

"My hips expand just thinking about them." She grabbed one anyway.

"You look amazing, as always."

"I feel amazing. I sealed a deal on the rental about a mile from you. Six-month lease, dead of winter. And to a celebrity."

"Whoa. Tell me it's Jennifer Lawrence. She owns my heart."

That earned an elbow poke and laugh. "I wish. But she's your kind of celebrity. You have to come meet her." She started scanning the crowd. "Her godmother moved here a few years ago, after a divorce, to get out of Dodge, so to speak. She's an old friend of Lorna's. And our celeb's here to spend some time with the godmother while she researches the area. And here she is! How's it going? Sebastian, I've got someone you have to meet."

He turned, and the world dropped away.

She'd drawn her hair back with two little braids over her ears so the rest fell, sun-drenched autumn leaves, down her back.

Those eyes, that witchy green, stared straight into his. He saw shock register.

"Miranda Emerson, bestselling novelist, Sebastian Booth. Sebastian's busy instilling a love for books and theater at Westbend High."

"Sebastian," she said, very slowly, very deliberately.

She could destroy everything with a word, and he couldn't

blame her. A word, and he'd get out, grab his go bag, and be gone.

It didn't seem to matter. Nothing did. But he reached out a hand, took hers. "It's nice to meet you. I really like your work."

"Do you?"

He wondered if only he heard that edge. "I do. I'm halfway through *Counterpoint*."

"Sebastian almost single-handedly keeps Books on Main in business. And it turns out the two of you are neighbors, or will be when you move in."

"Neighbors." Not an edge this time, he thought, but a kind of stunned laugh.

"Sebastian's house is about half a mile from yours, on the river. Oh, I see Marcy Babcock's cornered my Nick again. She's always wanting to sue somebody. Let me go save him."

He waited a beat, then said her name, just her name. "Miranda."

"Don't. I'm not going to make a scene and embarrass my godmother or Lorna. Not here, not now."

She walked away, and her scent lingered.

He couldn't just slip out, not without generating a lot of questions. Instead he poured himself a half glass of wine. He could stay out of her way for an hour. He didn't think his system could take more than an hour.

He gravitated toward a group, slid into it. Blended while everything inside him twisted and churned.

He'd have to leave, no question of that. How he left depended on Miranda. If she'd give him time, he'd create an emergency, list the house with Tracey, give Lorna a little time to replace him, or line up subs.

If she didn't, he'd pack up what he needed, say goodbye to Sebastian Booth, and disappear.

Maybe head west this time. Maybe freaking Alaska would be far enough away that fate couldn't put her in front of him again.

Couldn't put her where she stirred up all those old feelings. The ones he'd tried to lock away. Now she'd cracked the combination just by being. Those feelings were the only thing that hadn't changed in a dozen years.

He was still in love with her.

He talked, even laughed. He hugged Lorna and gave Jacob the man-version thereof. He nursed that half glass of wine for the full hour. He spotted her a couple times—that hair spilling down the back of a forest-green dress.

She met his eyes once, when she sat with Andy and Carolyn Stipper, the owners of the bookstore. And that look nearly dropped him to his knees.

He retrieved his coat, then slipped out the back like a—well, like a thief.

He drove home on autopilot, the festive mood shattered, and then just sat in his car. Put his head back, closed his eyes as everything she'd released swam through him.

His life—the life here he admitted now he'd wanted to keep, to build, to belong to, that was done. And he accepted that.

But how could he accept he'd never have a real life—anywhere, under any name—because he couldn't have her?

What kind of world was it that demanded he feel this, all of this, for the one woman out of his reach?

"Reality," he muttered as he slammed out of the car. "It's just fucking reality.

He'd nearly made it to the door when he spotted the headlights. His world shook one more time as the car pulled in behind his.

She hadn't wasted time.

He waited while she walked, the heels of her boots clicking on the slate. He started to speak without a clue what to say. And her fist plowed, with considerable force, into his gut.

She knocked the wind out of him. He had to suck it back in, ease it out again.

"I deserved that."

"You deserve a fist in the face, you absolute prick, but giving you a black eye would bring on too many questions."

"You're right, both counts. It's cold. Do you want to come in?"

"No, but I will."

He unlocked the door, reset the alarm once inside. "Let me take your coat."

"Don't touch me." She swung off the coat herself as she crossed the living room to toss it over a chair.

"Okay. Can I get you a drink, or—"

"Oh, please."

She looked like a warrior, ready for a battle she'd surely win. He saw pieces of the girl he'd known and loved, but the woman had a toughness she hadn't. She had a vibrating confidence and a lot of righteous fury.

"Sebastian Booth? What kind of bullshit is that? And you're teaching? Do you even have a degree? What the hell *is* your name?"

"Here and now, it's Sebastian Booth. Don't make me quote Shakespeare on names. I'm not going to tell you because it's better for both of us."

"You're a liar, and don't think I'm going to buy into your lies the way I did when I was twenty. Answer my questions, or I go straight to Lorna and your little game here's done."

"It's not a game, not the way you mean. But I'll go. I'll leave. If you could give me a few days, I'll—"

Fury had the roses in her cheeks blooming hot.

"Take off like before? Leave Lorna in the lurch, desert the kids she claims you teach so creatively? Just like you." She whirled away, whirled back. "Will your mythical aunt have another car accident?"

"She not mythical. She didn't have an accident, but she's not mythical."

"Anyone who'd lie about his mother dying of cancer would lie about anything."

"Stop." His voice whipped out on that, and he found some of his own temper simmering. "I was nine the first time my mother had cancer, the first time she went through the tests, through all the treatments and sicked up her guts from them. Think whatever you want about me, you're entitled. But don't diminish what she went through. She wasn't even thirty the first time, and she didn't live to see forty."

"Then why all the lies, Booth? You broke my goddamn heart, and made me ashamed of what I'd felt for you, what I did with you. You cheapened everything. You cheapened me."

"I meant to. I didn't know any other way. There was someone who wanted me to do something, who didn't give me a choice. To get it done, and get out, I had to go, just go. And I thought—I believed—making you hate me was better for you."

"That's not good enough, not even close. I cried buckets over you. You hurt me, Booth, the way no one ever had, or has again. 'Someone'? 'Something'? Not good enough. You're standing here in a house a high school teacher shouldn't be able to afford, you're using another name, and, according to Lorna, you graduated from Northwestern, which is another lie, and fraud. You were in North Carolina.

"So who and what and why."

She perched on the arm of a chair—didn't sit, he thought, as that was too casual, too friendly. She perched there, gestured to him.

"I get some truth or I swear to God, I will punch you in the face on my way to a serious conversation with Lorna."

He saw something he hadn't wanted to. Under the fury in those eyes lived hurt.

He was done here, he reminded himself. He could give her some truth first.

"His name's LaPorte, and he wanted me to steal a bronze sculpture. *Bella Donna*—it was worth several million then. Probably double that now since the theft."

She cocked her head, arched that eyebrow. "Why in the hell would somebody want or expect you to steal a statue?"

"Because that's what I do. I steal things." He sat now, partly because it took a weight off to just say it.

Chapter Eighteen

SHE CLEARLY DIDN'T BELIEVE him. Rather than shock at his revelation, she showed derision.

"So at about the age of twenty, you're forced by this LaPorte to steal a valuable piece of art. Successfully, I assume?"

"I'm good at what I do."

"Right." She pushed up. "I guess we're done here."

"Look it up. Take out your phone, Google it. *Bella Donna*, bronze, artist Julietta Castletti, stolen from the Hobart, a private museum in Baltimore. Just a few weeks after I left."

She took out her phone, and while she keyed in the details, he continued. "I took it to him at his place in Lake Charles, Louisiana—Christmas Day. Then I changed my name—and my look again. That's something else I'm good at. And I chartered a plane to Paris. I needed to keep away from him because he'd just do the same thing again, and again. It's a power trip for him."

She looked up from her phone. "Just because you know some details about this art theft doesn't mean you took it, or that anything you're telling me is the truth."

"For Christ's sake." He pushed up, moved toward the fireplace, brushing by her on the way. "I'm going to light the fire. What time is it?"

She looked immediately at her watch—a very nice Baume & Mercier. But it wasn't there.

He held it up. "This yours?"

Now he saw, if not shock, surprise.

"I've been picking pockets since I was a kid, a kid in Chicago with a sick mother in a mountain of debt."

He handed the watch back to her, then lit the starter under the kindling and logs. "I left and did the job for LaPorte, because he threatened to hurt Mags. My aunt. He sent someone to wreck her place when she wasn't there to prove he could. He would've hurt her, he might've hurt you, my friends, anybody I cared about. That's what he does, and he's good at it."

The firelight streamed across his face as he looked up at her. "So I left, and I hurt you."

"You're a thief."

"That's right." He pushed to his feet. "Jewelry and art, primarily. Stamps and coins, but they're not as satisfying."

"Satisfying?" She stood, stared at him. "You steal from people. You're a criminal, and it's *satisfying*."

"I'm trying not to lie to you."

"You—you break down doors and—"

"No, I don't. I deal with locks and security systems. I don't break anything. No violence against people or property. Major rule."

"You have rules?"

"Yeah, I have rules. A pretty long list, actually. I'm getting some wine. You can have some or not."

He walked back into the kitchen and chose a nice Chianti from the rack.

"You invade people's privacy and take what doesn't belong to you. For money."

He pulled the cork, got two glasses. He looked at her as he poured. Coolly.

"You never once, not once, had to worry about the roof of

that big, beautiful four-generation house staying over your head. Never once had to wonder if there was enough money to buy food. Never heard your mom crying at night when she thought you were asleep because the bills just kept coming.

"Hospital bills, doctor bills, mortgage payments, insurance that covered dick-all when it came down to it. You grew up privileged, so don't lecture me on what I've done for money."

"How I grew up has nothing to do with it."

"How I did has everything to do with it," he snapped back. "She did everything right. We lived within our means, bills got paid. She started a business and worked her ass off. She saved what she could—a cushion, she'd say. She wanted enough of one so we could take a vacation, a week at the beach. She wanted to see the ocean.

"Then none of that mattered anymore. Doing everything right didn't mean a damn thing. She got better for a while— remission. Yay. Then it came back, and a little harder. Bills, bills, bills, and her hair falling out in clumps again. Then remission again, and back again. Third strike, you're out.

"Have you ever watched somebody you love die of cancer?"

Miranda shook her head, picked up the wine. Drank.

"Don't lecture me about the choices I've made."

"Why are you here? Why are you teaching in a high school in Westbend, Virginia?"

"LaPorte got a little too close when I was still living and working in Europe. Maybe I got careless or too comfortable, I don't know, but he got too close. So I closed up shop there, so to speak, did some more traveling, and then came back to the States. Teaching's a good cover."

"A cover."

"You've developed an annoying habit of repeating what I say."

"Well, excuse me while I stand here and you tell me you're some international art thief. Jewel thief. Stamps and coins and pickpocket thief."

"You wanted to hear the truth, you're hearing it. I came here, to this school, because they clicked for me. This house clicked for me. I've stayed longer than I planned because I like it. I like it here, I like teaching, and putting on high school plays, watching kids light up. And I'm good at it. So, I've extended my sabbatical."

"Sabbatical."

"There you go again."

Her eyes flashed temper, but she took a slow sip of wine. "So, you've been taking a sabbatical from stealing things."

He drank again, let out a breath. "Mostly."

"And that means?"

"School breaks, I might take a trip. How's 'busman's holiday' sound?"

"Jesus, Booth."

"I don't do any nightwork here. I don't steal from people here. Not that people around here are ass-deep in invaluable jewels and art, but I just don't."

"Another rule?"

"One of the first. I never planned on staying more than a couple years, but I'm going to be sorry to leave. I'm trying to be sorry I saw you again, but I can't. I never could put you all the way behind me."

No flash of temper this time, just cold steel. "You don't want to go there. You'll end up with that black eye."

"Okay. But consider I've got Wonder Woman's golden lasso around me, so I have to tell the truth."

"What's your real name?"

"Not telling you isn't lying."

"That's not how the golden lasso works."

"You got me on that. I'm amending it. I still have people to protect."

She wandered back to the fire, stood studying it. "I'm asking myself if I'm an idiot because I believe at least most of what you've told me."

"There's no reason to lie once I started."

"I'm sorry about your mother, Booth. I'm sorry things were so hard and sad for you as a kid. You're right, I've never experienced anything close to that fear and grief. But I can't justify stealing your way through your life."

"I don't expect you to. It's my choice. What are you going to do about it?"

"I don't know." She turned back. "Do you have a gun?"

"A gun? No. Why would I?"

"For when you steal?"

"Jesus, no. I don't have a gun. I've never even held a gun. I don't want to. I steal things, Miranda. They're things—beautiful things, sure. Shiny things. Even important things. But they're not human beings. Not flesh and blood."

"What do you do if you're stealing something and get caught?"

"It hasn't happened."

"Ever?"

"No, I'm good at it. Look, I get what you're asking. No, I've never bashed somebody or shot somebody, stabbed, choked, or otherwise physically hurt anyone. Things, Miranda. People matter a whole lot more than things."

He paced. "I don't, you know, pull a mask on and bust up somebody's house or some jewelry store. I don't smash and grab, it's not how I work."

It felt awkward and a little embarrassing, but he continued. "In Europe they started calling me the Chameleon. That's another reason I pulled out. Somebody's pinned down your style, your method, and that means somebody's too close. You can look that up, too—it's just speculative stuff, but you can look it up."

"I will. I won't talk to Lorna tonight, but—"

"If and when, if you could give me twenty-four hours. Just a day."

"If I agree to that, will you still be here in the morning?"

"Yes. Lasso's still on. My life's in your hands. I guess you deserve that, too. You're here for six months. I won't leave until you say it's time. I could finish out the school year. You may not believe it, but that's important to me. I've got some kids who . . . I'd like to see them through the year."

"If you're here in the morning, I'll agree to the twenty-four hours. If you're gone, I contact the police and tell them everything you told me."

"Harsh but fair. I'll be here."

She picked up her coat. "I'm going to think about everything you've told me. Then I'll let you know what I decide. If you're still here."

She picked up her coat, and, shrugging into it, started for the door.

"I really do love your work," he told her. "Even though you killed me pretty gruesomely in *Publish or Perish*."

She glanced back. "It felt good. Liberating."

"I bet," he murmured when she closed the door behind her.

He sat by the fire, just put his head in his hands.

He could run. Grab what he needed, wipe down the house. Get into the school, do the same with his classroom. The sensible thing to do. Take off, disappear again.

But this time around, he wouldn't do the sensible.

He'd put his life in her hands, and he'd leave it there.

MIRANDA SAT BLEARY-EYED OVER her first cup of coffee in the sweet little kitchen in her sweet little rental.

She hadn't slept well, not with her mind churning and a vague anxiety over the possibility of a break-in.

Clearly, she knew someone capable of it.

She believed him. She didn't want to believe him, because she'd gotten comfortable thinking of Booth as a lying bastard. Which he was, she reminded herself, so she could stay comfortable there.

But she believed him about being a thief—and traveling the world doing just that. On a side note, she had to admit she really wanted to know how he'd gotten the watch off her wrist in a snap without her feeling a thing.

She certainly believed him about his mother, and could see very well how that long-going childhood trauma had formed him.

But if she let herself believe him, fully, on this LaPorte character, it changed things. Made things very uncomfortable.

She slid off the stool at the counter to go into the living room—a short trip—and switch on the gas logs in the fireplace.

The cozy two-bedroom with its river view suited her needs for the short term, but it was a long way from the big, sprawling home she'd lived in most of her life.

She'd promised her godmother a visit, and since her father was living the dream as a guest lecturer at Oxford for the next few months, it seemed the right time.

Add in the idea of moving out of her—okay, comfort zone—by setting a book off her home turf, it all made sense.

Cesca, her godmother, also had a sweet little house, one right in town. Because she wanted—needed—more room, and the privacy to work, she'd lovingly but firmly rejected Cesca's entreaties to stay with her.

This worked. It all seemed to work perfectly. Until, days after she'd celebrated Christmas with her father at home, driven him to the airport on a bright Boxing Day morning, less than twenty-four hours after she'd snapped up the rental and moved in, she'd gone to the party at Lorna's.

And he'd been there, the boy who'd crushed her heart to pulp.

"What are you going to do about it, Miranda? Just what the hell are you going to do?"

She didn't know, and had spent much of the sleepless night on that single question.

What she did know? He held a teaching job without

accreditation. He held it under a name that wasn't his own. Or probably wasn't. How would she know?

Maybe, like Fagin, he trained impressionable kids into his personal gang of thieves.

A stretch, sure, but how would she know?

She did what she always did when tackling a problem. She sat down with a second cup of coffee and her notebook. She made a list.

> Make sure the son of a bitch didn't just take off.
> LaPorte—Lake Charles, LA—research.
> "Chameleon" (Europe)—research.
> Discuss—subtly—Sebastian Booth with Cesca/Lorna/Tracey.
> Visit high school. Observe.
> Visit bookstore, ask questions—carefully.

She'd add to the list, no doubt, but considered it a good start. And she decided to start, right away, crossing items off that list.

She dressed, braided her hair, and applied careful makeup to disguise a restless night. The school had to wait until after the holiday break, but she could start covering some ground.

Though it sat in the opposite direction from town, she drove by Booth's house first.

His car sat under the carport, and smoke curled up from the chimney. Not absolute proof, she thought, but proof enough he hadn't taken off.

She turned around, headed into town.

She liked the look of the area, the way the road followed the river, the glimpses of mountains, the thick stretches of woods. She could paint a solid story on this canvas, she thought. Pull herself off her home turf, and see what happened.

The town worked, too. Not so small you'd constantly trip over someone you knew every time you took a step, but small enough you'd likely see friendly and familiar faces often.

The little harbor added the feel of a water town, and just the right ambiance with a hearty Main Street and all the offshoots.

She liked seeing the lights and decorations on most stores, most houses, and wondered what everything looked like when it snowed. Really snowed.

She found parking and took a stroll in the brisk breeze off the water. At the party, she'd managed to dance around the requests for a book signing. Though she couldn't imagine there'd come a time when she didn't feel grateful and just a little amazed anyone wanted her to sign her work, she wanted to settle in first.

And really wanted to dig into the story she'd barely begun to write.

No question this bookstore visit would box her in there, but she'd pay that price.

Seeing her book on display in the front window gave her a happy little jolt—something else she couldn't imagine fading in time. She admired the way whoever did the window arranged books with sidelines like candles, tote bags, and already knew she'd walk out with one of the T-shirts that read:

I ENJOY LONG ROMANTIC WALKS
THROUGH THE BOOKSTORE

She stepped inside, and as often happened on romantic walks, fell a little in love.

She saw a cozy chair with a stack of books on the table beside it. Shelves of books, of course, with a rack of the best sellers. Hers stood there—more amazement.

Her second novel had crawled briefly onto the bottom of the list, and her third hit dead center, even stuck there for a few weeks. Now it clung to the bottom, but there it sat at lucky number thirteen for a total on the list of seven weeks.

She had seconds, really, to take in the shop: cookbooks and

candles on an old kitchen table, holiday-themed books beside a tree festooned with ornaments for sale—ten percent off.

The air smelled of books and coffee—the perfect perfume.

Behind the counter formed by a reclaimed book cabinet, Carolyn Stipper clapped her hands.

"Miranda! Welcome, welcome! I'm so glad you came in."

"What a wonderful bookstore."

"Oh, you haven't seen anything yet. Let me show you around."

She got her tour while Carolyn chattered, and found it a warm, inviting midsize independent in a charming midsize town.

She stopped by a wall of books under the banner:

westbend students recommend

"Students?"

"That's right. Elementary, middle, and high school. The teachers do a survey every month, send us a list of the top-ten student picks. If we don't have the title in stock, we order it."

"What a terrific idea. It has to pull some kids into the store, and into the books."

"It does. I wish I could take credit for the idea, but Sebastian suggested it."

Miranda turned her head, struggled to keep her voice neutral. "Sebastian?"

"Sebastian Booth, he teaches English and theater at the high school. I thought you'd met him last night at Lorna's."

"Oh, that's right. I did. I guess he's a creative teacher with good ideas?"

"He gets top marks from me. Our oldest grandson's a freshman at WHS, and you'd think with a Granny and Pop owning a bookstore, he'd be an avid reader. Not at all, until recently. Still, Robbie's not what you'd call avid, but he's reading. And he doesn't complain as much about the required reading now that he's in Sebastian's class. Every month the students get to free read—pick any book they want—that's what you see up here for the most part."

She tapped one of the books, and happy pride bubbled in her voice. "This one's Robbie's—he raved about it. It's about teenagers and zombies in London. I read it so we could talk about it. I had a book discussion with my teenage grandson. That's almost enough for me to kick Andy to the curb and run off to Aruba with Sebastian."

Carolyn sent Miranda a wide smile. "And, speaking of books . . ."

Miranda agreed to the signing, bought the T-shirt, three books, and half a dozen candles.

She made her way down to the real estate company and found Tracey just taking off her coat.

"Hi! You caught me walking in and just missed Derrick, who just walked out to meet a client. How's it going in your new place?"

"I love it." Miranda handed her a gift bag. "Thank you."

"Thank you!" Tracey peeked inside. "Oh, I love candles, and I'm crazy about this jasmine scent."

"So Carolyn said."

"Can you sit, have some coffee?"

"I've had three cups of coffee already this morning, but thanks. I just wanted to thank you again for finding me the perfect place, and making all the details go through so smooth and fast."

"Cesca's so excited to have you here for a while. Plus, we don't get bestselling authors moving here—even for a few months— every day of the week. Did Carolyn talk you into doing an event?"

"She did. An evening event—signing, mingling, conversation—the middle of March."

"That's great, and I see her method. She gets a big bump for the bookstore, Main Street, and the town, right before the spring musical. The high school will have flyers everywhere. I heard they're doing *Bye Bye Birdie* this year."

"That's, ah . . . the teacher you introduced me to last night. Booth?"

"Sebastian Booth, he runs the theater students. The spring musical's a big deal around here, and he brings it home. He tried to break in on Broadway in New York, but didn't make it. I honestly think it's their loss."

"So he was an actor?"

"The way he tells it, he was and always will be a wannabe. But he sure helps the kids shine. He's single, you know, in case you were wondering."

"No." Miranda made sure to laugh. "I'm really not here for that, which is another reason the house works so well for me. Plenty of quiet to write in. But I'll make sure to see the spring musical. Now I'm going to stop by and see Cesca before I dive right into that quiet."

She drove the few blocks to Cesca's, pulled in behind her godmother's sturdy sedan.

Maybe she felt guilty planning to secretly pump the woman who'd stood as her mom for most of her life, but it had to be done.

Cesca, ash-blond hair bundled up, the sweatpants and scent of orange peel indicating she'd done some cleaning, fisted a hand on her hip.

"Didn't I give you a key and say you never had to knock on my door?"

"You did, but I wasn't sure you'd be up."

"It's eleven! Middle of the day. I've got the afternoon shift at the library, but that doesn't mean I lay around in bed all day."

She pulled Miranda in, hugged her, swayed with it.

"You don't know what it means to me to have you around

awhile, to know you can pop in that door anytime like you used to back home."

Miranda hugged back. "Is it still home?"

Cesca sighed. "I'm working on that. I like my little house, and it's starting to feel like my little house. And Lorna, she's been a brick for me."

"I'm happy to have the chance to get to know her. I really enjoyed the party last night. I'm glad you talked me into it."

"You were a big hit. Now come on back and let's sit, have some coffee and coffee cake I baked hoping it would bring you by, and gossip."

"Your coffee cake could lure me in from Timbuktu."

They sat in the kitchen, as they had since Miranda had been a child. That kitchen had been big, sophisticated in its neutrals and shining stainless steel. This, though tiny in comparison, had soft yellow walls, sage-green cabinets, and a butcher-block table big enough for two.

She knew the divorce had shaken Cesca to the core, and couldn't understand how a man married for over thirty years could suddenly decide he didn't want to be married anymore.

They'd had no children, so the end of her marriage had left Cesca adrift. The move, Miranda thought as Cesca cut cake, poured coffee, had given her stability again.

"You're happy here. I needed to see it to be sure, but I can and do see it."

"I am. You know, I went straight from college into marriage. Never once lived on my own. I'm enjoying the independence more than I ever imagined. Now I miss you, your dad, and my friends from back—not going to keep saying 'home.' Back in Chapel Hill, but Lorna's making damn sure I make friends here. How's your dad liking Oxford?"

"He's a kid who wakes up to Christmas morning every day."

"And how do you feel about Deborah going with him?"

Miranda rested her chin on her fist. "I like her. I really do.

I don't think either of us—Dad or I—ever thought he'd have another relationship, a serious one. But she's brought a kind of lightness to his life the last couple of years, and a sense of adventure. He would've wanted to take that offer from Oxford, but I'm not sure he would have if she hadn't encouraged it. Taking a sabbatical from Carolina."

That word again, she thought.

"And leaving you. She was very kind to me after Marty left, and I won't forget it. You've spread your wings, Miranda, and we're all so proud of you. But I don't think you'd have spread them far enough to come here this way if he hadn't gone there."

"You're probably right." Comfort zones, she thought again. She'd burrowed into hers. "Emersons tend to root deep. I did take a short but interesting walking tour of Main Street this morning. I stopped in the bookstore."

"That made Carolyn and Andy's day."

"I'll be doing a signing there in March. I think they'd have booked me for tomorrow if I'd agreed." She shook her head.

"Now you've made their year. I can't wait!"

"I really liked their shop, the feel of it. I was seriously impressed with the idea of student recs. Carolyn told me that was the high school lit teacher's idea. Sebastian Booth?"

"Yes, apparently he talked the library into the same sort of thing, and it's a nice touch. I don't really know him—our paths haven't crossed since I moved here—but Lorna praises him to the moon and back."

"Does she?"

"She does, and she's no easy mark. I did meet him last night." Cesca let her eyebrows wing up. "Handsome, and single, I'm told."

"Stop."

"Just saying. Claudette, my supervisor at the library, said we have more Shakespeare checked out by students in the handful of years he's been here than we did in the ten years before. You'd appreciate that."

"I do."

"He started a Shakespeare Club."

"Did he?" she murmured.

"I doubt it's as, well, robust as your dad's, but for a small high school? It's an achievement. I'm going to warn you, Lorna's going to hit you up to come in, talk about writing to some of the students."

"Oh, well . . ."

Cesca patted Miranda's hand. "Fair warning, and another to warn you Lorna tends to get what she wants."

Miranda blamed the fourth cup of coffee before noon on the outsize burst of energy.

After she'd hugged Cesca goodbye, she drove around the town, out the other side, and back along the river, even stopped to take pictures with her phone.

To paint on this canvas, she had to know the canvas.

Since cooking didn't rank high—or much at all—on her list of accomplishments, she stopped to get a takeaway serving of soup to heat up later.

To double-check, she drove by Booth's house again—still there—before she went home.

What did he do in there, she wondered, on a school break?

Plan his next heist, contact his fence?

Did he have a fence? Is that how it worked?

Did he still cook? Because that hadn't been a lie. The man could cook. Or the boy could, anyway.

Maybe he baked bread and made soup while he planned his next heist.

She pulled into her drive, then sat as it struck her.

"That wasn't the idea," she reminded herself as she retrieved the take-out bag and started into the house. "It's a story about town secrets, and the killer hiding among them."

But being a thief rated as a damn secret, didn't it? A thief who cooks . . . maybe for a restaurant. She couldn't make him an English teacher. Far too close to the bone.

She put the soup in the fridge for dinner, then made a sandwich with the ham Lorna had loaded her up with the night before.

She carried it and a bottle of water into the second bedroom she'd barely set up much less used as her office.

She stared at her laptop, at the notebook already containing her obsessively careful and organized notes. She thought of the pages of the first draft already written, one that started with the bang of the murder of an unfaithful wife.

She could change that. She could adjust that.

What if the unfaithful wife lived, for now, but found the diamond—no, the ruby and diamond necklace, a family heirloom—missing.

No, no, not a necklace, she thought as she sat and booted up. An objet d'art, a priceless objet d'art, again, a family heirloom. A crystal bird, perched on the branch of a gold tree, by its nest. A nest that held a diamond egg.

The faithless wife, so easily seduced by the handsome thief/ chef. The woman who made it so easy for him to take the bird. And its loss would cost her her life.

"Okay, okay, this could work. Let's find out."

Chapter Nineteen

SHE WROTE THROUGH THE rest of the day, editing the draft as needed. The character of the wife still worked as written—except for being dead by the end of chapter one.

But the man she'd originally cast as her killer was now a thief, and *not* the killer. In a very real way, as she saw it, he became a victim, too.

Not, she thought, because she'd base him, very loosely, on Booth, but because having him as cause and effect, murder-wise, didn't work for her.

By the middle of the next day, she had her first two chapters redrafted.

She set them aside to let them simmer while she crossed another item off the list.

The first article she found on the Chameleon came from the French press—tabloid style.

She could read it, but it took a great deal of time and effort. So much she tried again, and found one from a London tabloid.

She read the article on the theft of an emerald and diamond pendant—valued at over eight hundred thousand pounds—from the vault of a Lady Stanwyke's country estate in the Lake District.

They believed the theft took place during a house party, sometime before Lady Stanwyke personally opened the vault, as she intended to wear the pendant for the ball she'd host that evening.

Authorities contacted, blah blah, all guests and staff interviewed, a thorough search. No signs of a break-in, no damage to the vault, no other item or items missing—though the lady was known for her impressive and valuable collection of jewelry and—ha—objets d'art.

"Some speculate," Miranda muttered out loud, "the clever and profitable theft as the work of the Chameleon, so termed as sources claim he uses disguise to mask his identity. Or hers! The Chameleon's modus operandi, these same sources state, is leaving no trace, and taking only one or possibly two valuable items."

She read on, though the bulk of the article leaned heavily on the sensational and lurid.

She backtracked to that single paragraph.

"One or two items, just like he told me."

She printed out what she wanted, moved on to LaPorte.

She didn't have a first name, but he popped when she googled the last name and Lake Charles.

She read half a dozen articles on him, all proving out the little Booth had told her.

A man of wealth and power—and maybe the story he'd told her put it there, but she saw cruelty in his eyes.

An avid collector of art—and a generous benefactor to the arts. A man who'd never married, but who often had a stunning woman on his arm.

She printed several articles, and decided he'd be the template for her killer. The look of him anyway, she thought, and some of the pieces, as the articles had, invariably, used terms like *charming, charismatic, powerful.*

"You cost me, asshole. So you can pay me back, my way."

She spent that evening, New Year's Eve, with Cesca, and stayed over, as the small celebration involved a lot of champagne.

But bright and early the next morning, she knocked on Booth's door.

He answered—after her knocking turned to banging. And he answered in what looked like an ancient Tulane University sweatshirt, flannel pants, and bare feet. He had enough stubble on his face to tell her he hadn't shaved in several days, and had the tousled hair and heavy eyes of a man who'd just rolled out of bed.

"Jesus, Miranda. It's, what, barely eight in the morning."

"Nearly eight-thirty." She added a heavy dose of sugar to her voice. "Sleeping in?"

"That was the plan. There was a party—New Year's Eve. Hell."

He turned away, gestured a come-ahead, and kept walking.

"Some of us plan to start the New Year working."

"I don't have to work until the day after tomorrow."

She followed him back to the kitchen—spotless, of course—and the jaw-dropping view behind it.

He got a Coke out of the fridge, made another vague gesture at a sleek coffee maker. "I'm not making coffee. Make it yourself if you want it."

"How gracious of you. I'll have one of those." She opened the fridge—again spotless, with the sort of supplies that told her yes, he still cooked—and got a Coke.

He got a bottle of Motrin from a cabinet, shook out three to down with the Coke.

"Hungover?" she said, piling on the sugar.

He just stared, stonily, and glugged down more Coke.

"I wouldn't be if I'd slept another couple hours. If you're here to tell me I've got twenty-four, take the Coke on the road so I can get started."

Instead she sat on one of his counter stools, then shrugged off her coat, unwound her scarf.

Maybe it was small of her, but she rejoiced a little that she'd taken time with her hair, her makeup, and her wardrobe.

She looked damn good, and he didn't.

"I'm here to strike a deal."

He shoved at his hair, and rather than sit, leaned back against the counter, the deep, dark blue eyes shadowed and heavy.

"What kind of deal?"

"First, I've done some discreet inquiries around Westbend about Sebastian Booth. *Bye Bye Birdie*?"

"That's right. I haven't decided whether to update it some or go full retro."

"Retro, adds the charm. Anyway, it shouldn't surprise me you're well liked. You were well liked at Carolina, too. But I'll concede you appear to take your job, your duty to your students seriously. But then you took your own studies seriously."

"It was my life then. This is my life now. What's the deal?"

"I also read up on Carter LaPorte. I don't like him."

"Get in line."

"And the Chameleon. The tabloids in Europe love him—or her. What did you do with Lady Stanwyke's pendant?"

"Broke it down for the stones and the platinum, sold it. I got . . . right around three hundred and fifteen thousand pounds. English pounds."

"The article said it was worth over twice that."

He rubbed at his temple and, she imagined, the headache inside it.

"And if I'd tried to sell it as a whole piece, I'd have netted about half what I got. Loose stones? About half's a solid take."

Fascinating, she thought. And a strange kind of business. "That's how it works—around half?"

"Usually a little less, depending on where and how you sell it. Why?"

"What do you do with the money?" she asked as she got out a notebook, began to write.

"Bank it—numbered or offshore, invest it. Depends. Why?" he repeated. "You writing a book?"

When she smiled and kept writing, he pushed off the counter. "No. Just no."

She set the notebook down, picked up the Coke. Yes, however small and petty, she enjoyed every second of this.

"Here's the deal, Booth—I'm never calling you stupid Sebastian, so you're lucky you used that last name. The deal. You want my cooperation so you can stay here, at least for now. I'll give that cooperation on the following terms. First, you're an educator only while you have that cooperation. No cat burgling."

"How would you know if I did?"

"Because you're going to make the deal, and if you break it and I do find out, no twenty-four hours." She paused a moment. "And I didn't like LaPorte—that's in your favor. Second, you'll tell me everything I need and want to know about this . . . profession of yours, because I am writing a book."

She held up a finger before he could object. "The character I'm crafting may be loosely based, but he won't look like you, sound like you. He's a chef, owns a restaurant in a town like Westbend. I can see you still cook, so I need you to help me out there, because I still don't."

"You stir and chop," he murmured.

"That's right. If I'm going to write about a thief, I'm going to write about a successful one. His motivations aren't yours, and I can alter his . . . style, I guess it is. You can help me there, too."

She lifted the Coke in toast. "You're my new research assistant, Booth, and that gives you at least six months. We'll negotiate again when I leave."

"Don't use my mother."

Her cheerful smile died. How could she hate him when his first demand sought to protect his mother? And how cynical did he believe her to be that he'd think she'd use his mother and her death to sell a book?

"No, I won't. I promise you I won't. I'll tell you this, even though you don't deserve it. You had a point the other night. I've never known that kind of loss, I've never had to worry about where or how I'd live. Other than my mother shrugging us off, and I know both of us were better off that way, my childhood was pretty much perfect. Other than you? The rest of it's cruised along, too. I won't use that loss."

He paced to the glass doors, stood and stared out.

She wondered why he didn't jump at the offer. She undoubtedly had the upper hand, but couldn't see a downside for him.

"You have to respect my schedule. It gets crowded when I go back."

"I'm the daughter of a college professor," she reminded him. "I know what goes into teaching. We'll work out a schedule that suits us both. We could do this by email or—"

"Jesus, you think I'm writing this down? No recordings either. Notes fine, but no recordings, no email, no texts, no phone conversations on the subject."

"Okay, I can see all that. In person only."

He kept looking out the doors, watched the river's lazy run, because that was the problem for him. The very big problem.

But to buy six months, he'd handle it.

He walked back to her. "Deal."

"Great. You must pick locks. Can you show me how?"

"You have to be kidding. I need a shower. I haven't even brushed my teeth. And now I'm hungry."

"All right then, pull it together. I'll come back in two hours."

She grabbed her coat, slid off the stool.

"I forgot how pushy you are."

"I don't believe that. You don't forget anything."

She took the Coke with her. He looked down at his own as she sailed out.

No, he didn't forget things. And now he'd have weeks or months of memories of her stuck in his head.

She sure as hell got the better part of the deal.

SHE CAME BACK, AND with a slew of questions. He decided to distract himself while he answered them, so he started making a pot of tortilla soup. Plus it gave him the advantage of leftovers once his schedule filled again.

Apparently his cooking distracted her.

"You're not using a recipe."

"I know the recipe."

"You're not measuring anything."

"My eye measures."

He found himself amused when she actually wrote that down.

"How the hell are you going to write about a chef when you don't know how to cook?"

"You do. People, mostly people who don't write, think you have to write about what you know. Oddly, I don't actually know how to murder somebody, as I've never done so myself. Yet." She smiled. "But on paper, I've killed—let's see—seven people by various means. I've never been a single parent or a veterinarian, but I've written about them."

She watched him get bags out of the freezer and take green cubes out of each to drop into the pot.

"What are those?"

"Herbs. I grow herbs, then I chop them and freeze them in ice cube trays so I can use them fall and winter. Do you want to know about stealing or cooking?"

"The central character does both, so both."

Booth replaced the bags, gave the pot a stir. "You know, cooking for and running a restaurant's not a part-time job."

"Neither's teaching," she pointed out. "You make it work. I want to know how."

"During the school year, teaching's the priority."

"So you don't steal things from, say, late August into June?"

"That's what school breaks are for."

"Okay. You just had winter break. What did you steal?"

"Nothing."

"Slacker."

Saying nothing, he got out a skillet.

He looked so irritated, so annoyed. Miranda couldn't say she minded that a bit.

"You seem to have misplaced your sense of humor during the last decade."

He got out the chicken he'd already marinated, began to cut it into chunks. "You're putting me in a bind, Miranda."

"Funny, from where I sit I'm giving you a major break. So why didn't you take advantage of your time off last week?"

"There's an excellent eight-carat pink diamond resting comfortably in a jewelry safe in a mansion in Potomac, Maryland, that didn't come into my hands last night because somebody decided to visit her godmother."

"I see." She noted down pink diamond because it sounded both romantic, sexy, and valuable. "But you went to a party last night. How would you have gotten out of that?"

"I wouldn't have. Leave the party shortly after midnight, drive to Potomac, do the job, come home, go to bed."

He said it, she thought, like someone talking about picking up a half gallon of milk after work.

"Just like that?"

"Not counting the man-hours researching and planning the job, yeah, like that."

"How did you find out about the diamond? Did you know the people?"

"Not personally. She shares entirely too much on social media." He added olive oil to the skillet, turned on the heat. "Her husband gave her the pendant last summer for their anniversary." While the oil heated, he juiced half a lemon in a little glass dish with a hump in the middle. "Tiffany's, New York. From there, it's a matter of authenticating the purchase, identifying their security system. Internet makes that easy."

"Does it?"

"They bought a ten-thousand-square-foot Colonial four years ago, have one kid—a boy, age three—no pets. She's allergic. A barking dog's more reliable than an alarm system."

She took notes as he sautéed the chicken, added, generously, a spice mix he'd obviously made up himself.

"He's a cosmetic surgeon, she's an estate lawyer—major estates. They own a summer home in the Hamptons and take a winter break in Vail. They like to ski. He's taking flying lessons, and they're both avid tennis players."

He added the lemon juice and a glug of tequila to the skillet. "They've been on my radar for a few months."

"You found out all that on social media?"

She made a side note to take a hard look at her own posts, and censor them as necessary.

"That's the springboard, in this case. She lists her employer, so that's another area of research."

None of the process, she thought, really ran along the lines she'd imagined.

"So you didn't even go there in person to, like, case the joint?"

He would've rolled his eyes, but it felt like too much effort. "Of course I went there. Twice. To check out the neighborhood. But you can call up a damn aerial view of any address, even walking views."

"How do you know they have a jewelry safe?"

"Because he bought one after the kid came along and he gave her a sapphire and diamond bracelet—blue stones because they had a boy. Burmese sapphires, double-A rated, and white diamonds—G on the GIA scale."

Now she frowned as she scribbled in her notebook. "A grade of G doesn't sound great—and what's GIA?"

"Gemological Institute," he supplied while he worked. "And G on the scale means the stones are nearly colorless, and IF—internally flawless."

"Then they should get a better grade, like an A or B."

"Scale starts at D, so take it up with the GIA. You know, you can look this up."

"Fine." And she would. "You got all that off social media?"

"The bracelet, yeah, because she posted a picture of herself wearing it while she held the baby. I got the rest by hacking his account."

"I see, okay, we'll have to get into how that works."

She wrote down HACKING and circled it.

"Question. The bracelet sounds like something you could break down like you did the Stanwyke piece. But you didn't plan to take it?"

"He gave it to her after she made a human, and after fifteen hours of labor."

Both baffled and intrigued, she studied him as he poured the chicken and the liquid into the big pot. "You're a puzzle, Booth. It's tempting to make my character equally sentimental, but—"

"It's not sentiment so much as targeting. My target's the pink diamond."

"You don't put that in the past tense."

"Because I'll get around to it."

She tapped her pen on her pad as he stirred his soup. "I think that makes me an accessory before the fact."

His shrug said, clearly: That's your problem.

"You're asking the questions."

"Let's switch to my character's public life while I think about that one. What kind of soup is that?"

"It'll be tortilla soup when I'm done with it."

"And you just toss it together, from scratch, from memory."

"If your guy's in a restaurant, he's going to have a commercial

279

kitchen and a sous-chef, a line cook, waitstaff, and all that. He won't be tossing something together at home."

"Which is why I'll be visiting some commercial kitchens and asking more questions. But you're here now. What kind of restaurant would you own?"

"None." No thought, no hesitation. "Too much work. I like to cook. I don't have to cook. And you're going to want a good bar area—margins are tight in restaurants. Not so tight in bars. Drinks make money."

"How do you know that?"

"I had friends in New Orleans who had a restaurant, and I dated a chef in France who wanted her own place."

"Did she get it?"

"I don't know. I moved on."

With a nod, Miranda closed her book. "And now I need to do the same and start working on this. What's the best evening this week for another round of this?"

"The first week back after the holidays is never a good week. Finals for this term are the end of the week."

"Okay, we'll stick with Sundays for now. Say, afternoon, about two?"

She rose to put on her coat. "Oh, and I might be talking to some of your students. Lorna's going to make a pitch—I got that heads-up—about me coming in and taking questions about writing."

"Great. Terrific."

The sour note in each syllable sort of perked her up.

"I'll see you next Sunday, and you can show me how to pick a lock." She wound her scarf. "Oh, one more. How do you open a safe, a vault, whatever? Something without a key?"

"It's mostly math."

"Really? We'll talk about that."

When she walked away to let herself out, he frowned at the soup. He didn't think she'd break the deal. Of course, she could, and he'd be truly screwed. But he didn't think she would.

And still, the idea that they had one baffled him.

SHE CAME BACK THE next Sunday, and the one after that.

He tried to put those . . . interludes into a box, set it aside except for Sunday afternoons.

He held auditions, did lesson plans, graded papers. And, for now, put his nightwork completely aside. He couldn't risk it.

Even though that pink diamond haunted him.

She did come in to talk to students, but at least he was spared having her directly address one of his classes. Still, the enthusiasm for her visit rolled through fellow teachers and students.

How approachable! Relatable! And funny, too!

He had kids building sets, painting backdrops, working on costumes. He had choreography and staging to deal with.

He had a student whose grades started sliding as his parents battled their way through a divorce, and another who decided her life was basically over after her boyfriend dumped her.

He pulled the boy in after the last class of the day, and met the wall of teenage misery in the form of I-don't-give-a-fuck insolence.

"I know it must be hard to focus right now."

"How would you know? Did your parents decide they hate each other's guts? Did your dad call your mom a bitch from hell?"

"No, because they never got married. Mine took off before I was born."

The boy shrugged, sulked, sneered. "You were probably better off. You didn't have him feeding you bull like it all has nothing to do with you."

"It has everything to do with you."

Insolent misery switched to outraged guilt. "It's not my fault!"

"That's not what I said, Barry." He didn't use his desk for this kind of session, but two folding chairs face-to-face. "Your family, the one you've grown up in, is changing, so that has everything to do with you. You're entitled to be hurt, pissed, unhappy. But the fact is, they're hurt, pissed, and unhappy with each other."

"Are you going to tell me I can't change that, I can only change my *reaction* to that?"

In class, Booth wouldn't have tolerated that ugly tone for a second. But here he let it roll.

"I'm not sure how you change your reaction when it's still going on, and you're stuck in the middle of the war."

Tears burned in Barry's eyes. Hot, furious, and desolate.

"He moved out, but they still go at each other every chance they get. My sister's freaking out, but they don't stop. My mom keeps saying shit like: You're the man of the house now, Barry, or telling my sister she has to be brave and help out more."

And Booth wondered why adults could be so shortsighted during a crisis.

"Here comes the standard question. Have you tried talking to them about it?"

"They don't listen! Now I'm grounded because of my grades, and my mom's saying she can't deal with another problem, and my dad's saying I'm lazy."

What Barry was, Booth thought, was close to a crying jag and desperate for his parents to stop tearing at each other long enough to *be* parents instead of mortal enemies.

"Here's what I want you to try."

"Don't start on family counseling." The words whipped out, sharp and fast. "They went to marriage counseling twice. It never got better."

"If they went to counseling, at least they tried." Booth held up a hand before Barry could speak. "Hold on. I don't and can't know anything about your parents' marriage. But I know you. You're a good student. I'm going to say again, you're entitled to everything you're feeling. I want you to write it all out."

"Oh, come on, Mr. Booth."

"Write it out, your way. Write out what they won't listen to. Write as little or as much as you want. I'll take that, and I'll grade that in place of the test you just flunked."

"If I write it out my way, I'll get suspended for language."

"No, you won't. Turn it in before class on Thursday."

At least the kid would have his say, Booth thought as he headed to the theater for rehearsals. Then they'd see.

SHE CAME AGAIN ON Sunday, and maybe he hated himself a little for starting to look forward to it.

As usual, they had their "meeting" in his kitchen. He had yet to allow her into his work space, but he'd brought out a few tools.

And as usual, he had something going on the stove, but hadn't yet invited her to share.

He'd shown her how to pick a simple lock, demonstrated how to beat a simple combination.

Miranda, of course, wanted more.

"Okay, but people aren't going to have a basic padlock on a safe with valuables inside."

"The same formula applies."

He'd set a small combination lockbox on the table, along with a notepad and a stethoscope.

"But on an actual safe, they'd be more complicated."

He applied the same patience and intractability to tutoring Miranda on thievery as he did to his students in language arts and theater.

"Same formula, more steps. The steps depend, like I told you before, on the number in the combination. I've already set this one to a simple three-number combo."

"If you already know the combination," she countered, "what's the point?"

"I'm not going to crack it, you are."

"I am?" Fascinated, she stared at the dial, then reached back to braid the hair she'd left loose.

"Do you remember the steps?"

"I think so, but I wrote them down anyway." She flipped back in her notebook. "I'm pretty sure—no, positive—I'm going to fail the math portion of the assignment."

"I'll give you a hand with it, this time."

Obviously delighted, she picked up the stethoscope, and in the kitchen fragrant with the beef stew he had simmering, started to fit the earpieces.

His doorbell rang.

"Shit." He picked up the box, took it and the rest into the mudroom. "We're discussing the possibility of you talking to my honors class," he said as he came back empty-handed.

"All right."

He woke up the laptop on the kitchen counter, then switched to the view of his front porch.

"You have a camera out—"

"It's Barry Kolber, one of my students. Just hold on a minute." He switched it off again before going to answer.

"Hey, Barry."

"Um, Mr. Booth, I . . ." He spotted Miranda, shifted his feet. "Sorry, you've got, like, company. I'll see you in class tomorrow."

"That's okay. Come on in."

Miranda rose. "I'm just going to use the powder room."

With her discreet exit, Booth gestured Barry in. "It's cold. Is everything okay?"

"Not exactly okay, but better. I know you had my parents come in after school on Friday, and you read them what I wrote. Anyway, Dad came over yesterday, and they talked to me and Becs—my sister. They really don't like each other right now, Mr. Booth, but they said they were sorry."

His voice cracked a little, so he paused, drew in some breath.

"They apologized to me and Becs, and that was weird. Great

and weird. They said how they were going to try to do better, not to talk to each other about anything but me and Becs. How they both loved us and all that. Anyway, we all said a lot of stuff, mostly without yelling. And I wanted to thank you. I didn't want to do it in school, you know. I just wanted to say thanks for making me write it out. You gave me an A."

"You deserved it."

"I gotta go. I got parole from grounding because they both felt crappy about it all." He shot out a grin. "Anyway, thanks."

"You're welcome."

"Ah, was it hard, not having a dad ever?"

"Harder, I think, on my mom than me. So maybe you can give them a break if their grades start slipping some."

He let out a laugh. "Yeah, right. Thanks."

Once Booth shut the door, he called the all clear to Miranda and went back for the lockbox.

"Can I ask, or was that confidential?"

He shrugged, got them both a Coke. "One of my students, parents in the middle of an ugly divorce and using him and his sister as weapons. I had him write out how he felt about it, then called them in and read what he wrote. They went right at each other, Jesus."

As it replayed in his head, verbatim, Booth rubbed the back of his neck.

"He this, she that, until I pointed out, not too diplomatically, they were proving out everything the kid wrote. And maybe they should listen again. I read it again."

He let out a sound, impatient disgust, before he sat back down. "I sweated that out, I'll tell you, because it started to look like I'd made it worse on the kids, but the second reading got through enough for them to stop trying to rip at each other. Barry said they all sat down yesterday, actually talked, so that's something."

"Something," Miranda said softly.

No matter how many times he'd seen it play out, it burned in his gut.

"I get how people can come to hate each other, or at least want to hurt each other because they're pissed and done. I don't get how parents can be so damn determined to cut each other to pieces they don't notice or care when their kids are bleeding out."

He thought of that long summer evening after the ball game, sitting on the front stoop with his mother. He could see her— so thin, so thin, with the fielder's cap over her short crown of pink hair.

"My mom never said a hard word about my biological father. Not one, in fact the opposite. She could've made him a villain, but she never did."

For a long moment, she said nothing.

"She loved you too much for that. We're lucky that the parent who loved us didn't have the need to villainize the other."

"Yeah. Most aren't so lucky there."

"No, but you validated Barry's feelings," she told Booth. "And that gives him support and a shield. More, he knows you made his parents listen, made them hear his voice when they probably didn't or couldn't over their own. He's never going to forget you."

"It wasn't about me."

"No, but he'll never forget someone listened when he needed to be heard. And maybe one day he'll be the one who listens because he remembers."

She picked up the stethoscope, and toyed with it a moment. "It's hard for me, Booth, to find these little pockets of like for you again. To remember why I had feelings for you once.

"So . . . if I open this lock, can I have some of what smells so damn good on the stove?"

"It's beef stew—sort of a not-as-fancy as the French beef bourguignon."

It was hard for him, too, just having her back in his life again. Just having her right there.

"If you open it, I'll get you a bowl."

Chapter Twenty

HE KNEW IT MADE him stupid, but Booth really anticipated their Sunday afternoons.

He concluded after a couple of lessons on finessing locks, she'd never get the hang of it—but not for lack of trying.

When he combined—at her request—safecracking with cooking, he reached the same conclusion about her talents in the kitchen.

In safecracking, the math defeated her. In cooking, her reliance on exact measurements did the same. She just didn't possess a feel for either.

On this February Sunday, with a thick, Hallmark Christmas movie-style snow falling outside, the fire snapping in the living room, she sat in his kitchen doggedly working on picking the lock of a standard dead bolt he'd installed in a panel for her practice.

He left her to it—it would take awhile—and punched down the bread dough he'd had rising. He set it aside to rest a few minutes, and watched her progress.

"You need to maintain tension with the wrench."

"Yeah, yeah, yeah."

His kitchen smelled like a farmhouse in Provence from the

chicken en cocotte he had on the stove. She, he had to admit as he bent over her shoulder, smelled even better.

"How many pins have you lifted?"

"One. No snide remarks."

Since she'd been at the dead bolt for close to ten minutes, and had four pins left to lift, she'd come in—at this rate—at nearly an hour.

He covered a baking sheet with parchment paper, lifted the dough onto a board, then cut it in two halves. With his hands he formed two boules, covered them, put them back in the oven—heat off, light on—for the second rising.

"Two! I got two! I got it now, I've got it. I'm just distracted by that incredible smell."

He'd told her to come early, since they'd combine her character's two professions—cookery and thievery. He'd had her peel, wash, chop the vegetables.

She was thorough about it, he thought. Methodical. Incredibly slow. As far as browning the chicken, he'd prevented her from burning it, but it'd been a close call.

He washed the bowl he'd used for the dough and thought she'd done a decent enough job at kneading once she'd found her rhythm. But that was a physical thing.

Like stirring and chopping.

Despite her lack of skill, which, he'd concluded, stemmed from a surprising lack of confidence, he enjoyed having her spend these Sundays with him in a way he knew equaled stupid mistake.

The long braid of her hair fascinated him. A little fancier today, he'd noticed, like a fishtail. Didn't it take nimble fingers to manage that? Why those same nimble fingers fumbled with simple picks confounded him.

"I got it! I got it! What's my time?"

"Forty-one minutes, twelve seconds."

"God!" She flopped back in her chair, flexed her cramping fingers. "How long does it take you?"

"It took me longer when I was learning." He got a nice Pouilly-Fuissé from his wine fridge in the butler's pantry.

"How long?"

He shrugged as he uncorked the bottle, but knew she wanted to know. "Eight-twenty-four."

"How old were you?"

"Ten. Almost ten. You haven't said when the character started."

"Young. His father was a thief, and his grandfather."

"Family business."

She took the wine he poured. "Exactly. He thinks of it that way, the same as if he'd grown up in a family of plumbers or lawyers. I'm doing some flashbacks to show just that. He's not a bad man, really. Morally squishy, but—"

"Squishy."

"Thou shalt not steal, Booth."

He countered that easily. "Thou shalt not a whole shitload of things people do regularly."

"Squishy," she repeated, and sipped her wine. "He doesn't have any problem seducing Allison Reed to gain easy entry into her home so he can outline his method for stealing the Covington Bird, the priceless family heirloom."

"That sounds sort of famous, so readily recognizable."

"Absolutely, it's very unique. Commissioned by the murdering husband's great-grandfather for his new bride. It's a Waterford crystal bird with sapphire eyes perched on a nest on a branch of a gold, jewel-encrusted tree. A twenty-eight-carat faceted Russian white diamond for the egg—D on the scale. And, ah, IF, internally flawless."

"Uh-huh." That would put the diamond alone at a couple million, he calculated. Before adding the rest, and the history.

"And what's he going to do with it when he gets it?"

"Sell it. Even for the half it's worth, the way you said, he'll net about five million. His biggest score, his last, as it'll set him up for—Why are you smiling?"

"Famous last words, 'last score.' Usually literally the last because you're just asking to get busted."

"That sounds like superstition."

"If you walk under the ladder some guy's standing on to paint a house, you could get beaned with a falling paint can. So don't walk under a ladder."

He walked over to take the bread dough out of the oven, turned it on to preheat.

But she liked the idea of her character planning his last job, his biggest job, and how things fall apart for him with the murder of his mark.

"The restaurant's taking most of his time, and he likes it. He wants to settle into it. Anyway, he'll plan to sell the bird."

"Who's buying?"

"I'm thinking a dark web auction."

Booth nodded as he checked the stew. "Could work, since he's going to get caught anyway."

Irritation flickered over her face. Who was writing the damn book?

"He's not going to get caught. That's the whole point."

"Then he needs a buyer. He's third generation, so he'd know you don't bag something like that on spec. He needs someone with a lot of money who wants it—for whatever reasons work for you—and can put it in a nice, private space to admire. It's too well-known otherwise, and breaking it down for pieces destroys the whole."

Irritation shifted to interest and new angles.

"You know people like that? Who'd pay millions just to horde away something beautiful?"

"Sure. The first—and I thought last—job I did for LaPorte was stealing a Turner from a guy who had it stolen so he could sit in his fancy locked room—filled with other beautiful, stolen things—smoke his cigar, and admire his collection."

"So you stole what had been stolen so this LaPorte could sit in some fancy locked room of his own with it?"

"Pretty much."

As she sat back with her wine, she began to see another plot-line opening up. "That's an interesting angle. I'm going to play around with that."

"Good. Now you can play around making an egg wash for the sourdough boules."

"An egg wash? I don't even know what that is."

He gestured for her to stand as he got out three small glass dishes. "It's just egg white and a little water. You're going to separate the white from the yolk, then whisk the white and the water together, brush it over the rounds."

He got a carton of eggs out of the refrigerator. "Like this."

He cracked an egg, then passed the yolk from half shell to half shell while letting the white drain into the dish. He plopped the yolk into the other dish.

"That looks doable. What's the third dish for?"

"For screwing up."

A challenge! "Twenty bucks says I don't."

He smiled at her. "How about a shiny quarter?"

She didn't smile back. He really wished she had.

"You really do remember everything. Okay, a shiny quarter." She cracked the egg, and broke the yolk on the first pass. "Damn it."

He handed her another egg. "Try again."

She didn't break the yolk this time, but bobbled the shell so it all plopped into the dish.

"That's fine. I'm going to make myself an omelet for breakfast. Try again."

"There must be a tool for this sort of thing."

"Sure. For sissies."

It took four attempts, but she finally managed it.

After she'd whisked, brushed, he handed her a jar of poppy seeds.

"How much?"

"Until it looks like you want it to."

Everything in her yearned for the precise and exact.

"Why can't there just be an answer?"

"That is the answer."

She started to shake the seeds. "You know, I can get why Nathan likes to steal, but I don't understand why he loves cooking. Loves it—it's his true calling. He's every bit as happy—actually happier in the long run—standing in a hot, noisy, chaotic restaurant kitchen making food as he is standing in a dark, silent house taking diamonds out of a safe.

"Does that look right?"

"It's your eye," Booth reminded her.

"I think it's right."

"Then it is." He slid the sheet into the oven, set the timer.

When he turned back, she stood at his kitchen door, looking out at the snow. He accepted the way his heart clutched in his chest. What else could he do?

"I wondered what all this would look like in the snow, and it doesn't disappoint. It seems to be tapering off, but you might get a day off tomorrow. Or at least a delay."

"Pretty sure the pop quiz I'd planned for first period's going to wait until Tuesday."

She laughed as she turned around, and their eyes met.

It was, for him, a punch in the gut, a warm embrace, a promise, a refusal all at once.

"Miranda—"

"I'd like to see your work space," she said quickly.

He gestured toward the glass-paneled door, the desk and laptop, the shelves of books behind them.

"Not where you do your lesson plans. Unless you don't have a separate space, for this." She tapped the dead bolt.

"Upstairs, second guest room."

"I've been coming here for over a month now, Booth. I'd like to see it. I have Nathan set up in the basement of his house. I'd just like to see if I've got a sense of things."

"I used the basement in the house in Chapel Hill. No basement here."

He coordinated the oven timer with the one on his phone before leading her upstairs.

She stood in the doorway, looked into what appeared to be an attractive, welcoming guest room. A white duvet over a queen bed, plumped pillows, a reading chair and lamp, an old dresser polished to a gleam with a mirror over it. Some framed street scenes of Paris on the wall.

"You don't lock the door?"

"People wonder about locked doors. I don't have a lot of people up here, but I do a big cookout in the summer, and I have a deal for my club students before winter break. Open, it's a room. Locked, it's a question."

Yes, of course. She'd keep Nathan's basement door unlocked.

"No overnight guests?"

"My aunt and Sebastien a couple of times." But he understood her. "No women, no. Asking for trouble."

He walked over to open the closet.

"I see a closet. One full of costumes, wardrobe, wigs—theater director things—organized in your ruthless way. And without a single stray dust bunny. I know you still do your own cleaning, because I asked Patti, who does mine every week."

"People who clean your house know more about you than most anyone else. Trust me. Anyway, that's what people see if they come up here. The rest's in my bedroom."

He walked out and down to the master.

Clean, she thought, organized, attractive with its misty gray walls and clever street art—and of course the gorgeous view through the glass doors to the snow-covered deck.

Not Spartan, not simple, she judged, and seriously appealing with the dark gray duvet, the strong blue accents in a cozy reading chair, a surely hand-knit throw. She recognized the bureau and chest of drawers as lovingly refinished antiques.

Maybe it leaned a little minimalist for her taste, and she imagined mounding pretty pillows on the bed, some interesting candles or bottles on the bureau, a tall green plant in a colorful pot by those doors before she caught herself.

To compensate for the mental slip, she nodded toward the doors. "It must be wonderful to wake to that view every morning."

"It never gets old," he agreed, and opened doors to another closet.

One so well outfitted it gave her a huge spurt of closet envy.

A dedicated space for shoes—not that he filled it with his three pairs of Chucks, a few dress shoes and boots. Two built-in bureaus where—considering Booth—he very likely kept off-season clothes. And rods where clothes, ruthlessly organized by type—shirts, pants, suits, jackets—hung with the additional insult to her own habits—coordinated by color.

"You can't possibly deserve this closet. I deserve this closet. You're obsessed, and so obsessed you could easily make do with half this size closet."

He wanted to touch her—just skim a hand down her braid, brush his fingers down her arm. Instead, he shoved his hands into his pockets.

"Using the space in an organized—not obsessive—way means you don't waste time trying to find a white dress shirt or a pair of black pants."

"You only have three white dress shirts anyway. Easy to count, as they're obsessively hung in trio."

"Three's the max anybody needs." He caught her quick, pitying glance. "How many do you have?"

"I have no idea, which is why I deserve this closet and you don't."

"On the other hand . . ."

He took out his phone, keyed in a code. She heard a faint beep.

"Electronic lock." Then he pressed a hand on the side wall of the closet.

It opened like a door—was a door, she corrected. Installed so seamlessly it became a wall.

Inside he had a desk and chair, a laptop, three monitors, a gun safe, shelves lined with locks, electronics she didn't understand along with a series of remote controls, several cell phones, more lock picks. A long, narrow counter—worktable, she supposed—ran under the shelves.

"Why so many phones?"

"Not all of them are just phones, or phones at all. I redesign them, basically, to read digital and electronic alarm codes, bypass electric locks, that sort of thing."

"That sort of thing," she murmured. "How did you learn how to do that?"

"Took some classes, and I have a friend with a talent for it who taught me more than I learned in classes."

In the compact space she turned to him, and their bodies brushed. "No place is really safe and secure, is it?"

"Not if somebody spends enough time figuring out how to get in. A heist from a major museum—the Louvre, the Smithsonian—that's going to take a lot of planning, and easier with a team or an inside man."

"Have you done that?"

"I don't like to steal from museums, and I don't work with a team."

"That's not a yes or no answer."

He slid his hands into his pockets again. "I broke into the Louvre. I didn't take anything. I just wanted to see if I could do it."

She stared at him, this man with his mop of hair just a few shades over needing a trim, the weekend stubble on that gorgeous face, the dark blue eyes now a little dreamy with the memory.

And this man, once a boy she'd loved, had broken into one of the most prestigious museums in the world.

Just to see if he could.

"If they'd caught you—"

"They didn't. It's magic without the crowds, and the guards, the motion detectors, the cameras. It's entirely different, and it's magic."

That's what she saw in his eyes. Remembered magic. "How different?"

If he looked back, he could still see it, still feel it.

"It breathes, the art. The canvases and the paintings on them, the marble and granite and bronze and porcelain. All those figures, landscapes, still lifes, all of it and what it took to create them."

"And that, seeing and feeling that, made the risk worth it?"

"Oh yeah. You think you know, say, the *Mona Lisa*. That image is everywhere, the iconic face, smile, all of her. You can see her with the crowds, in the light, with the noise and the movement around you, and she's so much more than you thought. You fall in love. But stand there alone, in that quiet with her, she takes your breath and trips your heart. She's alive. It's all alive in the quiet. Like hearing Stonehenge hum in the starlight."

"You're a romantic, Booth."

"Maybe." He'd ordered himself not to, but gave in and ran a hand over the braid that rested over her shoulder. "I can't paint, I can't take a piece of stone and see the life in it, bring it out, but I can admire the results and the genius that created it.

"Stand in, say, Cartier's in the dark—"

"Have you?"

He brushed that off. "The jewelry, it's stunning, even breathtaking. It took art to create those pieces out of stones and metal, but it's not the same. For me," he qualified.

"Why not?"

"Because you can pop those stones and create something else, something stunning. You can't create something else magnificent out of the *Mona Lisa*."

All at once, she thought she understood a key element of this part of him.

"You steal more jewels than art. That's why—because jewels are just beautiful stones and metal. Nathan doesn't have your sensibilities."

"Just my squishy morals."

She kept her face tipped up, and her eyes bewitched him. He thought the scent of her hair, her skin, simply enveloped the room. And him with it.

If he took what he wanted—just another light touch, just a taste—she might walk away and not come back. That might be a mercy.

He started to reach for her braid again, that twist of sunset. And the timer on his phone went off.

"That's the bread." He stepped back, away, he imagined, from a very steep edge. "I'll go take it out."

He moved fast and, she noted, all but soundlessly.

She let out the breath that clogged her lungs and rested her forehead on the wall until her brain stopped buzzing.

She couldn't let herself lean in this way, into him, into whatever happened to her around him.

No future in it, no real present either, she reminded herself. Only the painful past.

She had all she needed from him, at least for now, she thought as she stepped out of his secret room. She trailed her fingers over the suits, the coats, the ratty jeans, the pressed khakis.

She didn't have to spend her Sunday afternoons in his kitchen. If a question came up as she wrote, she could contact him, ask to meet.

She wished she didn't believe she'd seen the real Booth when he spoke of art, and his wonder of it. Or when he so patiently walked her through the steps of separating a damn egg.

She wished that squishy moral center didn't matter less and less the more time she spent around him.

And she wished she hadn't been ready to wrap herself around him when she'd seen the need and the intent in his eyes just now.

She'd stop coming. She'd take everything he'd told her, shown her, given her to think about and weave it into the book.

And when she went back home, she'd go back with her heart and her pride intact.

When she came back down, the scent of bread fresh from the oven added yet another perfume. He'd set the table—not fussy, just a couple of . . . friends sharing a meal on a snowy Sunday.

Her fault, she thought. She'd started that. The food, the wine, the conversation outside the deal they'd struck.

He'd kept his side of it, and she'd keep hers. And nothing more, either way.

"Snow's stopped." He spoke easily, as if that moment upstairs, and she knew it had been a moment for both of them, hadn't happened.

"I heard a plow go by," he continued, "so the road should be clear enough when you're ready to go."

She should go now, but he'd set the table. He'd topped off her wine.

Now he tapped a finger on the bread cooling on a rack on the counter. "Good job here."

"My famous egg wash."

"You helped make the dough and did most of the kneading."

He got a platter and began to fill it with the contents of the pot on the stove.

"Well, God." The scent drew her closer. "That looks amazing."

"You had a part in it, too."

"Where'd you learn to make this? The French chef?"

"No, actually, from a woman in Provence. I stayed there a few weeks once. A grandmotherly type," he added. "I convinced her to share her method."

He carried the platter to the table, came back to put a boule of bread on a board, set a bread knife beside it.

She walked over to join him. "I feel like I should take a picture, put it on my social media." Laughing, she sat as he gave her the jaundiced eye. "But I won't."

She took some chicken, the carrots, potatoes, celery, and onion, all smelling like glory, for her plate.

And told herself she'd firmly turned off whatever switch had flipped—in both of them—upstairs.

"Tell me how rehearsals are going."

"Not bad. Not exactly good yet, but not bad. We've got some strong voices, and Kim—that's Alicia Rohan playing Kim—can seriously dance. Our Hugo—Jonah Wyatt—seriously can't, but I'm using that awkwardness in his character. Jonah's making that work."

She listened to him, enjoyed listening to him, talking about "his kids," their strengths, their weaknesses, how tight the cast and crew had already knitted.

"Nobody's off-book yet, but we're getting there. And Jesus, Matt—he's playing Conrad Birdie—is a total ham. He's killing it. The sets are coming together, tech's still rough, but—and you better stop me."

"No. I was in the spring musical in high school—twice. I know how wild and wonderful. But just let me interject, you said a grandmotherly Frenchwoman taught you to make this. Are you sure she was human? And are you, not weighing in at six hundred pounds, eating your own cooking?"

"Her name's Marie-Terese."

He could see her in her big, colorful kitchen, her stone-gray hair in tight curls, those robin's-egg-blue eyes sparkling when her husband, in his floppy-brimmed gardening hat, came to the wide archway with a clutch of flowers in his hand.

"She has four children," he continued, "twelve grandchildren—probably more by now—and a husband who still adored her after, at the time, thirty-eight years of marriage."

"That's lovely, isn't it, a family cleaving together for decades. Neither one of us had that."

"You've got your dad. I've got Mags. How's your dad doing at Oxford?"

"Loving it. He and Deborah try to take some time every weekend to explore the area."

"Who? Who's Deborah?"

"Oh. She's . . . his—'lady friend' sounds stupid, 'girlfriend' sounds ridiculous. They've been together, involved, a couple of years now. She went with him to England."

"Well, that's big news. Good?"

"Yes." She ate more bread, still stupefied she'd had any part in making it. "She's wonderful, and they're really good together. She's a widow, two grown children, also very nice. She's an artist, a painter. Dad happened to go to one of her shows, and . . ." Miranda spread her hands.

"He asked her out."

"She asked him out for coffee, and I think he was too dazed to make an excuse, the way he might have. I like her a lot, and in no small part because she makes him really happy. Before they left he asked me how I'd feel about it if he asked her to move in."

"And how do you feel about it?"

"More than fine. So, Mags?"

They hadn't talked about family since they'd struck their deal.

"Is she still doing the phone psychic thing?"

"As part of the whole. She and another friend of mine have a psychic gift shop in the Quarter. Readings and magic stuff."

"A psychic gift shop. I really have to meet your aunt one of these days."

"She's hooked up with this Cajun guy, sort of like your father and the artist, I guess."

"Do you like him?"

"Sebastien, sure. He's, like Mags, unique. He—you could call it subcontracted me—for the LaPorte job because he'd tripped over his ugly little dog and bunged up his ankle. That dog—Bluto? Maybe weighed in at about five pounds, and had a deadeye stare that could scare the *cocodrils* away."

"Sebastien's a thief?"

And as he reached for his wineglass, Booth realized he'd gotten entirely too comfortable with her again. "That's right."

"Who works for this LaPorte?"

"No, it doesn't work that way. It's . . . like contracting. He took the job, then tripped over the dog and couldn't do the job. LaPorte's not the sort who'd take personal injury into consideration, so Sebastien contracted me."

"How did he know to contract you?"

Caution came back, even if, he admitted, a bit too late.

"A mutual friend."

"Another thief? Do you all know each other?"

"No, and no."

"You don't resent Sebastien for getting you tangled up with LaPorte?"

"I knew what I was getting into. Or thought I did—a job. If Sebastien had known, if I'd known, LaPorte would decide to add me to his collection of possessions, we'd have found another way."

His tone changed, went cool and final. "Look, Sebastien's the closest thing I've had to a father, okay? It's not his fault. It's not your world, Miranda."

"For the scope of the book, it is. So no den of thieves where y'all hang out and brag about your big scores?"

"Definitely not. Bragging gets you caught. Stay under the radar, don't get greedy, never carry a weapon, don't steal from friends or associates. Steal smart, live free."

"Why do you think LaPorte's so determined to own you?"

"Now, there's a question I've asked myself a few thousand times. First? I said no. He wanted me to turn on Sebastien and I said no. People aren't allowed to say no to LaPorte."

"Yeah, I got that impression reading between the lines of the articles and features I found on him. And?"

She might not have a feel for cracking a safe, but she sure as hell had one for prying out information. No harm filling her in, he thought. She already had plenty on him.

"And second, maybe I did the job too slick. It was a damn good vault, and I just have a knack for them. And, looking back, I should've lied, told him, yeah, I took a few other things, because it intrigued him I didn't."

"Why didn't you?"

"Because that wasn't the job," Booth said simply. "LaPorte's a man with a long reach and he found out enough about me to know how I worked. I was young, like, eighteen, and good at what I did, with the potential to be better yet. He needs to possess the best, the most valuable, the most desirable, the most whatever. He decided I fit that, or would.

"And I said no."

As he looked back, as he looked forward, Booth finally picked up his glass. "I'll take back that painting and that sculpture one day."

And there she saw what she hadn't before. A low fire simmering.

"Why would you do that?"

"The painting started it, and the sculpture cost me everything that mattered to me. I wanted to put on that damn cap and gown, even give grad school a shot. I wanted to hang out with the friends I'd made, and sit on my neighbors' porch and drink sweet tea."

His gaze shifted to hers, held. "I wanted you." Then he shrugged. "He won; I lost. But the game's not over."

Cap and gown, grad school. She'd thought—or convinced

herself, she admitted—he'd just used all that for cover. But she heard the ring of truth, and saw it in that low simmer.

And hearing it, seeing it, she felt a quick, hot spurt of anxiety for him.

"You should leave it alone, Booth. Leave him alone. You've made yourself a good place here, have a good place here. Looking to pay him back, taking some kind of revenge, isn't that breaking your rule about staying under the radar?"

"Exception proves it, right?"

It rubbed him just raw enough, even after all the years, to have him saying what he wanted.

"I was going to ask you to move in. After graduation, if I could wait that long. I'd ease off the nightwork and be Booth Harrison, maybe try teaching or figure out what I'd do. Maybe buy a house and fix you up a studio where you'd write. It all seemed clear as glass.

"Then he came to the door, and the glass shattered. He's a patient man, but so am I. And I'm not twenty and afraid anymore."

"I would have moved in with you," she said after a moment. "But we were twenty, Booth, and we can't know if we'd have made it work. If what we felt for each other at twenty would last."

"We never had the chance to find out."

Her eyes softened, and though she didn't reach out, he all but felt her hand on his.

"I think Sebastian Booth's had an impact on a number of young minds, and made himself a solid place in this community. That wouldn't have happened otherwise. Since you can't change what was, it's smarter to build on what is. Now, I have one more question."

"What?"

"What's a *cocodril*?"

It surprised him to find the laugh. "It's Cajun for alligator."

"I thought Cajun was French, or a kind of French."

"It is, and has its own idioms, slang, rhythm. You could do me a favor, and for this book anyway, not put any of that in."

"It doesn't fit anyway." She rose, and in the habit they'd developed on their Sundays, began to clear. "Do you speak Cajun?"

"*Mais, cher*, you pass by next Sunday I gotta make a grocery bill, me. Maybe you catch me some *bons amis* and we have us a *fais-dodo* and pass a good time."

Laughing, she shook her head. "That's another knack of yours. Not only the language but the accent. You sound like you were born in the bayou."

"Parts of me were. Sebastien has a cottage in the bayou. He taught me a lot."

She loaded the dishwasher while he divided up the leftovers. Some for him, some for her.

"Your psychic aunt lives in a cottage in the bayou?"

"No, she lives over the shop in the Quarter. They like having their own space, I guess, and it works for them. At first I thought—to my mortification—it was just sex with a healthy dose of affection. But they love each other."

"If I ever decide to set a book in New Orleans, would they show me around, give me some local flavor?"

"Sure. They like your books."

It always surprised her to hear it. And left her both flustered and proud. "They do?"

"They're both big readers—another attraction, I guess. I've never known Mags to go anywhere without a book in her bag. Or a bunch of crystals, five shades of lipstick, a tarot deck, and—since Sebastien—a baggie of dog treats."

"I seriously have to meet Mags."

She turned, bumped lightly into him. Rather than step back, Booth put his hands on her shoulders.

"I can't," she said, and she stepped back, began to gather up her things. "Thanks—as always—for an amazing meal. Meals, as you've again tubbed me up tomorrow's dinner."

"No problem. I like cooking for somebody other than myself. You ask the bulk of the questions, and that's the deal, but I have one."

She put on her coat, wound her scarf. "Okay."

"Is anything still there?"

"Yes." Keeping her distance, she met his eyes, and gave him the truth. "There's always been something there, which is why I can't. I'll see you next week."

PART THREE

THE RED GODDESS

Look with thine ears: see how yond
justice rails upon yond
simple thief. Hark, in
thine ear: change places; and,
handy-dandy, which
is the justice, which is the thief?

—WILLIAM SHAKESPEARE

Were beauty under twenty
locks kept fast,
Yet love breaks through and
picks them all at last.

—WILLIAM SHAKESPEARE

Chapter Twenty-One

SHE DIDN'T INTEND TO go into the theater. She'd wanted, for a scene and with Lorna's permission, a stroll through the school after hours.

But she heard the music, the voices, and slid through the heavy double doors.

A dozen teens had the stage, with Booth standing stage left.

Strong voices, he'd said, and she agreed as she slipped into a seat in the back row.

She identified the girl playing the lead, and agreed again on the dancing skill. She didn't appear to hold anything back, but then she played an angry teenager who snuck out for a night of rebellion.

A few in the chorus missed the beat, and one spun in the wrong direction.

"Cut the music."

"I'm sorry, Mr. B!"

"Don't worry about it, Carlene, that's what rehearsals are for. Remember, everyone, where you are. It's the Ice House, where you come to cut loose, and damn it, you've got a lot of living to do. Mark, give me those jazz hands, and, Alicia, a little sharper on the *pas de bourrée*. Nothing fluid here, sharp. Snap it."

When he demonstrated, Miranda's eyebrow winged up.

"From the top. Places. Music."

Some missteps, Miranda noted, which Booth no doubt saw and would deal with. But all in all, just fun.

So much fun she had to resist applauding at the end of the number.

She watched another ten minutes while Booth worked with a couple of individual dancers and the others took a break.

She considered the fact it was past five, and he'd already put in more than eight hours. And when he finally got home, she mused, he likely had papers to read and grade, or lesson plans to finish.

She hadn't followed her father into teaching for very good reasons, she thought now. To be a good one, you needed the education and training, but you had to have the passion.

Her father had it, and from where she sat, so did Booth.

She slipped through the doors again.

Kim and her friends had a lot of living to do, but she realized she had a lot of thinking to do.

Despite her best intentions, Miranda got roped into attending a book club meeting. She found it nearly impossible to refuse her godmother, and Cesca apparently found it equally impossible to stand up under Carolyn Stipper's pressure.

Just one meeting, she reminded herself as she parked in front of Cesca's house. To answer questions on her first book—cannily assigned that month—and drum up more interest in her upcoming signing.

The early March wind had fangs, and she wished, with every inch of her chilly bones, she could just curl up at home with someone else's book, in her pajamas, with a glass of wine, and listen to that damn wind rattle the windows.

Instead she'd dressed in what she considered her casual professional clothes. A black cashmere sweater with a bit of the tail and cuffs of the crisp white shirt showing, stone-gray trousers, and black, stubby-heeled boots.

She'd French-braided her hair and added simple studs to her

ears and a silver-framed moonstone pendant she'd found at the Treasure Chest on Main Street.

She started to knock, but over the wind heard voices and laughter, so just went in.

"There she is!" Cesca popped up from one of the living room chairs—several folding ones joined the usual—and hurried to embrace her.

"I'm sorry, am I late?"

"No, no. Let's have your coat. You're right on time. You haven't met everyone yet, so everyone, this is Miranda."

A chorus of female voices responded with, "Hi, Miranda!"

Some had wine, others what looked like coffee or tea. They ranged in age from their twenties to possibly eighties. And all looked at her with eager, curious faces.

She thought again, longingly, of her pajamas.

"Come sit down. We saved a chair just for you. Tracey, honey, get Miranda a glass of wine."

"No, I can—"

"I'm on it." Tracey popped up.

"We like to have a chatty little time before we get to our discussion. You know Lorna and Tracey—thanks, Tracey," Cesca added when the Realtor brought in the wine. "And Margo."

"The pendant looks great on you." Margo, proprietor of the Treasure Chest, beamed.

"And Carolyn, of course, and Layla—you spoke to some of her students last month."

She began introducing the rest so the names rattled around in Miranda's head.

She sucked at this, she thought. Just sucked at this part of writing.

But she put on her delighted-to-meet-you author face.

Oddly, it got easier when they began to pepper her with questions. Even, she realized, enjoyable when she sat back as they debated each other.

And who wouldn't find vast entertainment in listening to a couple of women argue—with considerable passion—about one of her characters?

The character she'd based—loosely—on Booth.

"He was an asshole," Margo insisted. "A himbo asshole."

Miranda held back a snicker, as that's exactly what she'd aimed for.

"He was so young," Lorna argued back. "Barely out of his teens."

"He used Fiona," one of the others put in. "Used that charm, that and the shy-boy pose, to lure her in. Just for the sex."

"Guys that age all think with their dicks."

"When does that stop?" Cesca wondered, and got a subtle pat from Lorna beside her.

The oldest member—Esther, retired librarian—cackled. "I'll let you know if and when."

"He did use her." This from Layla. "And then tossed her aside so coldly. But still, he paid such a terrible price for it."

"What do you say, Miranda? Asshole or victim?"

She smiled at Lorna. "It can be both. And y'all are right. He was an asshole, he did use her—and the way he tossed her aside played a part in her emotional life and her choices for a long time. But he never had the chance to redeem himself, to choose to redeem himself or not."

Because, Miranda could admit to herself, she hadn't wanted him to find redemption, or have a choice. She'd wanted to end him, and by the act of writing that end, close off her feelings.

It had worked, for a very long time.

She had more fun than she'd expected to, and realized her circle of female friends had spread out and scattered so much since her college days, contact found itself limited to occasional—and too-rare—dinners, and more often texts and emails.

She'd missed the casual intimacy of women gathered together.

As the evening broke up and Cesca chatted at the door with people heading home, Miranda carried glasses and dessert plates into the kitchen with Tracey.

"I'm really glad you came. It adds something to have the person who wrote the book right here."

"Adds something for the writer, too. And I loved seeing Cesca with good friends. She took a big leap moving here."

"She did, and that was really brave. We love her."

"I could see that. I'm glad I had a chance to really see that."

"Speaking of moving—even temporarily—how are you liking life on the river?"

"It's great. The house is perfect for what I need right now. I've got the quiet, the convenience, and the views."

"And a sexy neighbor," Tracey added. "I had an open house last Sunday out your way, and noticed your car at Sebastian Booth's house."

She thought: Whoops!, but kept the casual tone. "Oh, he's helping me with some research. I'm working on a character, a chef."

"And the man can cook. We dated some—way back—but I got a sample." She grinned when she said it. "He's a good guy."

"Seems to be," Miranda said easily. "I sat in a corner of the kitchen at Renalo's for a couple hours, so got a solid sense of how a restaurant kitchen works. Booth's giving me more a sense of—I'd say it's an art—of making food. My idea of cooking is to open a jar and call for Chinese."

"I hear you. Nick and I are trying to learn together to make actual food instead of grab and go. It's nice, cooking together. Sexy, too. Just saying."

She didn't want sexy, Miranda thought as she took the short drive to Booth's the following Sunday. Not for this area of the book, and not in her personal life.

But what she did want for the book was the sensuality of cooking. All those senses engaged—the scents, textures, the sizzle and simmer, the act of slicing, stirring, blending. And tasting.

She pulled in beside Booth's car and realized someone else could drive by, recognize hers. And speculate.

Didn't matter, she decided. She'd go back home in a few months, and Booth? He'd stay or he'd go.

Icicles dripped from the eaves of his house, and the quiet plop-plop reminded her spring lurked around the corner. Somehow March had arrived—and the book signing loomed.

Rather than think about it, she admired the snow.

He'd shoveled, plowed, snow-blown the drive and the walk, but the rest lay untouched, a white blanket with a thin glimmer of ice from melt, freeze, remelt.

Smoke curled up from the chimney, so she knew a fire waited inside.

And so did he.

Walking a fine line, she thought, coming here week after week, spending these hours with him inside all those scents, flavors, textures.

For her work, she reminded herself. And, admittedly, to prove to herself she could walk that fine line without slipping off.

If she still had feelings for him, she handled them.

She rang the bell, wiped her boots on the mat, and geared herself up to handle it.

He answered—jeans with a hole working into the knee, a sweatshirt, ancient Chucks that comprised his usual Sunday uniform.

"I told you you didn't have to knock."

"I rang, but in either case, blame my southern upbringing."

His house smelled of oranges and vanilla. The fire snapped; the floors gleamed.

"Did you polish the floors?"

"Yesterday."

She took off her coat, scarf, and, because he'd do it if she didn't, took them into his mudroom—depressingly organized, to her view—to hang beside what she decided was a work jacket.

For shoveling, plowing, or snow-blowing.

"I've got wood floors. Am I supposed to do that?"

"Wood needs to be cleaned. Plus, it gets thirsty. Plus, it looks better. You have those amazing floors in your family house. Didn't the cleaning crew clean and polish them?"

"Yes, now that you mention it." And she added a chore to her list for the rental. Rather than ask him how to do it, she'd look it up.

Less lowering.

"So. I'm planning a heist."

"Okay." He got them both Cokes. "What are you after?"

"Inspired by these private hoarding rooms, I want him to break into one, take a painting—artist to be determined—an antique ivory netsuke, I think, and a carved French porcelain vase from the Baroque period."

"That's quite a haul. Sticking with art?"

"That's his thing. So how does he do it?"

"You tell me."

When he sat, she slid onto the next stool. "It's an estate, inside a family compound," she began.

She described the house, the grounds, and gave him a good picture. He could imagine himself finding the weak spots, the blind spots, going over the wall, and gave that back to her.

For the first hour, he took her through the steps, the pitfalls, the tools while she took notes.

She'd fill in the drama, she thought, the tension, the risks and rewards, but he gave her the practicalities.

"Say there's also a vault in the room. Would he try for that, too?"

"It depends on how much time he has, and how greedy he is. It's going to be money, maybe bearer bonds, jewelry, or loose stones. If he's primarily an art thief, why not just take more of what's sitting right there?"

She frowned at that. "You wouldn't go for the vault?"

"Not unless what's in it is my target to begin with, no. But he's not me."

"No, he's not. I think he goes for it, because stealing's an addiction for him. It would be, for him, like an alcoholic on a binge saying no to one more round."

"It's a miracle he hasn't been caught before."

Maybe, she thought, but . . . "He's been lucky—that can happen—and that feeds the addiction. It's the murder of the woman he used that changes things for him. He liked her, but he slept with her purposefully to get the bird. He succeeds, and she's murdered. It looks like whoever stole the bird killed her. But he stole it, and didn't. Now it's like 'The Tell-Tale Heart' for him. The bird's haunting him, and finding out who killed her becomes more important than the addiction."

"So the heist is before the bird and the murder."

"I'm going to open with it." More editing, more redrafting, she thought, but worth it.

"I wasn't, but I realized I needed to set him up for the story and the reader right off. I want that impact, that tension straight off, showing who he is. That way the changes, the redemption—so to speak—and the outcome all have more impact.

"I hope," she qualified. "Then the juxtaposition of showing him cooking, his restaurant, his other life."

"There was a Renoir stolen from a home in Houston about a decade ago. Worth about a million back then. It might be a good choice. Most people know Renoir if not the painting. *Madeleine Leaning on Her Elbow with Flowers in Her Hair*. You can look it up."

"I'll do that. Did you steal it?"

"No. Armed nighttime robbery. I don't do armed or terrify people."

"Because I want him sympathetic—and because I see him pretty clearly—I'm taking a page from your book on that. He doesn't hurt people, and that makes his guilt over the woman sharper, because the theft caused her death."

Booth got up as she spoke, retrieved a large bag from the refrigerator, then a bowl, a pot, and some newspaper. He poured shrimp from the bag onto the paper.

"You got me thinking about New Orleans last time, so we're making shrimp étouffée."

She set her notebook aside, but close enough to scribble something down. "I've not only never made it, I've never eaten it."

"That changes today." He gave her an assessing look. "That's a nice sweater, so I'd roll up the sleeves. We start by peeling the shrimp. The shrimp go in the bowl, the peels in the pot to make the stock."

"We're making stock out of peels?"

"It's how it's done."

When he peeled about ten to her one, she hissed. "I've only peeled them after they're cooked—like spiced shrimp."

"You'll get there."

She got there, slowly, then washed her hands. A lot.

Booth set out an onion, celery, and a green pepper. "Behold, the holy trinity of New Orleans cooking."

"Do we pray over it? To it?"

"Neither. We're going to chop half the onion, a rib of celery, and use the top and bottom of the green pepper for the stock."

She had to detour to note it all down. "How does that make stock?"

"By adding water, chopping some garlic, tossing in some bay leaves, and cooking it for about forty-five minutes."

He sliced the onion, started chopping, so she took the celery.

"How is it your eyes don't water when you chop onions?"

"My steely will."

He guided her through the rest, then put the pot on the stove.

Then he had her kneading bread dough again.

Doing her best with it, she shot him a look. "Do you ever consider just buying bread?"

"You know what the difference is between a loaf of store-bought French bread and homemade? Everything. You've got a good hand for kneading. Form your ball, and we'll let it rise while we get started on the roux."

"I know the term, but what is it, exactly?"

"Flour and fat."

"Yum."

At that, he flashed a grin. "You're damn right, *cher*. Brown roux for étouffée." He glugged—no measuring—oil into another pot, got a whisk, and began adding flour. "You're going to stir it, constantly, over the heat. You don't want clumps."

"Nobody likes a clumpy roux."

"And you don't want it to burn."

Call for delivery, she thought, slap a sandwich together. You still got food.

"How long do you have to do that?"

"Ten, fifteen minutes. It'll go silky."

She decided cooking Booth's way meant she could skip a day of upper body work. Her bis, tris, and shoulders got a solid workout every damn Sunday.

"And after your arm falls off?"

"You have a nice, flavorful roux. Try it."

"My thief has an eclectic restaurant," she said as she tried her hand at whisking. "So I can see him making this." She leaned over to look at the other pot. "I guess it's starting to look like stock."

"Because it is. Keep whisking."

"Right, right. I'm going to have serious guns between all the kneading, the whisking, the stirring. Oh, I saw some of your rehearsal last week."

He'd crouched down to select a bottle of wine from his cooler, stopped to look up at her. "You did?"

"I have this scene in school, after hours, thought why not get a feel, and I heard the singing. You were doing 'A Lot of Livin' to Do.' They're really good, Booth."

"They're getting there."

"I sat in the back for—well, about as long as I have to stir this roux, and really enjoyed it. I didn't realize you did the choreography."

"We can't afford to pay somebody to do it, and I'm lucky to have a couple students and cast members who know dance. They've had some good input."

"It looked like fun. Like the kids were having fun."

"No point in it otherwise. They work hard, so fun's important."

He opened the wine, got out glasses.

"I'll take over, you can have a quick break before we do the vegetables."

"More chopping."

"The rest of the onion, the green pepper, a few jalapeños, more celery, more garlic."

She took the wine, leaned back on the counter while he continued with the roux. "I did the book club—Cesca's book club—a couple of days ago. That was more fun than I thought it would be. I really don't like sitting around analyzing a book, especially my own. But they're a nice and interesting group of women."

"Lorna tried to pull me in. We need a man, Booth. Be a man," he said in a very credible Lorna tone. "I like talking books, but the whole assigned reading? I have school for that."

"Tracey's one of them. She mentioned she saw my car here last Sunday."

He glanced over. "Is that a problem?"

"No, I told her you were helping me with research." She gestured to the pots. "This sort. I didn't realize the two of you had a previous thing."

"We didn't, not really. We liked each other. Still like each other. We just got together a few times. Is that a problem?"

"Of course not."

"Good. Get chopping."

She chopped. "You know, some of this is oddly soothing. Not quite zen, but soothing. More work than I'd put in making a meal for myself, but I might actually try something simple and have Dad and Deborah over for dinner."

"Over? I thought you lived at home."

Now she chopped and laughed. "God, Booth, I'm over thirty! I have my own town house. My own space. I see Dad all the time, but I moved out years ago. I actually toyed with—for about five minutes—following Zed and R.J.'s lead and trying New York. Did you know they moved to New York the summer after graduation?"

"I saw Zed on Broadway a few years ago."

"You did! Did you talk to him?"

He shook his head. "Better to avoid awkward questions. But he was really good—he played Billy Flynn in a revival of *Chicago*. Do you keep in touch?"

"Off and on. I know R.J. just got engaged. He didn't pop like Zed, but he's done off-Broadway and regional."

"How about Hayley?"

"She's in L.A. She's a screenwriter. She loves it out there. She got married last year."

"Would I have seen any of her stuff?"

"She's working on a streaming series. *Cold Play*. Second season."

It seemed normal, and soothing rather than prickly, to talk about the lives of people they both knew. Or had known, in his case.

"I'll take a look. Need those veg now, this is ready. Hold the garlic, but all the rest."

He switched to a wooden spoon, stirred and mixed as she added them. As they stood close inside the heat from the pots.

"That's going to cook a few minutes, then we'll add the garlic, cook it a couple more."

"Isn't it crowded in your brain?"

"Lots of rooms and boxes in there. Punch down the bread—remember how?"

"It's my favorite part but for the eating."

"Punch it down, use the tool to divide it, cover, then let it rest on the board."

It was . . . interesting, she decided, and satisfying—at least enough she could transfer the feeling to her character.

"I'm never going to love cooking, but I see how some do. All the scents, the colors, the feel of bread dough in your hands."

He showed her how to add the stock to the pot, then how to shape the bread before the next rising.

She sat with her wine. "This dish is labor intensive."

"Worth it. So, your book signing's coming up."

"All too soon."

He took a moment to sit next to her. "You don't like doing them?"

"It's not not like. I always feel just a little odd, at least at first. It's great, really, meeting readers. People who'll actually sit down and read what you wrote. I end up being energized and drained at the same time.

"I like the quiet," she said with a sigh. "Which is more odd, but it's why, in the end, I didn't go to New York, or L.A., or somewhere else. Traveling's wonderful. Seeing, experiencing, all great. But I like knowing I have the quiet after. Why not New York, for instance, for you? It seems like you could disappear there, if that's the goal for your sabbatical."

"I like the quiet."

He shifted to the view out his kitchen doors. "I like looking out at that instead of traffic or a street, people hurrying from one place to another."

So did she, oddly enough.

"How did we get so boring? Although I can't say what you do is."

"It's a job, it's work, a career choice." He shrugged it off. "And it takes a lot of quiet time. Like writing."

"I think that's the only similarity you can pull out on that."

"I don't know." After angling his chair, he stretched out his legs. "You plan, you plot, you have a goal, you make adjustments as needed, and you work alone. And now you're going to make another egg wash."

"Oh God."

"And we're going to add the shrimp, make some rice, bake the bread. Then we'll have a really good meal."

Chapter Twenty-Two

HE DIDN'T LIE.

Miranda sampled a bite, held up a finger, took another.

"This is great. It's got some nice heat on it. And it's pretty." She tried the bread, sighed. "Okay, maybe you've got a point about the difference being everything."

"You made it."

"I helped make it."

"No, I helped," he corrected. "You worked on every step of the meal. You should be able to show your chef character putting a meal together like this."

As she ate, she considered her character, his flaws and somewhat shaky virtues.

"He's attracted, drawn into, the sensuality of cooking. Even in the chaos of a commercial kitchen, that's part of it for him. Smoke, steam, sizzle, scents. The stealing, that's business—the family business, and an addiction. But cooking, that's passion. I may decide to have him retire—at least try to—from the business at the end. I'm not sure yet."

Then she considered Booth. "Do you ever think about that? It's not a family business, but you could say it's something you grew up in."

"I thought about it in college. Now I'm taking this longer break than I planned on, and I'm living this life."

She wanted to know for the book, but she couldn't deny she just wanted to know.

"Isn't that hard, even disorienting? Shifting from one life to another?"

"I don't know." He couldn't say he thought too deeply on it, but . . . "Basically, it's acting, and to inhabit a part, to really project the character, you just become. And sometimes it's liberating. Sort of tabula rasa, then you can see what you write on the next slate."

"That's interesting." She gestured with her fork. "I suppose everyone, at one point or another, wishes they could just wipe the slate clean, start over, do, be, have something else."

Thoughtfully, she scooped up more étouffée. "I guess that's what my mother did."

"Does that still sting?"

"No, no, not really. I can work it up to a sore spot at most, and do," she admitted, "when I'm feeling bitchy about it. But really, it's just part of my history."

"Is she still in Hawaii?"

"She is, though not with the guy she left with."

"Biff," he remembered, and made her laugh.

"No more Biff. That went south five, six, seven—not sure— years ago. Apparently, he did to her what she did to Dad, but took most of their money with him."

"Nice guy."

"Well, you get what you pay for, so to speak. I know all of this because she actually contacted Dad, begged for a loan. I objected, but he overruled me."

"She gave him you."

She nodded over a bite of bread. "That's exactly what he said, and shut down my objections. Anyway, he sent her money—not a loan, just here you go—so she could get back on her feet. She now owns a tattoo parlor, has her own tattoo sleeves, got a boob job, and has a boy toy—he looks about my age."

She sipped wine, smiled over the rim. "Social media. I couldn't resist."

"So she started another slate."

"It must be hard, being so dissatisfied with your life every few years, never finding the sweet spot. I'd feel sorry for her, but I just don't have that sort of generosity in me."

"It wouldn't matter to her," Booth pointed out. "Why waste it?"

"Excellent point. It's not like that for you. For you, it's part of what you do. Clearly, you're happy in the life you're living now."

"Sure. Part of it's the luck of where I landed, stumbling onto this house before I'd even nailed down the job. Some days it's drudgery, or you tangle with a kid who's determined to screw up his life, and yours if he can. And I'll think, hey, I could be sitting on the terrace of a villa on Corfu, looking out at the Ionian Sea, and sipping some ouzo."

And strangely, despite the sweatshirt and worn jeans, she could see him there.

"But you go back the next day."

"Because the next day lights some spark, and you see—actually see—something click in some kid's head, you see the door open. Or you see a bunch of kids onstage, reaching for something. And you know some of them are going to grab it and hold on to it."

He shrugged. "And the Ionian's not going anywhere."

"I've never been to Greece. Would I like it?"

"I did. The culture, the art, the antiquity, the food, all of it."

"I bet you learned the language."

"Enough to handle myself."

"Say something in Greek."

He looked in her eyes, her sea-witch eyes. "*Écheis ta mátia mias thalássias mágissas.*"

"Sounds like more than handling yourself. What did you say?"

"I said," he lied, "it's nice to have company for an excellent meal."

"It is. At home, on a day like this I'd probably open a can of soup and shake a portion out from a bag of salad."

He winced. "That actually hurt my heart."

She winged up the eyebrow. "I could go a little wild and squirt some Cheez Whiz on a few crackers."

"Stop."

"Quick, handy, tasty. Anyway, tell me about one of your jobs. No, not just any," she decided. "Your first. The first time you broke and entered."

He knew she'd circle back to the book, and told himself to accept it. "That's a pretty good one, actually. A client's neighbor was over during a cleaning job, and they sat in the dining room having coffee, talking. I'm doing the kitchen floor while the neighbor's complaining and joking about her husband's stamp collection. Obsessed with it, she claims, and tosses out big numbers he paid for this single stamp."

He picked up his wine. "I hadn't given stamps a lot of thought, but that got my attention."

"How old were you?"

"About twelve. I'm mulling over it while they're talking about this charity fundraiser they're doing, so I volunteer to help the neighbor haul out some of the stuff for the auction from her house to her car."

"So you walked right into her house."

"Helped her with the boxes, got a good look at the alarm system. I could take that. Actually saw the husband's study. It fell in my lap."

"Your twelve-year-old lap."

"Yeah. Biding my time. The neighbors had vacation plans, so I waited until I knew I'd have an empty house. Nice big house, nice, quiet neighborhood. It didn't take much to get through the locks or bypass the alarm."

He paused a moment while it rushed back, every detail. "It felt incredible. No point in pretending otherwise. Standing there in the dark, silent house where I had no business standing. I knew I could go all through it, take anything I wanted, and no one would ever know."

"Is that what you did?"

"What? No."

"Why not? You're twelve, and everything's there for the taking."

"Because that's not how it works, not for me. Knowing I could was the magic. The stamps were the job. Anyway, I'm in his study, going through his stamp albums. He had them well catalogued. I pick out what I'd researched, and . . .

"Lights flash on, music blasts."

Miranda actually jumped, then laughed at herself.

"They hadn't gone on vacation after all?"

"No, they'd gone, but what I didn't know is their son bopped in from college to party. Now I'm hunkered under the desk in the guy's den, and college boy's in the kitchen—right through glass doors—in his boxers. And he's with a girl, in her underwear. They're pouring wine, and sexy dancing."

Laughing until she had to press a hand to her stomach, Miranda pressed the other to her face. "Oh God. What did you do?"

"Well, I watched—and tried to figure out how to get out, with the stamps—but mostly just hunkered down in the dark and watched. Then she started stripping while sexy dancing, and we'll just say I had a strong reaction."

The next laugh snorted out before she could stop it. "I bet you did."

"I'd never seen a naked girl. A real live naked girl, and he's pulling off his boxers, then they're all over each other, right there in the kitchen. I knew how it was supposed to work, but I'd never seen it actually work in person, in progress."

Delighted, she propped her elbow on the table and her chin on her fist. "Stamps or live porn. What's a pubescent boy to do?"

"Hard choice, but I needed to get out while they were distracted, so I took the stamps, slithered out, kept slithering, reset the alarm, and took off."

He rose to clear. "They never copped to a break-in, but figured somebody helped themselves at one of the parties he had. And I paid a lot of bills with those stamps, and furthered my education."

At twelve, she thought as she helped him clear.

"So was that your transition from picking pockets?"

"I wouldn't say that. I just diversified."

She started to load the dishwasher, the signal their Sunday session wound down. If she regretted the wind-down, just a little, it seemed natural.

"Can you show me how you did that with my watch? How you got it off without me feeling it?"

"It just takes a light, quick touch."

He brushed a hand over her wrist.

"Like that."

She held up her arm. "I'm still wearing the watch."

"But you're not wearing this." He held up the necklace. "It's a nice moonstone. Distraction," he told her, "and a light, quick touch."

Her mouth opened in shock, then she let out a laugh. "That's ridiculous, and I wasn't that distracted."

"Just enough. You probably want this back." He draped the necklace back on, and from behind her, clasped it. Those fingers skimmed over the nape of her neck.

If she closed her eyes, just a moment, over the sensation, it seemed natural.

"I do, thanks. It's a new favorite piece."

"How about this?"

She turned, saw her watch dangling from his fingers.

"Booth! All right, that's past ridiculous into uncanny." She took back her watch, clasped it back on. "You could have a magic act."

"Nothing up my sleeve. Except . . ." He slid her necklace out of his sleeve. "This."

Her eyes sparked, both amusement and wonder. "I can see anytime I walk down the street now, I'm giving everyone else a ten-foot berth. And your aunt taught you?"

"The basics, yeah." He circled a finger so she turned again, and smiled when she deliberately closed a hand over the watch on her wrist. "In her defense, it was entertainment, not a guide. There you go. Moonstone, that very nice Baume and Mercier. I'll just keep these for the lesson fee."

He held up her earrings, grinned when she slapped her hands to her earlobes.

"Come on!"

"French wires. Easy pickings."

"I'll remember that." She held out her hand.

Instead, he moved in another few inches to slide one, then the other back in place.

"They look good on you."

"Thanks." She felt her heart slip and the longing rise. "You're blocking me in, Booth."

"Sorry." He stepped back, and those clever hands went into his pockets. "I'll finish up in here. I'll give you some to take home so you lay off the Cheez Whiz."

He walked to the island, got out a container.

Miranda stood where she was. "That's the thing about you. Another thing about you. You take no and don't push. Even though we both know, right now, a little push would be to your advantage."

"I don't want to push for advantage." He looked straight at her. Straight into her. "Not with you."

"I can't repeat a mistake."

Like a fire sparked, his eyes went molten. "It wasn't a mistake, and I'm damned if you'll call it one. You can say the way I handled things was, and okay, even though I don't know what I could've done otherwise. But that time with you, those last couple days, it was the best weekend of my life, before or since. It was perfect. It wasn't a goddamn mistake."

Temper kindled temper. "You could've told me the truth, that's an otherwise."

"Really? So in your scenario, I say, Hey, Miranda, the girl who's just spent an amazing weekend with me, whose father's not only one of my favorite professors, but who's had me in his home, I say, here's a fun fact about me. I'm a thief, plus, all those transcripts that got me into the university? Fake. And now some crazy rich guy I pulled a job for a few years ago is back. He wants me to do another, or he'll hurt my aunt, maybe you, maybe the handful of friends I've made. So now what?"

He shoved at the container, paced away. "Call the cops? The FB-fucking-I? And tell them what? This guy wants me to steal this statue? Oh, why me? Because that's what I do. My name? Oh, well, which one?"

"Maybe you're right. I don't know. Maybe I could've helped. You don't know."

"You don't know, I don't know. But what I do know is if I'd told you, he'd have more reason to hurt you. I didn't tell Mags until it was done for the same reason."

That stopped the rise of resentment cold. "You didn't tell your aunt?"

"Not until it was over, and I was on my way, basically, to France. She wasn't all that happy with me either, but she was safe."

She didn't know why that changed things, even a little. But

it did, it did, she thought, because he loved his aunt, and she'd been a constant in his life.

"How did you tell her if you left?"

"Burner phones. I got her and Sebastien burner phones. No emails, no letters, no other communication. I didn't see her until the next year. She goes to Mardi Gras, and she slipped out to the private plane I arranged and flew over. We'd promised each other we'd spend a few days together every year—no exceptions. On or before April first."

His only family, she thought. His only connection to home.

"And you've both found ways to keep your promise."

"Yeah, we find ways. So."

He walked back, finished filling the container. His tone was calm now, as if the spike of temper and emotion hadn't happened.

Holding himself back, she realized. Holding his true self in.

And wasn't she doing exactly the same?

"You must have enough for your book by now."

"Probably."

"It'd be easier on both of us if we cut out these Sundays."

"Probably," she repeated.

He held out the container. She took it, then set it down. Enough, she thought. Enough pretense, enough filters, enough denials, on both sides.

"Why don't you ask what I want?"

"What do you want?"

"Maybe I wanted you to push a little so I didn't have the responsibility, but that moment's past."

She crossed to him, laid her hands on his cheeks, touched her lips lightly to his.

And her heart did a slow turn as he looked at her so much like he had that first day in class, a thousand years before.

Intense, wary, a little pissed.

"Maybe I want to take back, even if it's just for today, what he stole from us. I loved you the way you can love at twenty. No restrictions, so sweeping, with the future all laid out in beautiful colors. Maybe I want a little of that back, even if it's just for today."

"I don't—"

"I think you owe me. I think you want to make it up to me for dimming those colors." She kissed him again, felt him hold back, pull back. "Make it up to me, Booth," she murmured.

She linked her arms around his neck, then boosted up to wrap her legs around his waist. "Take me upstairs." Her head swam, her kisses turned urgent. "Take me to bed, or I'll have to have my way with you on the kitchen counter."

"You're not allowed to regret it. You're not allowed to call it a mistake."

"We're adults now." She feasted on his throat as he carried her out of the kitchen. "It's just sex."

He stopped, drew back to meet her eyes. "We are, and it's not."

Undone, she dropped her forehead to his. Not a mistake to admit it, but a risk. She took the risk. "No, it's not." She did what she'd wanted to do for weeks, and combed her fingers through his hair. "I'm only going to ask you for one thing."

"I'm inclined to give it."

"Don't just leave again. I won't either. If and when it's time for one of us to leave, we don't just go."

"Deal." In the bedroom, he set her on her feet, then reached up to unbraid her hair. "If you change your mind about this . . . they'll find my broken body on the ground under the window."

"I can't be responsible for that." She tugged off his shirt, then skimmed her hands over his chest. "You've really kept in shape."

"A paunchy thief's a slow thief. God, your hair." With it loose, he buried his face in it. "I missed seeing it, touching it." With his eyes on hers, he lifted her sweater up and off. "Seeing you, touching you."

He gathered her up, gathered her in, and finally met her mouth with his and let himself take.

What he wanted, all he wanted. A dream come to life, a dream swimming in his senses until it saturated him.

With slow, sumptuous kisses, with her mouth yielding to his, taking from his, the past and present blurred together into something separate and only theirs.

A flower, long dormant, finally unfurled.

He laid her back on the bed, linked his fingers with hers. To draw out the moment, he feathered kisses on her brow, her eyelids, her cheeks. Then, with her lips against his, sank.

Everything in her woke and stretched and yearned. She hadn't slept, she thought. She'd had a life, lovers, work. But with that kiss, it felt as if some part of her, something elemental, woke again.

He kept her hands clasped in his while his lips roamed, and the sensation of helplessness overwhelmed and seduced and taunted her to surrender.

"I've dreamed of you." His tongue slid under her bra to find her, stir her. "Of you, of this, and I'd wake up with the scent of your hair all around me."

He trailed lips, teeth, tongue up her throat. "Now here you are. You tortured me, sitting or standing in my kitchen, all those questions."

"I know." Breathless now, wonderfully breathless now. "I wanted to."

"Bull's-eye." He lifted one of her hands, nibbled her knuckles. "I'm entitled to a little payback."

Her hips arched; her pulse pounded. "Help yourself."

"Gonna."

He released her hands, and, in a lightning move, released her bra. She reached for him as he slipped it off, but he gripped her hands again. This time he took her arms over her head.

"I'm helping myself."

Her heart stumbled under the lazy demands of his mouth. Had she forgotten, how could she have forgotten how he could take and take, and give such aching pleasure?

The pleasure built, built, built until she began to tremble, then began to writhe. With his mouth alone, he shot her to peak.

He felt her rise, and he felt her fall before he released her hands so his could touch. All that lovely skin, so smooth, just a bit damp now from the heat they brought each other.

All those sweet, subtle curves and long limbs he could finally, finally touch and explore and possess again.

Her hands moved over him urgently as her body moved under his and offered all he wanted.

Then they knelt on the bed, rushing to undress each other.

Her laugh hitched out. "Get those damn shoes off. And finish what you started."

"I'm still looking at you."

"Look later, finish now. Booth. Booth," she repeated, and got those endless legs around him to take him in.

Her nails dug into his shoulders as her head fell back. And still he looked, the fall of her hair, the need in her eyes, as they took each other.

Everything he wanted surrounding him. A dream so long out of reach now warm and vibrant in his arms. Whatever price to come, he gave himself to it, to her.

No regrets.

She didn't curl up against him as she'd once done. She wasn't the naive young girl she'd once been, certainly no longer a woman who believed love somehow forged a path for all.

And he wasn't the sweet, shy boy she'd fallen headlong in love with, but a man so much more complex and complicated.

In bed beside him she could admit the man fascinated her.

An honest assessment—and she wanted honesty—added excitement and appeal. But all of those reactions didn't add up to love, which, even if it did clear a path, still left that path with bumps and pitfalls and obstacles.

So, she concluded, all good.

Then he reached over, linked his hand with hers. She closed her eyes and dug for defenses she usually had at the ready.

"It's not just sex," he said. "And we're okay."

"I'm not looking for romance, relationship, or happy-ever-after, Booth."

"Those things aren't on the menu for someone like me. And we're still okay. There's something between us, Miranda, and always has been. I'm willing to take that, for now, and be glad of it."

He sat up, looked down at her. "I didn't run, straight off, when I saw you again, because of the kids. But that wasn't the only reason. You didn't go straight to Lorna or the cops because you wanted some answers, and you could use them. But that's not the only reason."

She sat up with him, and now in the full dark, studied the shadow of him. "No, it's not. I'm only here until July."

"See, that's glass half-empty. I see it like I've got three months with you. So let's take them."

"I always think, if the glass is half-empty, get off your ass and pour some more into it." Giving in wasn't giving up, she thought, and brushed a hand through his hair. "All right, Booth, we'll pour some more."

He leaned forward just enough to touch his lips to hers. "Stay."

"That may equal filling the glass so it overflows and spills all over the floor."

"We'll start slower. Stay for coffee and dessert."

"You don't drink coffee."

"I'll have a latte."

"If you want to call that coffee." She cocked her head. "What dessert?"

"We'll have hot fudge sundaes."

"You do not have hot fudge sundaes in your freezer."

"No, but I have ice cream in there, a jar of fudge topping in the pantry, and whipping cream in the fridge. Put them together, and you have sundaes."

"Whipping cream. What's wrong with the stuff that comes in a tub or a can?"

"Don't get me started."

Before she could get dressed, he handed her a robe and pulled on sweats. After due consideration, Miranda decided if you knew you were being maneuvered, you weren't actually being maneuvered.

She handled the coffee while Booth transformed a container of whipping cream. Then she sat at his kitchen counter, in his robe, and ate a hot fudge sundae.

"I thought I'd come to your signing next weekend."

"You don't have to do that."

"I teach lit," he pointed out. "We have a bestselling author in the house. What kind of example would I set skipping it? And you can reciprocate by coming to one of the performances of *Birdie*."

"I'd already planned to. Really, nobody's going to notice or care if you come by the signing."

Amused, he tapped his spoon in the air. "That's where you're wrong after three months in Westbend. You don't like doing them—the signings."

"I didn't say that."

"Your whole body said that. Why not?"

She sighed, played her spoon into the ice cream. "They always make me feel like someone I'm not. Writing's solitary, just you and the story. Then after it's all done, people want you to go out there and, well, perform."

"Stage fright?"

"I never worried about going out on a stage. I liked doing

plays in school. But you're supposed to be somebody else in a play, that's the whole point."

"Every actor brings something of themselves to a part. The bookstore, in this case, is your stage."

"I like meeting readers. I'm grateful people spend the time reading something I wrote. It just takes me out of my nice cozy comfort zone."

"Where it's just you and the story."

"Yeah. Then again, one of the reasons I'm taking this time in Westbend is to widen that comfort zone. You can get entirely too comfortable, and then routine—and I'm a fan of routine—becomes a rut."

She licked whipped cream from her spoon, then gestured with it. "Ruts aren't a problem for you because you change routines, locations, everything whenever it suits."

"It doesn't always suit. Sometimes it's just necessary."

"My character's too invested in his restaurant to change things up. Hmm. Do you steal from women you sleep with?"

"No. Jesus." Appalled, he dragged his hands through his hair. "That's a hell of a question when you're sitting there naked under that robe."

"He does. That's a major plot point. He's slept with the victim, and she's not the first he's slept with and stolen from. Just the first who ends up murdered. Why don't you? Intimacy as access."

"Because, in the first place, it's just rude."

She laughed, then set down her spoon and laughed some more. Then, leaning over, she cupped his face in her hands. "You would think that, and feel that. It's part of what makes you hard to resist, that odd moral code."

"Squishy."

"Odd, squishy, but genuine. And in the second place? There's usually a second if there's a first."

"In the second place, it's a direct connection. If you're not already in the wind, the cops are probably going to have some questions for you."

"Yeah, I'm using that part." She picked up her spoon again, smiled at him. "You make a damn good hot fudge sundae."

"I also make a damn good cheese omelet. You could get in on that if you stayed. You're already in on it because I'll be making it from the eggs you screwed up making the egg wash."

Instead of one arching up, her eyebrows drew together. "I didn't screw up that many."

"I have more eggs."

She studied a spoonful of fudge-laced ice cream before eating it. "Does it come with bacon?"

"And toasted French bread."

"Well . . . I guess we could mop up whatever spills out of the glass onto the floor."

"I happen to have a mop," he told her.

She stayed.

Chapter Twenty-Three

SHE STAYED AGAIN MIDWEEK, after rehearsal, and found it oddly relaxing to sit and read in front of his fire while he graded papers.

Not a routine, she assured herself, not even an expectation. Just a casual invitation to come over after rehearsal for some homemade pizza. And stay.

On the evening of the book signing, she put on a simple dress in soft gray and topped it with a leather jacket in strong blue. She left her hair down and slipped on heels that matched the jacket.

Polished, professional, she judged, but not stuffy.

When she stepped out of the bedroom, she blinked at the rainbow of tulips in a clear, square vase on her kitchen counter.

She picked up the note leaning on the vase.

Break a leg.

Booth, of course. It seemed the thief had come in and left something rather than taking something away.

She wished she didn't find it charming.

"I shouldn't be charmed," she muttered, even as she put the note in her wallet as a kind of talisman for luck.

When she got to town, she went in the back entrance of the

bookstore, as instructed. She found Carolyn vibrating with excitement, and a counter stacked with her books.

"I should've asked you to come an hour earlier instead of thirty minutes! We've been taking online and preorders all day! People are already lining up, and, would you believe it, there's a TV crew from DC out there. I did a quick interview, and they're talking to some customers. Of course, they want to talk to you."

Even as she pumped up an enthusiastic smile, Miranda's stomach sank to her knees. "Great."

"You don't have a thing to worry about. We have a good, smooth system in place for events. And I'm going to help you get through these orders. What can I get you to drink first?"

A good shot of whiskey, Miranda thought.

"Just water's good, thanks."

"Got you covered!" Carolyn sang. "I can't believe our store's going to be on the *News at Eleven*, and maybe get another shot in the morning."

Miranda kept that smile in place as Carolyn handed her the water. And said, "Yippee."

Andy had billed her as "almost local" with her connection to Cesca, and it worked, as did his extensive social media marketing.

When she stepped out into the event area, she saw an impressive sea of faces, including Booth's, who stood with Cesca and Lorna.

The Q and A part of an event never troubled her. She knew how to answer questions, and did her best to keep that hat on when she did the—mercifully brief—interview with the DC reporter.

If she noticed Booth avoid any pan of the camera, she doubted anyone else did. He proved as smooth there as the Stippers did with their event system.

She sat at the table, signed books, took pictures with

customers, chatted, and eventually the buzzing in her ears subsided until she felt almost normal.

When Cesca stepped up, Miranda shook her head. "You already have the book, signed."

"And you'll see this isn't for me, but a friend of mine. Ronda's always bragging about her daughter the doctor, her son the lawyer. Let's see her top this! Oh, I'm so proud of you."

Then she motioned to Booth. "Please take a picture of me with my famous goddaughter."

Once he had, he handed Miranda another book.

"I thought you'd read it."

"I have. This one can go in my collection of signed books. You did a solid Q and A."

"Always the easiest part for me."

"I'm glad I got to see it. I have to take off. I've got tech tonight. Probably won't get home until about nine."

She understood the question in the statement.

"I'm having a post-event thing with the book club. I think I'll get home about the same time."

"Have fun."

She did, and a surprising amount of it. And still, normally she'd have gone straight home, changed into sweats or pajamas, then flopped down for at least an hour to stare silently at the ceiling.

Instead, she drove to Booth's.

"Good timing," he said when she knocked. "I got home about five minutes ago."

He pulled her into his arms. The kiss did a lot more for her equilibrium than staring silently at the ceiling.

"I've got champagne."

"So did Cesca, but I kept that to one glass."

"Now you can have two." He drew her back. "You looked, and look, amazing."

"Not stuffy was the goal."

"You more than hit that mark. I think you made Carolyn's year." Taking her hand, he walked back to the kitchen, and the bottle he'd just taken out of the refrigerator to screw into a bucket of ice. "You know, with Cesca in her pocket, she'll hound you back here."

"She already started." She slipped out of the heels and let out a sound of pleasure only a woman who'd been in a pair for hours fully understood.

"Have a seat. I'll open this."

"Been sitting for hours. You broke into my house."

"I didn't break a thing."

On her walk by him, she poked his arm. "You could've knocked."

"Less surprise impact," he said as he popped the cork.

"I'll give you that, and the flowers are beautiful. Thank you."

"You're welcome." He handed her a glass, picked up his own. "Congratulations on a successful 'Evening with Miranda Emerson.'"

She drank, rolled her shoulders, sighed. "And I'm so glad it's over."

"I liked watching you, in the spotlight, in the moment. It gave me a lift."

"You mean that," she murmured.

"Why wouldn't I?"

"I don't know. I don't know. I guess . . . it should be small-time for you, a book signing in a town like Westbend."

"It's not. It's where I live. And it's you. Maybe you could get past what I do just for one night."

"I think I've done a pretty good job getting past that. And I didn't mean it as an insult or a dig."

She sat now, sipped again. "I watched you, too. It's not all an act with you. You're not pretending to relate to people. You do relate to them. You're not using the spring musical as part of your cover. You want those kids to shine."

"Again, why wouldn't I?"

How to explain, she wondered, what simply was for him, and a winding road for her?

"It's all the normal for you. It takes some of us—me, for instance—a little longer to find that normal. When I first met you? I thought: Oh, he's a little shy. And of course, that made me determined to get through. That's how I work. But what I saw as shyness was really more caution. Necessary for you. So I can look back, and I know you meant the things you said to me, but it was all through your filter of normal."

He couldn't argue with any of it. Remembered all of it. "I can't go back and fix what happened."

"No, that's not what I mean. Not at all. It's just . . . You're an incredibly honest person for someone who makes their living in a dishonest way. And what you said to me before, about how an actor brings something of himself into a part? I'm seeing that you may change your name, even your look, your cover, all of it, but it's still you.

"I'm coming to terms with that."

"You could let me know when you get there."

"All right. Meanwhile, why don't you sit down and tell me how things went with tech?"

"You really want to hear it?"

"I actually do. Especially since it'll give me an excuse to have a second glass of this and unwind before I lure you upstairs and seduce you."

He picked up the bottle. "I'll make it quick."

ON HIS LUNCH BREAK, Booth took a quick swing to the theater. Hammers and nail guns pounded, and he heard the whine of a drill. As he headed down the center aisle he smelled fresh paint where some students worked on the drop of the train station for the "We Love You, Conrad" number.

Jill Bester, his student lighting tech's mother and volunteer set designer, stood over another student while he drilled a screw into one of the lower cubicles for the opening number.

"Good job, Chuck. We got her done." Then she called to Booth and tapped the bill of her fielder's cap. "What do you think?"

He studied the cubicles of varying lengths, widths, and could already see the cast standing, sprawling, sitting inside them with prop phones.

"It's perfect."

"It will be when we paint it." She walked over to a folding table for her tablet and brought up the design. "Check, check, right?"

He looked at the screen, the bright, bold colors, thought about lighting cues that would accent, spotlight. "And one more perfect. I don't know what we'd do without you, Jill."

"I love working on the spring musical especially."

"You're not going to quit on me when Tod graduates, are you?"

"Try getting rid of me. I've only got this crew for another twenty, but Missy drafted some of her art students to help with the painting next period. You'll be able to use the cubes and the kitchen set for rehearsal tonight."

"You've nearly finished the builds. Right on schedule."

"That's how we like it. You've put plenty of time in on it." She propped her hands on her hips as she studied what some would see as chaos.

"The drops should be done by the end of the week. And we thank you for not putting time in there."

"Another dig at my artistic talents."

"You have none in the drawing and painting fields."

"Harsh, but true. Grab some lunch, Jill. I'll check in later."

He snagged a Coke and an apple from the teacher's lounge, did a spot check on wardrobe, then set up for his next class. The upcoming weeks would run on the same frantic schedule. And he was fine with that.

He thought about when that schedule would loosen up again,

and wondered how Miranda felt about hiking, kayaking. He'd never had time to find out.

Should they be dating? Dinner out, a movie, a drive to DC for a concert? How could he be so in love with her and not have figured the simple things out?

They'd talk about it, he decided as the last bell rang, and kids made their noisy dash for the door.

Except for Louis, who always seemed to have a question after that last bell.

"Hey, Mr. Booth."

"What's up, Louis?"

It only took about ten minutes to address Louis's anxiety over the upcoming test on *Julius Caesar*. A transfer student from Pennsylvania, and a freshman, Louis had yet to find his circle, his comfort zone, or his feet.

"You know, Louis, I could really use another stagehand."

"Oh, I don't know anything about that stuff."

"We can show you the ropes." And there was nothing, in Booth's judgment, that helped open up a shy, anxious kid like theater. On or backstage. "Why don't you check with your parents, see if it's okay for you to watch rehearsal."

Louis's caution and anxiety leaked through like water through a crack in a glass. "Just watch?"

"If you want. We start at four. I'm actually heading there now." Booth rose, packed his briefcase. "You can walk down with me. You don't take the bus, right? You walk to school."

And both parents worked, Booth recalled. No sibs.

"Yeah, it's only a couple blocks."

Booth started out so the boy would fall into step with him.

"We're still working on the sets, but most of the builds are done, and we've got the props situated."

"Are all the stagehands kids?"

"That's right. The stagehands, the techs, the property master, stage manager, the actors. Students build and paint the sets, too."

"How do they know how to do that?"

Worry, worry, trickle, trickle.

"We teach them—some learned from a parent, but we teach and supervise."

Some students loitered in the hallways, flirting by lockers or texting somebody they'd seen two minutes before, but the school already had that hollow feel of a building that had done the bulk of its job for the day.

He turned into the theater, deserted now before the cast and crew began to come in. Booth saw Jill had finished the cubes and left them standing center stage, bright, bold.

Booth hit the house lights. "The kids built that, with Mrs. Bester—the mom of one of the students—showing them."

"What's it for?"

"Hang out and see. Call your mom."

"I can just text her."

"Do that then."

"Okay, but what does a stagehand do?"

"Some set pieces like that are on casters. They lock so they don't go rolling around. Stagehands come on between scenes. They'd roll that away and put the next set on its marks."

"What marks?"

Booth gestured, started down the center aisle. "Text your mom."

Gotcha, Booth thought as Louis peppered him with questions, texting as he walked.

By four-fifteen, Booth had wrangled the cast members in the scene into the cubicle.

"Joley, lean back against the wall, stage right. Give me a leg extension and prop your foot on the opposite wall. Yeah, that's it. Phone in your other hand—don't block your face."

He directed other students, then stepped back. "What do you think, Louis?" he asked the boy in the front row.

"It looks really good."

"I think so, too. Curtain goes up. Hold positions, hold for applause. Hold them until the music cue and the first ring."

He cued the music and watched the run-through. It gave him a lift, a good, solid lift.

He called out a few new directions over the voices, nodded as the kids made the most of their spaces.

When the number ended, Louis broke into spontaneous applause.

"Man, sorry."

"No one on a stage ever objects to applause, pal."

By five, he had Louis onstage moving scenery and props.

By six-thirty, the boy looked as if he'd been given the keys to the kingdom.

"Can I really be a stagehand, Mr. Booth?"

"As long as your parents give the go-ahead. You caught on fast."

"It's fun."

"Yeah, it is."

"Hey, Lou! You're walking my way, right?"

Louis blinked at the boy who called out. "Yeah, I guess."

"Let's book it."

When everyone cleared out, and Booth shut off the lights, he thought there were no kids like theater kids.

His footsteps echoed on the way out, hollow feeling complete.

Outside, a breezy March wind blew, but he saw the start of greening on the trees, and a few hopeful daffodils already starting to pop. Spring riding in, he thought as cars carrying his kids pulled out of the lot. A couple tooted, so he waved as he walked.

He kept walking when he saw the sedan next to his car, and the man who got out to wait for him.

Not the one he remembered from a dozen or so years before, but the same type. Broad shoulders, stony face, hard eyes.

A second man got out—slightly older, a little taller.

He didn't feel anything, he realized. Not panic, not grief,

nothing. After all, he'd known this day would come sooner or later.

"Get in the car."

"I've got a car."

"Hand over your keys. He'll drive your car."

Take a stand now, Booth thought, or everything rolls over and flattens you.

"I'll keep my keys, drive my car."

"You don't want any trouble here."

"No trouble. Your friend here can ride with me. But I drive my own car. Tell LaPorte you can follow me home. Where else am I going to go?"

After a short stare down, the bodyguard nodded to his associate.

Booth got in, pressed the ignition. He turned off the radio, as music didn't seem appropriate with a spine-cracker riding beside him with a gun on his hip.

He drove in silence and considered his options. He had contingencies. He always did. Maybe Miranda changed them, once again, but he had contingencies.

First order of business. Keep LaPorte away from her. Keep him away from Mags and Sebastien, Dauphine and her family. And away from the people of Westbend.

Second? Avoid broken bones or gunshot wounds.

After that? He had a variety of scenarios.

LaPorte wanted something. He wanted Booth body and soul, but he'd want Booth to get something for him.

He could use that, whatever and wherever it was.

He didn't flick a glance at Miranda's house when he passed it, but he caught the gleam of lights in her windows as dusk settled toward night.

He'd said he'd text once he got home.

That would have to wait.

He pulled into his carport and got out without a word.

Instead of going in through the mudroom—friends used that entrance—he walked to the front of the house with his passenger close beside him.

He heard the second guard get out as he unlocked the front door. Ignoring them, he went inside, coded the alarm. And used the first contingency by engaging the recorders and cameras he'd attached to it.

"Check the house, Angelo," the first man told Booth's passenger.

"There's no one here."

"Check the house. Do you have any weapons, Mr. Booth?"

"Your boss would've told you I don't use guns. I've got a really good set of knives in the kitchen. I like to cook."

He pointed to a chair. "Sit."

"I'm going to take off my jacket and hang it up. In there."

When he pointed to the closet, the guard crossed to it, opened the door, checked it and his other jackets for the nonexistent weapons.

Booth waited him out, then hung up his coat. He sat, set the briefcase beside the chair.

The guard took it, checked it, set it down again.

The second guard came back down the stairs. "It's clear."

"Tell Mr. LaPorte, then you can wait outside."

Booth occupied his time speculating on just how LaPorte had found him—and thought he had a glimmer there. And just what LaPorte wanted him to steal. There he hadn't a clue.

The man himself came in. He had a languid, in-charge stroll. He wore a gray pin-striped suit, with a paler gray shirt and a blue-and-gray-striped tie.

Business mode, of course.

His hair still flowed, a golden mane, and without a hint of gray. Since LaPorte was in the middle of his fifties, Booth concluded he covered the gray. Just as he knew LaPorte had work done here and there to maintain a face that taut, that smooth.

Vanity, of course. Everything stemmed from vanity.

"It's been some time since we've had a chat." Before he sat, LaPorte glanced around the room. "A bit rustic, I'd think, for a man with your vast experiences."

"It does the job for now."

"Yes, for now is part and parcel, isn't it? You live a nomad's life, yet here you are, playing at high school teacher in a—I suppose I'd call it a three-horse town rather than a one. You must be unspeakably bored."

"Not yet. I've enjoyed the break. What do you want me to steal?"

"Oh, we'll get to that. I left you alone through your adventures in Europe, and through your odd choice of this place, this life for the last few years. I could have, of course, visited you at any time, but I'm a patient man."

Lies, Booth realized. He left out South America, Australia, New Zealand, New York, and elsewhere. He hadn't known until now. And the lies—vanity—added power to Booth's side of the scale.

"And," LaPorte went on, "I realized you'd do better, for me, with more seasoning. Now you've had that time, we can discuss what's next."

"I have no interest in working for you."

Supremely confident, LaPorte waved a hand. "Your interest doesn't concern me. But I imagine your aunt continues to concern you. And Sebastien, perhaps, though you elect not to spend time with them. Do I bear responsibility for that?"

Some bait on the water, but Booth didn't nibble. "I've been busy."

"As so often happens with families, with friends. I hear you're very involved with your students—educating young minds. All so young, so fresh, with so much ahead of them."

"Really?" Booth let out a short laugh that was all disgust. "Threatening kids now?"

"Accidents happen, even in a quiet sort of town, don't they?"

"I'd say that's beneath even you, but I see it's not."

"I could move straight to the woman. What a treat it must be to have your long-ago love back in your life."

He'd been ready for this, and met LaPorte's gleaming eyes levelly. "Not really, no. What we want at twenty changes. But she recognized me. I didn't know about her damn godmother." Booth shrugged it off. "But I know how to stir embers when needed, and turn them to my advantage. She's susceptible to a sad story and a good roll in the sheets."

Booth caught the flicker of interest, and suspicion.

"She doesn't know what you are?"

"What do you take me for? She'd hardly keep her mouth shut if she did. My aunt, you see, had an unfortunate drug addiction that led to trouble with the police. I had to help her, had to try. Things didn't go well, and so on. I finally changed my name, finished my education, and was much too ashamed to contact Miranda again."

"And your aunt?"

"Well, she's dead—tragic overdose—for the purposes of this play. Now my college flame walks back into my life, and those old feelings bloom again. For a clever woman, and she's clever enough, she's an easy mark."

With the faintest sneer, Booth shrugged. "Most are if you know how to find the soft spots. I'd be sorry to see her hurt—I don't like violence. It's messy. But she's just another woman, another mark. You may have had a part in curing me of making attachments, but cured I am."

LaPorte steepled his hands. The interest on his face now didn't strike Booth as entirely pleasant. More that of someone eyeing a strange smear under a microscope.

"But you didn't finish your education. No degree for you, certainly no certification. All lies, all fake. Your superior at the school, the community, the parents, the authorities would find that revelatory, I'd think, should I send word their way."

"No doubt about it, but you're not going to do that."

"Aren't I?"

"You want something, and this cover works for that as much as it does for me. Blow it for me, and the cops come sniffing."

At ease, the thief stretched out his legs.

"You want me, LaPorte, because I make sure they don't come sniffing. I've made sure of it since I was nine. You have others you can call on, and have, to acquire things you want. None of them can say the same."

Relaxed, faintly amused, Booth sat back. "You can set the cops on me, and they can—if they catch me—put me in prison. That won't get you what you're here for. So let's cut the bullshit. Tell me what you want me to steal."

"You've yet to learn your manners." LaPorte flicked a glance toward the bodyguard.

"Be careful." Booth spoke very quietly and had LaPorte holding up a finger. "You've got a new guard dog, and you can tell him to smack me around like the other, but that won't incentivize me to get you what you want. You need me incentivized. You have nothing to pressure me with now."

Booth leaned forward, eyes hard and cold. "I made sure of it."

"You want incentive? Three million dollars. That's what I'll pay you."

Booth sat back, crossed his ankles. "That's not the staggering amount to me it was when I was twenty. I name my own fee, and I don't name it until I know what I'm going after."

"I'd like a brandy."

"I'd like a pair of hot blondes waiting upstairs for me. Tell me what the fuck I'm going after and you've got a better chance of getting what you want tonight than I do."

"The Red Goddess."

At the name, Booth's mask of bored derision slipped. Seeing

the stunned reaction, LaPorte smiled. "Now, I'd like that brandy."

"Most believe the Red Goddess is a myth."

"Most are idiots. Most don't know exactly where she is. I'm not an idiot, and I know. If you'd like to know as well, fetch me a brandy."

Chapter Twenty-Four

BECAUSE HE NEEDED A moment—maybe several—to clear his head, Booth rose to walk to the butler's pantry and his liquor cabinet. Though he'd have preferred a Coke, that didn't suit the persona he'd adopted.

Not just a thief, but hard, cynical, a user. Confident, heartless, self-possessed.

After he poured the brandy, he poured himself three fingers of whiskey, straight up.

The Red Goddess. The stuff of legends, of blood and death and betrayal.

There wasn't anyone in his line of work who hadn't had a dream or two about her, including himself.

But then, he reminded himself, people dreamed of dragons and magic coins. It didn't make them real.

He took the brandy to LaPorte, then sat again.

"What makes you think you know not only the Red Goddess is real, but where to find it?"

"Because it was put on auction last year, for bidding by a select few."

Pulled too far out of the game, Booth admitted, because he hadn't heard a whisper of it.

"You authenticated it."

"Would I have bid otherwise?"

"You've seen it."

"In a very restrictive setting. I held her in my hands." As he swirled brandy with one, LaPorte stared down at the other as if seeing the stone. "She's well named. There's no other like her. Nothing approaching her. In all the world, she is the only of her kind."

"Why didn't you buy it at auction?"

Temper flared, briefly, before LaPorte sipped his brandy. "The final bid was three million a carat, and she, the largest raw red diamond ever mined, half again the weight of the Moussaieff. Nineteen point eight carats, pure red. Absolutely pure, without a hint of brown or blue or green."

He sipped again. "Why would I pay sixty million when I can pay you three to acquire it?"

"You won't get it for three." Booth dismissed the offer with a slow roll of his shoulders. "Five maybe, depending. Who bought it? Where is it?"

"You might think to take it for yourself. To vanish with it. I'd think carefully. I'll kill you in the most painful of ways if you don't deliver the Red Goddess into my hands."

Ice-cold, Booth stared him down. "If I take a job, I deliver. It's annoying enough to have you show up at my door when you please and threaten me. I sure as hell don't want that stone weighing me down. I'd never be able to sell it—too much risk. If I take the job, you're the client. That's how I work, and you know it. I wouldn't have lasted this long otherwise. But I'm not taking a job without the particulars."

In the silence, Booth sipped whiskey and waited. He felt the subtle power shift when LaPorte broke first.

"She's in Georgetown. Washington, DC. I think of that as fate, as it makes it convenient for you. Alan C. Mountjoy acquired it."

"It would've been a blind auction," Booth commented. "No one knowing the identity of the other bidders, or the top bidder."

"Of course. But there are ways."

In the same flat tone, Booth asked, "Who'd you kill?"

"I don't kill. The man who possessed the Goddess murdered his own father for it. Arranging an accident seems like a kind of justice. And his death helped the one who ran the auction see the wisdom in cooperating with my very simple request."

"What happened to him?"

"He appears to have gone missing." Another sip of brandy. "People do. All the time. You won't go missing if you try to refuse the job now that you have this information. But Edward here will beat you to death, and he and Angelo will stage a break-in. A tragedy along the river."

"I'm not about to refuse. Why would I refuse the opportunity to steal a legend? But the fee's five million. Don't nickel-and-dime me, LaPorte. I may need to hire some help for this. Half up front."

"One million up front."

"No." He had to set the terms, and the tone. "Half. I'm the best there is. I'm the goddamn GOAT, or you wouldn't be here. Half up front, half on delivery."

"I want her within six weeks."

"No," Booth said again, and began to enjoy the iced anger on LaPorte's face. "You're hiring me, and I set the terms. I have a musical to put on."

Booth held up a hand before LaPorte could fully surge out of his chair.

"If I take off before that, before the end of term, there'll be questions. If I poof, they'll look for me. I've been here three years, and I'm part of the community. It's not like college and a few months. Jesus, I'm friendly with the chief of police, the freaking mayor. They'll start digging."

He turned the hand he held in the air side to side as if

considering. "I can do a lot of the research remotely, and I can take a weekend trip or two—after the show. Nobody'd think twice. I can take a vacation after school's out. No questions, then work out how to get the stone. By August, I'd say. And it's probably better if I come back, put in another year. Another year holed up here after the job of a lifetime.

"After that," Booth murmured, and let pleasure eke through. "After that, I can shake this place loose. It'll be cool enough back in Europe now. Or anywhere else I want to land."

Putting excitement in his eyes, he lifted his glass. "Those are my terms. Five million, half up front, half on delivery. And stay out of my way while I'm working. I don't want to feel you breathing down my neck. The job of legends."

He shook his head, drank deep. "By August. I put it in your greedy hands by August. This isn't the beginning of a beautiful friendship, LaPorte, but it's a very lucrative contract on both sides. Now finish your brandy and hit the road. I've got a lot of work to do."

"Do you think your arrogance and rudeness are somehow charming?"

"I think you mistake confidence. And since you hijacked me at my current place of employment, have threatened to maim and/or kill me, I don't give a rat fuck if you consider me rude."

Booth waited to see if he'd gone too far, if the stone-faced Edward would knock the arrogance out of him, but LaPorte set the glass aside.

"I'll leave you a way to contact me."

"Really?" Gesturing with his glass, Booth pushed a bit more. "You expect me to steal the Red Goddess, but you don't think I can get your personal cell phone number? I'll let you know where to wire the up-front. Don't come back here. Somebody sees you, questions? Somebody recognizes you? Deal's off. Let me get to work."

As LaPorte walked to the door, his bodyguard opened it.

"If you fail and run, I'll find you. And I won't be so patient or accommodating."

Booth waited until he heard the car pull out, saw the sweep of headlights before he went upstairs, changed into a black long-sleeved tee, black jeans, black high-tops.

Just in case.

If LaPorte had someone watching his house for his initial reaction, his first moves, they'd see nothing.

He switched on the light in his office, drew down the shades. The light would show against the window, but nobody would see in. He checked the recording on his laptop, then did a search, and confirmed his suspicions.

He slipped out the back like a shadow, and was in the trees within seconds.

He knew the way, had hiked these woods countless times over the last three years. The thin moonlight didn't provide much, but he didn't need it.

He had gotta-run routes mapped out in his head. Maybe he'd relaxed enough—too much, he admitted—to believe he'd ever need to use one, but the route he wanted now came clear.

That thin moonlight silvered the near shadows while the deeper ones held midnight dark. An owl hooted its curious two-note call, and something splashed into the river to his left.

He jumped over a long, thick branch that must've come down in the buffeting March winds, and kept his ears tuned for the sounds of a car on the road, any rustle that said human rather than animal.

Her lights gleamed, spots of light in the dark.

At the edge of the woods, he paused, scanned toward the road, then back.

He could see her clearly through a kitchen window. Her hair braided and falling over the back of a baggy gray sweatshirt.

He waited a full two minutes, but not a single car passed. Still, he did a wide circle of her house, looking for signs anyone watched before he went to the back door.

She had music on—loud—and he saw her pull a bag of popcorn out of the microwave. Rather than knock, he tried the door. He found it unlocked, shook his head, then stepped in.

"Miranda."

She didn't scream, only made a strangled sound as she spun around. The bag of popcorn shot straight in the air.

He caught it, set it on the counter. Closed and locked the door behind him.

"Booth! What the hell! You scared the crap out of me."

"We need to talk. Right now."

He pulled the kitchen blinds.

"Get the living room."

"What?"

"The blinds, Miranda. Just go close the blinds. I don't think he's got anybody watching your place, but close them."

"Who? And what?"

"LaPorte. If you close those damn blinds, I'll explain. Just go close them, casually, like you're settling in for the night."

She'd never seen him like this—cool, dangerous, impatient. And her heart wouldn't stop drumming.

"If you're trying to scare me, you're doing a damn good job."

"Good. And make sure your front door's locked."

She crossed into the living room, drew down the wooden slats. When she went to the door and he heard the lock click, he stepped out.

"I'll lecture you about an unsecured house later. You should sit down."

"I'm not sitting down until you tell me what the hell's going on. What about LaPorte?"

"He found me. He and a couple of his goons were waiting outside the school when I came out from rehearsal."

"Booth." Irritation shifted hard to concern. "Did they hurt you?"

"No. That's never going to be his first move. He starts with intimidation, threats, demands. He wants you to think he's got all the power, holds all the cards. But he made a mistake."

Booth paced now, now that finding her safe defused the low-grade anxiety. He'd deal with his anger later. Now was the time to look at the whole, see the steps, work out the plan.

"He lied. He lied right off, telling me he'd known I was here all the time. That's ego, vanity, the power play, and a mistake."

"How do you know it's a lie?"

"If he'd known, he wouldn't have waited. The TV crew at the bookstore. They took a shot of the Westbend Students Recommend wall, and Carolyn mentioned me, by name. He'd have feelers out, or maybe he has someone running a program. Sebastian Booth—those names. And you. Put it together, he'd dig deeper. So the way I figure it, he lied about knowing because he just found me."

"Because I did that stupid signing. Because I—"

"No, Miranda." He cut her off. "Not because of anything you did. Because he's like a cat at a mouse hole, and he sees me as the mouse. He's dead wrong."

"What does he want? What are you going to do? What—"

"Take a breath. Sit down. Please."

She sat, linked her hands together, took that breath. She felt, actually felt, that scarred-over crack in her heart open again.

"You have to leave, disappear again. You wanted to tell me first this time."

"I'm not going anywhere. I have a spring musical to put on, and finals coming up right after."

"I don't understand."

"I ran before because I didn't know what else to do. He had all the power, and I was afraid of him. For Mags, for you, for myself. He's repeating the pattern, almost straight down the line, but he's not dealing with the same person this time. And he lied."

Booth smiled a little because he understood all the fear he'd lived with had vanished like smoke.

"He lied so I'd be crushed under the weight of believing he could reel me in anytime. But he can't, and I'm a better liar."

Booth sat now, on the coffee table facing her. "And this time, I'm going to tell you everything. He doesn't know Mags and I are still tight. As far as he knows, I haven't seen her in years—and I played that up. She's really nothing to me. Neither are you. My bad luck you came to the area, worse luck you saw me, recognized me. But I played on old feelings, spun you a sad story. I've got a recording of the whole thing, so you can hear it for yourself."

"A recording."

"A remote switch on my alarm system. The whole thing's on my laptop. But highlights. I told you Mags—my only family—got into trouble. Drug addiction, police, desperation. I had to go deal with it. Ashamed, then in trouble, and so on. She died."

"Oh my God, Booth."

"You felt sorry for me about that, and bought I'd changed my name. Anyway, once I'd covered that ground, I played you into bed."

Through the whirling in her head, one thing stuck. "You've made me out to be a spineless idiot."

"That's right, and one I don't care about. Just useful in the moment, just handy. Be pissed off if you want," he added as her body stiffened, her eyes hardened.

"Oh, believe me."

"Fine, but let me finish. He bought I have to finish the term so nobody goes looking for me, starts digging. He should've thought of that himself. I've been here three years, made connections. It's not like a few months in college. So instead of a deadline of a few weeks, I have months."

"A deadline for what?"

"What he wants me to steal. The Red Goddess." Booth looked off in the distance, like a man gazing at something holy.

"What's the Red Goddess? A statue? A painting?"

His gaze shifted back to her. "No. It's a red diamond, raw, uncut, nearly twenty carats, and pure. It's the fucking Holy Grail for someone like me. And most who know about it think, like the grail, it's the stuff of myth and legend. But he's seen it, verified it, even held it."

"If he has it, why does he need you?"

"He doesn't. He got outbid at auction, an underground auction. It's all on the recording. The Goddess has a bloody history. She's the biggest red diamond in existence. People have killed for her. I imagine he's weighing the option of killing me when I get it for him. He absolutely plans to kill me if I don't."

The way he spoke of murder made her throat dry.

"You have to go to the police, or the FBI or whatever authorities handle this kind of thing."

"That's the last thing I'm going to do, or should. I'd end up in prison, then dead—he'd make sure of it."

"Then you have to run, you have to go. What else can you do?"

"That's easy. I'm going to steal the Red Goddess."

"You're going to steal for him? You're going to let him use you again?"

He gave her a look of such infinite patience, she wanted to smack him.

"I'm not going to steal her *for* him, Miranda. I'm going to steal her, then I'm going to use her to make him pay. I bought the time I need to figure it out, just how to do it. And I'll figure it out. He's not my client this time. He's the goddamn mark."

Reaching out, he took her hands. "You could decide to spend some time with your dad at Oxford. He thinks I'm like him, Miranda. That I don't care about anyone. He's not going to bother with you if you're in England."

"I'm not going to England."

"Just hear me out."

"No." She pushed up. "No. I'm not letting someone I've never even laid eyes on run my life, push me into doing what I don't want to do. He wrecked my life before. Not again. And now I want a drink."

She stalked into the kitchen. "You're not the same person," she continued as she took a stopper out of a bottle of Sauvignon Blanc. "Neither am I. Do you want a glass of this?"

"Now I do. It would just be until August, maybe September. Sooner maybe, I have to work it out."

"No. I didn't even know diamonds could be red, and now this greedy bastard and some big red rock are going to dictate my life? Just no."

"Diamonds come in all colors, and red's the rarest, so more valuable per carat than any. Most are small. Anyway, what's important is he's fixed on it. I can use that. I will use that. I don't want you catching any of the blowback."

"Why would I?" She tossed back her braid, then some wine. "You said you convinced him you don't care about me. You're just using me as cover. Like you used Mags as cover in the story you supposedly told me. You're out for yourself, right? Did he believe that or not?"

"Yeah, yeah, he believed it. Why wouldn't he?" He drank some wine, set the glass down. Then began to pace again. "He doesn't understand love. He doesn't love anyone. He feels for no one. Possessing drives him, not feelings. He doesn't even love the possessions. He used what I felt for you before, something he saw as a weakness. He thought he could use it again, and that he won't do. He won't use you or what I feel for you as a weapon ever again."

He turned, saw her standing in the bright kitchen lights just staring at him.

"God, Miranda, you have to know. I've never felt for anyone what I feel for you. Not before you, not after. It's always been you. Just you."

"How can you think you can say that to me, that I could hear you say that to me, then pack up and fly off to Oxford?"

"There's nothing I can offer you beyond what I feel. We both know that. Now, right now, I need to figure out how to solve this problem, because until I do, you're never going to be fully off LaPorte's radar. Neither is Mags. You're the most important people in the world to me, so I'm going to solve the problem."

Her heart didn't drum now. It beat hard, but it beat steady. "The problem's the priority?"

"It has to be."

She considered her wine, then nodded. "All right. How can I help solve the problem?"

"I don't—"

"You don't get to say you don't want me to help, don't need me to help, and you just want me bundled off a few thousand miles away like some helpless, useless, spineless damsel in a tower."

She'd stalked up to him as she spoke, and accented her words by drilling a finger into his chest.

"I don't think you're helpless, useless, or spineless—and never have. Decisive, determined, direct. That's always been you, so I wasn't exactly going the princess-in-the-tower mode."

"You also don't get to say: But, Miranda, I'll be worried and distracted unless I know you're safe."

He couldn't help himself. He reached out to run a hand down her braid. "Maybe I was going toward that mode."

"My feelings count, too. Plus, I have a brain. So you get one more chance. How can I help solve the problem?"

"Just let me . . ." He lowered his forehead to hers. "Adjust."

"Make it snappy."

The laugh dropped the tension out of his shoulders. "Let's start here. Pack up what you need for now. Your house isn't secure. I can fix that if you want. But if you pack what you need and stay at my place for a while, it would help eliminate that worry and distraction and let me focus. And," he added before she could object, "it might help for me to bounce some ideas off you. You know how to plot."

"That's better, and I can agree to that. I'll need a place to work."

"You can take the guest room for that, or if that doesn't work, I can move my school stuff upstairs and you can take my office."

"The guest room's fine. Give me fifteen minutes." She started out, paused, and looked back at him with those sea-witch eyes cool. "You're going to have to keep adjusting, Booth. This particular production? You're not a solo act."

He couldn't be this time, he admitted while he wandered her kitchen. Too many factors, too much risk, too much to lay on the line. So while Miranda packed, he took out his phone and contacted Sebastien.

When she'd finished, and he had the first steps arranged, he loaded her things—more than he'd anticipated—into her car.

"We're going to take your car back in the morning," he told her. "Until I know who he's sent to keep an eye on me, it's smarter to look like you're going back and forth."

"Just booty calls?"

"For right now."

"I'm fine with that. How will you find out who—if he does send someone—is here to spy on you?"

"He'll send someone. He didn't expect me to insist on staying, so he doesn't have anyone in place now. But by tomorrow, the day after, latest. Finding out shouldn't be hard. Whoever he sends needs a place to live. Either close to my house or close to the school. Who knows everybody who's in the market for a house in and around Westbend?"

"Tracey. Of course." She pulled in beside his car. "I can take that one. We talked about having lunch, so I'll set it up. I can ask her about that without being obvious."

His hesitation was knee-jerk, and he knew it, so set it aside. "It'll most likely be a rental, but LaPorte may authorize a buy."

"I've got this one, Booth."

"Okay." He grabbed the suitcase, the laptop case, a messenger bag, and started to reach for a substantial tote before she beat him to it.

"I'll need keys, and the alarm code," she told him as they carried her things in and upstairs.

Adjust, adjust, he reminded himself.

"I can set up my work area in the morning. Laptop and messenger bag in there. I'll need your Wi-Fi password."

She went about it all so briskly, moving into his bedroom, opening the suitcase. "And a designated drawer, some closet space. Also at least one vanity drawer and some shelf space in the bath."

She turned, smiled. "Adjusting?"

"Yes."

"Does it hurt?"

"Little bit. Have you ever lived with anyone before?"

"Other than my father, no. But I think it's clear I'm more flexible about it. I need my space—personal and work spaces. I'm not a slob, but I'm never going to be as obsessively tidy as you are."

"I wouldn't call it 'obsessively.'"

"Because you're the one who's obsessed," she pointed out. "It's a good trait, but I'm not going to meet your scarily high standards. You'll adjust, and I'll do my best to be respectful. And once we have those practicalities out of the way, we can concentrate on solving the problem."

He opened a drawer, took out T-shirts—a lot of precisely folded T-shirts—transferred them to another drawer.

"Is that enough?"

Hardly, she noted, but nodded. "For the moment."

He went into the closet, shifted a few things. Hesitated, then shifted a few more.

"There's already plenty of room in here. Rods and hangers, shelves. And I'm only using two drawers in the bathroom vanity. It's got six."

"Great, I'll use the other four."

If he wondered what she could possibly need with four, he didn't ask. "Do you need any help?"

"No."

"Great, good. I'm going to throw some food together. I haven't had dinner. Do you want something?"

"I haven't had dinner either."

"You were making popcorn."

"For dinner."

Rather than gape, he just closed his eyes a moment. "I can't even address that. I'm going to pretend you never said that. I'll be downstairs."

Alone, Miranda filled the single drawer, made use of the hangers in the closet and the shelf space. As she unpacked her makeup, her skin care, her hair products, bath products, she laughed to herself.

It was, absolutely, a terrible situation, a very real and dangerous situation. Yet she couldn't deny she would enjoy it—already was enjoying it—on many different levels.

Oh, his face, she thought as she looked at her own in his bathroom mirror. The stunned, blank look on it when she'd reeled off her needs for space in *his* space.

So used to having it to himself, being on his own, running his own schedule. Now he had to make room, share his plans, his space, and—at least for now—his life.

"Things change, Booth," she murmured. "And not just your name this time."

She stepped out, and glanced in the spare room—her temporary office—as she started downstairs. It made her grin, just grin when she imagined how he'd *adjust* to the fact that her work space would turn the room into chaos—on his scale—within twenty-four hours.

So she'd shut the door, she thought as she kept going. He had more important things to worry about. And now, so did she.

Whether he liked it or not, she was in this for the duration.

LaPorte had shattered her hopes, her young and lovely dreams, once. She—they—wouldn't let him do so again.

As she approached the kitchen, she saw him working at the stove, a cloth tossed over one shoulder.

Her heart sighed, just as it had at twenty. It sighed, she thought, even though now she knew what he was.

She'd deal with that, she promised herself. She'd deal with her feelings, and any hopes and dreams that radiated from them.

After they'd solved the problem.

She stepped in.

"So, what's for dinner?"

Chapter Twenty-Five

HE PERFORMED SOME SORT of miracle with pasta, grape tomatoes, cannellini beans, some olives, some spinach. After he plated
it, he grated Parmesan on top.

When they sat, she sampled the first bite.

"I don't know how you put this together in the time it took
me to unpack."

"Mad skills."

"You joke, but you have them. So what mad skills do you
need to deal with the problem? Idea bouncing," she reminded
him when he hesitated. "I'm not just here for the food and sex."

"It's a layered problem, so you deal with the layers. Once I
know who and where LaPorte's person or people are—I expect
at least two, probably a couple—two posing as a couple—I can
decide how to give them the impression I want reported back."

"And that way he thinks he's won the first round?"

"Sure. It might mean driving to Georgetown one night, or a
weekend morning, letting them tail me if they want."

More relaxed now that Miranda was where he needed her to
be, more focused on the steps and stages, he drank some wine.

"That also gives me a firsthand look at the target and its
environment. I'll need to do that two or three times, even when
I have the blueprints."

"You can just get the blueprints of a private home?"

He twirled some angel hair around his fork. "Mad hacking skills, and if mine aren't mad enough, I know a guy. The treasure room's likely near Mountjoy's private space—the guy who has the Goddess now."

"His name is actually Mountjoy?"

"Alan C. Oddly enough I have his place on my list of potentials." He caught her look. "Which has been tucked away since we struck our deal.

"Anyway, his treasure room's likely near his home office, den, or the master suite. It's going to be heavily secured, so I'll need to get the security schematics.

"What's he got?" Booth went on as they ate. "Alarms, cameras, maybe motion detectors, security lights, possibly a human element. Guards doing a ground patrol. Does he have a dog? He didn't last year when I put him on the list, but things change. I have to know if he has a dog. A pet, a guard dog. I normally give a pass if there's a dog, but if he has any, we'll deal with it."

She looked him dead in the eye. "You're not going to hurt the dog."

"Right now it's a possible dog, Miranda, and if it turns into a reality dog, no, I'm not going to hurt it. Red meat. A dog's a dog, and dogs go for a nice, fat steak. If I can't get by it that way, I find another. One of us will lure it away."

"One of us?"

He gave her a level look in return. "In this case, that doesn't include you. I contacted Sebastien. He'll start dealing with another layer of the problem. LaPorte has a kind of network," Booth continued. "People in my line of work, researchers, information gatherers, muscle. His own bodyguards and security, and ones who can travel if there's someone he wants to intimidate, threaten, pressure. Or worse."

Outwardly, she ate calmly, but her insides shuddered. "You're talking about assassins? Murder for hire?"

"That's right. Say he wants a piece of property in Lyon and the owners don't want to sell—and certainly not at his price. He sends someone to persuade them. One way or the other."

He'd told her some things about LaPorte, he thought, but she simply didn't understand the full power and twisted nature of the man.

And she'd need to.

"He covets things, Miranda, especially if they belong to someone else. Important things, unique things, priceless things, and when he covets something, nothing gets in the way of possessing it. Killing—ordering a killing—it's just removing an obstacle."

"He's evil."

Booth lifted his shoulders. "I think of him more as warped, but you can have 'evil.' He doesn't know I've spent a lot of years studying his patterns, his methods. I know some of that network, and Sebastien will work that level."

"What is that level?"

"I need a patsy. I've got someone in mind, but we have to work out the logistics."

"A patsy? That's not a word you hear every day." She stabbed a tomato. "What do you need a patsy for?"

"To take the fall, and connect to LaPorte so he goes down, too."

"Wait, wait." She'd reached for her wine, now set it down again. "Booth, you're going to frame someone? One of your own . . . associates?"

"Not an associate. Someone in my line of work who doesn't have what you called my squishy moral center. Somebody who really gets off on home invasions, and terrorizing the people in those homes. And hey, if the only way to get the combo of the safe is to pound on the guy's wife, or worse, that's a bonus. Fuckers like that give the rest of us a bad name.

"So yeah." With a shrug he wound more pasta. "I'm going

to frame him. LaPorte's going to hire him to steal the Goddess, instruct him it's a quiet job. Meaning, no violence, no trace. He'll leave trace, and plenty."

"I don't understand. Why would LaPorte hire him when he has you?"

"The patsy will think it's LaPorte, but I'll do the hiring." Booth smiled at her, and his voice became soft, arrogant, and southern. "A million cash ought to do it, with a deal for two more on delivery."

"That's good. That's what he sounds like?"

"You can hear for yourself on the recording." He considered as he ate, began to wind the plan like he wound the pasta. "I need a place in Lake Charles, something comparable to LaPorte's. We need to find the time and the place—and work it so LaPorte's shaky on an alibi for that time. I lure the patsy to that place at that time."

He looked off, visualizing it. "We'd need time to set it up, need the house empty for five to ten hours to do it right. Bring him in at night, have the meeting in what will look like LaPorte's office, make the deal, then break down the set and move out."

"You're making it sound easy. It can't be."

"Not easy. Layers, steps, timing. Details." He frowned over the ones already running through his head. "It'll take some work to fine it down."

"But hasn't this patsy seen LaPorte, and been to his house?"

"I can't confirm—yet—if he's been to Lake Charles, but he's dealt with LaPorte in person. That part's not a problem. I earned the name 'Chameleon' for a reason. I need to stay behind a desk. I've got a good three inches in height on LaPorte, but I can make it work. I need the location and that five to ten hours. I'll work on that."

He topped off her wine. "You've seen *The Sting*, right?"

"Newman and Redford? A classic. Sure."

"This won't be as elaborate or involve as many people, but it's the same concept at the base of it. And we bag two bad guys at the end. It'll work. I'll make it work."

Absolute confidence, she thought. She could admire that even if she didn't share it.

"You sound like you're looking forward to it now."

"I am. If I've had one goal since I left Chapel Hill, it's been to pay him back, to bring him down hard. I've got a clear shot at that goal now. I've got the endgame, so I just have to figure out how to get to it."

"What if this patsy contacts LaPorte?"

"I'll make sure he doesn't. I know the pattern. LaPorte doesn't want to be bothered, or leave any trail back to him. You take the job, you do the job, and you don't make contact—unless he gives you a contact. Maybe you get caught, and some get caught. Maybe you pull out his name to try to make a deal. Some investigator might go have a chat with LaPorte, but that's as far as it goes because there's no connection, no evidence linking him."

"But this time there will be?"

"Oh yeah." He smiled now, not only confident but with a trace of humor. "Trust me."

"Apparently, I do. I've got a good hand with research myself. I'm going to use some of those mad skills to learn more about this diamond. And I'd like to see the recording."

"Okay. I need you to remember I was playing him. The things I said . . ."

"I wasn't wrong about you twelve years ago. I'm not wrong now. Just one more question. What do you plan to do with the Red Goddess once you have it?"

"I've got some ideas—working that out. But none of them involve keeping it or selling it."

"That's good enough for the moment. I'll make a date with Tracey, find out what she knows about rentals or purchases, and tell her I want to extend my lease through August."

"Miranda—"

"For the duration, remember? I'm in this, Booth. Not on the periphery, not at a distance, but in it."

"If something goes wrong, if I get caught—"

"You won't. Didn't you just say you'd make it work? If you're that confident in yourself, spare a little for me. This time you've got backup. You've got a team. Get used to it," she suggested, then rose. "You cook, I do the dishes. I think that works out best for both of us."

She carried plates to the sink. "Oh, don't forget. I need the keys and the code."

HE'D LIVED HIS WAY for a long time—his space, his schedule, his rhythm. Booth didn't see himself as a man who'd have issues with making room, sharing, merging. More, he wanted her there—for her own safety, for himself.

He just wanted her.

Still, he experienced quick, unexpected jolts at seeing her clothes in his—in *the*—closet, and her toothbrush on the bathroom vanity.

She had, in short order, set up her work area. And within the first twenty-four hours turned the casual charm of the guest room into a kind of creative chaos.

Because part of him actually itched to straighten it all up, he began to wonder if he did have a problem.

He told himself he'd learn to ignore it, and, more importantly, he had other things to worry about besides scattered papers and stray coffee cups.

As always, he compartmentalized, the only way he could manage the lives he'd chosen.

He taught his classes, graded papers, dealt with the occasional unruly student—or worse, whining parent.

He had rehearsals, and first dress loomed.

He spoke with Sebastien, and filed the accumulated data.

And he planned the multiple levels of his job.

Most of all, he wanted to separate Miranda from all those plans. Maybe he did want to bundle her away in a tower—and what was so damn wrong with that?

He hadn't been able to protect his mother from cancer, and he'd lost her.

He wouldn't lose Miranda.

But she stood firm.

He taught his junior class on *The Tempest*—the brave new world, the sorcery, the betrayal, the romance. And thought about her lunch with Tracey.

She'd handle it, he told himself, and put it away for Prospero and Caliban.

SHE'D HANDLE IT, MIRANDA thought as she breezed into Water's Edge ten minutes early. She wanted to be settled at the pretty outdoor table in the sweet little breeze with her glass of lunchtime Pinot Grigio before Tracey arrived.

An easy assignment, she thought, and an enjoyable one, as she liked Tracey. She rarely if ever did the lunch-with-a-girlfriend thing back home, as she kept to a fairly strict writing schedule. So this equaled a nice break—the cherry on top.

A semi-fancy lunch with a friend in the frisky spring breeze by the water. And, hopefully, some solid information that helped Booth.

She wanted to help him, and—another cherry on top—wanted the excitement of being a part of a heist.

She didn't feel the slightest guilt, which surprised her more than a little. But what Booth intended to steal had already been stolen, and involved cold-blooded murder.

No stealing for profit in this case, as she didn't think her own moral code was quite that squishy. Simply a vehicle to right wrongs.

Since revenge equaled a gray area for her, she labeled it justice.

She strongly believed in justice.

She ordered her drink and settled in. She dressed for girl to girl. Bold purple suede jacket, linen pants and top, kicky boots, and she'd tossed on a fun scarf.

She spotted Tracey, in bright red and cream, rush in ten minutes late—exactly as Miranda had expected.

"Sorry, so sorry!"

"Oh, stop!" Laughing it off, Miranda picked up her wine. "I've been enjoying the view, the wine. I hope you're going to have some so I don't feel like an afternoon lush."

"Twist my arm. What she's having," Tracey told the waiter. "Thanks, Rod. This is so great. I didn't think I'd ever talk you into lunch."

"I really wanted the break, and to thank you for arranging the extension on my lease."

"Thrilled to do it. I can't wait to read the book. It's all so exciting. I hope you're having some time to enjoy the house, the water, the gardens. Things are popping."

"They are, and it's gorgeous. I was afraid someone else had the house booked, and I'd need to move. You must have bookings back-to-back, especially for river properties."

"Things are good. Thanks, Rod," she said again as the waiter brought her wine.

He rattled off the lunch specials, told them to take their time.

"You've got to try the calamari appetizer. How about we split it?"

"Sounds good."

"We'll start there, Rod, and figure the rest."

That done, Tracey sat back, took a sip of wine, said: "Ahhh." Miranda nudged. "You've been busy?"

"We have, and no complaints."

Nudged again. "Any new arrivals?"

"I actually just closed a three-month rental on a house just down from you. It usually rents by the week in season, but this

376

couple wanted a three-month lease. Nice people if you have a chance to meet them. He works in DC, and when he can't work remotely, he'll commute. She's a photographer working on a series of nature photos and wanted the location."

"Really? That's so interesting. Would I know her work?"

"Well, I didn't. They're out of DC, and this is, apparently, a new direction for her. I kind of think it's more a hobby, or has been, and he's indulging her. The house is seasonal—shuts down late fall to spring, and hasn't been updated in a decade, so this is a lucky break for the owners and for us."

"Sounds like it." Miranda broke a fat, soft, herbed bread-stick in half, offered some to Tracey. "What kind of work does he do?"

"I think it's supersecret government work, because he was really cagey about it."

Miranda wiggled her shoulders. "I love a mystery. You screen applicants, right?"

"Absolutely. He works for something called Legacy Consultants, and no flags there. She's freelance, and it does strike me as hobby time. Whatever, their credit rating was thumbs-up, they paid the first month and the security, and didn't complain about the dated kitchen and bath. The proper-ty's a hard sell for more than a week, and even then. I figured it would sit most of the season, again, and bam. Got the inquiry just a few days ago, and they're moving in tomorrow."

"Congratulations." Miranda tapped her glass to Tracey's.

"Thanks. Now, enough about real estate. How are things going with you?"

They split the appetizer, had salads, split an enormous fudge brownie with vanilla bean ice cream.

An easy assignment, Miranda mused when she drove back to Booth's. And a thoroughly enjoyable one.

Next time, she thought, she'd make a lunch date with Tracey just for the girlfriend factor.

But for now, she figured a drive by the river rental wouldn't hurt a thing.

WHEN BOOTH CAME IN after a long rehearsal, he found Miranda sitting at the kitchen counter with her tablet and a glass of wine. The fact that she looked completely at home brought on a tug-of-war of sensations. The oddity of having anyone so ensconced in his space pulled against the pleasure of having that anyone be Miranda.

He caught the mixed scent of sweet and savory in the air as she pushed her tablet aside and smiled at him.

"Hi. How'd it go?"

"Could've been worse." He veered into his office to lay his briefcase on his desk.

She rose and moved in to kiss him—such a strange normal, he thought.

"I took care of dinner," she told him.

"You cooked?"

"You sound both shocked and concerned. I took care of dinner, and my way of doing that is ordering Chinese. And I hope you're hungry, because since I didn't know what you'd want, I got a little of a lot. Grab some wine and sit down. I'll set it up."

"Just a Coke. I've still got work. Miranda . . . thanks for this."

"It's called teamwork, remember?" Very much at home, she got cartons and containers out of the oven, then began to fill bowls and serving dishes. "You may be used to cooking every night, but there's no need to when you're putting in ten- and twelve-hour days at school. Then dealing with the problem after you get home."

With a whip of her head, she tossed her braid back as she carried dishes to the table. "I thought, unless you have issues, I can order something in every couple of days, at least until after the show closes."

"That would be great."

"Consider it done. I'll mix it up."

He turned off the warming oven, as she'd forgotten to. He got a Coke, then joined her at the table. And took her hand.

"I appreciate this."

"It's Chinese takeout, Booth."

"It's food I didn't have to think about. It's been a long time since anybody took care of dinner for me."

She wasn't sure why that made her heart twist, but she gave his hand a quick squeeze. "The benefits of having a housemate. Oh, and I noticed something today. Not sure how I missed it before."

"Noticed what?"

"You have a kayak hanging from the ceiling of the carport."

"Yeah, I usually have it in the water by now, but things've been a little busy. You could rent one if you want and I'd teach you."

"You forget I grew up by a lake." She started with some General Tso's chicken. "I've been kayaking since I was a kid. Maybe we'll try out the river together when things aren't as busy."

More normal, he thought. Just easy, pleasant normal. "Weekend's looking good weather-wise."

"If the book cooperates tomorrow, maybe I'll go into town and see about a kayak. Meanwhile, I had a very pleasant lunch with Tracey today, if you're interested."

"Jesus. You moved fast. I thought you'd booked that for the end of the week."

"She had a lunch opening today, so I bumped it up. Here's a little more to push in that brain of yours—which must be crowded. First, I didn't even get a chance to use my crafty wiles to find out you were absolutely right about LaPorte sending people."

She let out a little gasp as she stared out the glass doors. Booth was on his feet in an instant.

379

"Sorry, it's nothing. I saw a hummingbird. Like a moving sapphire at your feeder out there. They're a favorite of mine, and it's the first I've seen this spring."

"It's okay. I didn't need those last five years of my life anyway. Who are you talking about, and how do you know LaPorte sent them?"

"She didn't tell me their names—I should've used those crafty wiles to get them, but I didn't think of it. A couple, and he supposedly works—remotely, for the most part—in DC for a consulting firm. Legacy Consultants. She's claiming to be a freelance photographer who wants to focus on wildlife. You know the house just about a half mile from here? The little one, older. Tracey says it needs some serious updating and only rents by the week—and rarely at that—in the season. They took it for three months, on the spot. Moved in today."

"I know the place." So easily brought it into his head. "The owner brings his buddies down for long weekends, fishing. More like a gut job than an update. Doesn't have much of a view either, but it's secluded. Private."

"There's a shiny black Mercedes G-Wagon in the drive, along with a BMW two-seater convertible. And yes, I had to look both of them up, as I don't know one car from another. That tells me they could afford a lot better for a seasonal rental, so my sleuthing senses say the location won. Secluded, within half a mile. And a nature hunter armed with a camera doesn't raise eyebrows hiking the woods, the river trails up this way, right?"

"It will now. How do you know about the cars?"

"I looked them up."

"I meant, how did you know to look them up?"

"I saw them—and could see the make sort of thing—when I drove by. It's a public road, Booth," she replied before he could say more. "And a road I live on right now. Driving by is normal, natural, and expected. I took note of the cars, and of the fact all the shades were drawn. Those same sleuthing skills tell me they're doing something in there, during their move in, they don't want anyone to see."

"Installing some security, setting up a work area. Smart thing would be to install a few outdoor wildlife cameras in the woods aimed toward my house. I'll think of something I can do, something they can send to LaPorte to keep him satisfied."

"I could bake some cookies—or better, do the fake-bake thing and put some from the town bakery on a plate. Take them over, welcome to the neighborhood."

"First, no." He ate a spring roll, chased it with Coke. "Next, 'fake bake'?"

"If I wanted to welcome someone, I wouldn't expose them to my cookies. It's a common thing, especially where I'm from. The taking over of baked goods, I mean, not the fake bake necessarily. It's just hi, y'all, and welcome. Then you hope they invite you in out of obliged politeness so you can be nosy."

"And again, no. I'll get their names, see what I can find out about them."

"How are you going to get their names unless you ask them? And you need those baked goods for that."

"No, I just need to hack Tracey's rental files. I could ask her if I ran into her, but this is quicker."

"Oh."

He could actually see her examining her ethics on the hacking.

"If Tracey knew, she'd help, but we can't tell her, so I guess this is a work-around. But wouldn't they use fake names?"

"Most likely, and most likely she has their fake driver's licenses on file. I can run facial recognition."

Both stunned and intrigued, she sat back. "You can do that?"

"Haven't had much call to, but yeah, I can do it. Or Jacques—a guy I know—can. Or Sebastien." He spoke absently as he looked outside.

"It's nearly dark. Too late for a casual walk in the woods," he considered, "and they probably wouldn't set up cameras until tomorrow, when I'm at school. I want a look at their equipment, but we'll see what we can find out about them first."

"You're going to sneak over there, aren't you?"

"Eventually, but I don't consider it sneaking."

"What then?"

"Work. We'll carve out some time this weekend for that kayaking. It's a pretty ride down that part of the river. Okay, I've got the dishes."

"No, clearly your crowded brain is a hundred miles away. I've got them. Go do the hacking thing."

Not used to it at all, he admitted. "Thanks. It shouldn't take long."

She considered that as he went upstairs. Was not taking long a bad thing, as it proved him adept at hacking into personal and business information? Or a good thing, as it wouldn't eat up much of his time learning about who LaPorte hired to watch him—or potentially do worse if they didn't like what they saw?

She tubbed up leftovers—she'd ordered far too much—loaded the dishwasher. Since she'd recognized the lofty standards of her housemate, she thoroughly cleaned all surfaces.

And because she wanted to see him hack, she went upstairs.

Chapter Twenty-Six

SHE HEARD HIS VOICE, and the laugh in it, as she approached the bedroom. He sat at the computer in his secret room talking to a man on the screen.

A good-looking older man, craggy face, a shock of silvery-gray hair, a stubbly little beard, and lively eyes. From the accent, she thought, surely Sebastien.

Then a strange, bug-eyed little dog leaped up and lapped at the screen.

"*Mais*, he has nothing but love for you, my Wiley."

"Why would you humiliate him with a rhinestone collar?"

"A gift from our Mags. He likes it. And so, you're sure this is Cannery?"

"A hundred percent. I recognized him from our near miss in Calais. It's been a few years, and he added the beard, dyed his hair brown, but I don't forget faces."

"Or anything else. I think LaPorte sends more than spies, me. Cannery's an enforcer."

"I won't give him any reason for that. I need to run the woman. She's going by Lori Slade, but that'll be bullshit. But knowing he's brought in someone like Cannery, I wanted you on watch. You keep an eye on Mags, Sebastien, just in case."

"*Cher*, I keep my eye on our Mags always, and the rest of me whenever I can."

"Jesus, Sebastien, she's still my aunt." Booth rubbed both hands over his face. The dog leaped up again with a little stuffed mouse clamped in his teeth like an offering.

"Wiley would share Coquette with you."

"Next time. I'm going to do a pass by later, just to see if I can get a look at their setup. Over the weekend, I'll get a look from the river. As soon as the show's done, I'll find you a place in Georgetown."

"No, I do that. That's for me, my part. LaPorte hounds you because I gave him your scent."

"Sebastien—"

"This is for me. *C'est tout!*"

"All right, okay." In a gesture of peace, Booth held up a hand. "Let me know when you have that set up."

"Send me the pictures of your new neighbors. I'll run the woman. I have a new program." His gaze drifted over, and he smiled—flirtatious now. "This is the Miranda. I'm very pleased to meet you at last."

"I'm sorry to intrude."

"Beautiful women never intrude, only enhance." Now he grinned at Booth. "*Ta rousse est glorieuse, mon ami.*"

"*Merci beaucoup*," Miranda replied. "*Je parle assez bien française.*"

"Then you come to my bayou and we'll have many conversations. You can bring *mon bon ami* if you wish."

"You're coming north."

"*Bien sûr*, when the time is right. No worries for you, *ma belle*. This one is mine, too, and I don't let harm come to mine. Send me the pictures. I'll have her name for you, her true one, before morning."

"I'll send now. Eyes sharp, Sebastien."

"As ever, *cher. À bientôt.*" He blew a kiss to Miranda, and broke the connection.

"I eavesdropped, and that's not an apology."

"It's not eavesdropping if I knew you were there. And I did."

"Tell me about this Cannery and Calais."

"In a second." He did something—sent the picture, Miranda assumed—then brought up a split screen of a man and a woman. The man looked to be late thirties, early forties, short brown hair, trim brown beard, cold brown eyes. The woman, a beauty, looked about a decade younger, sharp features, wide hazel eyes, her raven-wing hair worn short—sharp like her features—with a fringe.

"The neighbors," Booth told her.

"And John Madison is actually this Cannery."

"Lucius Cannery, and LaPorte sent him hunting me in France. He got close, too close, which is how I spotted him. Not that long after I was working a job in Paris and spotted LaPorte. So I decided to leave Europe."

"He's an enforcer, Sebastien said. Which means he hurts people, or worse."

"For a price, sure. But LaPorte wants me alive and well, at least for now. Cannery's insurance. The woman's the one who'll keep tabs. You just need to keep your distance."

At her steady stare, he amended: "We need to keep our distance. We run into them, we're casually friendly."

"Won't Cannery know you know?"

"He doesn't know I made him in France. LaPorte would never send someone he thinks I'd recognize." He reached up, took her hand. "I'm not keeping anything from you. Knowledge is power. It's a weapon. I want you to have both."

"So you were going to tell me you intended to—not sneak— pass by their house?"

"Maybe," he said after a moment. "I don't know. But I'd have told you if I found anything."

"What if I'd woken up and you weren't here? I'd've been worried, upset."

"You're right. I'm not used to having someone who'll worry or be upset. Maybe you could grade me on a curve for now."

"For now," she said, and took his face in her hands. "But the curve isn't endless."

"Got it." He rose, wrapped his arms around her. "I'm a pretty fast learner."

"Good, because I intend to educate you. But for now I imagine you have work to deal with."

"A couple things, yeah."

"You can add this if it's helpful." She took a flash drive out of her pocket. "It's everything I found on the Red Goddess. I imagine you already know all of it. How it was mined in Western Australia eighty-four years ago, its weight, its worth then and now, and so on. The untimely end of Carl Santis, the owner of the mine, before he completed the sale of the stone to a Lady Jane Dubois, a wealthy British aristocrat."

He knew the story, and all its varieties, but let her tell it.

"The unfortunate owner's partner then put the stone up for auction," Miranda continued, "and Lady Jane, apparently determined, ended up paying nearly eight hundred pounds a carat—or about four million pounds more than the original agreed-on price."

"Santis needed the cash flow, and set the original price too low."

"And was likely murdered by his partner, but they never proved that. I suspect money changed hands to keep him in the clear."

Booth smiled. "Do you?"

"Clearly. In any case, the surely murderous partner absconded with the money, leaving the mine and Santis's family in dire financial straits. The oldest son committed suicide, the daughter died in childbirth, the younger son fled to America and was never heard from again."

"Victims—if you buy into it—of the Curse of the Red Goddess."

"A lot of tragedy for one family inside a year. And the partner ended up floating facedown in New York's East River shortly thereafter."

"Some pin that on the younger son, some on the Goddess."

"Dead either way," Miranda finished. "Then came the week-long house party at Lady Jane's estate, which was supposed to conclude with the cutting of the stone by the experts she'd engaged."

"She set it up like theater," Booth put in. "Had the press there, fellow aristocrats, servants, security. A stupid, indulgent show of wealth and privilege."

"She paid for it, didn't she, as the stone disappeared never to be—officially—seen again. Major investigation, of course, and not a trace. I'd look at you"—Miranda tapped a hand on his chest—"but you weren't born at the time."

"Reincarnation?"

"Always a possibility. Anyway, I added in the multitude of conspiracy theories, the mythos, the curses, the supposed mystical powers of the stone—the Goddess's revenge, among others. The various accounts of sightings over the last seventy-five years. And I have a question."

"I can't promise to have the answer, but go ahead."

"Obviously LaPorte's seen the stone, had it authenticated. Why in the eight decades since it was dug out of the mine hasn't anyone taken this big, ugly lump of rock and had it sensibly cut into bright, shiny, beautiful stones?"

It took him a moment to find his voice. "Ugly lump?"

"Well, yes. It's just . . ." She held out her hands, palms up, to mimic holding it. "A big, dull lump."

He couldn't respond until he found the breath she'd knocked out of him.

"There's nothing like it in the world. It's the only one of its kind."

"There's only one Red Shield, right? The five point eleven

carat red diamond cut from the Moussaieff Red. And it's stunning. Maybe I don't care for the setting, but that's just personal taste. But people have murdered for this lump of carbon and never revealed what it holds. It's like Michelangelo leaving *David* inside the massive slab of marble."

He decided he needed to sit down. "That's one school of thought."

"Obviously not yours. What is yours?"

"It's pure, Miranda. It's a legend. If you read into that legend, you know it's said that anyone who's planned to or attempted to cut it met with one of those untimely ends."

"I'd let out an amused laugh and say you don't actually believe that, but I see you do. You who scoff at psychics."

"I don't scoff, and I don't not believe it. Lady Jane died of influenza three months after the Goddess was stolen from her. Josh Stein, the expert she hired to cut the stone, died in a car crash—a single-car crash—outside London only weeks later. The two assistants with him at Lady Jane's both died within the year.

"That's a serious run of bad luck, and doesn't include others believed to have been hired after the theft who ended up dead."

"So you *do* buy into it."

"A pattern's a pattern. I respect a pattern."

"But you're not worried about stealing it?"

"I'm not going to cut it or hire anyone to. If LaPorte plans to—and I doubt it—he's not going to get to keep it anyway."

"Who will? You've never said."

"I'm guessing that's going to be a long, protracted battle between the authorities and anyone claiming to be one of Lady Jane's heirs. She bought it. Then again, Santis's heirs could try a claim. Not my circus by that point."

"It belongs in a museum."

"And I don't not believe that. It won't be my call."

"What if it were?"

"I'd opt for the museum. I think—and you can hold the amused laugh—I think she wants to be seen, admired, respected."

"I'm not laughing, and I have an idea on how we could—possibly—make that happen. Do you know any forgers?"

Baffled, he frowned. "Maybe."

"What if, on her deathbed, Lady Jane saw the error of her ways and left instructions regarding her wishes for the Red Goddess? Explicit instructions, witnessed and certified by her attorney. Like a codicil to her will. And what if that codicil suddenly came to light?"

Maybe it seemed like something out of a Gothic novel, but . . . he liked gothic novels. "It'd be a hell of a coincidence."

"True, but . . . not our circus."

He swiveled right and left in his chair. Details, he considered. More details.

"Let me think about it."

"Do that." She set the flash drive on his desk.

He would think about it, he decided. If he could work it, it would be something he could do for her as much as for the Goddess.

Any document like it would undergo thorough examination and authentication. The paper, the ink, the seal, over and above the handwriting. If he could work it, it would cost him—time and money. But, if he made it work, worth it.

A kind of justice, he thought. Righting wrongs.

But first he had to get the stone, and he wanted more than blueprints. He wanted a good look inside the house.

He had some ideas on that, and, swiveling to his desk, began to water seeds he'd already planted.

THE SHOW CAME FIRST, and he wouldn't let his kids down, so he set all he could aside for the week before opening night.

That didn't mean he couldn't take a hike in the woods on

a Saturday morning. With Miranda, as she refused to let him shake her off.

"Keep any conversation light. We're just taking a morning walk."

"I've got it, Booth." She took his hand when they stepped outside into cool April air. "You should get a dog."

"I work all day."

"It just feels like a walk in the woods should have a cheerful dog trotting along with you. A big, goofy dog, that's your type."

"Big and goofy's my type?" She'd nailed it—him—and that baffled him.

"For dogs, yes. One that likes to swim so he could play in the river. Everything's getting green." She took a deep breath of spring as they took the beaten path through the trees. "Your lilacs are glorious. Birds are singing. I like that you have bird feeders set up in the yard. I should do that at the rental."

"They have some nice ones in town," he told her. He'd already spotted two cameras, and expected to see more. "But you're only here for a few more months."

"Oh, you never know." She said it breezily, sent him a coy look.

The first time, he thought, he'd ever seen coy on her face. She did a damn good job of it.

"I can write anywhere, after all, and I've gotten really fond of the area. Especially my neighbors."

He kissed the top of her head, and deliberately rolled his eyes over it for the camera.

"We—I mean you—should really think about getting that dog. Can't you just see a happy Lab maybe running around the woods, splashing in the river?"

"Tracking mud through the house, barking at squirrels."

She laughed, elbow poked him. "Oh, you!"

"Oh, me."

He felt it—someone watching, and not just by the cameras. And he heard it—the faint rustle, the quiet footsteps. He didn't react, just draped an arm around Miranda's shoulders.

"I don't have a lot of time today. I've got tech this afternoon."

"Opening night on Friday. I can't wait to see what you've done."

"It's about the kids."

"Of course, but you're guiding them through it. I love how dedicated you are to— Did you hear something?"

"It's probably a—" He broke off when the woman stepped onto the path.

She had a camera on a strap around her neck and a camera bag on her shoulder he suspected held more than lenses. Lean to the point she looked whittled down to muscle and speed, she stood in hiking boots, jeans, and a camo hoodie with a black ball cap over her short black hair.

"I'm so sorry." She held up her hands in apology. "Did I cross the line?"

He caught the faintest accent buried in her voice. She hadn't completely eradicated her Arkansas roots.

He gave her an easy smile, but made sure she'd see suspicion in his eyes. "What line?"

"The property line. I wasn't paying attention. I'm sorry," she repeated. "I'm Lori Slade. We've rented the bungalow." She gestured vaguely. "I'm a photographer. I was taking some shots. I didn't mean to trespass."

"No problem, as long as you're taking shots with a camera. We're not real fussy about property lines. Sebastian Booth."

"It's nice to meet you."

"Miranda Emerson. I think I drove by the day y'all moved in. Welcome to the Rappahannock."

"Thanks. It's beautiful. Just what I was after for my project. I heard what I think was a woodpecker earlier, and I grabbed my equipment, but I haven't found it."

"Get yourself a suet feeder," Booth suggested, all friendly neighbor. "They'll come around."

"Suet? I'll look into that. Thanks. I should get back. I didn't even tell my husband I was going out."

"Enjoy your weekend," Miranda called out as the woman slipped away again. "She gave me a start."

Booth just shrugged. "I don't know why anybody who could afford that Nikon rented a dump like that bungalow. But it takes all kinds. We should get back, too. I've got some chores before I head into school."

"You and your Saturday chores." She hooked an arm around his waist as they turned back. "You know, you could hire someone to clean your house."

"It's good mind-clearing work."

"But kayaking tomorrow, right? I'm going into town to get my own today."

"Sure. That's mind-clearing recreation."

"The new neighbor? She's beautiful. I don't think she had a speck of makeup on. And she looked so slim and competent. Didn't she?"

"Can't say I noticed." Booth kissed the top of her head again, rolled his eyes again. "I like redheads."

She giggled, snuggled against him as they walked back to the house.

When he closed the door behind them, Miranda turned to him. "That was her. That was—"

"Selene Warwick." He hung his light jacket in the mud-room, gestured for Miranda to hand hers over. "Born in the Ozarks. Got her start in the drug trade—transporting and distributing, not using. Graduated to murder for hire before she was legally old enough to drink. She's damn good at what she does."

"I meant what I said about her being beautiful. She is. But it's hard." When she caught herself rubbing the chill from her arms, she stopped. "Everything about her reads hard, and a little scary."

"You were a little scary yourself." He moved into the kitchen, got Cokes for both of them. "All coy, clinging, and saccharine."

"Since all three go against my nature, I thought I pulled it off."

"Yeah, you did."

"Do you think she pokes around in the woods regularly, hoping to run into you?"

"She doesn't have to with the cameras letting her know if I walk in."

"You saw cameras?"

"I spotted four before she decided to cross paths."

"I'm pretty observant, and I didn't see any." She frowned, sipped at the Coke. "That's annoying."

"Don't walk in there alone. The job's to keep watch, but no point taking chances. I do have tech," he added, "and the chores."

"I'll help with the chores. That's what a coy, clinging, saccharine woman who's determined to bag you would do."

"Great. Let's go strip the bed. You can put on fresh sheets while I start the laundry. While we're cleaning, I'll tell you about the appointment I have two weeks from today with Mrs. Mountjoy."

"You—you have an appointment with the people you're going to steal from?"

"I'll tell you about it," he repeated.

When they kayaked the next day, Booth made sure they glided past the bungalow. He spotted Cannery in the yard, sent out a wave—a casual, hi-neighbor sort of gesture. Cannery lifted his in return, the same tone, added a kind of smirk.

Then he set all that aside to enjoy a couple of hours on the river with Miranda.

She wore a broad-brimmed hat—a redhead's shield against

the sun—and had strong, smooth strokes with the paddle. He relaxed as the river took them through sun and shade. One quiet afternoon, he thought, with deer grazing silently in the woods, a couple of boys sitting on rocks with their lines in the water, a hawk circling, endlessly patient, overhead.

"It really is beautiful here," Miranda said. "I've been so busy, or just haven't taken the time. I haven't been in a kayak for a year."

"You haven't lost your stroke. When there's more time, we can take a long one, head down to the bay. I can get someone to pick us up, drive us back."

She shot him a look. "What, do you think I can't handle the return trip?"

"It's a long one," he repeated. "Maybe . . . we could book a room, make it a weekend deal."

"Now you're talking."

"When this is all taken care of. Like, toward the end of August."

She tipped down her sunglasses. "I'll pencil you in. It's interesting that we're having this really lovely interlude as if it's all we have to do or think about."

"Today, it is." He reached across the water to take her hand. "Let's take today."

CHAOS REIGNED BACKSTAGE ON opening night. Nerves, the shaky edge of hysteria, breathless (sometimes literally) excitement played together in a crazed concert as teenagers donned costumes, applied makeup, worked hair into the style of the sixties.

Dancers stretched, singers vocalized.

Booth did his best to be everywhere at once. He calmed nerves, dried a few anxiety tears, walked through cues with the crew and his stage manager.

A peek from the wings showed him the house filling up, and

filling up nicely. Among the familiar faces he saw Miranda, program in hand, chatting with Lorna and Cesca.

He heard the call: *Fifteen minutes to curtain. Fifteen minutes.*

He walked through for another check and spotted Louis—now known as Lou—with the rest of the black-clad stagehands. One of the gang now, Booth thought. He checked costumes, makeup, the soundboard, the lighting board, checked on props.

He checked everything.

Then he called the cast together, a circle of nervous glee.

"Okay, gang, this is it. You've done the work, and I'm proud of every one of you. Now it's time for the payoff. You're not just going to take the stage, you're going to take the night. Are you ready?"

He got a chorus of *Yeah! We're ready! Damn right!* and stretched a hand into the circle's center. Hands joined his, slapped together.

"Are you ready?"

Louder now, hands gripping hands.

"Then take it! Three, two, one."

Hands flew up on shouts.

"Places," he said, and took his own in the wings.

He waited, watched his kids take their positions onstage.

"Dim the house lights. Open us up, Marlie."

"Good evening, and welcome to Westbend High School's production of Michael Stewart's *Bye Bye Birdie*, with music by Charles Strouse, lyrics by Lee Adams. Please turn off your cell phones and refrain from any flash photography or Principal Downey will personally scold you. You don't want that. Now sit back and enjoy the show."

"Curtain," Booth said, and knew every one of the cast and crew thrilled to the sound of applause. He cued the light on Kim and her friend, opposite sides of the stage, old-fashioned phones in hand for the opening dialogue.

Then the ringing phone, the lights washing over the cubicle

center stage. More applause with voices rising over it. *What's the story, morning glory? What's the tale, nightingale?*

Booth thought: Knock 'em dead.

Controlled chaos now backstage as kids scrambled off, stage-hands hurried on for scene changes. He heard laughter from the audience—at the right moments. Robust applause after every number.

A couple glitches and mangled lines here and there, but no one in the audience would know it.

He didn't relax until his Kim—and she shined so damn bright—finished the closing *Bye Bye Birdie* number, and the audience surged to its feet.

Then he watched those glowing faces come out for the curtain call, one by one or in pairs, line up together with that applause rolling over them.

Join hands, take the bow. Take it again, and again.

He walked onstage when the cast called for him, took a bow of his own.

One down, he thought as he helped reorganize costumes, two to go. He made sure all props had been secured, and turning out lights as he went, left by the side door.

He found Miranda sitting on the low stone wall by the parking lot.

"I didn't know you were waiting. I figured you had your car."

"Lorna drove me in, and I didn't mind waiting. Not only a pretty night, but I'm still riding on the show."

Pride just swelled through him. "They were great, weren't they? Really great."

"They were amazing. I've seen my share of high school musicals, Booth. I've been in my share. That was a serious cut above."

"They worked their asses off."

She laid a hand on his arm as he unlocked his car. "Take some credit."

"Oh, I do. I worked my ass off, too. Worth it," he added as

they got in the car. "Seriously beyond worth it. But two more to go."

"The girl who played Kim."

"Alicia."

"Does she have plans?"

"Her parents hope she'll go into teaching."

"Is that what she hopes?"

"Not really. They're supportive—the dance lessons, the school plays. She's done some community theater in the summer, and they're good with it. I like to think what they saw tonight—because she slayed—will help them give her a chance to take a real shot at what she wants."

"I hope she gets it. They love you. Your theater kids. They love you, and it shows."

"It's mutual."

He pulled under his carport, glanced at the mudroom door. He unlocked it, reset the alarm.

"I don't know about you, but I could go for some wine. I just need to check something in my office."

"Then I'll get the wine."

When she brought it into his office, she gasped at what she saw on his monitor. "That's your house, outside the house. LaPorte's people, breaking into the house."

"Trying to," he corrected. "They're not B and E men. They could bust down a door, break a window—which would bring the cops coming and let me know somebody wanted in. Still, that's probably what she's arguing for here."

He tapped the screen. "The lady's bored. No one to maim, no one to kill, day after day. It can wear on you."

Her heart stuck jaggedly in her throat. "Jesus, Booth."

"I got an alert on my phone when they tried the doors, but I had to focus on the show. Even if they got in—which they couldn't without that brute force—they wouldn't have found anything I didn't want them to."

"You were expecting this."

Nodding, he took the wine, ran through the videos again while he drank. "If I knew my target would be out of the house for a solid three hours, I'd want to take a nice tour of his place, get a feel, find what I could find."

"You could show this to the police. It would ruin their plans, and piss off LaPorte."

"I could, and wouldn't mind ruining their plans or pissing off LaPorte. But Warwick's good at what she does, and she's good at what she does because she likes to kill and maim. She's smart and she's skilled, but she's also sick and unstable. She could decide to kill whoever went over there to question them about this little visit."

Booth swiveled, then tugged Miranda into his lap.

"Are you happy about this?"

"I will, happily, send this video to LaPorte and tell him to pull his bullshit watchers out, or deal's off. I'll add considerable outrage."

He kissed the side of her neck. "That'll feel good," he murmured. "So does this."

"I take it having people who like to maim and kill try to break into your house makes you happy and stirs your sexual appetites."

"The show made me happy—the attempted break-in is just satisfying. And you stir up my sexual appetites. I liked looking out and seeing you in the audience." He skimmed a hand up her side, just brushing her breast. "I'd like to look out tomorrow night and see you."

"Because you don't want me here if they try to break in again."

"That's a bonus, but I liked seeing you when I looked out."

"Can I watch from the wings?" He managed to soothe her and arouse her at the same time. "It's been years since I felt that backstage rush."

"Sure. I'm just going to set my drink down because what I have in mind requires both my hands."

"Oh?" She tossed back her hair, lifted an eyebrow. "And what do you have in mind?"

"I'll show you."

He had her shirt unbuttoned in under five seconds, and the front snap of her bra released. Then he used his thumbs, just his thumbs.

And his teeth.

She had to grip his shoulder in one hand as her spine melted. "I think . . . God! I'm going to put my glass down, too."

"Good idea." He flipped open the hook of her pants. "Because I'm just getting started."

He didn't strip her clothes away. He found it erotic, exciting to take her when they were both half-dressed. Her shirt, so crisp and white, fell off her shoulders, caught at her wrists, and laid bare so much smooth skin.

The sounds she made with her mouth avid on his kindled fires in his blood, in his gut, in his loins. Urgent, desperate sounds as she grappled with his belt.

The chair rocked and swayed under them as he worked her pants over her hips. And with one arm locked tight around her, he slid his hand down, teased, stroked, tormented until his fingers penetrated the wet and the warm.

She cried out once, twice, shuddering, shuddering before her head dropped limply onto his shoulder.

"I can't. I can't."

She'd gone liquid, he thought, like wax in the sun. Still hot, so hot and fluid.

"Sure you can. Just a little more." Light strokes now, until her breath began to thicken, and her hips began to move against his hand. "Give me just a little more."

He'd wrecked her, destroyed her, renewed her. The pleasure, torturous, glorious, built again so she could only yield to it, to him, could only let him take what he wanted, how he wanted, as long as he wanted.

When at last, at last, he thrust inside her, she could only press her face against his neck and let him drive her.

WHEN BOOTH STEPPED ONSTAGE at the end of the final performance, the cast and crew presented him with a ham. It made him laugh through the odd sorrow of being done.

Then his Kim stepped forward. "We have something to go with it. Some of us will be back next year and look to you to turn another group of hams into a troupe. And some of us will graduate next month and move on. But none of us will forget you. So . . ."

She started it, a cappella, then the music flowed in, and the rest joined.

"We love you, Mr. B, oh yes we do. We love you, Mr. B, and we'll be true."

It floored him, left him speechless. All those voices filled his heart so he had to struggle for composure when they finished, when the applause died off.

When he looked at their faces, he knew love.

"Thank you. Thank you for the gift, and I don't mean the ham. You're treasures to me, every one of you. Take a last bow. And curtain."

After the curtain, the celebration, the cast party, he lay in bed beside Miranda. As he lay in the dark he wondered if he'd be one of those who came back next year, or one of those who moved on.

Chapter Twenty-Seven

HE HAD FINALS TO prepare, but since he'd been there, done that, he had a lot more time to spend on the Goddess and how he intended to steal her.

He had the rest of the week before he put his first step into play, one he'd fully intended to take solo. But Miranda had other ideas.

He considered ways to talk her out of it—all, he already knew, futile—as he took pleasure in one of his favorite spring after-school chores.

Mowing the lawn.

He thought he'd blacken some chicken for dinner, serve it with wild rice and asparagus.

Leaves had unfurled nicely in the woods and azaleas had popped. People took advantage of warm evenings and had boats out on the river.

The grass he mowed smelled like summer—one of his favorite perfumes.

He saw Selene step out of the woods—no camera this time—with a purposeful stride. He switched off the mower, and met her hard look coolly.

"I'd say you heard from the boss."

"You think you're a smart guy."

"No, I don't. I know I am. I'm smart enough to know you can shoot me dead right here on my half-mown lawn with that gun under your hoodie. And I figure we're both smart enough to know if you do, you'll have LaPorte hunting you until somebody puts a knife or bullet in you. And that would cut down hard on the projection of your career."

"You cost me fifty grand."

"You could look at it that way." Booth leaned casually against the lawn mower. "Or you could look at it another. You're not stuck in that dump of a house for the next two months, give or take, and with an asshole like Cannery."

"Fifty grand," she repeated.

"Well, don't look at me. You got made. It happens. Suck it up, Selene."

She stepped into him. "I can wait until you do whatever LaPorte wants you to do, kill you then. Or I can take out that useless redheaded slut."

Her eyes changed—mild surprise—as his did. She didn't back up at the threat in his. But neither did he.

"Do you know my rep as well as I know yours? If not, do some research. You hurt her, give her a goddamn hangnail, and I'll hunt you down. I'll never stop, and you'll never find me. I won't kill you—much too quick and over. But I'll make sure you spend the rest of your life in prison. And not a nice, regulated American prison. I know the places you've worked, Selene, and some of their prisons make the system here look like Disneyland."

"You don't scare me."

"No?" When he stepped back with her gun in his hand, her eyes widened. "I should. I could kill you here and now, bury your body in the woods, and lay it out so the fingers point at Cannery. Or you can walk away, consider the fifty a loss, and keep going. Because trust me, I'm going to know where you are and what you're doing from this point on. You made that a mission for me. Go look up Frank Javier and see what happened to him when he got in my way. It should help you decide how to play this."

"You think this ends it?"

"I think I'm pointing your own gun at your gut, and could end it right here. Now get off my lawn."

She turned, stalked toward the woods.

"Frank Javier, Lima, Peru," Booth called after her. "Look him up."

He heard the door open behind him as Selene disappeared into the woods. "Stay in the house," he said without turning around.

"She's gone. You're holding a gun. Would you have shot her?"

"No, but that's my failing. LaPorte doesn't have the same sensibilities, and he'll get an earful on this."

For safety, Booth ejected the magazine, made certain the chamber was empty. Just because he hated guns didn't mean he didn't know how they worked.

He turned then and saw Miranda on the patio with his kitchen cleaver in her hands.

"Jesus, Miranda. Go put that away."

"What are you going to do with that weapon?"

"I'm going to plant it in the bungalow after they leave. But now I'm going to let LaPorte know his hired gun cost him another million. Up front."

"Did you—" She broke off, then started again. "Booth, did you kill this Javier person?"

"I've never killed anyone, and don't intend to ever kill anyone." He walked to his garden shed to stow the gun and the magazine. Separately. "He's in a craphole prison in Peru."

"What did he do to have you make that happen?"

He turned, gave her a steady look. "He tried something along the lines she just did. He got in my way. Go put that away now," he said more gently. "I have to make a call."

She put the cleaver back, noted, as if looking at someone else's hand, hers was steady. But she couldn't quite will her heartbeat back to normal.

She'd come into the kitchen for a bottle of water after shutting down her work for the day. And glanced out the window because she heard voices through the screen. Just glanced out as she twisted off the top of the water bottle.

And there was Booth facing off against a hired killer.

She'd grabbed the cleaver. She still didn't have a clue exactly what she'd intended to do with it, but seconds later Booth had a gun in his hand.

Her gun. He'd taken a gun from a professional killer as easily as she might pluck a wildflower from a meadow.

How did she feel about that? Maybe she'd figure it out once her heart stopped banging against her ribs.

She took a long drink of water, then another while she watched Booth standing on the narrow pier, talking on his cell.

She grabbed another bottle of water and went outside.

He glanced back as she walked to the pier and looked mildly annoyed. The look didn't match the cold snap of his voice.

"I told you not to fuck with me, LaPorte. Sending your psycho killer to my goddamn house is fucking with me. I don't give a rat's ass if you did or didn't," he said after a brief pause. "You fucked with me, you broke the terms, and it's going to cost you another million. Pay up or find somebody else to get the rock. You know where to wire it. I'll check in twenty minutes. If the money's not there, deal's off. Oh, and if she comes back here, they're going to find her body on your fucking doorstep. Count on it."

He broke the connection, pocketed his phone, then took the water she held out. "You couldn't just stay in the house for ten minutes?"

"If she comes back to kill you, I don't think hiding in the house will stop her from coming after me."

"She won't touch you."

"Just you?"

"She won't come back. She's done here."

Behind him a bird swooped low over the river, then winged skyward again. He had a thin line of sweat down the center of his T-shirt. Not from fear, she thought, not even from fury.

From the simple and homey task of mowing the lawn on a sunny afternoon.

"How do you know she's done?"

"Because the satisfaction of killing me isn't worth having LaPorte hiring someone to kill her. And when the job's done, she'll be in prison."

"How do you know that?"

"Unless LaPorte has her taken out first, I'm going to make sure of it."

"Like you did with this Javier?"

"Yeah, like that. I've got to finish mowing the lawn."

Miranda just put a hand on his chest. "Tell me about Javier. I have a vested interest, Booth. If you hadn't taken the gun away from her, she might have used it. You said he got in your way. How?"

"He's a third-rate thief who tried to frame me for one of his jobs. Sloppy job, as most of his tended to be, and he put the man who wasn't supposed to be home that night in the hospital. Told the guy he was beating half to death he was the Chameleon, and topped it off by calling in an anonymous tip."

He paused, tipped back the water, and drank.

"Weak because sloppy and physical violence isn't my style, but it brought some heat. So I hired him."

"You hired him."

"A wealthy Peruvian named—what did I use? Right, Lejandro Vega—and I also purchased the twelve-carat diamond solitaire he'd stolen from the man he'd beaten at the same meeting. I planted it and a couple other items in his flat, and alerted the authorities to a break-in, in progress. They rounded him up, solved two cases at once. And he's doing a very long stretch in a very inhospitable Peruvian prison. I slipped in once, just to let him know who sent him there, and why."

Her throat had gone dry, but she'd already finished the water. "You 'slipped in' to a Peruvian prison."

"Not that hard, and necessary from my perspective. I wanted the word out." With eyes calm and cool, he scanned the water, and over to the woods where Selene had retreated.

"I pay my debts."

He finished off the water, handed her the empty bottle. "I need to finish mowing the back. I'll deal with the front tomorrow. We're having blackened chicken for dinner, and I want to marinate it for an hour."

She stopped him again, this time with a hand to his cheek. "You're so angry."

"Damn right I'm angry. She came here, armed. You were in the house."

"I had a cleaver."

He let out a half laugh, then turned her hand to press his lips to her palm. "She won't be back. LaPorte will make sure of it. More, in the end, all this turned to our advantage."

"How's that?"

"He was rattled. I could hear it. He didn't control her. I did. And now I'm controlling him. It's costing him another million."

"Will he pay?"

Booth took out his phone, checked. "He already has."

She realized, from her viewpoint, Booth could do anything, handle anything. So she nodded.

"Good. Go perform your miracle with chicken. I'll finish mowing. I have a very cute backyard at my town house," she said when he hesitated. "I take care of it myself. I like taking care of it myself."

"Okay. All right. I'm sorry about all of this."

She handed him back the water bottle. "How stupid is it to

apologize for having the spine and the skill to chase off a professional killer?"

"I had a redhead with a cleaver as backup."

He went back inside, washed his hands.

He figured the angry phone call to LaPorte—and the demand for the additional million—not only removed Warwick from the area, removed the threat to Miranda, but had likely guaranteed Warwick's death warrant.

He'd done what he'd had to do, he thought as he watched Miranda mow the lawn. And he could live with it.

AFTER DINNER, AFTER DARK, Miranda went with him to the bungalow. He took the route through the woods because he wanted to make sure they'd taken down the cameras.

They had.

Miranda tapped a finger on the bag he carried over his shoulder. "I didn't realize you'd need so many tools to get into the house."

"I don't. Lights are off," he said. "We'll go around the back."

"What's in the bag, Booth?"

"Just a few things I picked up on a previous visit."

"A previous visit when?"

"After they tried to get into my place. I left you a note in case you woke up, so you wouldn't worry."

"How considerate."

He ignored the pissy tone because he figured she was entitled.

"I thought so. Listen, I never figured I'd have her gun to plant when they left. I wanted a little insurance."

Both cars gone, he noted, and when he checked, he found the trash bins empty. Smart to clean them out.

He took a pair of surgical gloves out of his bag. "Put these on."

"Really? Why would anyone look for fingerprints?"

"Because I'm going to give them some reasons to." He put on another pair, tried the back door. "Didn't bother to lock up."

"Oh." Disappointment rang in the single syllable. "I was looking forward to watching how you get in."

"In this case, I just open the door." After he did, he turned on the kitchen lights.

She jumped back a foot. "You turned on the lights!"

"Leaving a light on's a lot less suspicious than a couple of flashlights bobbing around in a dark house." He walked through, pulled down the shades on the front windows, then took a survey.

"They really should put some money into this place. Kitchen drawer for the gun, I think."

"It's got your prints on it."

"I wiped it down, like they'd have wiped down the house before they left. But her prints are going to be on the magazine, and I was careful with it."

He opened drawers, found one with a pitiful collection of plastic kitchen tools, and put the gun in the rear behind a slotted spoon.

He set his bag on the kitchen table. "So, what might people in a hurry to get out inadvertently leave behind? I got a few things out of their bins after they rolled them out the night before trash pickup."

The beer bottle went under the sink, beside rather than in the kitchen can, a magazine found a home under the saggy living room cushions. He shoved an empty bottle of tequila in a dusty corner of an upper cabinet.

He took out a single black sock and started toward a bedroom.

"You found that in the trash?"

"In a basket of dirty clothes in the laundry area after I broke in." He tossed it under the bed.

He retrieved a bright red sports bra, kicked it under the dresser in the second bedroom, then balled up a pillowcase from his bag to stuff between the washer and dryer.

"They were here, sleeping, when you broke in."

"It's what I do, Miranda. Stand back."

He got out a second beer bottle, smashed it on the side of the table. Then he picked up one of the kitchen chairs, slammed it against the counter. And gave a satisfied nod to the little dent he left in the ancient Formica.

"Don't want to break my hand," he commented, and wrapped it in a thick towel before punching his fist into a hollow core door.

"You're making it look like they had a fight—a physical fight."

"With just enough damage to raise some alarms. I'm doing the owners a favor, really. Insurance'll cover it, and they'll get more out of the place with a halfway-decent upgrade."

"That's not why you're doing all this."

He nearly made an excuse, but stopped himself. She deserved truth.

"This should get the cops going. Hopefully get their real names, their backgrounds. Maybe, the cops catch up with her before LaPorte does. She cost him a million. He pays his debts, too."

"You'd rather see her in prison than in the ground."

He stood, long and lean in his battered jeans and ancient Chucks. "I would, but she chose her path just like I chose mine."

"She would've killed you, and me. And . . . she wouldn't have given either of us another thought. What happens to her now isn't your responsibility."

"No, but either way, I'm staging a fight, bringing trouble down on her and Cannery."

"All right." All in, Miranda thought as she glanced around. "What next?"

"We'll take more of the glass and wood away, like they tried to hide it. But we'll leave some behind. I figure they wiped the place down, but odds are they missed some spots. They're paid up, who's going to care they took off early? So you don't worry too much."

"But Tracey, the owners, and the police are going to care when they find damage, what looks like a physical fight, and a loaded gun."

"There you go. I've got a couple more things to toss around, then we'll pick up and go home. Since we're neighbors, we're going to get some questions. Hit the truth—to a point. We ran into her one morning walking in the woods between my place and the bungalow. She had a camera, talked about all that. She stopped by tonight while I was mowing the grass, no camera, seemed upset, but just said she was out walking."

"Close enough."

THE QUESTIONS CAME AT the end of the week with a knock on her door. She'd come home to pack for the weekend in Georgetown—a trip Booth didn't want her to take.

The knock interrupted her consideration of what to wear when meeting his aunt and his father figure. Then going with him—like it or not—when he, well, cased the joint.

Though she'd never met him, she recognized the chief of police when she opened the door.

"Sorry to bother you, Miss Emerson. I'm Greg Capton. Chief of police."

"Oh, of course." She extended her hand, hoped it hadn't gone clammy.

"I wonder if you've got a couple of minutes."

"Sure. Come in. Is there a problem?"

"Might be. It's about your neighbors down the road."

"Neighbors? Oh, sorry, sit down. Can I get you some coffee?"

"I appreciate it, but I won't keep you long." He did sit, smiled a rather disarming smile. "Can you tell me the last time you saw the couple who rented the bungalow? The little place on the other side of Sebastian Booth's? You know Booth, right?"

"Yes, I know Booth." She put a laugh with it. "I imagine as police chief you're aware Booth and I are seeing each other. But as for the people in the bungalow, I'm not really sure. I've never met him. Booth and I did meet her. We were all taking a walk in the woods one morning. Not sure when . . . two or three weeks ago maybe? She was out taking pictures. Has something happened?"

"I can't say. Tracey—you know Tracey—got worried when she heard they'd missed two trash pickups this week. It looks like they've packed up and gone."

"Oh? That's strange, isn't it? She seemed excited to have the chance to take photos—wildlife photos, she said. But, you know, I was at Booth's the other night. I think Monday night, evening," she corrected. "She walked over while he was mowing the lawn—the back. I saw her out the window, and wondered if I should offer her a drink, but she left. Booth mentioned she seemed upset. Didn't they let Tracey know they were moving out?"

"It doesn't seem so. And you didn't talk to her yourself Monday evening?"

"No. I was finishing up some work, and came in for some water, noticed her talking to Booth. She walked back in the direction of the bungalow, through the woods. When I went out, Booth said she'd just sort of wandered over, and said she wanted a walk or some air, or . . . I'm not exactly sure, sorry. And he said she seemed upset. Maybe she was, maybe she was upset they were moving out."

"Could be. Well, thanks for the time."

No mention of the gun, the damage, Miranda thought as she closed the door behind him. She took out her phone. She'd get a more detailed account from Tracey.

As she packed, Miranda put the phone on speaker.

"And when they didn't answer their phones, I drove over. No cars, shades down. I walked around the back, and the back door was unlocked! When I went in, I could see something was really wrong, Miranda. It looked like they'd had a fight. A real fight."

"Oh my God." The black dress, she decided, in case they went out to dinner.

"One of the kitchen chairs was missing, and I saw some broken pieces of it under the table. Broken glass, too. And there's a big dent in the broom closet door, like somebody punched it!"

"That's awful. Do you think he hurt her?"

"I don't know, I just don't know. But I can tell you I don't think they slept together. I think they slept in separate bedrooms. They took their trash off with them. Who does that? But they missed some things. Beer bottles, a tequila bottle, all empty. I think one of them might've been a closet drinker."

She let Tracey vent it out while she finished packing.

"I hope you find out what happened, and you've *got* to let me know when you do."

"Count on it."

"I'm heading out now. Booth and I are taking a weekend getaway."

"Romantic!"

"I hope so. I'll let you know if it lives up to my hopes when I get back. Good luck with the case of the missing tenants."

"Have fun!"

Miranda loaded her suitcase, her laptop, her purse into the car. She'd wait for Booth at his house. It would be harder for him to come up with more reasons she should stay home if she made it a fait accompli.

He tried.

"I'm starting to think you don't want me to meet your aunt or Sebastien."

"We'll go to New Orleans when this is finished, and you can meet them."

"They're only a few hours away right now, and I'm looking forward to meeting them. And playing my role tomorrow."

"There's no need for you to—"

"A man like . . . What's your name again?" She laughed

when he just closed his eyes. "You're Monsieur Henri Dubeck, the great eccentric, exclusive, and difficult interior designer. You're also discreet, never reveal, much less discuss a client. I'm Mademoiselle Marguerite Gavier, your faithful and long-suffering assistant."

She pointed at her suitcase, pointed at the door. "We agreed, Booth."

"I was in a weakened state, after wine and sex."

"A deal's a deal, and you'll have two sets of eyes." She sailed out with her laptop case and her purse, and waited for him to load her suitcase.

He'd saved it till last in vain hope.

"You'll note I packed light, and you didn't."

"Dubeck and Gavier are in those bags."

She got in the car, smiled as she put on her seat belt. "See? You knew I was coming."

"Apparently."

"We can go over my character again, but first, you never told me how you got Regal—stupid name—Regal Mountjoy, Alan C.'s newish trophy wife, to bite on Dubeck."

"Newish trophy wives, logically, want to put their stamp on spaces previously decorated and occupied by the ex. And I have a connection in France—an important woman—with a connection to a connection of Regal's. She planted the seed for me."

"A past lover?"

"No, a former client."

Miranda settled back for the drive. And whatever the hell it said about her, she no longer cared. She loved his stories.

"You stole for the Frenchwoman."

"I reacquired her property. Her great-grandmother was an artist, of some import. The Nazis stole a portrait of my client's grandmother, one of her grandmother as a young girl. Her grandmother survived the Holocaust. None of the rest of the family did."

"That's horrible. It's just horrible."

"My client wanted the portrait back, had exhausted all other avenues, then hired me. I took the job pro bono because . . . because."

Miranda laid a hand over his. "Because."

"She said if I ever needed a favor, ever needed anything. So she let drop to a friend of a friend of Regal's that Dubeck was coming to DC to meet a client. A famous client. And intended to stay for several days. Dubeck was persuaded to meet with Regal and consider awarding her his great talent."

"Now the question becomes how are you going to pull off playing, convincingly, a snooty French interior designer."

"I've done it before, a few times. Though Dubeck will retire after this one."

"You actually designed?"

"I've been in plenty of fancy houses, ornate, minimalistic, retro, ultramodern. It's just a matter of gauging the client, what they really want—or expect. Talking the talk, doing the math."

"Math."

"You gotta measure, Miranda. I did a place in Provence about eight years ago. I went with modern farmhouse with some provincial touches. It worked. I made a fat fee and walked away with a thirty-three-carat emerald necklace, twenty carats of white diamonds, platinum setting."

Oh yes, she loved his stories.

"You decorated their house, then stole the jewels?"

"I never steal from a client. This is the exception and why Dubeck will retire. I took it from a neighboring villa, then oversaw the installation of the azure linen drapes in my client's master suite. We were all shocked and horrified."

"I bet."

She thought, as she often did, what a fascinating, complicated man she'd fallen in love with.

She'd never been to Georgetown so enjoyed the change of

scene. The tall brick homes, the busy streets and mad traffic, the bright spots of shops and restaurants.

"It's like a town within a city, isn't it? It's got dignity, history, and action all together. I might like to spend some time here when we're not on a caper."

He looked at her. "A caper."

"It's a good word, and stands the test of time. What do you call it?"

"Work," he said simply, and pulled up to a small garage beside a lovely, three-story brick house. Flowers carpeted the tiny front yard on both sides of a low brick walk. The walk led to a trio of steps and a covered front door.

The door flew open, and a woman rushed out, hair—plum colored, Miranda decided—flying. A tiny dog ran out behind her to stand on the top step and dance on its stubby legs.

The woman threw her arms around Booth, and when he wrapped around her, Miranda's eyes stung. Love, she thought. Absolute and unquestionable.

"I missed you, pal. I missed you hard."

"I missed you." He drew back to brush a hand at her hair. "What color's this?"

"Jack Horner."

"Because?"

"He pulled out a plum," Miranda finished, and earned a teary grin from Mags.

With a wild laugh, Mags threw herself around Miranda. She smelled, Miranda thought, of Chanel, roses, and fresh bread.

"You're the one," Mags murmured, then drew back. "Mags."

"Miranda."

"Come in, come in. We'll let the men deal with the bags and have some of the wine breathing on the bar. This is Wiley," she added as they walked to the steps.

The dog leaped straight into Miranda's arms, then stared up at her with bulging, love-drenched eyes.

"Oh God, you're adorable."

"Isn't he?" Mags led her inside while Booth just looked on in wonder.

Sebastien strolled toward them, a dishcloth over one shoulder, his gray hair tied back in a tail as stubby as Wiley's legs.

"Ah, *ma belle amie, bienvenue!*"

Miranda not only got a hug, but a kiss on both cheeks.

"Booth needs help with the bags. Sebastien's made a feast," Mags continued as she walked Miranda out of the foyer, down a hallway toward a massive great room with a glass wall of doors open to a paved courtyard complete with fountain.

The air smelled like heaven must.

"I watch him when he prepares a feast. Occasionally I stir. On special events, I may chop, even mince."

"That's what I do."

Mags just beamed at her. "Aren't we clever girls? Let's have some wine."

Chapter Twenty-Eight

THE WINE FLOWED, AND the food kept coming. Conversation rolled through it, nonstop, as Miranda sampled boudin balls. She didn't know what they were, other than delicious.

Conversation did not roll anywhere near LaPorte, the Red Goddess, or any aspect of what loomed ahead. It jumped around from food, New Orleans, Westbend, Miranda's books, and back to food as they moved from the spacious kitchen into the formal dining area with the table set charmingly with flowers and candles.

Sebastien, clearly enjoying himself, set down a platter of beautifully presented crab cakes on mixed greens served with his own rémoulade.

One bite had Miranda lifting her glass to him. "Amazing, and I see where Booth got his culinary skills."

"I polished up a rough diamond, me. Tonight, we bring New Orleans to you."

"I don't think I'd taste better on Bourbon Street."

"If my heart didn't belong to your aunt"—Sebastien patted it—"I'd steal this one from you, *mon ami*. You come visit me in the bayou, *cher*, and we'll have us a *fais-dodo*."

"I'd love to see your bayou." Would see it, Miranda determined. "Booth says you have three daughters."

"My three jewels. And now, I'm a Paw-Paw, me. I got me four grandbabies, and another coming."

"Which makes me an honorary grandmother," Mags put in. "They call me Magma. Time goes," she added with a wink at Sebastien. "The smart ones go with it and enjoy the ride."

The purpose of the visit didn't come up until they sat with servings of bread pudding and caramel sauce.

"*Mais*," Sebastien began, "tomorrow."

"Tomorrow," Booth repeated. "The appointment's at two, so we should leave here at two. Dubeck keeps them waiting. You've got the transportation arranged?"

Sebastien nodded. "*Bien sûr.*"

"I figure about ninety minutes should do it, and I'll give the client a business card—or Miranda will—with the direct line to the drop phone. Dauphine has that?"

"She's set," Mags confirmed. "Monsieur Dubeck's administrative assistant."

"I'll assess the security—electronic and human—evaluate the weak spots, locate the target area, and get the client's schedule for the next three months."

"You'll do all that in ninety minutes?"

Booth glanced at Miranda. "Less, but ninety for the flourishes. Dubeck's a busy man. If it takes longer, it's because she's giving me more than I expect."

"She's a talker." Looking smug, Mags sipped coffee. "I got a mani-pedi at her salon when she was in. You wouldn't believe what they charge in that place for nails."

"You need to bill me."

"Oh, stop." She waved Booth away. "I got a glass of good champagne and some time watching your target out of it. Plus a damn good pedicure. She brags, she name-drops, and spent a lot of her time there on her phone gossiping with friends. Otherwise flipping through fashion magazines. She struck me as about as deep as a puddle of rainwater, harmless, and on the giddy side.

"Her aura's got touches of brown with the rosy pink. She actually loves her husband, but his money sure doesn't hurt."

"Wait." Miranda's hand shot up. "You read auras?"

"Madame Magdelaine sees what she sees," Mags said, piling on the drama. "Yours? Red, touches of orange and yellow. Confident, direct, creative. You need as much as want to learn through experience."

"I could've told you all that without reading auras," Booth pointed out, and Mags fluttered her lashes at him.

"I'll add you're a lucky bastard, pal. Those orange lights mean sexual as well as creative energy."

"And moving on," Booth said as Miranda let out a quick laugh. "The mark?"

Mags winked at Miranda. "We'll talk later."

"Oh, yes, please."

"So . . . as a casual conversation starter, I admired her earrings—canary diamond studs, Graff, about two carats each—and she told me her husband had given them to her on a romantic weekend in Paris for Valentine's Day. He's a doll baby. Her words."

"And you were?"

"She didn't ask for my name or anything else about me. We only spoke for a few minutes, and still she managed to drop in the fact she was consulting with the famous designer Dubeck over reimagining her master suite. I acted suitably impressed."

Her eyes laughed over her spoon. "More, I think you'll be interested to know she's doing all this as a surprise for her husband for their third anniversary. He's currently on a golf trip in Hilton Head."

"All the better." Booth turned to Sebastien. "And the setup for Lake Charles?"

"We have a house from the ones you picked. A good choice, I think. We find a coordination with LaPorte's schedule, then move the family and staff out."

"And how do you arrange that?" Miranda wondered.

"Maybe we get lucky and work it in with a family vacation. Then it's only the staff to deal with," Booth told her. "Or we find a reason everyone has to vacate overnight."

"Pests work," Sebastien said. "Or the gas leak." And Booth nodded.

"Quick and easy. I think the gas leak—if I can work the timing. If not, a couple rats, a few mice. Time to call the exterminator. Which," he told Miranda, "will be one of us. We suggest they leave—all humans and pets—and we'll solve this problem overnight."

He looked back at Sebastien. "I'm targeting—best scenario— the middle of June."

"We'll aim for it."

"It's all about the illusion and the timing."

"Isn't there also the matter of stealing a big hunk of diamond?"

This time Booth patted Miranda's hand. "Not yet, but we'll get there."

She supposed preparations the next morning for casing the joint equaled the start of getting there.

After an elaborate brunch, she sat in the back courtyard with Mags while Wiley, after a walk, napped under the table.

"I'm not going to poke and pry," Mags began. "But I want to say you make my boy happy."

"I hope I do."

"He's had a lot of sad and mad and bad in his life. He's had some happy, too, but nothing happier than you."

The words struck her heart, and just held there. "That's . . . that's an amazing thing to hear."

"When he first told me about you, back in college? I could hear that happy, that all-the-way happy, and I thought: My boy's in love. It cut a piece of his heart out to walk away from you. And he walked because of me."

"No, Mags." Direct, determined, decisive Miranda reached out to grip Mags's hand hard. "No. He walked because of LaPorte. I wanted to blame Booth—I did blame him," she admitted.

"Of course you did," Mags said quietly. "He wanted you to."

"But I know better now. I know there's only one villain here. It crushed me, I won't deny it. And it changed me, my attitudes, my outlook. But . . . Do you believe in fate?"

"Oh, honey." Mags barked out a laugh. "Do I."

"Well, we were both so young, and who knows how we'd have handled all we felt in the long run. But we're older now. Smarter now, we've lived more now. And in the past few months I've gotten to know Booth more than I ever did during that rush of falling."

She glanced back toward the house, and up to the windows of the room where they'd spent the night.

"Did he tell you about Selene Warwick?"

"He said LaPorte called her and Cannery off."

"He did, but only after Booth threatened him. And ran Selene off himself."

As she related the story to Mags, Mags poured more of Sebastien's sun tea into glasses.

"He never tells me about that sort of thing." Mags sighed with the words. "I don't think he often tells Sebastien either."

"I doubt he'd have told me, but I saw it myself. And one of the things I saw was a man who can handle himself. He took her gun, and ran her off, threatened LaPorte—hell, bullied him," she corrected, "out of another million dollars. Then he set up the house they'd rented so they'd be identified, so authorities would look for them. Finding them's another thing, but he did all of that so . . . smoothly. He did all of that, and what he's doing now, while teaching full-time and putting on a really impressive high school musical.

"I think he could do anything he wanted to do."

"Preaching to the choir. You love him. That's not a question, because I see what I see. You'll decide what to do about it."

"Oh, I've decided." Miranda glanced toward the window again. "It just has to wait until this is finished."

Sebastien stepped out before Mags could ask. He slapped a hand on his heart. "Ah! *Les belles femmes!*"

Hearing his voice, Wiley scrambled up to race over and dance on his hind legs. Sebastien scooped him up, nuzzled.

"Booth's ready for you, *cher.*"

Miranda went in, and up the arrow straight staircase to the landing, turned left.

The bedroom door stood open, so she walked in. Jolted back.

The man who stood studying himself in the cheval-glass mirror boasted a two-toned pompadour—stone-gray topped with snow-white. His goatee, stone-gray, came to a sharp white point.

Under the palest of pale gray suits with a royal-blue waistcoat he had broad shoulders, a broad chest.

Rings sparkled on both pinkies. An elaborate lapel pin in the shape of a phoenix glimmered.

She didn't see Booth until he spoke.

"Good. We need to get started on you."

"You— I would've passed you on the street. You look older, and—and fuller. Your eyes are brown."

"Colored contacts." He spoke briskly—work mode, she realized. "Strip it down and put on the robe. I need to do your hair and makeup."

"Thanks, but I've been doing my own since I was twelve."

"Not like this. That's your hair."

He pointed to a short, blunt blond wig with full bangs.

"Okay. It sort of looks like the one Julia Roberts wore at the beginning of *Pretty Woman.*"

"I guess it does."

She walked back to close the door before she undressed. "I take it I don't get the facial hair."

"Not this time." He took off his suit jacket, laid it on the bed as she put on the robe and sat. Then he turned her chair so her back was to the mirror.

Immediately, she tried to turn it back. "I want to watch!"

"No. When I'm done, you'll get the full effect." He began to work her hair into a skullcap. "This'll keep it out of the way while I do the face. I'm going to build on what you're already wearing."

"Can you do a beauty mark? I always wondered how I'd look with one." Then she actually bounced in the chair when he opened a train case. "Oh my God, look at all those brushes! The palettes! Let me—"

He slapped her hand away. "Mine. I'll share later. I've got a schedule going here."

"Your face is fuller, too, around the jaw."

"Mm-hmm."

"Are you going to make mine fuller?"

"No," he said as he worked. "Just stronger makeup, especially the eyes. Bold red on the lips."

"Red lipstick doesn't work on me."

"It will today."

He brushed, he dabbed, he penciled and powdered. He astonished her by applying false eyelashes—and ignored her claim they'd look cheap and cheesy.

He changed her earrings, and he tugged the wig on, studied her with narrowed eyes before he slipped black-framed glasses on her.

When she tried to turn and look, he pulled her out of the chair and away from the mirror. "Not yet. You need to put this on."

He held up the bodysuit, watched her mouth fall open.

"Is that going to be my *ass*? You're giving me a big ass, and those are my . . ." She laid a hand, protectively, across her breasts. "I'm going to have a big butt, wide hips, and huge boobs."

"They're not huge. They're in proportion to the rest. If she ever describes you, she won't say 'willow slim,' won't say 'lanky,' she'll say 'curvy.'"

"How about 'robust'?"

"That works, too. You wanted the part, Miranda," he reminded her. "This is your wardrobe."

She muttered, but tossed the robe aside and let him help her into the bodysuit. "It's a little tight, and it's shoving my own girls way up."

"It's supposed to be tight, and it's supposed to push them up. Here's the rest."

She studied the little skirt, the jacket, the silky white tank. "That's a really short skirt."

"Miranda."

"All right, all right. I don't know if my new ass will fit into this."

It did, of course, it all fit, and so did the black stilettos. After tying a scarf in red, black, and gold around her neck with the knot on the side, he stood back, circled his finger so she did a turn.

"Good. Very good. Now you can look."

She stepped to the mirror, just stared.

She'd have passed herself on the street, too, she realized. Her eyes looked huge and madly shadowed. Rather than cheap and cheesy, the lashes came off exotic in contrast to the studious glasses. The red lips looked somehow French, and with a deeper dip in the top lip than she could claim.

"It doesn't look like me. It doesn't look like a wig. And with this body, I think I'd make a damn good living as an exotic dancer. Am I sleeping with Dubeck?"

"*Mais non!*" He pulled out his accent. "You are but another tool to him, no more than a measuring tape."

"Okay. Do I detect a hint of Poirot in Dubeck's voice?"

"A *soupçon.*"

Still fascinated, she turned this way and that. "He was Belgian."

She missed Booth's delighted grin. "He was, but it still works. Let's hear yours."

She'd practiced, privately. "I am at *monsieur's* disposal, and beneath his notice. But I have dreams."

Soft, low, a little breathy, with the accent subtle.

Better, he thought, than overdone.

"That'll do it. Can you hold it?"

She stared, a little fiercely, at her new face in the mirror. "I can hold it."

"When I speak to you in French, respond in French. In English, respond in English. You won't have to say much, just follow my lead."

"I know, we covered this."

"Repetition carves it in. Take off the watch—she couldn't afford it. Try those three bangles. You'll carry this bag—it holds your tablet for notes, measuring tape, pencils, pens, a paper notebook, the business card case—his—and other tools.

"Look at me, don't smile."

When she did he snapped a photo. "You'll want to familiarize yourself with the contents. Move things around if you want, as long as you know where you've put things. I'll be right back."

"Okay. I'm a little nervous. But I think it suits my personality."

She sat, opened the bag to go through the contents, saw he'd organized them as she would. She tried out the tablet, attempted some notes in French.

While she waited, she got up to check out his makeup case, and found it awesome.

"Here's your wallet," he said when he came back in. "It's got your ID, a credit card, some cash—euros and US."

She opened it, stared. "I have a French driver's license with a photo that looks like I do now."

"It's a quick job. It's a just in case. The credit card's only for show—another just in case. We should go. Don't overplay it, stay in the background."

"Looking like this?"

"Did you hear Mags's rundown of her? It's all about her and who's important. She doesn't care about you—you're not important. She'll see a young, blond Frenchwoman with a good bag and cheap shoes—"

"Like Clarice Starling."

"Jesus, no wonder I'm crazy about you. Yeah, like Clarice. But you're tall, you're built, and you only speak when spoken to."

"*Oui, monsieur*," she murmured, casting down her heavily lashed eyes. "*Je ne suis personne.*"

"*Exactement.*" He kissed her hand, and led her out.

At the bottom of the stairs, Mags fisted her hands on her hips. "Nice work, pal. You look damn good as a blonde, sweetie. The red's you, but you look damn good. Now break a leg."

"I might in these heels." She gripped Mags's hand. "Hold good thoughts, will you? It's my debut."

"I've got you covered. Sebastien's outside."

He stood by a black limo in a gray suit, a chauffeur's cap. He rolled his eyes at Miranda and said, "Ooh la la."

She laughed, slid in. "A limo?"

"*Bien sûr.*" Booth—or, she realized, Dubeck—slid in beside her. "I am Dubeck. How else would I travel? Put on the accent, and keep it on. Get inside her and stay there."

She took the little compact out of her bag, studied her new face in its mirror. And carved it into her brain.

The house was gorgeous, she couldn't deny it. It stood massive and elegant in the heart of Georgetown with its three stories, bride-white trim against the palest of yellows. Its front gardens rejoiced in spring.

"Not walled or gated," she commented with her soft accent. "I expected more security."

"It's there. The outbuilding to the left? That's the security station. And it'll be manned twenty-four/seven."

Sebastien eased to a stop on the brick driveway in front of a white portico that protected the double front doors.

He opened the door for Booth, circled around, and did the same for Miranda.

In character, Miranda walked two steps behind Booth as he strode up to ring the bell.

It opened promptly. The middle-aged woman in a black uniform looked exceptionally fit. Booth imagined security blended with her housekeeper responsibilities.

Dutifully, Miranda produced one of Dubeck's business cards.

"Monsieur Dubeck," she said. "He has an appointment with Madame Mountjoy."

"Please come in." The housekeeper invited them into a grand foyer with soaring ceilings. The floors gleamed under a perfectly faded Aubusson carpet. Antique mirrors were interspersed with art on the walls and complemented the furnishings of polished mahogany and quiet colors.

The air smelled a little too strongly of roses and gardenias.

"Please make yourselves comfortable in the parlor."

She led the way into a large room with an Adam fireplace, three tall windows, more art, more quiet colors. "Mrs. Mountjoy will be right with you. May I offer you refreshments?"

"Coffee, strong and black." Booth put a considering frown on his face as he wandered the room, assessing it.

Miranda kept her gaze down, nodded. "Yes, please. Thank you." She stood where she was, hands folded, while the housekeeper left, and Booth continued to circle and study the room.

He started to speak in rapid French, shot her an impatient look, gave an equally impatient gesture. Miranda pulled her tablet from the bag and did her best to make notes while frantically interpreting in her head.

Tasteful, cautious, good art, dignified and respectful of the architecture of the house. Beautiful millwork. Original plaster walls.

As he finished, she heard the sound of heels—likely as high as her own—clicking rapidly.

The newish wife, a bombshell blonde dressed in bold red Versace, all but pranced into the room. Her joy sparkled as brightly as the diamonds in her ears, on her wrist, on her fingers.

"Monsieur Dubeck!" (It came out "mon-sure.") She extended a hand. "Welcome. Thank you so much for coming."

"Madame." Booth held her fingers lightly, kissed the back of her hand. "My time is limited, as you know."

"I do, I do. I'm absolutely thrilled you'd give some of that time to me."

Another uniformed woman, younger, wheeled in a caddy.

"I hope you can take a moment to sit, have coffee."

"So I will."

He sat, waited to be served. Miranda took a seat on the edge of a chair, knees pressed together. She remained silent, as she understood for these purposes, she was just another piece of furniture.

"This house, she has age," Booth began, and continued before Regal could apologize for it. "And she wears it well, a great beauty."

"Oh, thank you!"

"This is her gift, not yours." He said it dismissively while sipping coffee. "But it seems she's been well tended and respected. I must see the whole of her before I agree to take your master suite and enhance her."

"Of course. I'm thrilled to show you the house. I'm so excited you agreed to consider designing the master. I just feel it doesn't reflect me—or us, my husband and me. It . . . There's too much of his former wife in there, if you understand."

"All who live in a house leave something of themselves behind. *Mais oui*, you wish to . . . exorcise your predecessor."

"Yes!" As if in prayer, Regal pressed her palms together. "Thank you for understanding."

Booth set the coffee aside. "Let us begin."

He gestured at Miranda. Regal didn't so much as glance at her.

She took notes. Occasionally Booth tossed an order in French at her, but otherwise she simply trailed behind them through rooms.

A study, a larger parlor with a grand piano, an actual orangery where orange, lemon, lime trees thrived and their blossoms filled the air.

She toured a library, a reading room (why have both?), a formal dining room with a table that could have seated thirty people, a family dining area and morning room with glass-wall views of expansive gardens, a pool, a pool house, another garage.

The kitchen, thoroughly modernized under a decor of classic charm, the staff rooms, more sitting areas.

It went on and on before they took the stairs down to a home theater with a bar, rows of wide leather seats, and two half baths.

Storage areas, utility areas. Then up again to take the grand staircase to the second floor.

Regal chattered the whole time. Booth—Dubeck—said little unless he tossed a comment or order at his faithful assistant. He stopped Regal before she could open the double doors to the master.

"*Mais non.* I will see the next floor before I view the master. This is for the last."

There they saw a kind of ballroom with a trio of Waterford chandeliers, a catering kitchen bigger than the one in Miranda's town house, two full baths, two powder rooms, sitting rooms.

And a locked door. Not an original door, but one Booth recognized had been fabricated to appear as one. He tapped on it casually and confirmed his assessment of wood veneer over steel.

"And that?"

"Oh, that leads to the attic. My husband has a kind of man cave up there, you could say. He keeps it locked. Nobody's allowed up there."

"Perhaps the madwoman in the attic?" When she just looked blank, he gave a very French shrug. "*Maintenant*, a man must have his secrets, yes? Now you may show me what you wish to change."

She all but bounced in her Louboutins.

The master suite consisted of the bedroom itself with its tall windows, coffered ceiling, fireplace, massive four-poster bed, along with two en suite baths, two dressing areas, a sitting room.

Miranda found the furnishings and decor lovely if a little too feminine with the florals and touches of pink.

Booth looked at everything, including the custom-made closets. He strode, he paced, he paused, he studied, he touched, all while Regal, finally silent, stood with her hands clasped between her breasts.

"This is space well used." He barked in French at Miranda, who dutifully took notes. "But this is not you. There is elegance, yes, but no romance, no sexuality. You like good sex, yes?"

Regal blinked. "Well, yes. My husband and I . . . Yes."

"I think when this room was last enhanced, there was no thought of sex, only style. The style is . . . ah, tasteful. Conservative. This is not what I see for you."

"I really want more modern," Regal began. "More color and—"

She broke off hard at Booth's cool stare.

"Modern? Modern is wrong!" He chopped a hand through the air like an ax through wood. "It is an abomination in this space, in this house. You have the old and must respect it. *Mais*, you will have romance, sensuality. In here, the colors must be soft, a dream, a first kiss. The softest gray, like an embrace in a summer rain, the quiet greens and blues of the sea in the twilight. This bed, this magnificent bed, he sleeps with the other wife in this bed?"

"Yes."

Now he flicked a hand. "It must go away. Live in another space. You will have your own."

"That alone, oh, Monsieur Dubeck, that alone would make me so happy."

"I will make you happy. And this house, I will keep her happy." He snapped his fingers at Miranda, demanded in French she measure the drapes. "They must go, these drapes. They are too heavy, and the color too bold. Soft, soft. The rug, no! Upholstery must change, here, in all the suite."

He looked up at the chandelier, frowned. "Here, I think, you can have a whisper of the modern. For tension, just a touch. I have something in mind. We will see."

He paced, he frowned. "We will see," he repeated. "The mantel is good, this oak. Who painted it white should be shot in the public streets. This we will strip down to its original glory."

He went through each space, spouting his vision, leaving Miranda to marvel and measure.

Regal actually wept her gratitude and didn't blink at the astronomical price he set for his design work alone. Labor and materials would come as they came.

He gave her instructions for wiring the first half of his fee, and left her weeping happily in the doorway.

Miranda didn't speak until they'd driven off the property. "It took more than ninety minutes."

"Yeah, a little. Big house. Pretty fabulous house."

"The only thing I really envied was the orangery. First time I've seen one, and now it'll be a life goal to have one. The door to the attic, right?"

"Yeah. Steel door, Sebastien. Nice wood veneer, nice reproduction of the original panel doors throughout."

"Ah. Change of shift in security at three. Two men in, two out."

"Good to know. No interior cameras—surprising. Exterior

north, south, east, west—leaves a lot of gaps. I saw the security stations—one in the kitchen utility, one in the basement. He's got a smart home setup. I can take that down remotely, bypass the alarms and motion detectors."

Thinking, imagining, he rubbed at his two-toned goatee.

"I'll work out how to keep it up for live security. Once I get in, it's just a matter of getting through the door. It's a good lock, but he didn't want to draw attention to it. No dead bolt or digital. I can scan it for an alarm, but it looks to me like he doesn't think anybody can get that far. And he loves the house, he loves the age and architecture. You can feel that walking through it."

He turned to Miranda, smiled at her. "You did great."

"I didn't do anything."

"You did exactly what you were supposed to do. Jump to my orders and otherwise fade into the background."

"I guess good. She didn't even know I was there, basically."

"Sure she did. She gave you a couple thorough look-overs, wondered if I'd nailed you yet. You envied her orangery, she envied your legs. But you're the hired help. She won't think of you much, if at all, again."

"She's going to be crushed when you—when Dubeck doesn't fully enhance that space."

"No, she won't, because he will. And she's going to love it. You took notes, right?"

Stunned, Miranda blanched. "Yes, I tried, but—"

"Joking." He leaned over to kiss her. "I remember what I saw, what I said. It'll be fun."

"She's paying you—just you—mid-six figures for the fun."

"You get what you pay for." He said it cheerfully. "Give us about thirty to ditch the wardrobe, Sebastien, then we'll get down to it."

"It'll take me that long to get the limo back."

Booth reached over Miranda to open the door when Sebastien parked again.

"We'll have cocktails in the courtyard and talk this through," Sebastien suggested.

"That's a plan." Booth took Miranda's hand as they walked to the door.

"I have to confess something."

"What's that?"

"I had fun. I really liked doing this, all of this, from playing this silly part, to touring that amazing house, to watching you spout off orders and insults and compliments. It should feel wrong. It just doesn't."

Inside the door, he took her shoulders, drew her in for a kiss. "We're righting wrongs with this one. I'm not going to claim that's what I always do, even mostly do. But that's what this is."

"I wanted to feel sorry for her. She was so eager, Booth, and she didn't get your reference to *Jane Eyre*. You could've said she needed rainbow polka dots, puce velvet drapes, and a brick bed, and she'd have gone with it."

"Never go with puce for velvet," he said, and made her laugh.

"So noted. It's just . . . She was so enthralled. And I did feel sorry for her, a little, because she shouldn't have to sleep in the same bed her husband slept in with his ex-wife, and she only wants to make that one space hers. Just that."

"There's the bonus." He gave the shoulders he still held a quick rub. "We'll give her that. She'll get that, and we'll take something from her husband he shouldn't have. And we'll make LaPorte pay. If we do this right, everybody wins."

"Okay." She let out a breath. "Let's do it right."

Chapter Twenty-Nine

AS THE SCHOOL YEAR ran down, Booth budgeted his time. Papers to grade, finals to prep for. He juggled that with poring over paint and fabric samples and consulting with Sebastien on security and how to circumvent it.

He found the perfect bedroom chandelier, all dreamy and dripping blue glass with rust metal accents, and the bed he wanted—both shipping from France.

He made two more trips to Georgetown, once as a painting contractor and the next, along with Mags, as upholsterers. Both times Regal smuggled them in during a window when her husband wouldn't be at home.

He worked all through May, while his vision—in various areas—grew clearer and clearer.

On the Friday of Memorial Day weekend, he told Miranda he'd be a little late.

When he got home, she stood in the kitchen arranging some of his Knock Out roses in a vase.

"Hi. You look pleased with yourself."

"Feeling pretty good. Those look nice."

"I think so, too." She stepped back to admire her work. "Holiday weekend. Time for some wine on the patio. Maybe we can take the kayaks out tomorrow. It's supposed to be sunny and hot."

"Might be a little busy." He hefted a bag onto the table, opened it. And set a large red stone beside it.

Her jolt nearly knocked over the Knock Outs.

"Oh my God! Is that it? You've already done it. How did you—When did you? Oh God, Booth." She punched him before picking it up. "It's got weight. You didn't tell me! What the hell."

"That's not the Goddess. It's a replica I had made. I picked it up tonight. That's why I'm late. It's the exact size, shape, weight, color. Damn good job."

"It's a fake? Why do you need a fake? You're not going to try to pass off a fake on LaPorte. He'll have it tested, won't he? Jesus, it's just a big, ugly, dull red lump."

"That looks just like the real thing. At least enough to pass a visual. And I need the fake to put in the place of the real thing when I take it. Tomorrow night."

"What?" She swallowed hard. "Tomorrow. But you talked about June, the end of June. When school's finished. When—"

"The Mountjoys are traveling to a weekend party at a friend's in Kennebunkport." He glanced at the kitchen clock. "And the landing gear on their private jet should be coming down right about now. I'd go tonight, but tomorrow's better. I needed to make sure the replica worked. It does. It will. And this timing works."

She didn't panic—wasn't a woman who panicked, she assured herself. She panicked.

"I don't understand the timing. I don't understand anything. I thought there was more time. You should take more time."

"Don't need more, and now you have less time to worry." He rubbed his hands up and down her arms. "I know what I'm doing. Take a few breaths. Trust me."

He turned away and into the butler's pantry, took a bottle of Pinot Grigio from the rack. He thought it would go well with the fish he planned to grill.

"Let's have that wine on the patio and I'll explain."

"I don't think I can sit. I really don't. What if—"

"The river tends to calm things down. LaPorte doesn't expect me to take the Goddess until well into August. I made it clear I couldn't start serious planning until after the school year. No blowing my cover. Regal's kept her mouth shut about Dubeck because she knows if her husband finds out, he may put the skids on the remodel.

"Come on."

He took the wine, the glasses, headed out the door.

"I need the replica," he continued, "because Mountjoy's bound to spend some time in his treasure room before they leave for Europe. As long as the fake's there, all good."

He poured the wine, sat, stretched out his long legs.

"Next month, end of school year, my annual cookout to celebrate that—"

"A cookout." Madness, she decided. She'd fallen for a madman. "With all this going on, you're having a cookout?"

"It's a tradition, it's expected. We keep doing what's expected. Meanwhile, the Mountjoys head to Europe, and all the sub-contractors Dubeck hired get to work. He'll make several appearances. And while that's going on, I—as LaPorte—call in Russell—the patsy. We meet at the house in Lake Charles, at night. I hire him to steal the Goddess, give him more than enough details to make the job reasonably smooth."

"But he'll steal the fake."

"Yeah, or try to."

"I don't understand." She sat after all, picked up her wine. "I'm lost."

"Russell's good enough to get in, with what I'll give him. And I'll make sure of it—or Sebastien will. He'll not only find the Goddess, but he sure as hell won't leave that house or that room without helping himself to more. And he won't get away due to our setting off the alarms remotely, which will have Mountjoy's security and the cops swarming."

"You want him—the patsy—to get caught."

"Key detail." Content, Booth stretched out his legs and admired the river. "When they grab him up, with whatever he's grabbed, he'll roll on LaPorte."

"What if he doesn't?"

"If he doesn't, they'll easily trace the big chunk of new money in Russell's account back to LaPorte."

Frustrated, Miranda slapped both hands to her head. "But LaPorte didn't pay this Russell, you did."

"Didn't he?" Booth smiled and sipped and enjoyed the spring breeze, the flowers, the buzz of bees. "LaPorte's wired three million dollars to an account I set up in his name, with his data. The half million he advanced Russell will come out of it, so will a few other suspicious transactions."

Now she began to see, so picked up her wine again.

"You're setting him up with his own money. That's brilliant."

"Thanks. I like it. And more than his own money. But that's the crescendo. I need to marinate that tuna, and prep the peppers I'm going to grill."

"You're not leaving me hanging."

"I'll tell you the rest."

She rose with him. "I'm going with you tomorrow."

"You're going, and you're staying with Mags. You're not going on the job. That's not on the table."

"Because I'd be in the way."

"I love you, Miranda. That's pure truth. And yeah, you'd be in the way. But I'll tell you the rest."

It all seemed impossibly complicated and ridiculously simple at the same time. She examined her conscience countless times over the next twenty-four hours.

And still, when she stood with Booth, Mags, Sebastien, and the little dog in Georgetown, she didn't know exactly what she felt.

She considered what her father would think if he knew what she'd become part of. And didn't know.

437

She only knew she'd passed the point of no return.

"I love stones," Mags commented as they all studied the fake goddess on the table. "Raw, tumbled, faceted, they have a kind of life to them that fascinates me. This one just sits there."

"Because it's not a stone. It's a composite."

"It's a good one." Sebastien hefted it, studied it from all sides. "Looks like the pictures—not many of them to see, but the ones you can. *Mais*, *mon ami*, you can't be sure it fools the man who's held it, stroked it, gloated over it."

"If it doesn't, plans change. We'll have our ears to the ground and know if it's clear before they head to Europe. If we get that far, we keep following the steps until it's done."

He rolled his shoulders. "I'm going to check my equipment before I change."

"You'll have a meal first," Sebastien insisted. "Keep your energy up."

"A light one, no alcohol."

Miranda ate a little, but mostly pretended to. She'd expected to worry. She hadn't expected to feel nearly sick with worry even as Booth appeared absolutely calm.

When he went upstairs with Sebastien, she helped Mags with the dishes.

"It's okay to worry. It's natural to worry."

"Are you worried?"

"I always worry some," Mags admitted. "I worried when he'd sneak out of the house as a kid. Dana so sick, the bills piling up so high. Then there was money for the mortgage, for the medical bills. I worried he was dealing drugs, or himself, my sister's sweet boy. But he wasn't."

"Oh, Mags. You carried so much weight."

Mags shook her head. "Dana wasn't weight, and neither was Booth. They were—and are—lights in my life."

She touched the celestite crystal she wore on a chain in memory of her sister.

"After I pinned Booth down on what he was doing, I worried. But he kept the roof over his mom's head, food on the table. We couldn't have done it with the cleaning business alone. It was too much."

She closed the dishwasher. "I worried about Sebastien, but he's pretty much retired now. His girls are grown and set. He has enough. My business with Dauphine's doing fine, and he helps out there. Keeps him occupied."

"But you're worried about both of them tonight."

Mags gave Miranda's hand a squeeze. "Waiting just sucks, doesn't it? We're going to light candles. Some good white magic."

"I don't know if I believe in that kind of magic."

"Oh, I believe enough for both of us." With the next thought, Mags's smile turned to cold fury. "If I didn't, I'd make a goddamn voodoo doll or poppet of LaPorte and burn it to ashes. He wouldn't know what hit him."

"You actually believe you could do that?"

"If I couldn't, I know a few back home who could. But it's not the way. This is the way."

"So says the Mandalorian."

With a wild laugh, Mags grabbed Miranda, gave her a noisy kiss. "Booth must be circus-clown crazy about you."

"Do you know any circus clowns?"

"Dated one. Moody bastard." Mags gave the kitchen a last glance. "Okay. So we light candles, and we wait until they're back again."

When he came down, Miranda realized Booth looked like her image of a cat burglar. Long, lean, lanky in black jeans, a long-sleeved black tee, black high-tops.

She decided against asking herself what finding that outrageously sexy said about her.

"You're not going now. It's barely ten."

"I've got the dark, the house is empty. Nobody around but

security. That doesn't change if I wait." He put his hands on her shoulders. "It's going to be fine. I'll be back soon."

Don't panic, don't panic.

Too late.

"I don't know what I'm supposed to do. How to feel."

"Think of it as me getting called into work for a couple hours." He kissed her, light and casual, before he glanced at Mags. "I'll bring your boyfriend back."

"See that you do."

"I do the driving, me, so I do the bringing back. *À bientôt, ma belle.*" Sebastien's kiss was neither light nor casual.

Then they walked out the door, two men in thievery black, and drove away in a black SUV.

"Oh God, this is really happening." Riding on the panic, Miranda took two steps outside as if she'd run after the car.

Mags just curled her fingers around Miranda's arm. "Do you play Scrabble?"

"What?" Wild-eyed, baffled, Miranda stared. "*What?*"

"We're going to light the candles, then I'm going to show you how we play Scrabble in my family. It requires wine."

SEBASTIEN DROVE BY THE mansion. Security lights beamed. More lights glowed against the windows of the outbuildings. The carriage lights flanking the entrance doors burned a soft gold.

"There." Sebastien jutted his chin. "The man and the big curly dog."

"Labradoodle."

"They head home now. He walks the dog this time every night. Not much foot traffic otherwise, see? Ah, but there?"

Booth glanced across and down the street. "Somebody's having a party. Might have some walkers when it breaks up. Turn left here. I'll backtrack. I'll signal when I'm ready for pickup."

"The Goddess waits for you, *cher*. She wants you to take her."

"Then I hope she's packed and ready."

"No, no, I mean what I say, me. I feel this inside my bones. She's been used for greed, for envy, for blood and death. Now it's for justice, for payment overdue. She's the answer, and I think she's always been your answer. She waits for you."

Taking a moment, Booth let himself feel. "I want a life, Sebastien. All I've ever wanted was a life of my own choosing."

"Then go get her."

Booth slipped out of the car. A couple stepped out of a restaurant half a block down and into a waiting cab. He walked on as it passed him, just a man taking a stroll on a pleasant night in spring.

He smelled roses from someone's garden, then heliotrope; he heard the thump of bass from the open windows of a car driving by.

He thought of nothing, set everything else aside, but the next step.

And in the shadows between streetlights, in the narrow gap between security cameras, he took that next step.

In his head he saw, as clearly as the map he'd made, the lights, the cameras. He took a wide berth, used the trees, the shrubs, caught the scent of night-blooming jasmine, as he crab-walked through another gap.

He took a short run, crouched, and paused when he saw the door to the security house open.

The man stepped out, and Booth saw the 9mm on his hip as he lit a cigarette. And through the roses and jasmine Booth caught the sting of smoke as he exhaled.

The man strolled as he smoked, a well-built man with blond hair cut high and tight. Military, but not on patrol, Booth decided. The cameras handled things. Just a smoke break, a leg stretch.

And a short delay in the schedule.

He waited it out. Once or twice the guard strolled by close enough Booth could have reached out and grabbed his leg.

Then he field-dressed the smoke—*semper fi*—put the butt into an Altoids tin, and made his way back to the guardhouse.

Booth gave it another full minute before he took the next run.

Now he crouched by the far side of the house under a Japanese maple. Tricky here, he thought. While the guards couldn't see him—except through the cameras—he couldn't see them either.

But he could see the way in he'd selected—side door into the orangery—and took out his remote.

Seven seconds, he thought. Interrupt the feed—he hoped—for seven seconds. Some static, a quick glitch, all he needed. Inside, ten seconds to reset the alarm. They'd likely programmed it to at least thirty, or more. Most did. But in his calculations, anything over ten could—and should—alert the guards to a breach.

If he went over either time, he had—maybe—thirty seconds to run.

And screw that, he thought. The Goddess waited for him. Miranda waited for him. His life—one of his choosing—waited for him.

Running wasn't an option this time.

He engaged the remote, and, counting off the seconds, bolted to the door. The lock wasn't the real problem. Not leaving any signs of forced entry—that was the issue.

He finessed the lock, stepped in, restarted his internal clock. He pulled off the cover, attached his digital reader.

Counting, counting as the numbers flashed on the display.

It hit the last of the six-digit code in ten flat.

So he stood surrounded by the heady scents of oranges, lemons, blossoms, eyes closed, orienting himself.

It came back to him, rose up inside him, that visceral thrill. It had been nearly a year now. One job the previous summer, just to keep the muscles tuned. Then back to school.

Then Miranda.

Now he embraced it as he moved through the house. He used no light, stayed well away from windows not only because someone might see movement but to avoid any chance of setting off a motion detector.

The housekeeper/interior security had quarters off the kitchen, so he avoided that area. He knew she was up—he'd seen the light. He got close enough only to hear the murmur behind the door. Some laughter.

Television, he concluded. One of the late-night shows.

All the better. He'd do what he came to do, and she'd report no disturbances.

Other live-in staff had separate quarters on the property— he'd seen lights in the staff house, some movement behind the windows.

He'd keep a careful eye on departure.

He used the main staircase to the second floor, then the third.

He walked as he had with Miranda and the lady of the house, carefully avoiding the two treads he'd noted let out quiet creaks.

He walked directly to the locked door. He didn't worry about leaving some subtle signs of lock tampering. In fact, he'd intended to leave more than he ever would, still subtle, but signs any decent cop would find.

Russell would leave more, he knew.

He got through, shut the door behind him. And waited for any sounds, waited for his eyes to adjust yet again.

Darker here, he thought, and more creaks in the damn stairs. Still the odds of house security hearing them down on the main floor and through a steel door hit nil.

At the top of the steps, he made out two windows—both with blackout shades drawn. He pulled out his penlight, scanned the space—large, many shapes, angled ceilings.

And a camera.

"Well, shit."

He considered it while he stood out of range and once again calculated the odds. No way Mountjoy would trust paid employees with a view of his private collection. This was for him.

He could look in on it while he was away, or record himself in the midst of his treasures.

Either way, he had to disable it long enough to do what he came to do.

He used the remote again, let out a long breath when the camera light went from green to red.

With no time to waste, he took a chance, hit the light switch, and flooded the room.

He'd seen this sort of thing before, but admitted Alan C. Mountjoy had created a very sumptuous space for himself. Antique furniture, artfully arranged, a small but well-stocked bar. Art, of course. He counted eight exquisite paintings, twice that in sculptures. The glint of jewelry in glass displays.

And an impressive, very impressive, collection of gems—raw and faceted.

And the centerpiece stood on a gold column with the top shaped like an open palm to hold her.

She was gorgeous. Raw, elemental, pure. The only one of her kind.

She took his breath away.

Everything else in the room faded beside her. The Degas, the Rodin, the ice-white diamonds, the bloodred rubies faded to nothing in comparison.

When he touched her, when he lifted her, he would have sworn he heard her breathing.

He set the replica in her place. Perfect fit in that golden palm.

He heard his own heart knocking as he reverently placed her in the velvet bag, and the bag in his leather satchel.

Backing away, he turned off the lights, restarted the camera.

"I think you were waiting," he murmured as he went down the stairs. "And I hope I'm taking you where you want to go."

It occurred to him if that wasn't the case, legend claimed she'd let him know in a fatal sort of way.

When he reached the second floor, he saw the lights on in the main. And sincerely hoped that fatal sort of way hadn't arrived.

He ducked into the shadows.

Housekeeper, doing a sweep, he realized. Would she come upstairs? If so, he could evade her, wait her out.

He heard her humming, caught the tune. Okay, a Gaga fan. She couldn't be all bad. And if she caught him, she'd kick his ass or shoot him. He preferred avoiding either.

He caught sight of her crossing the foyer to the front door. Short robe, pockets drooping some. Good legs, bare feet.

She checked the front door, the alarm.

Then took out the phone in her pocket.

"This is Rena, giving the all clear. I'm turning in for the night."

"Copy that. All clear. We've got the watch."

She put the phone back in her pocket. Booth suspected the second pocket drooped from the weight of a weapon.

She moved out of sight, and the lights went off.

He waited, giving her time, plenty of time, to settle back into her quarters. Then he added more, just to top it off, before he slipped through the dark down the stairs, and back to the orangery.

For the hell of it, he plucked an orange, put it in his bag.

He dealt with the alarm, the door, and was out, retracing his steps.

No elation, not yet. He wouldn't allow it. He texted Sebastien as he headed away from the mansion, toward the bars, the restaurants, the people, the nightlife.

Four blocks away, Sebastien glided to the curb.

"*C'est fini?*" Sebastien asked when Booth got in beside him.

"You bet your ass."

"You took a little longer than planned."

"Still inside the window." Booth leaned his head back. No elation, he thought again, not until all, not just this phase, was finished.

Hell, maybe just a little elation.

"I just stole the Red Goddess. No one's ever going to know but you, Mags, and Miranda. And, eventually, LaPorte."

"*Mon ami*, you will always know."

"Yeah. Holy shit. Yeah." He scrubbed his hands over his face. "I couldn't get my breath, and my ears started ringing when I picked her up. Maybe nobody should know that part but you."

Smoothly, Sebastien pulled up to the house. "You make me proud. You've done what no one has."

"She's been stolen before."

"With blood and pain and death. And, to me, *cher*, you freed her. And this is a different thing."

"It's what it felt like." Still a little shaken, Booth got out of the car. "Swear to God."

The door to the house swung open. Miranda stood in the backwash of light with Mags behind her. She rubbed a hand on her heart and worked up a smile.

"Welcome back. You're okay. You're both okay."

"All good." He walked up to kiss her, felt her trembling. "I'm sorry you worried." He reached into the bag, pulled out the orange. "Brought you a souvenir."

She stared at it, began to laugh. Took it, pressed it to her face to draw in the scent. "Thanks."

"No trouble?" Mags reached out, just to touch both of them. "No problems?"

"One of the guards had a smoke and a stroll, the housekeeper does a final check of the main floor, and Mountjoy has a camera in his collection room. Took me a little longer to get around those."

"For God's sake—or the Goddess's," Mags corrected, "let's see her."

Booth took the bag back to the kitchen, and, lifting the stone out, set it on the counter. Pure, raw red, wider than it was long, it sat—a kind of large fist on the granite.

"It looks the same as the fake," Miranda said after a moment. "But it doesn't . . . feel the same."

Mesmerized, Booth traced a finger over the stone. "Why?"

"I don't know. Maybe because I know it's not. But it feels more potent. It's the word that comes to mind."

Sebastien cradled the stone, then lifted it. And let out a long, soft "Ahhhh" before he smiled at Mags. "If I could, I would give her to you."

She laid her hands over his with the Goddess under them. "I'll take you instead. Potent." Mags nodded at Miranda. "It's a good word."

"You could keep it." In turn, Miranda laid a hand over Mags's. "You must be tempted."

"No." Not even a little tempted, he thought. Not even a little. "She has a purpose." He put his hand over the others'. "When she's fulfilled it, she belongs to the world. No more hiding."

With a nod, Miranda stepped back and waited until he put the stone back in velvet. "What's next?"

"Finals week."

Laughing, she put her arms around him and held on tight.

Chapter Thirty

FINALS WEEKS RUSHED RIGHT into graduation. As always, Booth felt a lift when he watched his seniors cross the stage in cap and gown.

And as always, he wondered what they'd do, where they'd go, what mark they'd leave on the world.

The school year wound down for the rest of his students, and for him.

And as he always did before he left on the last day, he walked the halls, walked through the theater, and backstage. Because he could never be sure he'd come back.

This year, more than any other, everything hung in the balance.

He had a ten-day lag until his annual party—and plenty to fill it.

When he got home, Miranda met him at the doors with her suitcase—and his.

"You said you wanted to get going as soon as possible."

"Yeah." His rubbed his hands along her arms. "I wish—"

"No point going over all that again. We agreed I would go. And I have a part to play."

"You agreed," Booth corrected, then gave those arms a squeeze. "No, I think the word's 'insisted.'"

"I'm looking forward to seeing New Orleans, Sebastien's bayou, Lake Charles. I'm a prop again, just like before, that's understood. But I have that role to play, and I'm looking forward to that, too.

"Plus," she added, "you're the one who bumped up the timeline."

"Because LaPorte's in seclusion for the next few days after getting a tune-up." Doing his best to set aside worry, Booth waved a hand in front of his face. "And, thanks to Sebastien, the Moren family and staff are about to vacate the premises until tomorrow morning. Dangerous gas leak."

"Then we're set."

Boxed in again—she had a way of boxing him in—he gave the house a last check before the drive to the airport, and the private charter that would take them to New Orleans.

"I COULD GET USED to this, you know." Miranda snuggled back in her cushy leather seat on the plane and sipped champagne. "I may have grown up with a certain level of privilege, but it didn't include private jets."

"It's work."

"Are you nervous about this part?"

"No." He couldn't allow nerves. "LaPorte's vanity just gave us a smoother ride. As long as Russell sticks to the timetable—and he'll be too afraid of LaPorte, too wrapped up in the opportunity, to deviate—it'll go fine."

With his mind focused on the steps, the stages, he gave her hand an absent pat. "I really can't show you New Orleans this time. We're going to change, then drive to Lake Charles. The schedule's tight there, and we need to be out and heading home within four hours, all told."

He checked the time. "Jacques will meet us at the airport, drive us to Sebastien's. We get into character there while Sebastien and Mags set up LaPorte's fake office."

"Why don't we change in Lake Charles?"

"Timing, and that leaves more chance of making a mistake. Leaving some trace."

"Okay, then we drive to Lake Charles."

"Jacques drives us. He has a role to play, too. Russell comes in at eleven, I make the deal. We break down the set, drive back to New Orleans, break character. We'll be home by morning."

"And when Regal and her husband are off in Europe—and Dubeck's crew's busy on the redecorating—Russell breaks in to steal the Goddess, takes the fake, gets caught."

Timing, he thought, and one piece dovetailing into the next. One by one.

"That's the plan."

"Because you're going to set off the alarms, have the place surrounded. Then you plant the real Goddess in LaPorte's place, alert authorities—which could be helped along if Russell rolls."

"Even if he doesn't—"

"Even if he doesn't," Miranda continued, "you left the money trail. There's one thing I keep circling back to. What happens if LaPorte brings you into it?"

"He can try, but he'd have to admit to various crimes, and I'm just a high school teacher." He shrugged, then gave his shoulders an extra roll. "The background I created will hold unless they keep digging. And since the Chameleon's hit a couple times this year—in France, in Italy—and I haven't left the country—why would they?"

"How did you manage that when you haven't been in France or Italy this year?"

Relax, he ordered himself, and managed a smile.

"Called a couple of . . . colleagues. Just asked them to use my particular signature on an upcoming job. One, when I was holding a Drama Club meeting in late March, another on the spring musical's closing night. LaPorte can try to implicate me, but it just adds to his troubles."

"Here's what I think. LaPorte only tries to implicate you—if he does—because of me."

He turned, pinned her with a sharp look. "What do you have to do with it?"

"I met him briefly when we were both in New York."

"No. Miranda—"

"Hear me out. I gave Sebastien some cities and dates, and he looked into all that, found we were both in New York for three days—actually four for me—a few years ago."

Obviously pleased with her idea—and determined—she barreled on.

"We had a moment, Carter and I, which I very much regret, as he made harsh demands, and was unpleasant when I refused them. He's contacted me a few times since, but I've continued to refuse, as I felt he made veiled threats. Nothing specific, but he made me uncomfortable. He seemed obsessed with me—it felt like possession."

"Just no."

She drank again. "You don't think a man could be obsessed with me?"

"No, I buy that, but—"

"If it ever gets there, I can make that work. I haven't had a real relationship until you—and that moment is part of the reason."

She blinked at him, all emotion. Tears glimmered, actually trembled.

"He must've found out, and he sent those two horrible people to watch me, and you because of me. All because of me. I haven't told you any of this before because . . ."

A single tear slid slowly down her cheek as she turned into him, gripped his arm. Struggled off a sob.

"I was afraid. Of him, of telling you that even once I . . . I was afraid he'd hurt you or you'd leave me. Oh, Booth. Forgive me!"

Fact was fact, he thought, and he had to admit it. "That's pretty damn good."

She tossed back her hair. "I worked it out with Mags. If it comes down to it, I can make that sing like a Shakespearean sonnet."

She just . . . dazzled him. "I think you could."

"Oh, I could, and you should let me, because I'll do it anyway. It takes the focus off you, puts it on me. And I have nothing to hide."

"Lying to the cops—"

"That ship's sailed." She floated a hand in the air as if sending that ship over the horizon. "I know who you are, what you do. I've been part of it—made sure of that."

Sure of herself, she brushed the single tear away, flicked it into the air.

"I haven't turned you in. He took from me, too, and you know how I feel about it. If the authorities give you a push, it's going to be all about me and my lapse of judgment four years—almost five years ago, when a charming older man seduced me."

She finished the drink, set the flute aside. The amusement in them faded as those witchy eyes met his.

"I don't want diamonds, Booth, or paintings by the masters. This is what I want, and I need you to give it to me. I'll do and say it anyway, but it would mean a lot if I didn't have to go around you."

"Let's take the next step, okay? One at a time." He took her hand, brought it to his lips. "It's a good plan."

As promised, Jacques met them at the airport. Miranda saw a scarecrow of a man about her age in ripped baggy jeans and a New Orleans Saints tee. He wore his hair in short twists and sported a tiny silver hoop in one ear.

His grin nearly split his face when he spotted Booth.

"My man." They did a hand slap, a fist bump, then a solid hug. "Looking good. This one looks even better."

"Miranda Emerson, Jacques Xavier."

"*Bienvenue.*" Jacques took her hand, gave her a charming kiss on the knuckles. "We got you set, so pile on in." He opened the front passenger door. "You sit up front so you can tell me your life story."

"It's not over yet," Miranda said as she slid in. "But I'll tell you mine if you tell me yours."

Booth sat in the back while they talked like old friends, and pulled out his drop phone to check on the progress in Lake Charles.

Timing, he thought again. It all came down to timing.

She got a glimpse—it hardly seemed like more—of New Orleans, and none of the Quarter as Jacques drove from the airport to the bayou and Sebastien's cottage.

"Oh, it's wonderful!" She turned in a circle beside the car.

Heat lay heavy; the water moved lazily; moss hung like lace.

"It's beautiful—it's exotic and primitive at the same time. And look at his house. It's charming."

"He'll be happy you think so. We've gotta—"

Booth broke off when the cottage door opened, and a pregnant Dauphine stepped out.

In a poppy-colored tank dress that showed off her—third—baby bump, she walked onto the porch, set a hand on her hip.

"So this is the one." She gave Miranda a long study. "The girl you left behind."

"Tried to," Miranda corrected.

"I'm Dauphine. An old friend."

"Do you have many absolutely stunning old friends, Booth?"

"Not like this one." He walked to her, caught her in a hug. "Where are the kids?"

"With their Grann and Papi."

"Luc?"

"In Lake Charles, helping."

"Dauphine, he didn't have to—"

"It's not have to, it is. I would be there myself, but for this." She laid her hand on her belly. "But I'm here to help. Jacques."

"We're family," Jacques reminded him, and tossed a suit bag over his shoulder. "I have my fancy suit in here."

"And I have lemonade and wine, some food—not so good as yours or Sebastien's. I missed your face," she said, and kissed Booth. "And wanted to see yours." She offered Miranda a hand.

Miranda accepted it. "I won't say any friend of Booth's, because I'm not sure about that. But I will say any friend of Mags's. It's really good to meet you."

"Come in, take a moment. Yes, yes, your schedule," Dauphine said to Booth. "But take a moment. I'll help with the transformations."

Maybe it didn't fit neatly into his steps or schedule—only one of the reasons he'd worked solo through the bulk of his career—but he found it fascinating just how quickly Miranda melded with his two old friends.

They had lemonade—no wine while they worked, by his decree—and some damn good shrimp Creole.

Then Booth brought out Miranda's wardrobe.

"No big ass this time, so that's a plus." She tapped the fake breasts and bra. "Just gigantic boobs."

"Not gigantic, just . . . enhanced. Noticeably enhanced."

"You're perfect as you are," Jacques told her. "But this is for the play. A kind of play with me in my fancy suit and a hard look."

He changed his face into what Miranda had to admit equaled a very hard look.

She studied the stern black suit—stern, but perfectly cut. Slim. And the shoulder holster and weapon.

"I'm going to wear a gun."

"A prop. A fake gun. You're security as well as in charge of the house. You're former MI6."

"Like a spy? This is great. I'm an ass-kicker."

"You'll bring Russell into the office and go away. You'll lead him out and say nothing."

"I'm a walk-on," she said to Dauphine.

"Let's get to makeup."

"Miranda and I can handle that on our own," Dauphine told him. "I have the picture of who she needs to be."

"Okay. Don't worry about exact." He could always fiddle with it after, he decided. "Here's the wig." Booth took the long fall of perfectly highlighted golden brown out of the case, then held it up against Miranda's face. "Don't use any bronzer. She's a Brit. Lily Cross—and the real Lily Cross has a small tattoo of a butterfly. I have the fake to apply."

"I get a tattoo!"

"Temp. Do you know how to apply it?"

"We'll handle it, *cher*." Dauphine patted his cheek. "Where do you want it?"

"It's on the center back of her left wrist. The jewelry—"

"We have this." Dauphine grabbed the case, swept up the wardrobe. "Come, Miranda, or he'll talk us to death."

They went into Sebastien's bedroom, shut the door. Seconds later, he heard a burst of laughter.

"You found a jewel, I think."

Still looking at the closed door, Booth nodded. "She's that, and a constant surprise. I appreciate your help on this, Jacques."

"I get to wear a fine suit, drive a fine car, and look mean and dangerous." That grin flashed out again. "I like this job."

"We're going to slick back your hair," Booth decided. "And I'm going to give you some facial hair. You'll need to lose the earring for this."

Behind schedule, Booth thought, once he adjusted Jacques's look. While Jacques changed into his suit, he worked on his transformation into Carter LaPorte.

Over the next hour he heard more laughter, several exclamations, and a lot of muttering and murmuring. He did his best to ignore it as he worked with face putty to round out his face, added some color to any visible skin—just a subtle, rich man's tan. He added some facial bruising around the jaw, around the eyes to depict someone recently out of cosmetic surgery.

"You're not so pretty now," Jacques commented as he drank more lemonade and watched. "The nips and tucks he gets can't change that. You look older, too. It's some damn skill you got with all that stuff."

"It comes in handy."

With the wig, the colored contacts, the padding under the suit—he'd pass. In good light, close up, he wouldn't, but he'd planned for that.

Then Dauphine stepped out. She did a classic double take, then laughed. "At first glance, you look too much like him for comfort. But you're too tall."

"I'll be sitting behind the desk. I'll pass."

"Yes, I think you will. And so, I give you Lily Cross."

Miranda strode out, her expression as stern as the suit.

Her nose looked just a bit longer, slightly more narrow—good work there, he admitted. They'd styled the wig into a sleek and severe tail. She wore the jacket open so a hint of the weapon showed.

"Good job. Damn good."

Her eyes beamed a hard, bright blue.

"You managed the contacts. How are they working for you?"

"I'm getting used to them."

The fact she added a faint and fruity British accent made him grin.

Yes, a constant surprise to him.

"Not bad, not bad at all."

"I saw my ID, read the background. Lily's from London. Educated, a risk-taker, an ass-kicker."

"All good, but you're still window dressing for this."

"Understood. I don't like how you look."

"It won't be for long. You saved me time, Dauphine."

"I'd do more if I could. You." She turned to Miranda, took

her hands. "Come back, meet the rest of my family, and we'll show you New Orleans."

"I will. Thank you, Dauphine, for everything."

"Ah, *c'est rien*."

"We're running a little behind. Miranda, grab that black bag. I stocked it with spare contacts, makeup if you need to boost it."

"Got it."

"We can drop you home," Booth began, but Dauphine waved that away.

"My parents are coming to get me. I have a lovely half hour or so to sit and drink lemonade on the porch. In the quiet. You'll tell me when it's done?"

"I will." He took another moment, gathered her in. "You're a great love in my life."

"And you in mine."

Dauphine stepped out with them, then turned to Miranda.

"You're *the* love. You know that."

"I do. I'm glad he had you. And now so do I."

This time both Booth and Miranda sat in the back, and Booth handed her a file. "Lady Jane Dubois's codicil on the Goddess."

"Really? I didn't think you had time to work this part. You never said anything more about it."

"I didn't work it, Jacques did. He's a hell of a good forger."

Jacques shot a wide grin in the rearview.

Miranda opened the folder, studied the papers protected by plastic sleeves.

"Well, wow. It looks old—the paper—and authentic. I guess I don't have to ask if this matches her signature, or those of the lawyer and the witness."

"They'll hold up," Jacques assured her. "Booth gave me plenty of time to work. And to age the paper, the ink. A fun job this, but he pays more than he should."

"LaPorte's paying," Booth reminded him.

"That's why I took the money."

Miranda handed the file back to Booth, leaned forward. "So, this is what you do?"

"It's one thing I do."

Since he chattered cheerfully, Miranda learned he worked as a computer programmer now—one hundred percent legit! A little side work here and there, especially for good friends or good money. He had a girl, and she played in a zydeco band. He thought maybe they'd get married. Maybe.

They streamed to Lake Charles under a half-moon that shimmered on the water.

Booth gestured out the window. "That's LaPorte's place."

"Some place," she replied as the moonlight gave her glimpses of gardens and walls and gates, and the massive house, the outbuildings.

"You're sure he's there."

"Oh yeah. And alone, other than his security team and house staff." Booth tapped the bruising and light swelling on his face. "Vanity. He gets tune-ups every few years, and closes everything down for a couple days—at least—after. No guests, no visitors, no interruptions."

Booth smiled as he imagined LaPorte alone in his massive suite of rooms.

"He likes to believe nobody but the medical team knows he gets the work done."

"How'd you discover all this?"

"I've made it my damn mission to know absolutely everything about him over the last dozen years."

Booth's eyes—LaPorte brown—stared straight ahead. "I know him inside and out. I've been prepping for this job a long time. It was always going to come down to this."

Jacques drove on, another half mile to another gated estate. This time, the gates slid silently open.

Miranda's heart tripped once when the man—broad shoulders in a dark suit—stepped up to the car.

Jacques rolled down the window, said, "Hey, cousin, where you at?"

"All good." Luc shot a finger at Booth. "I'd've thought you were the man himself."

"We keep the light dim, we've got it. Miranda, this is Luc, Dauphine's Luc. You can meet up later, but we've got to get inside."

"They're ready for you."

He stepped back, and Jacques drove down the paved drive. The gates slid closed again.

Under her fake breasts, Miranda's heartbeat picked up its pace.

"This doesn't feel quite real."

Booth put a hand on hers. "It'll be done soon."

They'd cut the security lights back as planned, Booth noted. The houses, the grounds, while big, elegant, sprawling, and rich, weren't like LaPorte's. He had to count on Russell not paying close attention to the exterior, the lack of light.

All his research indicated LaPorte had only met once with Russell at his Lake Charles estate, and eight years before.

Add to that fact, in his experience, people usually saw what they expected to see, it should work.

The door opened as they pulled to a stop.

Another man in a suit, she thought. A wiry one this time, with a steel-gray crew cut and prominent nose.

She didn't recognize Sebastien until he spoke.

"You're a little late, chickens."

"I know. We'll make it up."

With a nod, Sebastien smiled at Miranda. "You look scary. I don't cross such as you."

"I'll say the same. I honestly didn't recognize you."

"Neither will Russell. How you like my bayou?"

"It's wonderful. It's magic. I didn't have a chance to see a *cocodril*."

"Next time."

"I'll signal you if you have to delay," Booth told Jacques. "You've got this."

"I got it." He gave a quick salute and drove off again.

"Let's get inside."

The generous foyer had towering ceilings and a trio of chandeliers. Their light beamed over an elaborate tile rug and a massive table standing on it.

The grand staircase rivaled *Gone with the Wind*.

"This is . . . impressive," Miranda decided. "Wouldn't Russell realize this isn't LaPorte's entrance?"

"He's only been here once, but that's why you're bringing him in the side door to LaPorte's office. Mags will show you the route. Where's Mags?"

"Needed to fuss with her . . ." Sebastien waved a hand around his face and hair.

"The family and staff all tucked away?"

"Left fast, too. Internal gas leak—very dangerous. But the gas company, they work through the night, make it all safe again. They don't have so many as LaPorte anyway living right here. The family, they go to New Orleans, to a hotel. And I tell the man I check in to give him updates. Did one half hour ago, tell him we find the problem, and should be done by two, and does he want me to call then? He says no, to call in the morning unless more problems."

"Good. I want us out before one. Let's see the office."

"Gonna make you happy."

He led the way, out of the foyer, through a wide doorway, through a kind of fancy sitting room, past what Miranda saw was a music room with a glossy white grand piano, and to a set of doors.

Sebastien threw them open, said, "*Et voilà!*"

And Booth grinned. "It's perfect. Smaller, a little smaller than LaPorte's, wall paint's different, but it's neutral. The desk, the chairs, the wall behind the desk. Perfect. It's damn good work."

"We thank Luc for most of that."

"And I do."

Booth circled the room, one dominated by the ornate desk. Because he knew, because his eyes looked keenly, he saw the false fronts, the props, the cagey reproduction of LaPorte's Victorian vitrine.

"Bring him in that door. Keep the lights low, keep him focused on me. It'll work. He's got no reason to doubt he's where he's supposed to be."

He turned as Mags came in.

She wore a stiff black uniform and ugly practical shoes. Her hair, mouse gray, sat in a kind of crown of short curls.

"Only for you would I let myself look like this."

"I see you in there, and you're beautiful." Booth walked over to take her hands.

"Can it. I look like Aunt Lydia. And you look too much like that bastard. You?" She pointed at Miranda. "Look like one tough cookie."

"I have a gun and a tattoo. They're fake, like these." She patted her breasts. "But I have them."

"How about you show Miranda the route to bring Russell in and take him out again?"

"Come with me, killer." Mags walked Miranda out the side door, where the air smelled of gardenias. "How's my boy doing?"

"He's focused. Very focused, but you'd have seen that. I don't think he's been getting a lot of sleep, but he seems steady. Rock steady."

"And you?"

"Sometimes it feels like some great adventure, and then I think it's all just madness. I really want it over, and at the same time, I'm never going to forget a minute of it."

"Sounds healthy to me. Okay, let's walk your route. I hate that these shoes are comfortable."

"They're hideous."

"Yeah, that's why I hate they feel like I'm walking on clouds. So Jacques drives Russell around the lake side of the house. You'll be waiting at the end of the walkway."

"Booth went over it with me about a dozen times, but it's good to actually see it."

"When you bring him in, Booth'll be sitting at the desk. I'll just be leaving by the interior doors. I close mine, you—when Booth gives you the nod—step back and close yours."

They came to the end of the path with the moonlit lake. More gardenia, joined by roses, perfumed the air. She imagined the pergola with its climbing vines smothered in bright red flowers offered shade for that view of the lake on a sun-drenched day.

"Less than two minutes both ways. You're okay with it?"

"Yes. I'm fine with it."

Mags gave her arm a squeeze. "Not everyone—probably most—would be. I want to say how much it means to me you're with him on this."

"I'm with him," Miranda said simply. "And Booth isn't the only one looking for some payback. LaPorte's earned everything that's coming his way, and when he gets it, I'll know I had a part in making it happen."

She took a long breath. "It matters to me, Mags, that I have a part in it."

In the office, Booth set out papers. Coming together, he thought, going over every remaining step, every contingency for a step that went south. Every action and its potential consequence.

He had an escape route for Miranda, should everything go south, and counted on Mags and Sebastien to convince her to take it.

Because if he failed, he'd go down, and hard. But he wouldn't take her with him.

Sebastien set the crystal lowball glass with strong tea—bourbon-colored tea—on a coaster on the desk.

Booth nudged it an inch over, adjusted the angle of the antique inkwell.

"You're worried, *mon ami*?"

"I've covered everything every way I know how, and I can see every piece fit together. But there's Miranda. If one of the pieces jams, I need to know you'll make sure she cuts herself loose."

"Love makes us worriers. A step at a time, just a step at a time."

"With contingencies in place," Booth added. "If it busts, you do whatever you have to. Convince her to say she didn't know anything. She's been a pawn, a ploy, a cover—just like I said to LaPorte in the recording. You make sure of that. I had another woman all along, the one who posed as my assistant, then the one I brought here. They'll believe her. Why wouldn't they?"

"That's what you think of me?" Miranda asked from the side door. "You think I'd just toss you aside to save myself?"

"Miranda—"

"Be smart. Shut up. Don't say another word." She strode to him, jabbed a finger into his arm. "I make my own choices. I decide my own fate. And I choose you. You're stupid if you piss me off, but even if you do, I still choose you."

"I make my own decisions, too, and decided my own fate a long time ago. If this goes south, I'm tossing you over. I'll tell them I sucked you in, lied every step of the way."

"Who're you going to tell?" She jabbed him again. "The cops, the FBI, Interpol? You've been doing this since you were in freaking grade school, you idiot, and suddenly you're going to screw it all up because of me? That's bullshit. Knock it off.

"Focus," she ordered. "Take the next step, then the one after. Do the work and stop picking fights with me. I fight dirtier than you."

"You have no idea."

She grabbed his face—ignoring LaPorte's mask—kissed him hard. "You're wrong. Now, we're here to do what's next."

"Fine. Fine. I need to check some things."

"I'm in love." Sebastien laid a hand on his heart when Booth walked out. "I think I have four beautiful daughters now."

"What a lovely thing to say." She went to him, sighed, leaned against him. "I don't want to make it harder for him."

"You don't. But you give him higher stakes, you see. Before, if he failed, he could run. He won't run now."

"He won't fail now."

"No, *ma chère amie*, he won't. He's tired, and worried—for you. He's out of sorts with it."

"Well, that's good. LaPorte would be both after a facelift."

"*Mais oui*, I have four beautiful girls now."

She went back out to walk her route again—rehearsing her walk—long, purposeful strides. And found Booth at the end of the path, facing the lake.

He put away the phone in his hand. "Jacques is on his way back with Russell."

"Good."

"I'm not trying to take your choices away."

"Aren't you?"

"No. I just don't want you to pay a price for stepping onto a road I've been traveling most of my life."

"Then don't screw this up."

"I'm not going to screw it up, but—"

"Then stop talking about it." Frustration rose up, spilled out. "You don't say 'Macbeth' inside a theater or wish a performer good luck before they go onstage. And you should damn well not talk about what terrible thing might happen while you're working."

Inside, she longed to pull the damn contacts out, but she continued in the same no-nonsense tone.

"You say 'the Scottish play.' You say 'break a leg,' or '*merde*.' And you shut the hell up about what-ifs. And you don't make me feel like I'm a weight around your ankle instead of a partner with another oar."

"You're not a weight." He turned her to him. "You're not. I never had to worry about anyone before, so—"

"Oh, bullshit! Listen to you." She shoved him back. "You're standing in this spot at this moment because as a boy you worried about your mom. You worried about Mags. You worried about me. You've worried about Dauphine and her family and your kids, your friends."

She threw her hands up, then inadvertently slapped one on the butt of her fake gun.

And looked like she could kick some serious ass.

"It's who you are, and it's how LaPorte's used you. He knows you'll do whatever you have to do to protect the people who matter to you. What he doesn't know—it's not in him to know—is you've had years and years to think up ways to pay him back, or that I'd be not only willing, but goddamn eager to help you do just that. So stop all this, and let's pay that bastard back."

When he started to speak, she pointed. "The Scottish play, Booth. Don't ask for bad luck."

Since he couldn't think of a single logical argument, he said the thing most clear in his mind. "I love you."

"Then let's get this show started."

Shortly before midnight, they stood together, Booth, Miranda, Mags, Sebastien, in what would be LaPorte's office. He glanced at the phone.

"Luc's letting them in the gate. Let's wrap this fish and fry it."

Sebastien walked out the interior doors to take his place outside—just a guard on duty.

Miranda walked to the side door, glanced back. "*Merde*," she said, and closed it behind her.

"She's one in a million." Mags walked to the office doors, took her place.

"Only one of her kind. I guess that makes her my Red Goddess." Then he sat, became LaPorte.

While he waited, he booted up his computer, and switched on the recording.

Moments later, Miranda tapped on the side door.

"Yes."

She eased it open. "Mr. Russell, sir."

Booth just gestured a come-ahead.

Miranda stepped aside to let Russell through, gave Booth one last glance, and shut the doors.

She walked away—long, purposeful strides. Then simply stood in the fragrant air, staring blindly at the lake, and waited.

Booth picked up the lowball glass of tea.

A man going soft in the middle, one trying to claw his way back from fifty, Russell sported a short brown ponytail. He had cagey blue eyes, a square jaw, and a mouthful of caps as straight as piano keys.

He knew LaPorte well enough to have worn a suit, though the seersucker was, perhaps, a dubious choice.

In the dimly lit room with the curtains drawn, Booth gestured him to the chair on the other side of the desk.

"It's good to see you, Mr. LaPorte. How are you?"

"I'm taking a few days' holiday, to rest. But I have work for you that can't wait."

"Always happy to do business with you."

"I'm going to give you the name and address of a man and a location. There is something this man has at that location I want. You'll acquire it for me."

"Sounds good."

"I had intended to hire another for this particular task, but after paying for the initial . . . research, this individual proved unsatisfactory. You'll benefit from that research, and from the fact that in a few days' time, the man whose information I give you will be in Europe."

Booth studied Russell coolly out of LaPorte's faintly bruised eyes.

"You'll have three weeks to acquire what I want. The location is in Washington, DC, in Georgetown. I will pay ten thousand for your expenses for these three weeks. I will advance you one million U.S. dollars, and when you deliver what I wish you to acquire, pay another million.

"These terms aren't negotiable. You take them, or you leave them. Leave them, you won't work for me again."

"We've done good business in the past," Russell said quickly.

"And you're not my first choice, as you haven't completed your work satisfactorily in the past."

The way Russell shifted, Booth knew he'd hit the right tone.

"I know you weren't completely satisfied with our last deal, the porcelain peacock."

"And why is that?" Booth asked dryly.

"The little chip, but as I explained, it was chipped when I took it. Even though you cut my fee in half, I—"

He broke off when Booth held up a hand.

"Don't make me regret giving you another chance, Mr. Russell. You have three weeks, from today, to make delivery to me here."

"What am I after?"

"You'll circumvent the security—both electronic and human—at the location I give you. As I said, much of the work on this was done by another. You will enter the private room in the attic of this home and acquire for me the Red Goddess."

Those cagey eyes popped into saucers. "The Red— Are you shitting me?"

Booth's mouth thinned, his eyes slitted. "Your language does you no credit."

"Beg your pardon. I've heard some rumors about the stone, but most people don't buy into them."

"One million advance, ten thousand expenses. One million on delivery. Take it or don't. The rumors are fact. I've seen the stone with my own eyes. I've held it in my own hands. I want it. If you want future employment from me, you'll get it."

"Three weeks isn't much time."

"I have blueprints of the house, I have all the data on the security. I have the exact location in the house of the stone. But for a female security member, the house itself will be unoccupied. Take it, or don't. I haven't the time to waste or the inclination to waste it."

"I'll take it."

Booth used LaPorte's superior smirk.

"Wise choice. Give me your banking information and the money will be in your account by morning. Do not contact me. If you must relay any information, I'll give you a number where you can leave a message. Don't think about running with the stone. I'll hunt you down, as I have others. You know their fate."

"What the hell would I do with that stone? I'll take the two million. I know what to do with that. If I have to handle human security?"

"Do what you feel is necessary. Get the stone. Give me your information and take this." He shoved the packet of papers across the desk and signaled Miranda. After noting down the account information, he picked up his glass again. "That concludes our business for today."

"You won't regret this." Russell rose. "I'll see you in three weeks, or less."

When Russell went out, Miranda stood at the door to lead him back to Jacques and the car. Booth shut off the recording.

He sat back, gave himself time to breathe in, breathe out.

Three weeks at most, he thought. Things had to move fast now.

Miranda stepped in again. "He's driving away. How did it go?"

"Bought it, top to bottom. Hitting him with the Goddess? He couldn't see or think straight."

"So this part's good. We did it."

"We need to strike the set and get out, but yeah. Listen, I'm sorry about before."

"I'm not." She walked to him, sat on the edge of the desk. "We're who we are, both of us. We're going to disagree—strongly—again. Maybe we could try to hold off on that until this is all finished."

"Three weeks, tops. Probably less, because once Russell looks at the prep already done, he's going to want to move. I think we can handle it. Let's strike the set."

"Then we're going home?"

"Yeah." He rose, wrapped around her. "Let's go home."

Chapter Thirty-One

BOOTH SPENT THE DAY before his annual cookout as usual: in the kitchen making sides, sauces, marinades. This year, he had Miranda with him, doing some of the chopping, the stirring and mixing.

She sat at the counter, hair braided back, a frown on her face as she peeled potatoes from a mountain for his Cajun potato salad.

"I don't know how you can do all this."

"You're doing a lot of the grunt work, which is appreciated. Making a lot of this—like the potato salad today—gives a chance for the flavors to blend. Plus, tomorrow's for the fun."

"I mean I don't know how you can cook and host a party for a hundred people or more with all that's going on."

"If I don't have it, people will wonder why. And when this is all done, it'll stick out that I didn't have it." He took the pasta shells—al dente—from the stove and put them into the colander he had in the sink to drain for his shrimp salad supreme.

"I have a favor to ask you."

"Besides peeling a million potatoes?"

"You're doing a real good job."

The eyebrow winged up an instant before she tossed a glare at him. "I know when I'm being patronized. What's the favor?"

"Before I get to it, I'm telling you it's not about taking choices away or protecting you. It's more about protecting me if . . ."

"Scottish play, Booth."

"Not that if. If LaPorte tries to implicate me. What you said before—about it being about you, that regrettable moment in New York. I'm playing on that. I've got a file I made up, with information on me—high school teacher me—and some others who have connections with some women he's been with."

She sat back, rubbed her nose with the back of her hand. "Oh, I see where you're going. He's kept files on men—you should add a woman or two in case some of his formers preferred women or fell for another woman."

"That's good." He should've thought of it. "Okay."

"He's kept files, kept track because he's an obsessive and vindictive personality. And if he tries to implicate you, that file just adds weight to my story."

"Exactly. There's more to the favor. I need you to be my alibi."

"For what?"

"I need to go to Lake Charles, and I need you to stay here."

"Wait a minute."

"My alibi, Miranda. I have to go down, break into his house, plant the Goddess and the files and a few other things. At the same time, I have to be here. Right here. You can swear I was."

"So your alibi can't be there for the payoff?"

"I won't be either. I'll be back, I'll be here. But it's going to take time for me to get to DC, fly to New Orleans, drive to Lake Charles, do what I need to do, and get back here. I need twenty-four hours, and I'm asking you to give them to me."

"This helps you."

"Even more than peeling those potatoes."

"When do you leave?"

"Sebastien and Mags are watching Russell. Russell booked himself a fancy suite in Georgetown, and Sebastien's been in a couple times. He was in this morning while Russell was using the hotel gym. He checked Russell's agenda on his laptop. He's planning to hit tomorrow night."

He poured the pasta into a bowl, added onion, celery, black and green olives he'd already prepped, then the shrimp he'd peeled and boiled.

"The night after this cookout? But—"

"So I need to leave right after everyone's gone. I need to leave you with the cleanup, and I'm sorry about that. The timing's going to work. It's all going to work. If someone comes over or calls, you say I'm sleeping, or hungover, or taking a walk, whatever works. But I don't anticipate anyone will. I'll be back in twenty-four hours."

"You've never told me how you plan to get into his house."

"That's the easy part. It's nightwork I've planned for about twelve years now."

"Will you go over it with me, so I can imagine it as it's happening? So I can see you?"

"I can do that."

"Then we have another deal. Start from the beginning, will you? Start with how you're going to make sure Russell's caught with the fake rock and whatever else he takes."

With a nod, Booth began chopping herbs from his garden. "Okay. Here's how it's going to go."

SHE THOUGHT SHE DID well with the party, playing hostess when everything wanted to blur around her. She talked and ate and served and replenished. She watched Booth grill ribs and chicken and burgers as if it was just another summer party on a Sunday afternoon.

She played cornhole and bocce, screwed more beer and wine into ice-filled galvanized tubs. She dodged, as best she could, the broad hints and direct questions about her and Booth.

And finally took a break from it all in the shade with Tracey and a frozen margarita.

"No party like Booth's summer bash."

"I can believe it. People brought enough food to feed an army on top of what he made—which was enough to feed an army. I've never in my life spent that many hours in the kitchen."

"You look so good together. No, no, I'm not asking," she said when Miranda gave her a sidelong look. "I'm just saying. I know people have asked or pretended not to ask. Everybody loves Booth. You're the first woman he's had co-host this party, the first he's been with this long. You extended your lease, but . . ."

Miranda looked over to where Booth tossed horseshoes. So relaxed, so calm, exchanging high fives with his partner when he tossed a ringer.

"We're working a few things out. I have a feeling we're going to lie around tomorrow like slugs, then work those things out."

"I like both of you a lot, so I'm just going to say I know how I hope things work out."

She handled it, Miranda thought, handled all of it—even though the last stragglers didn't leave until after ten. She handled it until Booth came downstairs in a blond wig, with a goatee, and carrying a bag.

"Mags'll be here in a minute to pick me up. Twenty-four hours, Miranda."

"Don't be late." She grabbed him, held on. "Please don't be late."

"It'd be best if you stayed in the house. It's supposed to rain anyway. We stayed in all day, slept in, cleaned up—sorry about leaving you with that."

"It's nothing. People insisted on helping clean up when I just wanted them out."

"We stayed in, we slept in, we had sex—I'd appreciate having sex. Watched movies, took naps. What did we eat?"

"Party leftovers." Her breath wanted to back up in her lungs. "You never left the house, neither of us did. Don't worry about that. It's an if anyway."

"That's Mags," he said when he checked his phone. "She's picking me up down the road. I have to go." He kissed her, ran a hand down her braid. "Get some sleep. See you tomorrow night."

"God. Okay. Break a leg. *Merde*. Don't be late."

"I've got this," he said, and left her.

She looked at her watch, and started the countdown.

HE CHANGED IN MAGS's apartment into his work clothes, and was on his way to Lake Charles when Sebastien called the drop phone.

"Russell's through the first layer."

"Stick to the timetable, and let me know when you hit the alarms."

"How close are you?"

"About twenty minutes out." He looked at Jacques for confirmation.

"About. I'm sticking close to the speed limit. Driving like an old lady in bifocals."

"I'll let you know when we go silent."

When he ended the call, Jacques looked at him. "You're sure this one's good enough to get in?"

"I laid it out for him. He wants the money. He'll get in."

But he started to sweat it when Jacques pulled up to the drop-off point.

"I've got to go silent from here. Drive around if you have to. I'll signal when I'm in the clear."

"Don't worry about me. I've got you."

He had just started to call Sebastien when the phone signaled.

"Thank you, Jesus."

"Thank me, *mon ami*. Do you hear that?"

Through the phone, Booth heard the alarms, the sirens, and closed his eyes. "Yeah, I hear."

"I wish you could see. Lights, so many lights. The house is bright as Christmas."

"Where's he?"

"He nearly made it out of the house. Nearly. The woman tackled him as he ran through the door, and now he's on the ground with her gun pointed at his head. The police are nearly there. And you?"

"At the drop-off. Going silent. I'll get back to you."

"Trap that pig of a man," Jacques said as Booth got out of the car.

"That's the plan."

He had a ten-minute hike and took it at a light jog. He could see it all in his mind, the various ways he'd planned it out over the years. Refined it after making this same trip every time he'd visited New Orleans.

Not for profit this time, he thought. Not altogether for survival. This was a very nice blend of payback and justice.

And whatever happened after, if the final part fell, he'd pay whatever price was demanded for delivering that blend.

When he reached the compound, he deactivated the sensors and climbed the wall in the gap between cameras. There was always a gap if you knew how to find it.

He reset the sensors and kept going, fast and steady.

He stopped and crouched at the first outbuilding—storage for the landscape crew that came twice weekly. Security lights beamed, added a wash to the gardens and grass. A fountain tinkled musically, and in the near grove of trees, an owl called.

He looked toward the gatehouse. Lights on there, as guards monitored the cameras on six-hour shifts.

Exterior and interior—except for certain, more private areas.

LaPorte's bedroom suite, his treasure room.

He made the next dash with the map of the cameras in his head and from the shelter of trees studied the sturdy trellis of purple bougainvillea. A short sprint.

He bounced for a moment, then hit the remote that bobbled the power for two seconds.

When it steadied, he was climbing.

Weak spot. Second-floor terrace. French doors, locked, with a six-digit alarm code. He dealt with the dead bolt first, then the lockset. He suspected LaPorte programmed no more than thirty seconds for the alarm—one he'd learned changed every six days, one with a secondary four-digit backup. Maybe ten seconds for that.

He got to work, focused on the flashing numbers, then reset for the backup.

And took the moment.

Dark, silent house. LaPorte sleeping in his sumptuous bed in his sumptuous suite, perhaps with a sumptuous companion.

Tomorrow won't be a good day for you, he thought. Not a good day at all.

He started out, scanned the hallway, stepped over the red beams of motion detectors, and made his way downstairs.

The office would be locked, of course, and there'd be the camera to deal with. But they wouldn't record on the guard's monitors. Those were for LaPorte.

He dealt with the lock, eased the door open, shut the cameras down. If LaPorte had insomnia, checked his office feed, it all went to hell.

He checked the bookcase behind the desk for a mechanism and ignored the line of sweat running down his back. It would be there. It had to be. Because there was a room behind this one, and this was the only way in, or out.

Too long, too long, he thought as he searched. He needed the cameras back on.

He glanced back at the desk, crouched down.

"Idiot," he muttered, and pressed the button. The bookcase eased open to the vault door behind it.

"Okay, a little more time here."

Once again, he got to work. He worked the tumblers, worked the grid. Tricky, tricky. He paused, circled his neck, and got back to it.

Longer, much longer than he'd anticipated. More than an hour inside, he thought. He needed to get the hell out. He could still run. Back to Miranda, ask her to run with him. Anywhere.

And once again, LaPorte would take his life, his choices, his fate away.

Not this time.

Two hours until sunrise, and he was close, too close to toss it in.

When the last tumbler fell, he pulled open the door.

Of all the rooms of its kind he'd seen, this was the most plush. A palace designed for one man, one ruler, one tyrant.

The red beams crisscrossed the room.

Booth took out a phone, recorded it, every inch. The gold, the ivory, the porcelain and marble. The jewels, the art. Priceless antiques, exquisite lamps. Ming vases, figures carved in alabaster.

He looked at the painting he'd stolen, the glory of that Turner sunrise. He took a photo of it, and of the sculpture that had cost him all those years with Miranda.

He recognized other pieces taken from museums, private homes, rooms like this one. Some of those thefts had cost lives; he knew that, too.

He danced over, under, around the beams to an empty pedestal.

He noted the single downlight that would illuminate it. He wondered if LaPorte had had it custom made in anticipation.

Booth took out the Goddess, set her on the marble. "Only for a little while," he murmured. "He won't keep you here. I swear it. He won't keep any of you."

He made the next recording, took another photo.

Then stepping out, he locked the vault, recorded, closed the bookcase, recorded.

He retraced his steps, just a shadow drifting through a dark house. When he climbed down, he hit the remote for his quick sprint.

When he landed on the far side of the wall, he checked the time.

Two hours forty-three. A solid forty-three longer than planned. He might be a little late after all.

Once he signaled Jacques, he started his jog back as the sun broke the night and bloomed rosy in the east. Birds woke to sing to it.

When he checked in with Sebastien, he learned Russell sang with them.

"You took your time, *cher*," Jacques said when Booth got in the car.

"Just a little extra complication, but we're good." He set the phone between them. "It's all on there. You can do your magic."

"Can and will. Why don't you drive, and I'll start now?"

"You can do it from the car?"

"I think by the time we get home, the police, the FBI will have a very nice gift, wrapped pretty and tied in a big, fat bow."

"Pull over."

AT MIDNIGHT, MIRANDA WALKED the floor. He was late, damn it. Already an hour late. Mags had assured her he was fine, had boarded the flight from New Orleans to DC, and wasn't currently in custody.

But all she could imagine was him being dragged off the plane at the airport, cuffed and charged.

Otherwise, he should be back. They said everything went according to plan, but this wasn't the plan.

Then she heard the door open. She raced downstairs, and there he was, holding a very sad bouquet of flowers in cellophane.

"You're late," she said, then sat down on the steps and burst into tears.

"Don't, don't. Please. I'm sorry. And the flowers are really lame. Mags told you everything was fine, didn't she?"

"But you weren't here. Give me those damn flowers." After snatching them, she buried her face in them and shed more tears. "Are the cops on their way?"

"Not here," he said, and smiled and brushed away her tears. "Everything's fine. Everything worked. Not only did Russell roll, but there's the money trail, and the anonymous tip—a recording of LaPorte's treasure room, the Goddess. There's also another payment he made, to another account they won't be able to track back. Looks like the Chameleon to me. He hired him, right? But the deal went sour, so he hired Russell."

"But the Chameleon put the fake in place, then set LaPorte up. He sent the recording."

"Renege on a deal," Booth said cheerfully, "pay the price. I really want a Coke. Let me get a Coke, and I'll walk you through the whole thing."

"You're not even tired."

"Pumped. Really pumped." He could have danced his way to the moon and back. "Might sleep for a week once I crash, but pumped. Let's have a Coke."

"I'm having wine. I didn't want to drink anything in case I had to bail you out, or bake a cake—my first—with a file in it."

In the kitchen, he opened the doors to let the night in.

"I needed to make sure it all worked. At LaPorte's, in DC. A lot of threads, Miranda."

"I don't know what you're talking about. We've been home all day. It rained all morning and into the afternoon."

He poured her wine, opened a Coke for himself. "Anybody call, come by?"

"Cesca called midafternoon, just to say what a great party. I told her you'd fallen asleep watching *Casablanca*, and I might take a nap myself."

"I don't see me falling asleep during *Casablanca*."

"You were really tired after all that sex."

He grinned. "Okay then. The cops might come by. I'm thinking not for more than a tie-up, since it's all right there, every step he took, and the files he kept on me, you, others. We're the latest, which is why—if he tries to push it on me—he chose us."

"I'm not worried about it. I'm really not. I'm going to put these sad, sweet flowers in water."

"He had this emerald ring that would look great on you—a little flashy at about ten carats, but you could pull it off. I resisted it."

"Good choice."

"I've been in the house twice before."

"I know."

"No, you don't. I've been in the house twice when he wasn't there. To see if I could get in, to see the setup. He didn't have the vault last time, or the desk button, but it's been a few years. So it took longer."

"You've broken into his house before?"

"Practice runs." He drank some Coke. "And he's really beefed up his personal museum. There's a diamond, Russian white, beautiful teardrop pendant. I don't know who did that job for him, not for certain, but I know the woman it belonged to was beaten to death for it."

"And you think it was Russell." Because she understood now, clearly now, she nodded. "That's why you chose Russell."

"It factored in. He sang on LaPorte, I think LaPorte will return the favor. What I know is it's done. And they're both going to spend pretty much forever behind bars."

She studied him now, carefully. Pumped, as he'd said, that came across loud and clear. But adrenaline faded. "Is it enough for you, Harry?"

He opened his mouth, shut it again.

"Mags told me."

"I haven't been Harry in a really long time."

"And you're Booth to me. You'll always be Booth to me. But I'm asking Harry, is it enough?"

"Yeah." He let out a breath and met her eyes directly. "It's enough. More than enough. It's right."

"Good. For me, too. Now, I want you to tell me about it, start to finish, but I have some things to say first."

"I'll get better flowers next time I'm late."

She touched a very droopy rose. "I should hope so, but that's not it." She sat, swiveled to him on the counter stool. "I've never understood why some people say they love someone—and I think they mean it—and want to build a life with that someone, and mean that, too. But then they start trying to change that other person, the one they love. If you love someone, you love them, and that's it. Would you agree?"

"Sure."

"Good. So I'm not going to ask you if you're going to continue your nightwork. I'd expect you to be honest with me about it."

"Hold on."

"I'm not done."

"But—"

"Not done. My father's coming back in a week or two, and he and Deborah plan to stop in DC, drive down to see me. I have to tell him."

"Tell him what?"

"Everything. Not done," she said before he could object. "I don't lie to my dad, that's a hard line. He's certainly not going to turn his only child over to the police. But to seal the deal, to cover all the ground, you're going to have to marry me."

"Wait. What?"

"I will insist you buy, not steal, my ring, but that's my only requirement on that. And it's another hard line."

Satisfied, she picked up her wine.

"Let's walk outside. I've been cooped up all day."

"Miranda." He pushed up to follow her.

"Gorgeous night. So, to continue. I don't want a big, splashy wedding. I will want the most fabulous dress, but that's on me. I think we should get married here, because people love you here, and I've gotten very attached to here. We can work it around spring break. Or winter break if you're in a hurry. I'm flexible. You are going to keep teaching, aren't you?"

"Miranda—"

"Of course you are." She rolled right over him as smoothly as she had over getting coffee between classes at college. "You love it. About kids."

The flutter—bat wings—that started in his stomach spread up to his chest.

"Kids."

"We're both only children, and I'd like to break that cycle. I insist on two. We'll see how we do, then I'm open to a third if we're both on that page. But two is firm."

On a half turn, she gave the house a considering study, then nodded.

"We'll probably have to add on to the house at some point, but that's down the road. In the immediate, I need a lot more room for my clothes, and personal items. I think that covers it for now. I should've made a list."

"Can we back up? Way, way up," he said with a wide, rolling gesture. "Back to that part where you said if you love somebody, you don't try to change them."

"You want me to go through everything again?"

"No, no, let's just start there. Do you love me?"

"Of course I love you." Her eyebrow quirked up. "Are you suddenly stupid?"

Not just bat wings flapping now, but a swarm in the entire Batcave.

"You never said. After we . . . When I told you, you never said."

"Timing, Booth, it's about timing. Now's the time I wanted to tell you. The ugly stuff is behind. We start from here."

She loved him. And that equaled, for him, the alpha and omega.

"You don't care that I'm a thief?"

"I love you." She laid a hand on his cheek, rubbed the stubble. "All the way through."

He grabbed that hand, held it.

"I don't need to do that anymore. I was going to tell you, ask you to give me a chance. I don't need that when I have you. The empty spaces, the lost places, you fill them up. This was my last job. You don't say you're going into your last job or you'll wreck it. But I can after it's done. It's done. I'm done."

"I'm okay with that, too."

"The house, your family home."

"I expect my father and Deborah to have a lot of happy years there. I called a Realtor about selling my town house this afternoon. This was, of course, after we talked some of this through, had all that sex."

"Sure, that follows."

"One day we might want to move into that generational family house, or we might not. I don't care. But I'm firm on marriage, on two, possibly three kids, and more room for my stuff. Oh, and I'll continue to chop and stir, and order takeout, but don't expect more. So are you going to marry me or not?"

Miranda, he thought. His Miranda. And couldn't help himself.

"'Ay, with a heart as willing as bondage e'er of freedom: here's my hand.'"

Tears swirled into her eyes as she gripped it. "'And mine with my heart in't.'"

"Can we make it winter break? It would be like a year since you came back to me."

"We came back to each other. I'd love a winter wedding. You really should kiss the hell out of me now."

"I'm going to get to that. Would you like an orangery?"

She laughed. "Yes!"

"And we could add a third floor. You'd have a hell of a view from your office, and since I can open up the master closet now, take out that area, plenty more room for your stuff."

"Looks like I have to kiss the hell out of you." She set down her wine, laid both hands on his face. "You told me once it was always me. Just me. And you said just now I filled up all the empty spaces and lost places. It's always been you, Booth. Just you. No empty or lost for either of us now."

They kissed by the river under the moonlight. Held close, kissed again.

"About telling your father—"

"Hard line, Booth."

"Okay. Okay."

He drew her in, rested his forehead on hers. And knew while the Red Goddess would find her home now, his had come home to him.

Epilogue

One year later

Fingers linked with Miranda's, Booth stood in London's great museum. Just part of the crowd, he thought, one of the many who came to view the extraordinary diamond known as the Red Goddess.

She sat—thanks to the generosity of Lady Jane Dubois—on a marble pedestal behind thick glass.

He knew, of course, the pedestal would be wired, the glass blast proof.

He also figured he could find ways around all that—if he were still in the business.

But the Goddess had found her home, her place, her purpose just as he had found his.

"She looks right here. And, I have to say, happy here."

When Miranda tipped her head to his shoulder, he nodded. "Yeah, she does."

"I'm glad we came to see her. I'm glad so many others have and will. No regrets?"

He brought her hand with its wedding set—bought and paid for—to his lips. "Not a single one."

He said goodbye to the stone, and heard someone remark in tones of deep disappointment:

"It's not even shiny. It looks like a big, red lump."

When Miranda laughed, Booth shook his head before he walked away with his personal red goddess.

"Why don't we find a nice café, sit down for something to eat?"

"Booth, the baby's the size of a pea. I don't have to sit every ten minutes, or eat every hour."

"It's still in there." And that was a wonder.

"And both of us are ready for our first trip to Florence. Detouring here closed one door. Let's go open another."

He could do that. But one more door first.

"LaPorte fired another team of lawyers."

Smiling, Miranda shook back the hair she'd left loose. "It must be frustrating for him. Nobody's giving him what he wants."

"Even with the deal he made, Russell will never get out of prison. Most of LaPorte's assets are frozen, his treasure room's empty, and he's got a tracker on his ankle until his trial."

He smiled himself. "I'm hearing buzz there's talk about revoking his bail."

"Aww."

Booth swung an arm around Miranda's shoulders as they walked out of the museum into a cloudy day in London.

"It already feels like justice," Miranda commented. "But I barely got to emote about my horrible mistake in New York."

"They had him cold." Hadn't he made sure of it? "We were just threads to snip off."

He didn't tell her, and hoped she never learned, they'd found Selene Warwick's body—what was left of it—washed up on a beach in Cannes just days after he'd planted the stone on LaPorte.

She hadn't run far enough, or fast enough.

Doors closed, he thought. Time to leave them that way.

"You're sure you don't want to sit, eat something?"

"I'm absolutely sure. Are you going to nag at me for the next eight months?"

"Probably. You're my first wife, and that's my first kid in there."

The Smokies, the ocean, New Orleans. The redhead in Shakespeare class.

"I get caught up on firsts."

"I'm your last wife, and don't forget it. Let's just head back to the airport. Maybe Mr. Private Plane can get them to take off a little early."

"I can work with that."

Before he could try to hail a cab, she shuffled him over to the far end of the sidewalk, looked up at him with those sea-witch eyes.

"I'm glad we stopped here first. I'm glad we're going to have two fabulous weeks in Italy, where my well-traveled husband will show me everything before we go home and get a puppy."

"With the baby coming—"

"They'll grow up together, and the dog gets to keep me company when I work and you're at school. Hard line, Booth. I was right about my father, and I'm right about a puppy."

He couldn't deny the first part, since Ben hadn't killed or maimed him.

"Before we go get started on all that," she continued, "I'm going to tell you I love you, and you make me stupidly happy. Now kiss the hell out of me."

"I can do that."

So he did.

And when they got into a cab to start the next part of the journey, he thought of his mother, of the lives he'd led. He thought about the thrill and simple satisfaction of knowing his nightwork now meant Miranda, a baby, and a big sloppy dog.

A life of his choosing, he thought, and linked his fingers with hers.

More precious than diamonds.

Keep reading for a sneak peek at Nora Roberts' latest novel, *Identity*...

Chapter One

HER DREAMS AND GOALS were simple and few. As a former army brat, Morgan Albright spent her childhood moving across countries and continents. Her roots, directed by her father's work, grew short and shallow to allow for quick transplanting. From base to base, from house to house, state to state, country to country for her first fourteen years, before her parents divorced.

She'd never had a choice.

For the three years following the divorce, her mother had pulled her from place to place. A small town here, a big city there, looking for . . . Morgan had never been sure.

At seventeen, closing in on eighteen, she'd dug those roots up herself to plant at college. And there she'd explored those goals and dreams and choices.

She studied hard, focused in on a double major. Business and hospitality—choices that led directly to her dream.

Planting herself. Her own home, her own business.

Her own.

She studied maps, neighborhoods, climate, while narrowing her choices on just where to plant those roots once she'd earned those degrees. She wanted neighborhood, maybe old and established, close to shops, restaurants, bars—people.

And one day she'd not only own her own home, but her own bar.

Simple goals.

And with those degrees hot in her hand, she settled on a neighborhood outside of Baltimore, Maryland. Old houses with yards, and as yet to be gentrified, so affordable.

She'd worked her way through college, waiting tables, then tending bar when she'd hit twenty-one. And she'd saved.

Her father—the Colonel—didn't make her graduation. And though she'd graduated with honors, he sent no acknowledgment of her accomplishments.

It hadn't surprised her, as she knew she'd simply ceased to exist for him even before his signature on the divorce papers dried.

Her mother and her maternal grandparents attended. She hadn't known it would be the last time she'd see her grandfather. A robust seventy, an active man, a healthy man, he died the winter after her graduation. He'd slipped off a ladder. One slip. Here, then gone.

Even in her grief, it was a lesson Morgan took to heart.

He left her twenty thousand dollars and memories, as precious, of hiking the Green Mountains of Vermont on summer visits.

With the money, Morgan moved out of her tiny apartment and into a small house. Her house. One that needed work, but had a yard—that needed work.

The three small bedrooms, two tiny baths meant she could take in a housemate to offset the mortgage, help pay for that work.

And she worked two jobs. She tended bar five or six nights a week at a neighborhood bar, a happy place called the Next Round. Considering homeownership, she took a second job as office manager at a family-owned construction firm.

She met her housemate at the local garden center as she puzzled over foundation plants. Nina Ramos worked in the greenhouses and knew her stuff. Handy with a yard that needed help, Nina turned puzzlement into joy, and in that first blooming spring in a house of her own, Nina moved in.

They enjoyed each other's company, and knew when to give the other quiet and space.

At twenty-five, Morgan had achieved her first dream, and by her calculations would reach goal number two before her thirtieth birthday.

Her one splurge sat in her narrow driveway. The Prius would take her a few years to pay off, but it would get her to work and back dependably and economically.

In good weather, she rode her bike to her day job, but when she needed a car, she had one. Nina called the car Morgan's subgoal.

The little house on Newberry Street boasted a pretty yard, fresh white paint, and a new front door she'd painted a soft, happy blue.

Her boss at Greenwald's Builders helped her refinish the old hardwood floors, sold her paint at cost, and guided her along the path of repairs and maintenance.

She'd planted those roots, and felt herself blooming.

It made her smile to see daffodils playing their bright trumpets along her—newly—paved walkway. Late March brought changeable weather, but all those lovely signs of spring. She and Nina had planted a dogwood in the front yard the previous fall, and she could see the buds wanted to burst.

Soon, she thought as she walked her bike to its rack and locked it.

A good neighborhood, but she didn't see the point in tempting anyone.

She unlocked the door, and since Nina's not-very-dependable car sat at the curb, called out.

"It's me, running late." She crossed the living room, and as always, thought about how much more open it would be when she took out the wall that blocked off the kitchen.

She had the money for that project earmarked, so maybe in the fall. Maybe before Christmas. Maybe.

"I'm not running late," Nina called back. "And I've got a date!"

Nina always had a date. But then again, Morgan thought, she was gorgeous and vivacious and only worked one job.

She paused at the open bedroom door.

Several outfits—obviously rejects—littered the bed while Nina modeled another in front of a full-length mirror. Her raven-black hair spilled down the back of a red dress that hugged every curve on her tiny body. Dark eyes sparkled as they met Morgan's in the glass.

"What do you think?"

"I often think I hate you. Okay, where are you going and who are you going with?"

"Sam's taking me to Fresco's for dinner."

"Fancy! Yeah, the red's a killer."

Which she envied a little. The only genuine disappointment between the housemates came from the fact that with Morgan's long, coltish frame and Nina's petite, curvy one, they couldn't trade clothes.

"Go for it. Isn't this nearly three solid weeks of dates exclusively with the hunkified Sam?"

"Almost four." Nina did a twirl. "So . . ."

"I'll be very quiet when I get home."

"I really like him, Morgan."

"So do I."

"No, I mean *really*."

"Oh." Angling her head, Morgan studied her friend. "I already know he's in seriously like and more when it comes to you. It's all over him. If you're heading there, I'm giving you the full friend approval."

After flipping that gorgeous hair, Nina let out one of her dreamy sighs. "Pretty sure I've already headed there."

"Full approval. I've got to change for work."

"From work for work. I've got to put all this away and clean up this room. I don't want Sam to think I'm a slob."

"You're not a slob." Chaotic, Morgan thought, but Nina kept her chaos contained to her own space.

Unlike Nina's cheerful chaos, lavender walls, a vanity top littered with makeup, hair products, and God knew, Morgan's space was just contained.

She used the third bedroom—closet-sized—as an office, so this was sanctuary. Quiet blue walls, some art she'd bought from street artists in Baltimore, the white duvet and pillows, a small but cozy reading chair.

She took off office manager—gray pants, white shirt, navy blue blazer—put on bartender—black pants, black shirt. In the bathroom, she opened the drawer where she kept her makeup organized for easy choices. And changed day to night.

The short, angled cut of her blond hair worked fine for both jobs, but the bartender went for more drama on the eyes, deeper on the lips.

With years of practice, she finished the transition inside twenty minutes.

Since she wouldn't be eating fancy at Fresco's, she dashed to the kitchen, grabbed a yogurt out of the fridge. She ate standing up, imagining the wall gone, new cabinet doors and hardware, some open shelves, some—

"*Amiga mia*, you need to eat food."

"Yogurt's food."

Nina, now in a robe, put her hands on her hips. "Something that requires a knife and fork, and chewing. You've got that long, slim build naturally—bitch—but if you don't eat, it'll turn to skinny and gaunt. Seriously, one of us has to learn to cook." She shot up a coral-tipped finger, then pointed it at Morgan. "I nominate you."

"Yeah, I'll take that up in my spare time. Besides, you're the one with a mother who cooks like a goddess."

"You'll come with me for Sunday dinner. Don't say you've got work—your spreadsheets, or whatever. You know Mama and Papa love you. And my brother, Rick, will be there."

With the yogurt in one, the spoon in the other, Morgan waved her hands as if erasing a board. "I am not dating your brother, no matter how cute he is. That way lies madness. I'm not losing you as a roommate because your brother and I date, have sex, break up."

Nina held up a gold hoop at one ear, a dangle of three circles at the other. "Which?"

Morgan pointed at the dangles. "Fancier."

"Good. And maybe you'll date Rick, have sex, and fall in love."

"I don't have time. Give me two years, maybe three, then I'll have time."

"I like schedules, too, but not for love. Now you've distracted me. You have to eat."

"I'll get something at the bar."

"Dinner Sunday," Nina insisted when Morgan tossed the container, rinsed the spoon. "I'm telling Mama you're coming, and once I tell Mama, it's done."

"I'd love to go, honestly. Let me get through this week. We've been so damn busy at Greenwald's. Spring makes everybody think of remodeling or painting or building decks."

She grabbed her purse and kept going. "Have a great time tonight."

"You can take that to the bank. I'm calling Mama before I get my gorgeous on."

"Your gorgeous is never off."

Morgan jogged to the car. Pleased she'd already made up a little time, she drove the five-point-four miles to the town center.

The shops along what the locals called Market Mile (actually one-point-six) would close within the hour. But the restaurants and cafés would keep Market Street lit and busy well into the night.

Most of the buildings—rosy or white-painted brick—kept the retail to street level and held apartments above. The Next Round was no exception and tended to rent to patrons or employees who had no issue living above a bar.

She swung off Market, circled around the back of the bar to the parking lot. With her car secured, she crunched across the gravel to the back kitchen door and stepped into the heat and noise.

The Round ran to burgers, steamers, nachos with sides of fries, onion rings, fried pickles, and three varieties of wings.

When she opened her own tavern, she intended to spread out to a few more, hopefully surprising, choices of bar food.

And she should probably learn how to cook first, because you never knew when you'd have to pitch in.

"Hey, Frankie," she called out to the woman working the grill as she put her jacket on a peg. "How's it going?"

"Good enough." With her poof of ink-black hair tucked under a white cap, Frankie flipped three fat burgers. "Roddy and his brothers are grabbing some dinner before their dart tournament. Be glad you weren't on for happy hour. We were slammed."

"I like slammed."

She exchanged greetings with the two line chefs, the teenage dishwasher, and the waitress who swung in to pick up an order of loaded nachos.

Though she had ten minutes before her shift, she walked through the door and into the bar.

A different kind of noise, she thought. Not the sizzle of meat on a grill, the whack of knives, the clatter of dishes. Here voices filled the big room with its long black bar, its tables and booths. Music pumped from the juke, but not loud enough to overwhelm conversation.

She saw Roddy and his brothers—regulars—at their usual booth near the dartboard, drinking beer and chowing down on bar nuts. Coors for Roddy and his brother Mike, she thought, and Heineken for brother Ted. If their father joined them, he'd order a beer—on tap—and a bump.

She took the pass-through behind the bar where the bartenders worked.

She'd relieve Wayne, currently adding a slice of lime to a bottle of Corona.

"Got a little bit of a lull," he told her, and gave her his full-wattage smile. "Guy at the end of the bar's running a tab. He's on his second vodka tonic, so keep an eye."

He served the Corona to another stool sitter, exchanged a few words before he slipped back to Morgan.

"Waiting for his date—Match.com—first time. She's late, he's nervous."

Cute, Morgan decided, on the nerdy side. She'd put down money he had a full gaming system in his living room.

"Got it."

"I'm gonna clock out then. Have a good one."

As always, she checked her supplies—the ice, the limes and lemons, the olives, the cherries. She filled a couple of orders for tables, and was about to work her way down to Corona when she spotted a woman of about thirty step in, look anxiously around before she approached the guy at the bar.

"Dave? I'm Tandy. I'm so sorry I'm a little late."

He brightened right up. "Oh, don't worry about it. It's nice to meet you. Do you want to get a table?"

"This is fine. Is this fine?" She slid onto the stool beside him.

Morgan shifted down the bar as they smiled at each other with expressions of anxiety and hope.

"Hi. What can I get you tonight?"

"Oh. Um. Could I get a glass of Chardonnay?"

"You sure can. I love your earrings."

"Oh." Tandy put one hand up to her left ear. "Thanks."

"They're really pretty," Dave added. "You look great."

"Thanks. So do you." She laughed as Morgan poured the wine. "You really just don't know, do you? I was so nervous, I walked around the block. That's why I'm a little late."

"I was so nervous I got here twenty minutes early."

Ice broken, Morgan thought as she served the wine.

And this, she admitted, was one of the reasons she loved working in a bar. You never knew what might start, might finish, might bloom or break in a friendly neighborhood bar.

By the time Roddy and his brothers plowed through their burgers, the place started filling up. The Match.com couple decided to get a table after all, and a platter of nachos.

Morgan made a mental bet on a second date there.

Vodka Tonic cashed out, left a miserly tip.

Darts thwacked against the board to cheers and catcalls of onlookers.

A man in his early thirties came in. He made her think of an incognito movie star with his dark blond hair, chiseled features, gym-fit body in jeans, boots, and pale blue sweater—looked like cashmere. He slid onto a stool.

She stepped down to him. "Welcome to the Next Round. What's your pleasure?"

"I've got a lot of them." He grinned at her—easy, charming. "But we'll start with a beer. Any local beer on tap?"

"Of course." Though they had lists printed in holders on the bar, she reeled them off.

"Maybe you can pick one for me."

"What're you looking for?"

"Another loaded question."

She shot him a smile. Looking for some conversation, she judged, along with the drink. And that was fine.

"In a beer."

499

"Smooth, but not bland. Rich, but not overpowering. Toward the dark side."

"Let's try this." She got a tasting glass, pulled a tap.

As he sampled it, he watched her over the rim. "That'll do. Good choice."

"That's my job."

Before he could speak again, one of the waitresses came up. "Girl table over there's stuck in the nineties. Four Cosmos, Morgan."

She carried the tray of empties into the kitchen while Morgan got to work.

"You know what you're doing," the new guy commented as she mixed the drinks.

"I'd better. Are you in town on business?"

"Don't I look like I belong?"

Close enough, she thought. His clothes said upscale, but not in-your-face. "Haven't seen you in here before."

A cheer erupted across the room.

"Dart tourney," she said.

"So I see. Serious?"

"Oh, in its way. Can I get you anything else? Would you like to see a menu?"

"Is the food any good?"

"It is." She pulled out a menu, laid it beside him. "Have a look, take your time."

With the Cosmos ready, she moved down the bar. Took orders, filled orders, chatting with regulars as she did. She worked her way back.

"I'll try a Market Street Burger, unless you tell me I'm making a mistake."

"It's a classic for a reason. If you like a kick, a little heat, go with the spicy fries."

He lifted his hands. "You've never steered me wrong."

She laughed, plugged his order in the machine.

Roddy, all six-four and two hundred fifty pounds, walked over to the bar. "Another round, sweets. How's it going?" he said idly to Handsome Guy while Morgan filled the order.

"Cold beer, beautiful bartender, live sports. It's a good deal."

"Yeah, it is. I took the lead in the semis. Give me some luck for the finals, Morgan."

She leaned over, touched her lips to his. "Go get 'em."

"Damn right." He took the beers and walked off.

"Boyfriend?"

She looked over at her customer. "Oh, no. Roddy and his brothers—the dart players—are regulars. I actually work with his girlfriend at my other job."

"Two jobs? Ambitious. What's the other?"

"Office manager for a construction company. What do you do?"

"I'd like to say as I please, because at least I try. I'm in IT. I'm in the area for a couple of months doing some consulting."

"Where are you from?"

"I travel a lot. San Francisco originally, but I'm based in New York now, or for the most part. Is this hometown for you?"

"It is now."

Another waitress came up, rattled off another order.

"Army brat," she said as she filled it.

"Then you know the traveling life."

"I do. And I'm happy to have left that behind."

When his order came out, he gave the plate a long look. "You don't skimp on portions here."

"We don't. Would you like a table?"

He sent her that charming smile. "I like the view right here. I'm Luke," he added. "Luke Hudson."

"Morgan. Nice to meet you."

He ate, ordered a second beer, stayed through the tournament.

He asked questions but didn't seem intrusive. Bar conversation, in Morgan's mind. She asked her own.

He was staying at a local hotel. His company would rent a house for him, but he liked hotels, and enjoyed getting into the local flavor wherever he traveled.

He asked where her father had been stationed, which places she'd lived she liked best. Easy breezy while she mixed drinks, mopped the bar, chattered with other customers.

"I should get along," he said. "I didn't intend to stay so long, but it looks like I've found my local watering hole."

"It's a good one."

"I'll see you again." When he rose, he surprised her by offering a hand to shake. And held hers while he smiled into her eyes. "It's really been great spending time with you, Morgan."

"It's been nice talking to you."

"We'll do it again."

He paid in cash, leaving a very generous tip.

A COUPLE NIGHTS LATER, Luke wandered in later in her shift. It was trivia night at the Round, and the noise level boomed as various tables and groups shouted out answers.

"Pick another local draft," he told Morgan. "Something . . . adventurous." He glanced behind him at the game players. "No darts tonight?"

"Trivia night. It's a free-for-all, so shout out whenever you want."

"What's the prize?"

"Satisfaction." She offered him a tasting glass.

"Interesting and adventurous," he decided. "Got some dark cherries going. Let's go for it."

As she pulled the tap, she smiled over. "Anything to go with it?"

"Just the beer for now. Had a long day."

"Life in the tech world?"

"Like the beer, it's interesting and adventurous. How are things in your world?"

"Busy, but I like busy."

She filled orders, working her way up and down the bar, but with trivia in full swing, she had a lull.

"What do you do when you're not busy?" Luke asked her.

"I'll let you know if I ever get there."

"Gotta take some downtime. Mind, body, spirit, and all that. Paint me a day off."

"Paint's accurate. My house needs more of that, but it's not quite ready. And with spring coming on, we'll work on planting."

"We?"

"My housemate."

"So he's handy?"

"She, and she's terrific when it comes to curb appeal, planting. She works for a garden center. Inside, Nina's not so much, but I'm not bad."

"Construction company job." He pointed at her. "Handy."

"It helps."

"A lot of maintenance when you're a homeowner. I guess that's why I've never gone there. I'm not handy. And there's the job." He pointed at her again. "Army brat, so you wanted to plant roots."

"Exactly right."

She mixed a whiskey sour, pulled two beers before he caught her attention again.

"What made you pick this area—if you don't mind me asking."

"It had what I wanted. Four seasons, close enough to the city without being in it, not a small town, not a big one. Right in the middle."

She set out a fresh bowl of pretzels for him.

"It's a nice area, prime for some of the upgrading you seem to be doing with your place. That's why I'm here. Homeowners and businesses looking to bump up their tech, a couple of developments where people want to option smart homes. Old houses, new buyers looking to flip or just refresh."

He shrugged. "What I do is part of the infrastructure. Everyone has home offices now, and I can set them up. You must have one."

"I do. It's not especially smart, but it works."

Trivia ended with cheers and boos, and a run on drinks and snacks. As she worked, she noted he chatted up another stool sitter. Baseball. He appeared to know enough to keep that conversation lively.

"Ready for another?"

"Yeah, thanks. How about you, Larry? On me."

"Don't mind if I do. How's Nina's car running?"

"Barely."

Larry shook his head, rubbed at his short beard. "She's gotta bring it in."

"I tell her. Larry's the best mechanic from here to Baltimore," she told Luke. "He's kept Nina's car running well beyond its expiration date."

"I do what I can. You still liking that Prius?"

"It's perfect."

She set their drinks in front of them, filled another round for a table of six. Larry's conversation turned to cars and engines, and Luke appeared to know enough again to hold up his end.

"Gotta get on." Larry pushed to his feet. "The wife'll be home or getting there. It's her book club night, which is a front for drinking wine and gabbing. Nice talking with you, Luke. Thanks for the drink."

"Anytime."

"Another round?" Morgan asked him.

"Two's the limit. I should get on, I've got my own busy day tomorrow." He paid his tab, tipped more than well. "I'd say don't work too hard, but pretty sure you will. Nice seeing you again."

"Good luck in tech world."

He sent her a grin and strolled out.

HE SHOWED UP AGAIN on a packed Friday night. She worked with the part-time weekend bartender to handle the crowd. Luke leaned on her end of the bar, as butts filled every stool.

"Surprise me. It's been a damn good week."

"Congratulations. Weekend off?"

"Ah, some paperwork and planning tomorrow, but yeah. Any suggestions on how I should spend the rest of it?"

"You could drive into Baltimore. Inner Harbor, aquarium, and it's opening day for the O's at Camden Yards."

"Want to keep me company, show me around?"

She couldn't say the offer came out of the blue. She knew when a man was interested. She played it light—part of the job.

"Can't do it. Homeowner's stuff on Saturday, and I'll be right here Saturday night. Sunday's already booked. But I appreciate the offer."

He sampled the beer she offered. "I'm getting an education on the local brews. It's nice, draw me one." He waited until she served him. "Look, if it's pushy or you're already involved, just say. No harm, no foul. But would you like to go out to dinner some night? A night when you're actually not working?

"No pressure," he added when she hesitated. "Just a meal and conversation. Do you like pizza?"

For whatever reason, the casual tone relaxed her. "I'm suspect of anyone who doesn't."

"The pizza at Luigi's is good."

"You hit the top of the line around here."

"So maybe pizza, some wine. I could just meet you there."

She hadn't had an actual date in . . . she didn't want to think about it. Why the hell not?

"I'm free Monday night."

"Seven o'clock at Luigi's?"

"Sure. Sounds good."

"Okay with you if we exchange phone numbers? I'm hoping you don't change your mind, but in case you do . . ."

She pulled her phone out of her pocket, took his so they could add their contacts.

"If you're planning on staying awhile and want a seat, the couple three and four stools down should be leaving after they finish their drinks and nachos."

"Thanks. I'll hover."

She shot him a smile, went back to work.

He grabbed a stool, had his two beers, and left just after midnight.

"Monday night," he said. "Enjoy the weekend."

"You, too."

"That is one fine specimen." Gracie the waitress looked after him. "And he's got his eyes on you, cutie."

"Maybe. He seems nice, steady—and he's only in the area for a few months."

"Strike while the iron's sizzling."

"Maybe," she said again.